Buried Alive

An Alexis Parker Novel

G.K. Parks

This is a work of fiction. Names, characters, places, events, and other concepts are the product of the author's imagination or are used fictitiously. Any resemblance to actual persons, living or dead, places, establishments, events, and locations is entirely coincidental.

A Modus Operandi imprint

ISBN:
ISBN-13: 978-1-942710-35-6

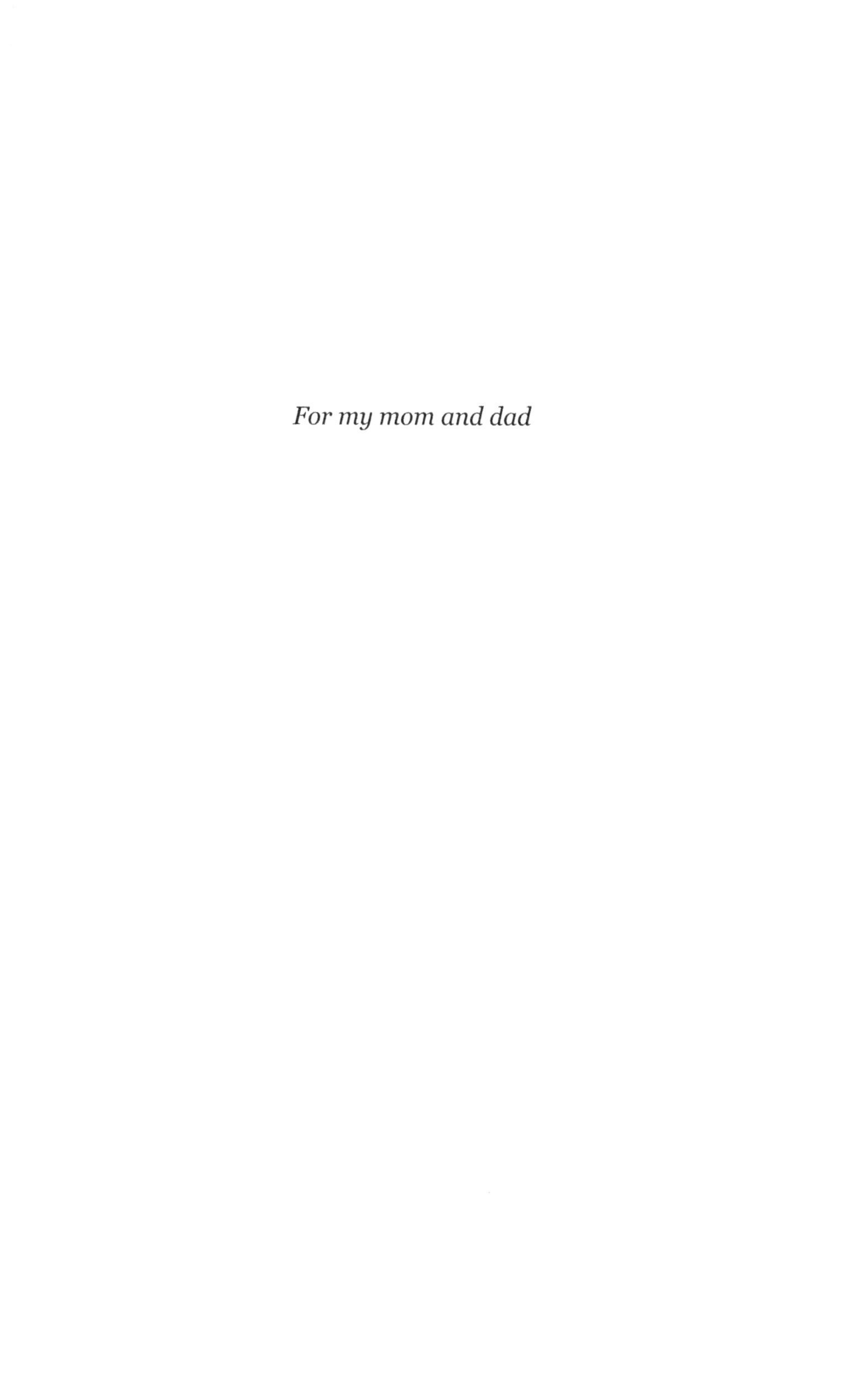

For my mom and dad

BOOKS IN THE LIV DEMARCO SERIES:

Dangerous Stakes
Operation Stakeout
Unforeseen Danger
Deadly Dealings
High Risk
Fatal Mistake
Imminent Threat
Mistaken Identity
Malicious Intent

BOOKS IN THE ALEXIS PARKER SERIES:

Likely Suspects
The Warhol Incident
Mimicry of Banshees
Suspicion of Murder
Racing Through Darkness
Camels and Corpses
Lack of Jurisdiction
Dying for a Fix
Intended Target
Muffled Echoes
Crisis of Conscience
Misplaced Trust
Whitewashed Lies
On Tilt
Purview of Flashbulbs
The Long Game
Burning Embers
Thick Fog
Warning Signs
Past Crimes
Sinister Secret
Zero Sum
Buried Alive
Trouble Brewing

BOOKS IN THE JULIAN MERCER SERIES:

Condemned
Betrayal
Subversion
Reparation
Retaliation
Hunting Grounds

BOOKS IN THE CROSS SECURITY INVESTIGATIONS SERIES:

Fallen Angel
Calculated Risk

ONE

I hated meetings, not just these. But these were the worst. I ran a hand down my face and filled my lungs with air. It'd be over soon, just fifteen more minutes.

James Martin sat beside me. His folding chair had a cushion, unlike mine, but it squeaked every time he moved, which made things interesting since his phone had been going off nonstop since we arrived. As predicted, it buzzed again.

Squeak. He shifted, crossing his legs to hide the phone screen from view.

"You're terrible at stealth," I whispered. "How many times did you get detention for passing notes?"

He glanced at me, a smile tugging at his lips. "Never."

"Not possible."

"Completely possible." Those sparkling green eyes and devilish grin could get him out of anything. His phone vibrated again, but since it was already in his hand, he saved everyone from having to listen to his chair let out another protest. He read the screen before anxiously tapping his phone against his thigh.

"What's wrong?"

"Nothing." He ran a hand through his hair. "It can wait."

"Bullshit." I jerked my head toward the door, which was only a few feet behind us. "We can sneak out. No one will care."

"I thought this was the last one of these for a while. Shouldn't we stay to the end?"

"Fine. I'll stay. But you should take care of that. We're getting ready to wrap up anyway. I'll meet you outside in a few minutes."

"Are you sure? This can wait." The expression on his face said otherwise.

"I'm fine. Go."

He gave me a quick kiss on the cheek and whispered in my ear, "Promise me you'll stick it out."

"If it'll make you happy."

As silently as possible, he slid out of the chair and ducked out of the room. My first instinct was to make a break for it, but I made a promise, even if it was under duress.

"Does anyone else have anything they'd like to share with the group?" the counselor asked, his eyes stopping on me.

Somehow, I resisted the urge to ask if we could call it quits. If no one else said anything, I'd be in the clear. *Come on, keep quiet. It's been a long day. Everyone just wants to go home.*

A woman timidly raised her hand. I'd seen her before, but she'd never spoken in front of the group.

"Yes, you." The counselor turned his focus to her. "Why don't you stand up and tell us what's on your mind tonight?"

"Um...hi. I'm Iris. I...uh...used to be a paramedic." Her face contorted, and she stifled a bitter laugh. "My job was to save people. Obviously, that didn't work out so well."

"What happened?" the counselor asked.

"It'd be easier to ask what didn't," she said bitterly.

I already knew this was going to be one of those gut-wrenching stories that would make me want to cry. And I really didn't want to cry. I glanced at the door, hoping Martin would return. But I didn't spot him through the tiny glass window. Toughing out these last few minutes seemed like a terrible idea, but she started talking before I could escape out the back.

"About ten months ago, we received a call. Drive-by victim. The cops were already there when we arrived. The shooters were gone. We loaded the kid into the back of our rig. He had been shot four times. Blood everywhere. One of those messy situations that makes you wonder how someone could still be alive." She bit her lip, nodding a few times and blinking while the scene played out behind her eyelids. "My partner, Gary, asked if I wanted to drive to the hospital. We always took turns driving. It was his turn, but we had two bad calls before that one, and I didn't want to see someone else code in the back of the rig. He wanted to make things easier for me. He was always considerate like that. But I shouldn't have let him." She opened her mouth but closed it. "Yeah. This was dumb."

"No, it's not. You're okay. You're among friends. It might help if you talk it out," the counselor said.

"We were almost at the hospital when a green SUV t-boned us in the middle of the intersection and knocked us on our side. I didn't see them coming. I did everything I was supposed to as we approached the light. At least, I thought I did."

"Accidents happen," someone else said. "But it's hard not to blame ourselves for these things."

"It wasn't an accident." Anger burned in Iris's eyes. "They targeted us. Gary was yelling at me. He wanted to make sure I was okay, and he needed my help to save the kid. But I didn't move fast enough. I'd gotten pinned beneath the steering column. Before I could say a word to him, the assholes," her chin trembled and she swallowed a few times, "opened the rear door." With a shaking hand, she tucked her hair behind her ear and stared at the wall. "They wanted drugs. They forced Gary to unlock the cabinets, and then they shot him in the head." Tears fell, and she took another shaky breath. "They got what they wanted. They had no reason to kill him. It should have been me. It was my turn."

"That's survivor's guilt talking," the counselor said.

"I know." Iris's heels anxiously tapped against the floor. "But after that, I couldn't do the job anymore. I couldn't face it. I had to leave. I had to do something new. For the longest time, every RA unit I saw, that's all I could think about. But I was doing better. I thought I was over the hump, that I was getting my life back together. Lord knows this affected everything. My job, my marriage, my relationships. I'm so tired of being broken. I just want things to be normal again. But they aren't. The other day, I was driving home from the grocery store and had to pull over because an ambulance blew through the intersection with lights and sirens which gave me a panic attack. Now, I can't stop wondering what I missed, if I could have avoided the green SUV, if Gary might still be alive, and if I'd still be the person I used to be. I know what happened wasn't my fault, but it feels like it. It just isn't fair. He shouldn't be dead."

"It's important you understand grieving is a process. Some days are easier than others. Setbacks don't mean we haven't learned or grown, but we have to give ourselves time."

"How much time?"

"As much as you need. And you need to be patient and kind to yourself, even when it's hard. Especially when it's hard." The counselor looked at his watch. "Unfortunately, we're out of time for tonight, but Iris, if you have a few minutes to talk, I'm here."

She nodded in that noncommittal way which meant she'd bolt as soon as he turned his back. I didn't blame her. Talking about these things was difficult, almost as much as hearing about them.

I maneuvered around the group congregated in front of the snack table and headed out the door. Just being out of the room eased the tension in my shoulders. But only one of Martin's patented massages could work the kink out of my neck. Admittedly, grief counseling had been instrumental in getting me off the crazy train, but now it hurt more than it helped. I was glad it was over.

"Hey," I found Martin sitting on the steps, the phone pressed to his ear, "can we get out of here?"

He nodded at me. "Right. The second quarter projections show the potential for a slight profit, but if we monetize the research, we'll have a cushion. Extra funds will give us more to play around with and more time to fine-tune development. We could expand into other areas." He paused. "Run the numbers again. Let's do a conservative estimate for the low-end, and use the offers we've gotten to calculate a more realistic projection. That'll tell me if we can move forward on the expansion this quarter or if we need to hold off."

After he tucked the phone back into his pocket, I snaked my arms around him and pressed my cheek against the center of his chest. "I need a drink. About seventeen of them."

He kissed my hair. "That can be arranged. Are you okay?"

"I will be." I clung to his side as we made our way to the waiting town car. Marcal, his driver, got out and opened the rear door as we approached. "Thanks, but you don't have to do that."

"No worries, Ms. Parker," he said. "I thought you'd appreciate a gentleman after Mr. Martin abandoned you for a work call."

I laughed. Marcal rarely picked on his boss, but Martin didn't mind.

He clapped his driver on the shoulder. "Good man. I always trust you'll pick up my slack."

"Yes, sir. That's why you dragged me across the country for half a year." Marcal met my eyes, but he and his family didn't mind the change of scenery. His daughters were young enough to see this as an adventure, along with the many trips they were taking to all the major theme parks, courtesy of Martin's generosity. "Where to?"

"Nearest bar," I said.

Marcal glanced at Martin. "Sir?"

"You heard the lady."

The nearest bar was a few blocks from the rec center where the grief counseling meeting was held. Had I known that, we could have walked. Marcal dropped us off and promised to stay close, so he'd be ready to pick us up whenever we wanted to leave.

"What happened after I left?" Martin asked.

"The usual."

"I should have been there to hold your hand."

"I'm a big girl. Hand-holding isn't required, but it is preferred."

He lifted my hand to his lips and gently kissed my knuckles. "I'm sorry. I shouldn't have taken that call. I know you don't like attending these meetings by yourself."

"It's okay." I nodded down at his phone, which he had placed in front of him on the bar. "What's going on at work?"

"Exciting things, I hope." Despite our evening of utter morbidity, he remained upbeat, bordering on manic. "I have a dozen meetings tomorrow, but the latest numbers look promising. The research into biotextiles has so many applications, I think we're going to be able to turn a profit within six months. That means we'll have additional funding to expand the project. We might even be able to cover Lucien's concept without sourcing it out."

"Does that mean my boss will have to make another visit?"

"I don't know. Maybe."

"Can we avoid telling him the good news for a while?"

Martin laughed. "Dare I ask how work is?"

"I started a jigsaw puzzle today. If I stay on schedule, I should finish it tomorrow. But I won't be able to keep up that pace if Cross decides to check up on the West Coast branch again. He has this weird idea that I should perform tedious tasks rather than doing something fun during business hours."

"What does he want you to do instead of puzzle-solving?"

"Run background checks, coordinate with our security teams, conduct interviews, and select an office manager."

"I may have asked you to do something similar when you worked for Martin Technologies."

"And when you needed a bodyguard vetted," I said. "But this is different."

"How?"

Before I could come up with some ridiculous reason to explain the difference, the bartender sauntered over. He wore a backward baseball cap and a heather blue t-shirt that looked like it had swallowed him whole. "What can I get you?" he asked.

"Lemon drop," I said.

"Macallan. The eighteen." Martin pointed to the bottle on the top shelf. "And a menu." The bartender pulled a laminated sheet from under the counter. Martin quickly scanned it. "An extra large order of fries and the sampler platter."

"What kind of sliders and wings?" the bartender asked.

Martin looked at me. "Honey glazed?"

"Yes." I read the options. "And cheeseburgers." Since Martin was ordering wings for me, I could order burgers for him.

The bartender nodded. "It'll be about twenty minutes."

"Great." Martin pulled out his credit card. "Can I start a tab?"

"Sure." The bartender took the card, poured Martin's scotch, and went to work on my martini.

"I'm not very hungry." I curled the edges of the napkin.

"I only ordered appetizers. You can pick at them if you change your mind." Martin sipped the scotch, savoring the first taste. "Remind me to order a case for the house, the twenty-five, not the eighteen, and I should get some Jameson for when Mark comes to visit."

"Why not the fifty?"

"At the present, I don't think I have the time to savor it. It'd be a shame to waste it like that."

"But the twenty-five you can waste?"

He grinned. "I like what I like."

"You don't have to bother with the Jameson. Mark will help you drink the twenty-five." I glanced at the calendar hanging on the wall behind the bar. "His visit is coming up soon. Are you taking off any time to hang out with him? Because I have zero desire to go with him to a basketball game."

"I'll figure it out. He won't be here for a few more weeks." Martin took another sip. "There's a chance I might have to make a trip home before then, depending on this new project. I have to call Luc Guillot first thing in the morning. He's going to teleconference for two of my meetings, but I want to make sure we're on the same page."

"He's your VP. Of course, he'll be on the same page."

"We still have 'I's to dot and 'T's to cross." The giddy energy radiated off him, but despite his excitement, I couldn't get Iris's story out of my head. Martin nudged me, and I forced myself to stop staring a hole into the bar. I didn't know how long I'd zoned out, but during that time, my martini arrived. "Sweetheart, talk to me. What happened after I left the meeting that has you so shaken?"

"I'm not shaken. I'm just in a weird headspace. Her story reminded me of some things. We're in California. This was where Michael had been assigned before our cases crossed and he got transferred. And this is where I ran when we broke up."

"When you broke up with me." Martin swirled the remainder of the scotch around his glass before draining it and gesturing for another. "That was three months of hell. Well, six weeks of hell followed by six weeks of hopeful desperation." He brushed my hair out of my face. "Were you working in L.A.? Did you lose someone here?"

"No, nothing like that. The compound we infiltrated was over an hour away, between here and Vegas. It's just being in this part of the country that reminds me of all these other things. Things I'd rather not think about."

"And listening to people share in group makes it worse." Martin scooted closer, wrapping an arm around me, so I could lean against his shoulder. "We can go to a meeting anytime you want. But I'm leaving that up to you. You said you were good. I'm choosing to trust you can make that assessment."

"Thanks." I tapped his phone. "Can you call Heathcliff and tell him that?"

"I'll tell him the next time I see him in person."

"When will that be? You originally said six months."

"We'll see. It depends on how things go."

TWO

I picked at the fries, more out of habit than hunger. The bartender gestured to my empty glass, and I nodded. A refill didn't seem like a bad idea. I could handle two, even if I hadn't had much to eat today.

Martin had just put the phone down when it rang again. "I can turn it off."

"No, you can't."

"This is the last call tonight."

"Liar." I jerked my chin toward the offending sound. "Answer your phone. It's important."

"Are you sure you're okay? If you want to talk—"

"I don't. I want to drink in peace." I pointed to the device. "A little quiet would be nice."

"Okay. Fine. I'm thinking the next meeting we go to should be one of those WA meetings you always threatened to drag me to. I think I could use one right about now."

"Find one and we'll go," I said as he pressed answer, "if you think you can squeeze it into your schedule."

He squinted, not hearing a word I said. "Hang on. I don't have a great signal." *Two minutes*, he mouthed to me before climbing off the barstool and heading toward one of the high-top tables near the door.

"Workaholic." But I couldn't fault him for that, even if tonight had been nonstop calls and texts. We should have stayed home. I'd be sprawled out on the couch or working out, not feeling like I'd been punched in the gut and run over by a train, while Martin dealt with ways to save the Los Angeles branch of MT by making his current project take off. "It looks like it's just you and me tonight, old friend."

The bartender quirked an eyebrow. "What?"

"Nothing." I pointed to the fresh lemon drop. "I was talking to it."

"Whatever floats your boat, but when it starts talking back, let me know."

"If I do, you'll cut me off."

"Appetizers should be out in ten minutes." He winked and moved to the other side to refill a pitcher of beer.

Resting my head in my hands, I stared at the red and white checkered paper surrounding the fries. My thoughts were on my late partner. Truthfully, not a day went by that I didn't think about him. But I didn't dwell. I'd come to terms with that. A much more recent death had put me in therapy, but months had passed. I'd come to terms with that too. But after hearing Iris talk about her dead partner, I found myself thinking about mine.

Had he ever been to this bar or any of the other places I'd visited? Did he have a favorite hangout in Los Angeles? From what I recalled, he never mentioned any places by name. But it had been years. I might not remember. I wondered if Mark Jablonsky did.

While I debated if I should text Mark and ask, a woman moved closer to the bar. "Excuse me," she said, "is someone sitting here?"

I looked up, recognizing her from the meeting. *Iris.* "Yeah. He just went to take a call. He'll be right back." I pointed to the stools on the other side of me. "But no one's sitting in any of these seats."

"Thanks." She narrowed her eyes. "Hey, I know you."

"Small world."

She slid onto the stool two away from me. "Alex, right? I heard you talking to someone a few weeks ago after the meeting. You're a private eye or security consultant, something like that."

"A bit of both."

"Are you taking new clients?"

I hesitated. "If this is about what you said in group, I don't have any local law enforcement connections, so I—"

"No, with twelve years on the job, I have plenty of those. This is...um...personal."

The bartender headed in her direction. "What can I get you?"

"A bottle of Moscato and a glass, unless you have a really long straw."

"Coming up." He placed a glass in front of her before uncorking a fresh bottle.

"You could just drink out of the bottle. I won't judge," I said.

She snickered. "Good to know." Once the bartender disappeared, she took a healthy sip. "I think my husband's having an affair."

That wasn't what I was expecting. "I'm sorry."

She gave the empty scotch glass beside me a look. "Are you married?"

"Not exactly."

"Divorced?"

"No."

"Did he die?" She swallowed. "God, I'm sorry. Pretend I didn't ask that. I don't know what's wrong with me tonight. It's those damn meetings. They make me crazy, like I want to crawl out of my skin." She picked up the glass and reached for the bottle. "I'm going to go sit in the corner and keep my mouth shut. I'm sorry I bothered you."

I turned to make sure Martin was still at the table, but he had migrated away and was standing near the door. He had a finger in one ear while he tried to hear over the noise. "Wait," I said, "why do you think your husband's having an affair?"

"He's been acting strangely. It's my fault. After what happened with Gary..."

"It's not your fault. Weren't you listening in group?"

Her eyes went skyward. "I should have that phrase

printed on t-shirts."

"I had to put it on a coffee mug so I'd see it every damn day."

"Did it help?"

"It didn't hurt. My boss doesn't always buy it, though."

"My husband probably wouldn't either." She tugged on her sleeves, and I couldn't help but wonder if he beat her. "We used to be happy. We were so in love. Don't get me wrong. We were always super busy. Things were never perfect. I worked twenty-four hour shifts and was off forty-eight, and he worked ridiculous hours too. Sometimes, we'd go days without seeing each other, but when we did, it was special."

"What does he do?" I asked.

"He's a nurse. We met at the hospital. I was always there, and we sort of bumped into each other and kept bumping into each other."

"How long have you been married?"

"Nine years."

"Do you have children?"

"We couldn't."

I resisted the urge to jot anything down. "When did you stop being happy?"

"I stopped after the accident." Her hand trembled as she lifted the wine glass to her lips. "I fell apart. Theo, my husband, couldn't understand. He was so relieved I survived. He didn't get why I wasn't elated. I guess that's when we started to drift apart." She finished the glass and poured another one. "I felt like I was buried alive beneath all that pain and misery. I couldn't get out from under it. I'm still not out from under it. He just doesn't get it."

"Have you considered couples counseling?"

"I have, but he won't hear of it. He doesn't think we have problems. He thinks I need to work on me and that will fix whatever isn't working with us." She drained her glass again. "He's been so cold and emotionally distant for the last, I don't know, eight months. I have to give him credit. After it happened, he tried. I had six weeks recovery, but everything changed for me after that. I lost interest in everything." She blinked a few times. "I don't want to lose him, but I want to know what he's been doing and who he's been doing. If it's just sex, I think we can get past it, but if he's found a girlfriend, someone he cares about, I...I don't know. Maybe she can give him children and a family. That was never his priority, but maybe it is now. I have no idea what he wants. He seems like a stranger, rather than my husband."

"Back up." I gestured that she slow down. "These circumstances can strain even the strongest relationships, but why do you think he's stepping out? Has he made or received any calls at odd hours or from strange numbers? Have you seen him with someone? Has he come home smelling of perfume or with lipstick smears on his collar?"

"I'm not sure. He's always so secretive. He hides everything from me. He won't let me near his phone. He sneaks out after he thinks I'm asleep, usually on the weekends. But yesterday, I woke up and found him gone. When I got up, he was in the kitchen. He said he couldn't sleep and went for a run. But I don't buy it."

That wasn't good. I sipped my drink, debating if taking this case would cause more harm than good. "Have you been fighting a lot recently?"

"Not really. Not in a traditional sense. His mood's been volatile. He gets mad at the drop of a hat. He'll storm off and disappear for hours at a time. He says he's been going to the gym. Sure, he's been getting into shape these last few months, but I don't think it's because he wants to take care of himself. I think it's for her."

"Have you ever seen her? Has he mentioned anyone? Maybe you overheard him talking to her or someone else?"

"No. And when I've asked, he acts like I'm crazy for even suggesting it. He says he loves me. But I can tell he can't stand being around me, not when I'm like this. I just can't seem to snap out of it for more than a day or two at a time."

"Have you considered anti-depressants?"

"They didn't help, not the way I hoped. I became numb to everything. I'd rather hurt. That must sound crazy."

"It doesn't."

"Ah," she grinned bitterly, "a fellow masochist."

"Guilty."

She drank more wine. “Even when we’re both home, Theo’s usually in another room or tinkering in the garage. At first, I thought he might be on drugs. As a first responder, I know the warning signs. He’s exhibited a lot of them, but I don’t think that’s it. As soon as he comes home from one of his mysterious outings, he showers. He won’t even let me wash his clothes. He does them himself. It’s like he’s afraid I’m going to find out what he’s been doing. Please, I need to know. He acts like I’m insane, but I’m not. At least, I hope not.”

“Has he ever hit you or been violent?”

“Never, but he gets so angry sometimes. He keeps it bottled up in front of me, but he’ll lock himself in the garage and explode. I can hear him throwing things and hitting things.”

“Has he always had such a volatile temperament?”

“No. It started after the incident.”

Anger was a reasonable response, but I wondered if Theo had anything to do with the incident. Maybe he wanted his wife dead and was angry she wasn’t. “Did the police catch the guys responsible?”

“They’re awaiting trial.”

“Has Theo said anything about them to you?”

“He doesn’t talk to me about it. Whenever I bring it up, he shuts down and walks out.”

That made the warning bells ring a little louder inside my head. “Where does he say he goes when he disappears? Is it always to the gym?”

“Most of the time. On occasion, he’ll say he picked up extra shifts at work, but I know that’s bullshit. He’s lying to me, Alex. Please. You must understand how hard this is. I know Theo doesn’t get it. We used to be so close. He always comforted me. We’d cuddle and kiss and share intimate moments, but we’ve lost all of that. We haven’t been intimate in months, since the incident. I pushed him away. I know I did. Maybe I pushed him too far. What if it’s already too late? I want to fix it, but I can’t until I know how broken we are. And he won’t tell me. He won’t tell me what he wants.”

“Have you tried to rekindle that old flame? Maybe he

doesn't want to pressure you." Even as I said it, I didn't believe it, but Iris was too wrapped up in the situation to notice.

"Yes and no. I asked him the other night if he wanted to have sex, and he said he didn't know why I bothered asking when he knew I wasn't in the mood. An hour later, he's sneaking out of the house, and he didn't get home until the next morning. What does that say to you?"

"Something's going on." I exhaled. "Are you sure you want someone looking into this? I don't know what you'll find if you keep digging, and once the truth is out, you can't exactly put the genie back in the bottle."

"I have to know."

My phone chimed. Martin sent me a message that he had gone outside to make another call and would be back in a few minutes. Two minutes, my ass. "Let's say you're right, and Theo's having an affair. What kind of proof would you want?"

"Proof?"

"A lot of times, I'm hired to provide proof of an affair for divorce proceedings."

"Divorce?" She emptied the rest of the wine bottle into her glass. "I don't want a divorce, unless he does. I just want to know I'm not crazy. He acts like I am, but he's gaslighting me every time he denies it. I want to be able to confront him, so we can get help. So he can finally tell me what he wants. I want my life back. I'll never get there if he keeps treating me like a crazy, depressed psycho."

The bartender placed another lemon drop in front of me. I must have looked like I could use it. "All right. I'll look into it. First, I need some basic information, starting with your name."

"Iris Stapleton. My husband is Theodore Stapleton." She gave me her address, their phone numbers, the make, model, and license plate numbers for the cars they drove, her husband's work schedule for the next two weeks, and the name of the hospital where he worked.

"I'll need access to his computer and phone. I'd like to look around your house when he's not there. And I'll need you to call me whenever he disappears."

"Of course, whatever I can do to help."

"I'll have a contract drafted. Once that's signed, we'll take it from there. You can stop by my office to sign the papers." I handed her my card, wondering if she'd change her mind when she wasn't full of liquid courage.

"Thanks." She tucked my card into her wallet and called a rideshare to take her home.

By the time Martin returned, the appetizer platter had gotten cold and I had knocked back three lemon drops without realizing it. Picking at the wings, I found I had no appetite. I went back to the fries, but they were cold and soggy. I was ready to cut my losses and leave before something else could happen.

"What was that about?" Martin asked, sliding onto the stool. "I noticed you gave your card to that woman."

"Jealous?" I asked.

"Not in the least." He played with the ends of my hair. "You look drained. Is everything okay?"

"Apparently, if you can work from the bar, so can I."

"What is that supposed to mean?"

"Iris hired me to spy on her cheating husband." I moved to stand, finding the room wobbly. Too many lemon drops, not enough fries.

"Easy, sweetheart." He asked the bartender for a coconut water and made me drink it while he wrapped up the appetizers.

When we got home, he reheated the sliders and placed a sports drink beside me. "Eat something and drink that." He went to the bathroom and returned with a bottle of aspirin. "Take two."

"Fine." I picked up the bottle, glaring when his phone rang again. "It's for you."

"Give me one sec."

One sec turned into two hours. By the time Martin hung up, I had eaten my dinner and part of his and had gone to bed. I was no longer drunk, just stiff and tired. But I couldn't sleep.

Martin slid under the covers beside me and rubbed my back. "I owe you an apology for tonight."

"No, you don't." I rolled over and laid my head against

his shoulder. "You've put up with so much. You never have to apologize for work. You know that. I'm just frustrated."

"Those are the lemon drops talking." He ran his thumb against my cheek and kissed me. "Tell me what I can do to make it up to you. I can always tell when you're mad."

"I'm not mad at you. I'm mad at Theo."

"Who's Theo?"

"The guy I was hired to follow."

THREE

Martin's alarm buzzed. I reached for it, finding his side of the bed empty and cold. No wonder Iris hated this feeling. I wasn't a fan either.

I looked at the clock. It was six a.m. We'd gone to bed at midnight, but I could have slept for another six hours. In fact, I had half a mind to do it.

Rolling over, I pulled up the blankets and buried my head in the pillow. On the plus side, I didn't have a hangover. I'd almost fallen back to sleep when Martin entered the bedroom.

"Did you finish your workout?" I asked.

"I haven't started yet. I had that call with Luc."

"Oh."

He opened a few drawers. "The waves are big this morning. It's the perfect day to surf. What do you say?"

"Shark."

"C'mon, gorgeous. You'll feel better once you're out there."

"I doubt it."

He pulled the long-sleeve rash guard he bought me out of the drawer, along with my black bikini. "You haven't had much chance to ride the waves. C'mon, this is why you've been doing all that prep with the board."

"You tricked me into it. I thought riding your long board was a euphemism."

Martin laughed. "Sometimes, it is."

"Hence your method of tricking me into this whole surfing thing. It's six a.m. The sun isn't even fully awake yet. I bet it's cold and wet out there."

"You're probably right." He slid his arms around me and gave me a kiss. "It'll be fun. We'll have an hour to ourselves. It'll give me a chance to make up for last night."

"No phone calls?"

"None." He straightened. "I'm going to change and stretch. I hope you'll join me." He peeled his shirt off, his back muscles flexing as he grabbed some things from the drawer.

"Fine."

I went into the guest bathroom to get ready. On the plus side, I didn't have to worry about showering or looking presentable. That would come later.

My reflection looked like shit. Dark bags hung beneath my bloodshot eyes. Sleep would have been the smart decision. Hopefully, Martin knew how much I loved him. First, I agreed to a temporary relocation to be near him. Now, I was giving up valuable sleep and the warmth of our bed for ice cold water, wind, and sand. Perhaps I should ask for a wetsuit. At least then, I'd be warm or warmer.

After a quick stretch, half a glass of juice, and some water, I met Martin on the beach. He'd dragged our boards down to the water. Several other Malibu residents were already out. They were just as crazy as he was. It was probably all the damn sunshine.

"You ready?" Martin asked.

"No."

His green eyes danced. "I'll make it worth your while when we get back to the house."

"You better."

He stole a kiss before offering me the leash which would tether me to the surfboard. The two women who always flirted with him jogged toward us as they walked their dogs. "Morning," they called.

"Good morning," Martin said as they neared.

The brunette with the fancy highlights gave him an unnaturally white smile. Her perky enhanced breasts bounced inside her bikini top as she flipped her hair back, slowing as she ran past us.

"Ugh." I watched as they giggled, continuing to run in the opposite direction. "I'm going back to bed. You want to continue that, go fetch."

"Hey," he grabbed me around the waist, "you're the most beautiful thing out here." He pulled me against him and kissed me like he had no business doing out in public. "You're so damn hot when you're jealous."

"I carry a gun. Remember that." I pushed against his chest and looked around, but no one was interested in our romantic exchange. Then again, the beach wasn't that crowded. Most of the people out were more concerned with catching the next wave. "Why do you think that's hot? Jealousy leads to murder."

He gave me that cocky smirk. "You think I'm something special."

"No shit. If I didn't, I wouldn't be out here."

The smirk turned into a full-blown grin. "I love you too." He tightened the Velcro around his ankle. "Let's go."

We carried our boards into the water. After I was deep enough, I climbed on top of the board. We paddled farther out. We took turns on the first few waves. I'd barely managed to stand up the first time. Lack of sleep impaired my balance, and I crashed into the water.

Martin rode the next wave back to shore. "Come on, sweetheart," he called.

I sat on the board, bobbing up and down as the water got choppier. When I saw the next one approaching, I paddled out, my arms pumping hard. Timing it right, I popped up on the board and tightened my core. *Don't fall.* The water continued to rise behind me, curling around me. My board didn't feel level, so I overcorrected.

I hit the water hard. The wave crashed down on top of me, forcing me beneath the surface. This must have been what the spin cycle felt like. My world flipped around. Which way was up? I couldn't tell. *Don't panic, Parker.* This had happened before, but usually, the light clued me in. But this morning, everything was murky.

The leash yanked my ankle to the point of pain. That must be up. The board should float.

I scrambled beneath the water's surface, unsure with all the bubbles if the light was coming from below or above. A current shoved me sideways, sending me tumbling head over heels. The board stopped me from hurtling too far by slowing me down.

Stretching out my arms, I turned and swam toward the light. Before I could breach the surface, a dark shadow came over me. My lungs burned from lack of oxygen. I kicked harder, propelling myself upward. Momentarily, I felt the sun on my face and opened my mouth to breathe.

Without warning, a solid object cracked down on my back. Damn surfboard. The impact forced my breath out in a gasp and me back underneath the water. The void in my lungs quickly filled with salt water, which turned the burning into a stabbing. I choked, coughing to expel the water which only forced more water down my windpipe. In my dazed state, I got turned around again. Now which way was up?

I kicked more furiously, my limbs flailing. This is why it wasn't safe to rescue a drowning person. But I knew how to swim. I wasn't drowning, except my lungs disagreed.

The waves pushed me sideways. I forced myself to stop fighting. My eyes teared to the point I couldn't see. But everything was bubbles and streaks of light amid the murky blue. I moved with the water, nothing more than a rag doll in the sea. Hopefully, I'd float to the top.

Before I drifted too far, something grabbed my ankle and dragged me backward. It turned me in the water until we were moving in the other direction. By then, dark bubbles floated in front of my eyes, making it impossible to see.

A moment later, wet sand was beneath my heels. Little pebbles and shells scratched against my bare feet, and then the sun was on my face.

"Breathe, Alexis. Breathe." Martin hauled me onto the beach, laying me on my side while I sputtered and choked.

I coughed up mouthfuls of warm ocean water while I

desperately tried to get air into my lungs. My head hurt, but my vision cleared.

Martin pulled my wet hair back so it wouldn't get in the way. "Take it easy. Long, deep breaths." He propped me up as soon as my choking turned into irritated, unending coughs.

"Is she okay?" the brunette from earlier asked. "I called 9-1-1. An ambulance is on the way."

"I'm fine," I croaked between coughs. But she ignored me.

Someone else approached us from the water. "Here." He moved closer and shoved the end of the surfboard into the sand. "That was a gnarly wipeout."

If my primary focus wasn't on breathing and hoping the warm fluid I kept coughing up wasn't blood, I would have had a snarky reply. Instead, Martin thanked the guy, but he wasn't worried about the surfboard, which he'd ripped free from the tether. He was worried about me.

I clung to Martin's arm, glad he was holding me in a tight hug. When I was finally able to stop coughing, I rested my head against him. "I'm never surfing again."

He kissed my temple, a tremble moving through him. "I shouldn't have made you come out this morning."

"I told you this was a bad idea. Mother Nature hates me. I use too much plastic and waste too much paper. She decided to get even. Remind me to donate to one of those save the ocean places."

"The lifeguards are in charge of a fundraiser," the brunette said.

I looked up at her. "Great."

Martin nuzzled against me. His fingers found the inside of my wrist while he checked my pulse. Slowly, he released the death grip he had on me and eased me back onto the sand. "You sound crazy."

"I always sound crazy." I coughed a few more times. "God, my head hurts."

He gently felt around the back of my neck, cringing when I winced at his touch. He looked up at the woman. "Does the lifeguard station have a first aid kit?"

"Let me check." She ran across the beach toward the

stand. Her dog, which her friend had been watching, raced after her, excited to run free again.

A moment later, she returned and handed Martin the kit. Martin took out a flashlight and shined it in my face.

"Stop that." I held my palm up to shield my eyes from the light. "I do not have a concussion. The board hit my back, not my head."

"Humor me," he said.

I hated when he played doctor. A shiver went through me. Right now, I wanted to be clean and dry and cuddled up in bed. My head pounded and my chest hurt, which made my ribs hurt, which made my back hurt. Or maybe it was the other way around. Regardless, it didn't matter. "I'm fine. Let's go home. I want to dry off." I moved to stand, but Martin stopped me.

"Too late. The ambulance is here. You're going to get checked out." Martin stared at me, his expression somber, his green eyes intense. "I can't lose you, Alex. I never meant for this to happen. This was supposed to be fun. An activity we could enjoy together. I never imagined." He shook his head. "I should have. You kept saying how dangerous it is."

"I'm just glad it wasn't a shark." That had been my main excuse to avoid surfing. I hadn't considered the ocean would try to swallow me whole.

"You should get looked at," the brunette said. "I can take your boards back to your house. It's that one, right?" She pointed to the fenced in pool farther up the beach. "I've seen you guys come out before," she clarified, realizing she sounded like a stalker. "I'll leave them inside your fence."

"Thanks." Martin nodded to her.

Realizing there was no point in arguing, I let the paramedics check me out and take me to the emergency room. After four hours, I was released since my lungs were clear and there was nothing wrong with me.

The doctor gave Martin a million signs and symptoms to watch for in case of complications or if I started to show signs of a concussion, which didn't seem likely since my brain hadn't gotten scrambled by the surfboard. Only my neck and back did. But Martin dutifully paid attention to everything the doctor said, even though I'd been in enough scrapes that he should have had this memorized.

Martin's driver picked us up and took us home. Martin hadn't taken his eyes off of me since he pulled me out of the water. Even when they'd taken me to get x-rays and CTs, he'd stood outside the door, waiting for me to come out.

The two surfboards were beside the fence gate. At least Martin's new girlfriend had kept her word. Still, I didn't like how much attention she'd been paying him, but that was my issue.

"You're late for work. If you hurry and change, you might make it by one. That's when everyone gets back from lunch, isn't it?" I asked.

"I'm not going anywhere." He ran a hand through my tangled hair. "You heard the doctor. Complications may present within the first twelve hours."

"I didn't drown. I swallowed some water. It happens, especially in the pool. You never worry about that."

"Alex, I'm not leaving you. I can't believe I dragged you into something else that nearly proved fatal."

"Excuse me? I'm the one who causes gunmen to come to our home. Not you."

He ignored my comment. "Do you want to take a hot bath, or is that too traumatic?"

"It depends. Are you joining me?"

"If you don't mind."

"Are you going to hold my head under the water?"

His jaw clenched, and he fought to keep from saying whatever came to mind. Instead, he pulled me into his chest and hugged me hard. "I promised I'd do my best not to hurt you. I made a vow."

I pulled back so I could look into his eyes. "Accidents happen. I'm okay. You grabbed me and pulled me out of the water. Maybe if you hadn't, we wouldn't be having this conversation, but we are because you did. I'm okay. This isn't your fault." I cracked a smile. "Isn't that what you tell me all the time? Don't you like to remind me that I can't control everything? Shouldn't the same rules apply to you?"

He smirked, but the teasing didn't quite reach his eyes. "I like to make my own rules."

"Me too." I kissed him. "You prepped most of last night for your meetings today. You can't take the entire day off."

"Wanna bet? It's my company." The smile finally reached his eyes. "My rules."

"How about after we wash up and dry off, you drop me off at work on the way to the office?"

"Alex—"

"I'll be okay. There are plenty of people to keep an eye on me. Plus, if I don't show up, Lucien Cross will send one of his tactical teams to find me." I dug the phone out of the pocket of his board shorts, ignoring the amused look on his face. "Here. Send another text to your assistant or whoever you've been messaging for the last four hours and tell him you'll be there by two. You do your thing. I'll do mine. And we'll put this morning out of our minds. You can't dwell on this, or you'll outfit me with another tracking device or decide, instead of working with biotextiles, you should invent some kind of underwater breathing apparatus."

"That wouldn't be a bad idea."

"It's a terrible idea. They already exist. Have you ever heard of scuba gear or oxygen tanks?"

"When did you become the rational one in this relationship?"

"It must be all those group therapy sessions." I moved to the dresser and pulled out some clean clothes. "Worst case, I drop dead and you start dating the brunette with the dog."

"Don't say shit like that."

"Why? She'd be all for it."

For the first time, he took his eyes off of me and went to the closet to pull out one of his suits. "Fine. I'll have Marcal stock up on lint removers because that dog will shed all over my suits."

"Good."

His thumb rubbed the wedding band on his finger. "Alex—"

"I know. I'm sorry. I have no intention of dropping dead, especially when a twenty-something is desperate to ride your long board."

FOUR

After I walked into the high-rise which housed the West Coast branch of Cross Security, I reached into my pocket for the key. A couple of people were getting off the elevator as I made my way down the hallway to 1D. From their chattiness and laughter, I had to assume not everyone was having a terrible day. But when I looked up, I wondered if mine was about to get worse.

"It's about damn time." Sgt. Will Russo tapped his watch. "Most people came back from lunch an hour ago."

"I wasn't at lunch." I took off my sunglasses and unlocked the door. "How long have you been standing here?"

"About an hour."

"Why?"

"I was hoping to get a cup of coffee."

"You mean to tell me San Diego doesn't have any coffee shops?"

"They all ran out."

"What about donut shops?"

"Same thing. There's been a huge run on coffee. Everyone's out. Not a drop in sight."

"Did you happen to pick up donuts while searching for

coffee?"

He shook his head, following me inside. "I find it hard to believe you eat donuts. You look more like the kale salad type."

"No wonder you never made detective."

"I never tried. I preferred the uniform."

"Regardless, unless you come bearing donuts, I can't help you." I jerked my chin toward the door. "Even if San Diego somehow ran out of coffee, which we both know isn't true, Los Angeles has a million places. Go somewhere else. This isn't a coffee shop. The sign on the door should have clued you in."

"What if I come back with donuts? Then will you hear me out?"

I sighed, my headache getting worse. "Make it quick. I'm waiting for a client." But I wasn't sure if Iris was going to show up or if she had already stopped by before I arrived.

"This won't be quick. It's rather complicated. Maybe you should call your client and reschedule. First come, first served, right?"

I couldn't figure out why he was hesitating. "What do you want, Will? Standing outside my door for hours on end with no clue when or if I would show up means it must be important, so why are you playing these games?"

He stuck out his bottom lip and jerked his chin at the coffeemaker. "Please."

"Fine." I filled the machine and pressed the button. By the time I turned around, he had moved one of the waiting room chairs in front of the reception desk and placed a manila folder near the edge. I handed him the cup of coffee and sat down. "What's that?"

"A case I've been researching. Well, cases since I think they could be connected. I thought if you had some time, you wouldn't mind helping out. The way I see it, you owe me. And until your client shows up, it doesn't look like you've got anything better to do."

Besides getting the contracts ready for Iris, performing a few background checks, and finishing the jigsaw puzzle, he was right. But I resisted the urge to pick up the file. "The commute's a bitch. I'm guessing so is the pay."

"You hit the nail right on the head." He sipped the coffee. "Damn, this is good. Much better than the sludge at the police station."

"That doesn't take much." I eyed the folder. "Why are you bringing me a case? We're barely acquainted. What makes you think I can help? Don't you have a squadron of officers at your disposal?"

"They haven't made any progress."

"Evidence problem?"

"Not really. It's more a lack of motivation."

"How do you plan on motivating me?"

He smiled, confident he knew the answer, but he didn't share it with the class. "What time do you normally show up at the office? I didn't see any hours posted on the door. The Cross Security website directed me to the East Coast branch. I spoke to someone in reception who said you should be here by eight during the week. I should have asked if he meant a.m."

"More like eleven, and that's pushing it."

"You're more than two hours late. It's after one."

"Something came up."

"That settles it. I need to turn in my walking papers and join the private sector."

"Why haven't you?"

"I need to clear this case first."

"Is it a pride thing?"

"It's something." He stared at me, his brow furrowing. "You don't look so good. Are you feeling okay?"

"It's been a day." I rubbed the back of my neck, wincing. "If you must know, I spent my morning in the emergency room."

"Hazard of the job?"

"Not this time. It was a surfing accident."

He cocked an eyebrow. "You surf?"

"Obviously not."

"That explains the mood." He hid his chuckle in the rim of the mug. "Are you okay?"

"I'm fine." I wasn't even sure why I told him that. I barely knew the police sergeant. We'd crossed paths on my last case, when he decided to introduce himself with an unprovoked stun gun attack. I'd dug into his background, but things were murky. All I knew was he'd been involved in an incident that resulted in two officers' deaths. At the present, he hadn't been cleared to carry a firearm or work the field. "What's the case or cases?"

"You remember when I mentioned the string of attacks on homeless people?"

"Some of that rings a bell."

"Two members of the homeless community were found dead. The lead detective ruled them both suicides."

"It happens."

He slid the folder closer to me. "Take a look at this before you reach any conclusions."

I hesitated, sighing, which made me cough. I rubbed my chest which helped a little. "Stupid salt water."

"Alex, please."

"Give me a minute. I have some things to take care of first. As you pointed out, I just got here." I rocked a few times in the chair before powering on the computer and checking my inbox. Since I'd been tasked with staffing the West Coast branch of Cross Security, Justin, Lucien Cross's assistant, forwarded me notes from every morning meeting. As with most of those messages, I put the one from today in the trash.

Aside from several threatening messages from Cross, asking when he could expect me to make some staffing decisions, I hadn't been given any new assignments. The security teams knew what to do and how to do it. Nero, one of the team leaders, had taken it upon himself to organize their schedules and shift things around if circumstances warranted it. He didn't need me to tell him how to do his job. He'd been functioning independently for years.

Clicking a few keys, I entered Iris's details as a potential new client, wrote a brief summary of her request, and sent it to legal to draft a contract. Then I skimmed the file I had on Will Russo. The official police version of events had been sanitized. Details had been withheld and omitted. It didn't tell me anything I didn't know. Cross's staff of hackers might be able to dig up more, but Cross cautioned me to stay away from Will. I didn't want the boss to know I was ignoring that order, along with all his other ones.

I closed the computer window before Will could see I had checked up on him and opened the manila folder. "Are you serious? You drove two hours to ask me to help on a murder investigation after the lead detective already closed the case."

"Cases. And yes." He pushed the folder closer. "Just take a look, unless you have something more pressing to do, in which case I'll wait." He stared at the door, but no one entered. "Shouldn't your client be here by now?"

"We didn't iron out a time." I pulled a blank legal pad from the top drawer and clicked my pen. "How did you know I'd even show up to work? Maybe today's my day off. Were you going to stand outside all day? You could have called. I'm pretty sure you have my number. You've used it before."

"I have it and your office number. By now, you should know I do my homework and keep my ear to the ground, which means you can be damn sure there's something off about these suicides."

"Okay." I reached for the folder, but he stopped me from picking it up.

"I don't want anyone to know about this. I don't want the SDPD to know I went to an outside source for help. Actions like that are frowned upon. It's why I didn't call."

"Are they tapping your phone?" I half-joked.

He shrugged.

That was not the answer I wanted to hear.

Deciding to see where this would lead, I read the details on the first victim. Sophie Marshman, forty-one, had a laundry list of mental illnesses. After her divorce, she was forced to move out of her home. Soon after, she ended up bouncing around from shelter to shelter.

Thirteen days ago, her body was found near a dumpster outside a fast-food restaurant. She clutched a bloody pocket knife in her right hand. Deep cuts marred her inner thighs. I studied the crime scene photos for a few seconds.

"Do you have the ME's report?" I asked.

"Keep reading. It's near the back."

I flipped to it, studying the copy of the printout. “She wasn’t a cutter. Lack of scars makes me think she never attempted suicide before. Do you have her medical history?”

“She swallowed a handful of pills with a bottle of Chardonnay once. Her soon-to-be ex-husband found her passed out in the living room and used that as an excuse to gain custody of their children and force her out of their home. But I don’t think it was a suicide attempt. She was angry and hurt and decided to self-medicate. She just got carried away.”

I scanned the rest of the file. Aside from that one incident, Sophie Marshman appeared to pose no danger to herself or others. She’d been picked up a few times for being a nuisance and urinating in public. Nothing in her history sent up red flags that she would turn violent. It seemed unlikely she’d harm herself in such a violent fashion.

“Did the canvass turn up anything?”

Will rolled his eyes. “No one saw or heard a thing. TOD was around three a.m. Everything closed at least an hour earlier.”

“Any idea why she wasn’t at one of the shelters?”

“They fill up fast. Too many unhoused, not enough beds. I’m guessing on those nights, she stayed at one of the homeless encampments.”

I went back to the photos, but aside from a tattered suede backpack, she didn’t have anything else with her. “Where are her things?”

“The detective reasoned if she had anything of value or use, scavengers took it with them.”

“Why wouldn’t they have taken the knife or her bag?”

“Hey, I’m on your side. I don’t think the official version makes sense, which is why I brought this to you. Detective Trevitt reasoned no one wanted to get blamed for killing her by walking around with that knife.”

“Did they print it?”

Will dragged the folder across the desk, pulled out the forensic report, and placed it in front of me. “There.”

“I could have found that myself. The reason I asked is

because it's easier if you tell me the answers instead of making me read them."

"The only prints on the knife were hers."

"What was in her knapsack?"

"A few bruised apples, a thermos with water, two pairs of socks, a sweatshirt, a prepaid cell phone and charger, a metro card, and twenty-three dollars."

"What time did officers find her body?"

"A little before four."

"She was dead less than an hour." I spread the photos out. "No one picked through her things. She died with what she had. But this can't be everything. She must have had a sleeping bag, maybe even a tent."

"We didn't recover those items."

None of this made sense. I read the inventory list, in case Will forgot to mention something, but nothing stuck out. I found Sophie's phone log. Every Monday and Friday, she called her children. Aside from that, the only other numbers she called were area shelters, food pantries, and soup kitchens. "She died on a Thursday."

Will arched an eyebrow. "Is that meaningful?"

"The detective questioned her family. According to his notes, no one suspected Sophie was suicidal. She didn't get into an argument or have a recent falling out with anyone. So why wouldn't she have called her children to say goodbye? She didn't leave a note or even send them a text."

"I said I didn't buy it."

"What about security cams?"

"What about them?"

"I was hoping one of them caught her cutting herself." I understood why this bothered him. It bothered me too. But I knew the statistics. Plenty of depressed people did their best to hide it. And Sophie had several mental health issues to contend with, in addition to depression and life kicking her in the teeth. She needed help, and I didn't think she'd gotten it. Everything could have gotten to be too much. But I didn't know why she wouldn't have wanted to speak to her children one last time. Why wouldn't she have called them or tried to see them?

"Nope."

"How did the police find her so quickly? Did they receive a 9-1-1 call?" I asked.

"No. Patrol spotted her, thought she was asleep, stopped to pick her up and take her somewhere safe, and realized she was dead. I was working that night and heard all about it. Homicide sent Trevitt. He looked into it for the next day or two, waited for the ME's report to come in, and closed the case."

"What about the other suicide?" I asked.

"Keep digging. I stuck them together."

FIVE

Robert Devers was the other alleged suicide. He was a nineteen-year-old opioid addict. He'd been an all-star high school athlete with a full soccer scholarship who'd gotten injured and hooked on prescription pain medication during his first semester in college.

After that, he dropped out and sold everything he had to pay for his habit. By the time his parents realized anything was wrong, months had passed. The police found Robert during a raid on a crackhouse. His parents forced him to go to rehab. It didn't last more than a few days before he ran.

The missing persons report was dated two months ago. He died two weeks after it was filed, roughly a month before Sophie Marshman. But Robert didn't die of an overdose. He had residual amounts of narcotics in his bloodstream, but he wasn't high at the time. He had hung himself.

I closed my eyes and took a moment. I'd seen and heard stories like these a thousand times and hated every single one of them. Addiction could happen to any of us at any time. A part of me feared one day that could be me, since I had an unknown family history, an obsessive personality, and shitty luck. Normally, that meant white-knuckling it through injuries, but that wasn't a solution either. Unfortunately, it was the only one I had that kept the paranoid part of my psyche happy.

"Alex?" Will raised an eyebrow. "Is it your naptime?"

"No, I just..." I pointed at the folder. "This sucks."

"No shit."

"The kid fell from grace, lost everything, and ended it. It's tragic, but it's not murder."

"Are you sure about that?" Will took the folder from me. "He hung himself from church rafters."

"It's probably sacrilege, but the church was open and empty. Robert must have gone there seeking answers and reached the wrong conclusion."

"Gimme a break." Will spread out the crime scene photos. "He broke the lock to gain access to the balcony where the choir rehearsed, brought in a ladder and rope, carried that shit up those narrow and winding stairs with his fucked up knee, climbed the ladder, tied a perfect hangman's knot, and jumped over the edge."

"Maybe he was making a statement." I narrowed my eyes at the evidence marker. An orange prescription pill bottle had rolled beneath the ladder. Inside were eight pills. Robert's prints were the only ones on the bottle.

I scanned the report. Detective Trevitt worked that case too. No one in Will's life seemed surprised by his death. Addiction took everything from him. If he hadn't killed himself, the pills would have, or so they believed. They didn't push the detective to investigate or question his findings.

But these two cases didn't have many similarities. The victimology was different. The suicide methods were different. Besides living on the streets, the only thing Robert and Sophie had in common was the detective who investigated their deaths.

Pushing the file away, I centered my keyboard and ran a search on Detective Gabriel Trevitt. "What kind of cop is Trevitt?" I glanced at Will before returning my attention to the computer screen.

"He does his job."

"That's not an answer." I didn't see any news articles

regarding the detective. That meant he hadn't worked any cases that made him famous or done anything terrible enough to become infamous. "Do you know if he's been the subject of any internal affairs investigations, past or present?"

"Not that I'm aware. Trevitt is like the rest of us, overworked and burnt out. Like you so kindly pointed out, I'm not a detective. But I've been a cop for a while. This doesn't pass the sniff test. I think it's connected to something larger."

"Would that be the assaults on the homeless you were looking into when we first met?" That explained why Will had pulled these two homicide investigations and why he'd examined the evidence so carefully. "Since you've been doing this so long, I'm sure you know why Trevitt reached the conclusions he did."

"He needed to clear the cases off his desk so he could focus on the more important ones." Disdain dripped from his words. "It's no secret certain sections of the population get preference over others."

"I don't disagree, but that's not why we're here." I understood why Trevitt closed the cases. Without a witness coming forward or the metaphorical smoking gun, the evidence remained inconclusive. But my gut said Will was right. Someone with that many pills and a bum knee would find an easier way to off himself, unless he wanted to send a big F.U. to the man upstairs. But even if that were the case, someone should have seen Robert dragging a ladder into the church or heard him breaking the lock. But addicts didn't always act rationally.

I went back to Sophie Marshman's case. No matter how I twisted it, I couldn't come up with an explanation as to why she didn't reach out to her kids before slicing herself open. Maybe she was afraid they'd talk her out of it or have her committed. Or she'd gone to see them and been turned away.

The ex-husband claimed she hadn't been by their house since he'd filed to have her visitation rights revoked. And since she didn't have money for a lawyer and wasn't in an ideal situation to fight for her parental rights, he would have had no reason to lie if he had forced her to leave after she showed up. The neighbors didn't recall seeing her either, so I doubted she'd made a surprise visit.

I sent a request to the experts at Cross Security to do a deep dive on Sophie and Robert and pull whatever they could on Detective Gabriel Trevitt. While I waited for the phone to ring and Cross to ask me why I was looking into two different homicide investigations, which he considered forbidden, I conducted an internet search for any article, message board posting, or social media mention of violence against the homeless. Nothing recent popped up.

"You said you thought these deaths connected to the cases you're investigating. But these are suicides or murders. The last time we spoke about this, you feared the assaults could escalate, but Sophie and Robert weren't attacked or beaten. Why do you think they're related to your other cases?"

Will got up to freshen his coffee. "You don't think they are?"

"I have no idea. But from what I recall, the M.O. is off. You said the others had been assaulted."

"And forced into dumpsters at gunpoint. A guy almost died when he got trapped in the back of a garbage truck. Maybe whoever's doing this got smarter and decided to take it one step further. Sophie was found near a dumpster."

"True, but this is about fourteen steps beyond a random beating." I leafed through the cases again, checking Trevitt's work. From what I could tell, Sophie and Robert didn't stay at the same shelters, eat at the same soup kitchens, or hang out in the same neighborhoods. Sophie's problem involved not being properly medicated. Robert's was addiction. Neither had any other signs of injury or recent bruising. It didn't look like either had been attacked or beaten prior to their deaths. "I'm not sure this is the work of the same unsub."

"So you agree? You think they were murdered?"

"I'm not sure. The evidence is inconclusive, but they died under suspicious circumstances. The cases should have been given more time."

"But you don't think this connects to the assaults?"

"No."

"Why not? Isn't murder an escalation of repeat attacks? Think about most domestic cases."

"That's not the same." But the sergeant had a point. Killers often honed and refined their methods over time, improving as they went. But to go from unprovoked assaults to cleverly masked murders was a hell of a learning curve. "That'd be like apples and oranges."

"They're both fruit."

"But they don't come from the same tree."

"Look who's getting philosophical."

Before I could reply, the door opened. I expected to see Iris. Instead, a delivery guy pushed his way inside. "Ah, you must be Alexis." He placed the box on the desk in front of me. "These are for you."

"Who sent them?" I eyed the pink pastry box, wondering if Will had ordered donuts using an app on his phone.

He handed me a note. "Martin Technologies. The guy who called said to deliver them to the most beautiful woman in the room. Obviously, that's you."

"Hey," Will said.

One of my patented death glares shut him up, and he made himself useful by refilling the coffeemaker.

I read the note. *I wanted to send a bouquet of roses but knew you'd like these better. I love you. ~ J.M.*

Reaching for my wallet, I pulled out a twenty and held it out to the delivery guy. "Thanks."

He shook his head and held up his palms. "Don't worry about it. The guy who phoned in the order added a hefty gratuity." He backed toward the door. "You have a lovely day, beautiful."

Peeling away the tape, I untucked the lid and opened it. Inside were a dozen cupcakes, expertly iced to look like white roses. These were definitely my new favorite flower. My phone rang before I could decide which cupcake to eat.

"Why aren't you working?" I asked.

"I am," Martin said, "but I'm between meetings and thought you could use something to brighten your day. I hope that's enough to feed the office."

"There might be one or two left. I'll bring them home tonight. They're gorgeous, by the way. You should see them."

"How do they taste?"

"I was just about to find out."

"In that case, I'll let you go. How about I pick you up after work?"

"I'd like to get home before three a.m."

"I'm calling it quits at nine. Is that too late? Marcal can—"

"Nine's perfect. But isn't that too early for you?"

"Not tonight. I'll see you later. Save me a rose."

I hung up, hoping to erase the smile off my face before Will could see it.

Instead of paying any attention to me, he peered over my shoulder and into the box. "Those look good."

I selected one from the center that had two leaves in green fondant. The cupcake wrapper was a shiny rose gold foil. When I peeled it away, it revealed a rich, chocolate cake. Martin knew me well. "Help yourself."

Will refilled my coffee cup and took one of the cupcakes from the box. "Are you sure this isn't a coffee shop? Fancy coffee. Expensive desserts. That's pretty much every coffee place in America."

Ignoring him, I nibbled on the cake. This made the morning's ordeal almost worth it. But I didn't want Martin to feel guilty, and these cupcakes felt like apology cupcakes.

"Damn." Will smacked his lips. "These are insane." He leaned over to examine the note. Automatically, I tucked it into my desk drawer. "Unless you and the delivery guy are having an affair and are into roleplay, I'm guessing these came from someone special. Most men don't drop a c-note on cupcakes unless they royally fucked up. What'd the bastard do? Did you catch him cheating? Did his wife walk in on you?"

I narrowed my eyes. "I thought you wanted my help."

Will noticed the chain hanging around my neck. But the engagement ring was tucked inside my shirt, so he couldn't see it. "You didn't sound mad on the phone. Is it your birthday or anniversary?"

"No." I let out an exasperated sigh. "Do you want my input or not?"

"Fine." He held up his palms. "You were just about to tell me why I'm wrong about everything. So let's hear it." He removed the wrapper from the rest of the cupcake and took another bite, getting a smear of white frosting stuck to the tip of his nose.

"The attacks you described were sloppy. Whoever committed the assaults did so for no apparent reason. It could be scare tactics, a turf thing—"

"A gang initiation?"

I pointed at him. "Right. Something along those lines." I tapped the folder on my desk. "If these suicides turn out to be murders, whoever committed them went through a lot of meticulous planning. You already described the lengths one would have to go to hang Robert from the church rafters. And given his lack of defensive wounds, that would be a difficult feat to pull off. Robert was an athlete. He should have put up a fight or tried to run. But he didn't." I couldn't figure out why not. I leafed through the folder. "We have the tox report. Robert wasn't drugged."

"Are you saying Trevitt was right?"

"I don't know, but I'm sure the detective reached that conclusion for a reason."

"Even with the unexplained oddities?"

I flipped back to the ME's report on Sophie Marshman. She'd cut her palm, which could have happened if her grip on the pocket knife slipped or if she'd held up her hand to ward off an attack. Other than that, there were no other marks on her, except for the cuts on her thighs. "The only other explanation is they knew their killer. It'd have to be someone they trusted."

"That means one guy murdered both of them."

"I'm not saying that. These two cases are completely different. Everything is different. The victims didn't travel in the same circles or hang around the same places. San Diego might not be as massive as Los Angeles, but I'm sure the unsheltered are spread out."

"There are about a thousand, maybe more, living on the

streets and in cars."

"That's exactly my point. Robert and Sophie may have never crossed paths, just like you and the million other people who live there. So why were they targeted? How did the killer or killers find them? And why didn't Sophie or Robert put up a fight?" I looked back at Trevitt's interview notes. "If they stayed at the same shelters or went to the same soup kitchens, it'd be more likely that these crimes were committed by one individual. But as it is, that theory seems pretty farfetched. If these are murders, they were probably committed by two different people for two very different reasons."

Will finished his cupcake and tossed the wrapper in the trash. "Just so we're clear, you're saying these cases have nothing to do with the string of assaults or each other."

"Unless you have a jacket on one of the assaults handy for me to compare to this, I'd say no."

"And that's your professional opinion?"

"Professional? Is that the vibe you're getting?" I got up and opened the door to the middle office. The computer monitor was on the floor and a half-completed jigsaw puzzle covered the entirety of my desk. "I hate to break it to you, but this office is a joke."

He ignored the theatrics. "I looked into you, Alex. Former decorated federal agent turned private investigator, employed at one of the top personal security firms in the country, so I'm not buying this preschool recess thing you have going on here. You've seen a lot of shit. Tell me what I'm looking at with the assaults."

"I'd say look into gangs and hate groups."

"Done and done. Nothing panned."

"What about developers?"

"Real estate?"

I nodded.

"I've tried looking into them, but that will require a lot more manpower. I'll keep digging."

"Don't forget contractors and politicians. Any group that wants to gentrify the neighborhoods or has a stake in making the area more aesthetically pleasing could be hiring muscle to scare the unhoused out of certain neighborhoods, assuming the attacks have been isolated."

Will reached for my sticky notes, peeled one off the top, and jotted down a note. "The mayor's up for re-election. One of the hot button issues is helping those who lost their jobs find new ones. Maybe there's something to that."

"Were the attacks isolated to certain neighborhoods?"

"They were concentrated in business and tourist districts."

"Are any new businesses or hotels thinking of moving into the area? If the mayor's keen on bringing in new jobs, y'never know."

"If some businessman or politician is paying a bunch of knee-cappers to scare off the homeless, do you think they'd go so far as to hire killers too?"

"Anything's possible, but hiring a professional to conduct hits on the homeless wouldn't be worth the return on investment. Murder brings about a lot of negative publicity. That would deter businesses from entering the area." But I couldn't help but think if Robert's suicide turned out to be murder, it was expertly staged. The kid shouldn't have had enemies powerful enough to pull off something like that. He was a nobody with a habit. He wasn't an Ivy Leaguer and never had the chance to become a first draft pick for the pro teams.

"Thanks for the tips." Will shrugged into his jacket. "What about the suicides? Any last thoughts?"

"If the way Trevitt handled these cases bothers you, talk to him or go above him. Whatever you think needs to be done, Sergeant."

"Call me Will."

"Why does the title bother you? You must have worked hard to reach that rank."

"Let's just say I'm hoping to redefine myself."

I rocked back in the chair and selected another cupcake. When I peeled back the foil, it revealed a fluffy coconut cake underneath. "Are you ever going to tell me why you're stuck with desk duty and aren't allowed to carry?"

"It doesn't matter."

"It damn well does."

He shook his head while he placed the pages back inside

the folder. "That's a story for another time."

"When?"

"Why are you pushing this?"

"I'm trying to figure out if I should trust you."

He closed the folder and tucked it against his chest. "That's up to you." He reached into the pastry box and grabbed another cupcake for the road. "What's your donut preference?"

"Chocolate crème."

"And if they're out?"

"Vanilla crème."

"And if they don't carry crème?"

"I'd go to another donut shop." I saw the exasperated look in his eye. "Anything with chocolate frosting. Sprinkles work in a pinch."

He tapped his temple. "I'll try to remember that."

SIX

After Will left, I called the sandwich place and had them move up my daily delivery from six to now. Since the sergeant had brought a series of convoluted crimes to my attention, I couldn't afford to go into a sugar coma or caffeine frenzy.

While I waited for them to deliver, I printed out the drafted contracts and called Iris to let her know the paperwork was ready. I hoped she'd changed her mind, but she hadn't. Today wasn't a good day, and she hadn't felt like leaving her house. But she swore she'd stop by tomorrow to sign the forms and drop off the retainer. After that, I'd be back on the scarlet letter brigade. Tailing cheating spouses was one of the things I hated most about this job, and given Iris's recent tragedy, I hoped she was wrong. But my gut knew better.

After conducting a quick background check on the Stapletons, I discovered neither had a criminal record or history of instability. Iris was a licensed paramedic. Theo was licensed by the California Board of Registered Nurses. The licensing bodies had conducted thorough checks, but I wanted to make sure they hadn't missed anything.

An internet search turned up dozens of news stories

related to the fatal shooting following an ambulance crash. Every news outlet reported the same facts. Gary Smale had sustained a fatal gunshot wound to the head. Iris Stapleton had been shot in the chest and sustained additional injuries due to the crash. The shooter and his two accomplices had been caught and charged. They were being held without bail while they awaited trial.

I checked Iris's and Theo's social media pages. They were set to private, but Cross Security had ways around such things. Iris had never been very active online. She'd share recipes, health articles, and any news stories related to taking safety precautions around the holidays. For Fourth of July, she posted fireworks safety. At Christmas, she posted tips on preventing fires from candles and tree lights. Thanksgiving was all about deep-fried turkey safety. But none of her posts were personal. And after the incident, she dropped off social media completely.

Theo, on the other hand, had hundreds of friends and an active page. After checking the most recent posters on his page, I scanned his friends list. At least twenty percent of his friends were single women around his age or younger. This might be a rooster in a henhouse situation. For Iris's sake, that would be preferable. I read the posted conversations Theo had with some of these women, but his tone remained friendly, bordering on flirty, but he never crossed any lines. He was smart.

After sending a request to my coworkers across the country to search all the dating sites and apps for Theo, I settled back in my chair. Before I could decide what to do next, my dinner arrived.

I ate a cup of soup with the roll from one of the sandwiches and added the meat and cheese to the side salad, glad Cross insisted on having a daily platter delivered to feed his employees and clients, even if I was the only one in the office.

I was halfway through my salad when the phone rang. "Cross Security, how may I direct your call?"

"Alex," Lucien Cross was not amused, "I was just notified of the request you placed earlier today."

"Which one?"

"The one involving a police detective."

"Have the techs finished their deep dive yet?" Opening my e-mail, I found the background check they'd run on Gabriel Trevitt but nothing on Sophie or Robert.

"I doubt it." Cross cleared his throat. "Is Detective Trevitt causing problems? If so, contact Jason Ganz. He's on retainer. He'll provide whatever legal advice or defense you require."

"That won't be necessary."

"Did the detective apply for the open position? I don't recall his name on the list of applicants."

"It isn't."

"Which would explain why you need the background check, assuming he just applied."

"Sure," I said.

"Alex, it's best not to fuck with law enforcement. You said you didn't have any contacts there. According to Amir, Detective Trevitt works for the San Diego police department, the same place as your new friend. Did the detective ask for your input on two recent homicides? Because I can't fathom any other reason why you'd want a deep dive performed on the victims in two of his cases."

"They're not victims. Trevitt said they were suicides."

"Even more reason not to poke around. Do I have to remind you that establishing a symbiotic relationship with local law enforcement is one of the reasons I chose you to get the West Coast office up and running? What you're doing sounds more like making enemies."

That was bullshit, but I didn't feel the need to point it out. "Sgt. Russo brought those two cases to my attention. He wanted my opinion on them and wondered if they could be related to a string of recent assaults."

"And he couldn't find a consultant in San Diego?"

"I doubt it. The man couldn't even find a coffee shop."

Cross mumbled something to himself, but I couldn't quite make it out. Maybe we had a bad connection. "Don't make enemies, but don't get too chummy either. Russo's not to be trusted."

"Russo helped us save your friend."

"That's debatable, but I see your point. Keep me

apprised. But under no circumstances are you to reevaluate the SDPD's closed homicide cases. Do I make myself clear?"

"What if the victims' families hire us to look into it?"

"Don't."

"Don't what?"

"You know what. Right now, you have more than enough to keep you busy. You have a few dozen applicants to interview and a new client to deal with. I want you to select an office manager by the end of the week. You've already wasted enough time."

"I thought you didn't want me to rush."

"Get it done." Cross hung up before I could ask what would happen if I didn't.

A moment later, my computer let out a series of chimes. He flooded my dropbox with another ten potential applicants, half of which required background checks. Justin, his assistant, sent me interview questions and a notice that three of the applicants had contacted him, wondering when they might hear back. I replied to his message, asking him to schedule interviews every afternoon from now thru Friday.

My boss's solution to my boredom was to give me more mind-numbing work to keep me occupied. Instead of having the desired effect, it made me more likely to find something else to occupy my time.

I grabbed my notepad and went into the first office, moved my blanket off the chair, and grabbed a marker off the desk. The whiteboard on the wall begged me to write something on it, so I wrote the first thing that came to mind. *Sophie Marshman.* Then I wrote down every detail I recalled from the case file, drew a line down the middle, and wrote all the questions that came to mind surrounding her death. I needed to speak to her ex-husband, her children, her friends, and anyone she interacted with at the various shelters and kitchens.

Once I ran out of room on the whiteboard, I entered the third office, grabbed the whiteboard off the wall, and brought it into the first office. After going through the same process concerning Robert Devers, I rested my hips against the edge of the desk and stared at the two boards. Homicides or suicides? One of each? I had no idea. But I had a list of people to question.

This would be easier if I had my own Justin to make calls, schedule appointments, and dig up addresses and phone numbers. Despite having done this job for quite some time, I knew it would be better to appease Cross than defy him. After all, he signed my paychecks. And regardless of his motivation, he opened this branch of Cross Security so Martin and I could be together.

Leaving the whiteboards in the first office, I went back into the main area and ran background checks on Sophie Marshman and Robert Devers. When that didn't result in any new information, I ran the rest of the background checks on the potential new hires, narrowed down the applicant pool based on qualifications, and sent the list of approved interviewees to Justin. Within an hour, he'd filled my calendar for the next ten days.

Tell Lucien I'll need two weeks. We have too many potentials to sort through, I typed.

A moment later, Justin's response popped up on my screen. *He said it's fine. And it's about time.*

I sent back an emoji with the tongue out. Will had been wrong. This office was just like preschool recess. And since I'd done all I could for the day, I poured myself another cup of coffee and took a cupcake into the middle office. While I worked on my jigsaw puzzle, I thought about the two suicides.

Cross was right. It'd be best to steer clear of them. But I couldn't do that. The circumstances surrounding their deaths made no sense. They would drive me crazy until I figured them out. But I was sure of one thing, whatever happened to Sophie and Robert had nothing to do with the random assaults. I just hoped this wasn't the work of a serial killer.

The M.O.s were too different, as were the victims. The only thing Sophie and Robert had in common was their living situation. Other than that, they were as different as day and night.

I'd make some calls in the morning and make sure

nothing strange shook loose. Part of me wanted to get started now, but I wanted to see what Cross's resident experts found before I did anything. Maybe Sophie had a life insurance policy her ex-husband wanted to cash in, and Robert had been into autoerotic asphyxiation and literally took it to new heights. But that seemed unlikely since he'd been found fully clothed.

For the rest of the night, I worked on and off at the reception desk, searching for news articles, similar stories, and checking social media accounts for clues. When my searches failed to turn up anything profound, I'd go back to work on my puzzle until another thought struck. Then I'd head back to the computer.

After hitting another dead end, I picked up the phone and dialed a familiar number. After several rings, SSA Mark Jablonsky answered his office phone with a gruff, "What do you want?"

"How'd you know it was me?"

"Parker?"

"You didn't know it was me?"

"Stop being cute. It's almost midnight. What's going on?"

"Why aren't you at home? I was all prepared to leave you a voicemail message."

"Too bad. You can ask in person or hang up."

"You're cranky. You shouldn't work so hard."

He muttered a few curses under his breath. "I'm trying to get ahead on a few things since I'm coming out to see you in a couple of weeks. Remember?"

"Me? I thought it was all about Martin and the Laker Girls."

"Lakers Girls."

"Whatever."

"I'm hanging up now."

"I need a favor."

He sighed. "What?"

"I need you to look into an officer-involved shooting that happened in San Diego." I gave him the date of the incident. "Two officers were killed. Sgt. Will Russo was involved. Mercer pulled the official file, but he said it looked like a cover-up. Everything had been sanitized. I thought maybe the sheriff's department or FBI looked into it, given the circumstances."

"What am I looking for?" Mark asked.

"Whatever you can find. I want to know what happened."

"Why?"

"Russo's a wild card. I can't get a read on him."

"Why can't Cross Security look into this?"

"We don't have that kind of access out here."

"What'd Lucien say?"

"He wants me to stay away from Russo."

"Maybe you should listen." He laughed. "Yeah, I heard it. That was dumb. I know better. Unfortunately, you don't. I'll see what I can find."

"Thanks." I hesitated. "If you could put a rush on it, I'd appreciate it."

"You're gonna be the death of me."

"I hope not." I waited, but Mark didn't hang up. "If it's too much..."

"It's not. I'm just busting your chops. You staying out of trouble? Given the things Marty's been telling me, it doesn't sound like it."

"I'm trying, but Russo showed up with two suspicious suicides which he thinks might connect to a slew of assaults he's been looking into. I'm pretty sure they don't connect, but I'm not sure they're suicides."

"Why is this your problem?"

"It's not, but my gut says Russo's a good guy. And he wants my help, but past experience tells me he's trigger happy and doesn't follow protocol the way he should. He said he's burnt out. That would do it, but there could be more to the story. A lot more. I want to make sure he's not dangerous. On the bright side, he's not authorized to carry or be out in the field, so that limits his opportunities to hurt someone."

"Those aren't good things. Be careful around him until I find out what's what. In other words, don't do anything until you hear back from me. Do you understand?"

"Yep."

"Are you going to do what I say?"

"I'll avoid Russo, unless he has donuts. Then all bets are off. But I'm going to move on these suicides once I finish gathering intel."

"Who hired you to do it?"

"Oddly enough, no one."

"Shit. You're bored. That always means trouble. Can't Cross give you a case to work? Maybe Marty has something you can do for him at the office."

"I'll be fine. I have a cheating husband to track."

"No wonder you're looking for something else to do. I know how much you love those. Just be careful. I'm not flying across the country to save your ass. I'm only coming out for vacation. That's it. Vacation," he emphasized all three syllables, "understand?"

"Yes, sir."

After we hung up, I did a quick news article search on the two suicides, printed out everything I could find, and highlighted the details as I read the pages.

A knock sounded on the outer office door. It creaked open, and Martin called out, "Hello?"

"In here." I looked up from the articles. *9:33*. "I'm impressed. Then again, you're usually punctual, except when it comes to leaving work on time."

Martin stood in the doorway, his jacket thrown over one shoulder and looking every bit the part of a cologne model. "I thought I'd surprise you tonight." He took half a step inside, looking around the room. "Where is everyone? Did they go home already?"

"Something like that."

He gave me an odd look. "Okay."

"Just give me a few minutes." I paperclipped the articles inside a folder and closed it before he could see what I was reading. "I want to finish this before I leave tonight." I went around the desk, grabbed his tie, which hung in a loose knot around his neck and pulled him close for a quick kiss. "Make yourself comfortable. I'll only be two minutes."

"Take your time." He wandered toward the break area while I ducked into the middle office and placed the last few pieces into my jigsaw puzzle. Now that was done, I had nothing else to occupy my time except work. Cross would be pleased.

When I returned to the outer office, Martin was gone. I found him studying the whiteboards in the first office. "That's your writing," he said.

"Are you sure you aren't a detective?"

"Is this your office?"

"I use them all."

He grinned, dropping his jacket on top of the desk while he took my face in his hands and kissed me again. "Hi."

"Hi yourself."

"It looks like we have the place to ourselves." He glanced back into the reception area.

"Keep it in your pants, handsome. Cross has the place wired."

"How about you give me a tour instead?"

"Sure." I entwined my fingers with his and led him out of the room. "This is the reception area. That's the waiting area." I pointed to the chairs, couch, and tiny impractical end tables. "These are the offices."

"Seriously, Alex, which one's yours?"

"The middle one."

"And the other two?"

"TBD."

"No one else works here?"

"You sound like Lucien. Did he call and ask you to give me a hard time?"

"No." Martin tugged on my hand and pulled me back toward him before I could close the open office doors. "You said there'd be plenty of people to keep an eye on you."

"And there are. This building has tons of offices and people. Plus, Will was waiting when I arrived."

"Will?"

"The cop I told you about."

"The one who arrested you?"

"No, the other one."

Martin thought for a few moments. "Not the one who attacked you in an alley."

"We've moved past that."

Martin let out an uneasy sigh. "Why hasn't Cross hired

anyone else to assist?"

"It's a process. I have interviews scheduled." Pulling my hand free, I closed the doors, grabbed my things, handed Martin the half-empty pastry box, and took out the remaining lunch items from the fridge. "Did you eat?"

"I put steaks in the fridge to marinate before we left this afternoon."

"Right." But I hadn't been paying that much attention. After I ushered him out of the office and locked the door, I dropped the leftover lunch platter off with building security.

"Thanks, Alex," Buck said.

"You're the best." Howard opened the tray. "I love roast beef."

"I'll make sure to keep that in the rotation." I smiled at them. "Have a nice night, guys."

"You too," Howard called as we left the building.

"See," I nudged Martin, who didn't appear pleased I'd been left to my own devices all day, "Buck and Howard are people from the office. Their entire job is to keep an eye on me." And everyone else in the building, particularly after a recent incident involving two decapitations, but Martin didn't need to know everything. "I didn't lie to you. Building security keeps tabs on everyone and everything. If I didn't feel well or needed help, I would have called them."

"I'm glad you're in such good hands." He snaked an arm around my waist as we headed toward the car. "How are you feeling? Any coughing? Chills?" He pressed his lips to my temple as we walked. "Fever?"

"We are not playing doctor when we get home. I feel fine."

"I bet I can make you feel better."

"The cupcakes already did the trick. I doubt you could top that."

A devilish glint entered his eyes. "Wanna bet?"

SEVEN

Will Russo wasn't waiting outside my door when I arrived at work the next morning. I was the slightest bit disappointed, probably because I was hoping for donuts. But it was better he wasn't around. I had too much to do, and the last thing I needed was someone looking over my shoulder.

Amir had left full workups on Sophie Marshman and Robert Devers in my dropbox. There wasn't much to either of them. Robert was the only child of two working class parents. His athletic prowess is what made him stand out. Everyone believed the scholarship was his big break and opportunity for a better life.

From what I could tell, his mom and dad avoided the criminal element. They were scraping by without owing anyone anything. A professional would have no reason to want Robert dead. He didn't rip off a dealer or the cartel. His parents hadn't pissed off any crime lords or vengeful dictators. Robert was just another kid with a drug problem.

Robert's potential enemies were limited to soccer rivals, but his injury removed them from the equation. I stared at the attached financial statements. Robert attended a large public high school, which had a top-tier athletic program. He never had a private trainer or coach, like a lot of all-stars. Once he entered college, the school provided state-of-the-art facilities, coaches, and medical services. But after he got hurt and hooked, he lost all of it, along with the few friends he had.

Amir had combed through Robert's social media and forwarded me a list of Robert's friends and teammates. One of them must have realized Robert was spiraling. But aside from a few desperate text messages and phone calls around the time Robert quit school, all communications with these supposed friends ceased.

I called the last few people Robert had spoken to before becoming homeless. Everyone said the same thing. Robert begged them for money and a place to stay. One guy, a junior from the soccer team, let him crash at his apartment only to find the place cleared out the next day. Robert stole everything of value, even the kitchen appliances.

"Did you file a police report?" I asked.

"No. Robert was in a bad way. I didn't want to make it worse."

"Did you ever try to find him?"

"Not after that. He screwed me. I was done."

"Didn't you want to get your things back or get revenge?"

"It wasn't worth it. Looking for Robert would have been looking for trouble. And I didn't need that in my life."

That had been the consensus. "Do you have any idea where Robert was getting his pills?"

"He had a prescription."

"What about after it ran out?"

"I don't know. He probably found a hook-up. There are always plenty of parties. People know how to get things. That's why he wanted the money, I guess."

"But no specifics? You don't know anyone who could have supplied him with drugs?"

"Sorry."

I made a few more notes, but figuring out what happened to Robert would require tracking down his dealers and speaking to the rehab facility. Since I had my first interview scheduled in a couple of hours, I didn't have the time to make a trip to San Diego. That would have to wait.

Switching gears, I opened the file on Sophie Marshman. She'd been born and raised in Los Angeles. Her sister, Jenna, still lived here. Sophie was divorced twice. Her first marriage was to her college sweetheart. They married at twenty-two, divorced three years later, and had no children. After that, Sophie focused on her career as a reflexologist and acupuncturist.

She worked at an L.A. clinic until she married Nathan Marshman. Soon after, she quit her job. The couple moved to San Diego where Nathan worked as a staff veterinarian. Sophie found a job at a spa, but that didn't last for more than a few months before the place went under. Instead of getting a new job, she ended up pregnant and at home with two young children. Her oldest daughter, Pam, was now eleven. Her youngest, Erin, was six. The Marshmans had been divorced for a little over two years.

At first, Sophie remained in the house. Neither she nor Nathan could afford to move out. But after the incident with the wine and the pills, which were Sophie's anti-anxiety medication, the court changed their tune. She had to go.

When she could no longer afford a place to live, she bounced around shelters, but the incident with the pills and wine made spas and medical offices less willing to hire her. Without a stable job or place to live, she eventually fell through the cracks. Her mental health deteriorated further, and her visitation rights were revoked.

From the details Amir found, I couldn't help but think Sophie had been isolated and alone. She had no one to turn to for support. Her ex was a slimeball. Perhaps that had been his plan all along.

Even though I didn't know Nathan Marshman, I wanted to consider him a suspect, except Detective Trevitt had ruled him out. Nathan had been home all night with his daughters. His live-in girlfriend vouched for him, and so did the neighbors who remembered seeing him come home the day before. When the police came knocking first thing in the morning, Nathan had just rolled out of bed.

I checked Sophie's phone records, wondering why she didn't ask her sister for help. But they hadn't spoken in years. I wondered if Jenna even knew she had nieces or what kind of falling out led to that level of estrangement.

When I couldn't find the answers written in black and white, I looked up Jenna's address and phone number. But when I drove by her place, she'd already left for work, so I headed to the groomers.

"Pick-up or drop-off?" a harried-looking woman asked.

"I'm looking for Jenna Roth."

She squinted at me. "Why?"

"I'm Alexis Parker." I showed her my business card. "I wanted to express my condolences and see if she'd be willing to talk to me about her sister."

The woman snorted, refusing to take the card from my hand. "Save your sympathies. Sophie was a piece of work. I'm not sorry she's gone."

"You're Jenna?"

"Yeah, but I have a lot to do today. I don't want to waste any of it discussing my sister."

I scanned the list of services the groomers provided and the price list before placing four twenties on the counter. "I just have a few questions. This won't take long. You can consider me a paying customer."

"Keep your money. I doubt I can help you. Sophie and I haven't spoken in three years. The last time we talked, I begged her to come home. But she wouldn't. She left everyone behind for some loser guy."

"You mean Nathan."

She nodded. "I tried calling her when our mom was on her deathbed, but she didn't even come home for that. She didn't show up at the funeral or anything. That was the last time we ever spoke. After that, I was done trying."

Jenna had every reason to be bitter, but that wouldn't help me figure out what happened to Sophie. "Are you aware Sophie was divorced and living on the streets?" I asked.

"The police told me, but I had no idea."

"What about her history of mental illness?"

"Sophie always had some sort of problem. It was under control. At least, that's what I thought." She turned at the sound of a dog barking. "One second." She left to see what was going on in the back. When she returned, the front of her shirt was wet and a few soapsuds clung to the side of her forearm. "Rascal has the perfect name."

"What?"

"The dog. He's a real rascal." She picked up a smock and wiped the soap off her arm before putting it on over her wet clothes.

"Do you believe your sister would intentionally harm herself?" I asked.

Jenna stared at me as if I'd spoken Greek. "The police said she killed herself. Are you telling me that isn't true?"

"I don't know."

"Why are you looking into this? Who hired you? Did Nathan hire you?"

"No one hired me."

"Then what the hell are you doing? Do you get your kicks by screwing with people?"

I held up my palms. "A contact I have at the police department expressed concern over your sister's case. She died under suspicious circumstances. I wanted to make sure the police didn't miss anything."

"And you expect me to pay you? Are you shaking me down?"

"No. I don't want anything. I just wondered if Sophie ever tried or threatened to harm herself in the past."

"No."

"Do you know anything about her marriage or dissolution of her marriage?"

"I'm sure Nathan used her until he got bored and moved on to the next best thing. He's a pompous piece of shit. He thinks he's better than everyone else because he's a marine veterinarian. He's too good for a groomer."

I narrowed my eyes. "Were you acquainted?"

"We were fucking engaged until Sophie swooped in with her fancy practice, and that was it. She and Nathan strolled into the sunset and never looked back."

"Is that why you're estranged from your sister?"

"Sophie knew better than to show her face around here, even when I asked her to. Frankly, I'm not surprised they divorced. Nathan already showed his true colors. He has shiny object syndrome. He can't resist upgrading when it comes to girlfriends or wives or whatever. His newest fling is probably a doctor or lawyer or something. She's probably younger and prettier and perkier."

"Do you think he'd harm Sophie?"

Jenna shook her head. "He's a lot of terrible things, but he's not violent."

"But he's a vet. He has medical training. He'd know about arteries and cutting."

"Humans are a lot different than animals. Frankly, Nathan's too much of a pussy to wander into some dark alley to attack his ex-wife."

"What about their children? Nathan had full custody. Sophie didn't even have supervised visitation, but she called them twice a week. Nathan might have been afraid his kids would turn against him or Sophie would fight for custody and support. He already had to pay her alimony." It just wasn't enough to get her off the streets.

"I can't picture him physically harming her. Manipulating, shaming, and screwing around behind her back, sure, I can see those things, but not killing her. I don't think he has that in him."

"But you think your sister would kill herself without reaching out to anyone."

Jenna looked me straight in the eye. "Who would she have called? She had no one left. And she hated being alone. So I guess, to answer your question, I'm not surprised my sister killed herself." She played with the touchscreen in front of her. "I have work to do. If you have any other questions about Sophie, I suggest you ask Nathan. She chose him, so he can deal with this mess."

Before I could say anything, my phone rang. *Mark*. I hit ignore, but Jenna was done talking. I left my card on the counter. "I'm sorry to pick at old wounds. If you think of anything, please reach out." But Jenna didn't take the card or acknowledge what I said. Instead, she went into the back. This interview was over.

I'd gotten the answer to one of my questions, but now I had a million more. I'd have to follow up with the social workers and volunteers Sophie had most recently interacted with. They'd be able to tell me more than her sister.

After I got back to my car, I returned Mark's call and put it on speaker while I checked the time and headed for the office. Depending on traffic, I might make it back before the first interviewee arrived.

"Hey, what's going on?" I asked.

"I called the L.A. field office to see what they know about the shooting. According to ballistics, one of the two dead cops took friendly fire. The slugs they pulled out of him matched Russo's service piece."

"Shit. Do we know what happened? From what I hear, Russo was cleared of any wrongdoing."

"I don't know how," Mark said. "The cop he killed was shot in the chest. They were facing each other."

"Maybe the cop tried to retreat and ran into the line of fire."

"He was double-tapped, just like the police are trained to do." Mark's cabinet drawer let out a shrill squeal. "I want you to be careful and stay away from Russo."

"Did the FBI investigate the shooting? What conclusion did they reach?"

"The FBI didn't touch it. The sheriff's department conducted the investigation. They cleared Russo, but I don't know how."

"Have you seen the reports?"

"You really think I'd call in favors like that for you?"

"Yep."

He chuckled. "Damn, you're getting as cocky as Marty. The report said it was a clean shoot. Russo acted reasonably and professionally. It was a justified homicide."

"What about body cam footage?"

"Funny thing about that. It went missing after the sheriff's department ruled on it."

"Do we know why?"

"Not a clue, but let me direct your attention to the writing on the wall. Russo and two officers ended up in a tight spot. They were at an abandoned garage in suspected gang territory when the firefight occurred. The other dead officer took a shotgun blast to the face. The cop Russo killed wasn't carrying a shotgun. In fact, no shotgun was found on the scene. And your buddy's the only one left to tell the story."

"He could have walked into a bad situation."

"Or he led the other two into a bad situation. Or there was a double-cross or any of a million other scenarios. Russo doesn't come out smelling like a rose in any of them."

"Wrong place, wrong time?" I suggested.

"Then why hasn't he come forward, pushed an investigation, denounced the actions the officers took? They were his subordinates. They were under his command. His word would hold more weight, but instead, they're dead and their families are receiving full benefits. That makes me think the dead officers weren't dirty, or they're all dirty. Keep your distance. Not everyone is as reliable as O'Connell, Thompson, and Heathcliff. But you shouldn't need me to tell you that. You've dealt with dirty cops before."

"But if Russo's dirty, why did he bench himself? Why is he reviewing closed cases for mistakes?"

"To make amends or throw everyone off the scent. It's also possible he could have had a change of heart, or he's afraid whoever killed the other officer will come for him if he causes any more trouble."

But something told me Will Russo wasn't worried about causing trouble.

EIGHT

My office door opened. "Alex?"

"I'll be right with you." I centered the computer monitor and wiped the remaining puzzle dust off my desk. After making sure everything was tucked away, I stepped out of the office. "Iris."

"You sound surprised." She looked uncertainly around the room. "If this is a bad time, I can come back."

"Now's great." I gestured toward a chair. "I didn't expect to see you this early. I was just tidying up. Please, make yourself comfortable."

She sat on the edge of the offered chair, clutching her purse on her lap. "Theo went to run some errands before work, so I figured now would be a good time to get this over with."

"Are you sure? You're more than welcome to change your mind."

"Wouldn't you want to know?"

"I wouldn't, but I'd have to."

"That's exactly how I feel."

I took two copies of the contract out of the filing cabinet and handed her one. We went over the terms and services Cross Security could provide, along with an estimate of projected costs. "It depends on how long the investigation takes and if I incur any additional expenses. Do you have any questions?"

"How long are you going to tail him?"

"As long as it takes. Generally, these things wrap up in about two weeks. Sometimes, a case is open and shut in a day. A lot depends on his schedule and his extracurriculars."

"With the way things have been going lately, you might not need an entire day."

"Do you know where Theo is now?"

"He went to pick up some groceries." She looked at her watch. "Usually, that takes at least an hour."

"That doesn't give me enough time." I wanted to put spyware on Theo's computer and phone. But the second would be trickier since he always had it on him and didn't want his wife near it. I'd also need to put a GPS tracker on his car. "Conducting surveillance solo is doable, but the more access you can provide, the easier it will be. It'll save us both time and you some money."

"Sure, anything you need." She picked at her cuticle. "What happens if you don't catch him with someone else?"

"Assuming there's another reason for his absences, I should be able to figure that out after I tail him for a few days."

"How likely is that?"

"I don't know."

She picked up the pen and signed the contract. "Do you take cash? I don't want him to know I hired you in case he checks our bank account or credit card charges. He doesn't look that often, but y'never know."

"Cash is fine. I just need the retainer. We'll square up after the job is complete." I printed out a receipt and tucked the money into the lockbox I kept in my drawer. Later on, I'd take it to the bank.

She stared at the receipt for a while before folding it into a tiny triangle and placing it into the decorative front flap of her purse. But she looked confused, like she didn't know what to do now. I'd seen other clients exhibit similar behavior.

"Would you like a cup of coffee? Or something to eat?" I

asked. "We need to go over how this works and what I need you to do."

She blinked, looking up at me. "Um...coffee, I guess."

"Cream? Sugar?"

"Both."

"Would you like to try a flavored creamer instead? My boss stocked the kitchen with all sorts of crazy things, and that's on top of the daily food deliveries. He's prepared for a buzzing business even though this branch is just getting off the ground."

"That sounds like something Theo would do. I used to tease him that he should have been a doomsday prepper." Her expression soured. "I guess we weren't prepared for everything."

"No one ever is." I led her into the kitchen and opened a few cabinets, pointing to the row of boxes. She gave me a confused look. No wonder Will thought this was a coffee shop. "Pick your flavor. Any flavor."

"Do you have vanilla?"

"French, Madagascar, or bean?"

She snorted and grabbed two creamers from one of the boxes, eyeing the contents of the cabinets as I filled a mug with coffee.

"Help yourself to anything you'd like. We have a few leftover pastries from this morning, too. They're in the box. Sandwiches and fruit are in the fridge."

"I didn't realize you served lunch." She reached for one of the individual salads and took a croissant from the box while I placed the cup on the desk and grabbed a stirrer. "Theo's probably picking up a couple of subs from the deli. One to eat now, and one to take to work." She stared at the desk. "He'll probably bring one home for me, too." She sighed. "I don't get it. Why does he bother being considerate when he's out banging some whore?"

"I don't know, but we live in a society that says innocent until proven guilty."

She scoffed, tearing off the top on the creamer and pouring it into her coffee. She repeated the process with a second one before giving it a stir and a tentative sip.

"Is it disgusting?" I asked. "I've been afraid to try them."

"Nah, it's not half bad. It's a decent replacement for a vanilla latte." She took another sip and settled into the chair. "If you hang a chalkboard right there, you could turn this into a nice little lunch place."

"I'll keep that in mind in the event the investigation thing doesn't work out. I'm pretty sure I can bet on at least one customer. Yesterday, a guy showed up to get some coffee."

"I'd believe it."

I laughed. "C'mon, you were a first responder. You know how much we like our snacks."

"The firehouse kitchen was always stocked. I didn't realize private detectives did the same thing."

"This is my boss's doing. He's fancy like that. A box of donuts and stale coffee is more my speed." I poured a cup of coffee for myself and moved some things around on the reception desk to make more room for her to eat. "Do you and your husband share a computer?"

"No, but he uses a desktop for almost everything. I can give you access." She stabbed at a tomato, spearing it with a few pieces of romaine.

"Have you ever checked his e-mail or browser history?"

She nodded while chewing. "I never found anything suspicious. He watches a lot of DIY stuff. Other than that, he listens to true crime podcasts and has a weird fascination with searching auction sites for car parts and power tools."

"He sounds like a stereotypical male." Almost too stereotypical. "Does he build cars or furniture?"

She snorted, nearly choking on a cucumber in the process. "A few of the surgeons he works with build kit cars. He's obsessed with them. They talk about them a lot during surgeries. He'd love to do it, but we don't have the money or time for that. But he looks online a lot to see what he can find, probably so he can be part of the conversation."

"Do you mind if I make a few notes?"

"Feel free, but I don't see how that's helpful."

"It probably isn't, but I don't want to overlook anything."

"He has a lot of car magazines. The ones with the half-naked ladies on the front with the big bazongas." She exhaled and put the salad container down. "With my luck, that's the woman he's found."

That seemed unlikely, but this was California. The place was lousy with attractive, single women. "Has he gone to any car shows?"

"One, I think. Maybe two." Iris rubbed her head. "These last ten months have been a blur. I don't know where he's gone or what he's been doing. I can barely tell you what I've done."

"I get it."

She tore off the edge of the croissant, focusing on it instead of me. "Do you mind if I ask how?"

"I do, but I'll tell you anyway. I used to be an FBI agent. My supervisor wanted to give me a taste of command, so he put me in charge of an op. I sent him, my partner, and another agent into a booby-trapped building. My supervisor's the only one who survived."

"That sucks."

"Yeah."

"No wonder you had *it's not my fault* printed on a coffee cup." She swallowed, abandoning the croissant. "How long did it take before you came to terms with everything?"

"You heard the counselor. It's a process. I'd say years, but whenever I lose anyone else, it becomes exponentially harder to move past it. It's like I have to get over the previous losses again. That's how I ended up in therapy. A fellow agent I'd worked with was...," just saying the words brought the horrific crime scene to mind, "killed."

"That's why I can't be a paramedic anymore. I'm tired of losing people. And to lose someone else in the back of an ambulance or to be thrust into another situation like that," she shook her head, "I can't do it. I won't do it."

"You don't have to."

"For the first few months after it happened, I was numb to everything else. If Theo had told me he was divorcing me or screwing around, I wouldn't have even cared. Now, I wonder what I'll do if he leaves me. I don't think I can lose anyone else. Not now. Not him."

"But you want me to look into this."

"I have to know. It's the only chance I have of fixing it."

"Before the incident, did you and Theo ever have problems? Any instances of infidelity?"

"No. We were solid. Our first two years were a little rocky, but that had to do with figuring out our schedules and how to live together. The usual things. We'd fight and throw stuff." A grin tugged at the corners of her mouth. "Laundry, mostly. Now, he just disappears. Again, that's probably my fault. After what happened, I avoid confrontation. I shake anytime things get tense. I can't even watch those stupid reality dating shows because the contestants fight too much. I guess that's when Theo started walking away. The rage he has bottled up is probably from all the fights we never had."

I made a few more notes, but it didn't tell me much. Iris tossed the container and uneaten portion of the croissant into the trash. "Is Theo on social media?" I asked, even though I'd already looked.

"He is. Actually, we both are. We're friends, so I can see his page. I haven't seen anything flirtatious pop up."

"What about private messages?"

"I don't log on to his account, and he won't let me check his phone. Maybe I should."

"There's no reason. I'll take care of it. I'll need access though."

"I don't have his password."

"But you can give me permission to access his phone records and internet history, right?"

"We're joint on the account, if that's what you mean. Everything we have is in both of our names."

"Great." I made a few more notes. That would make getting phone records easier.

"Theo's not one of those people who posts forty times a day or anything like that, but he gets on there when he's taking a break from work. He likes to watch funny videos and memes. Do you think that's where he met her?"

I shrugged. "Does Theo have any kinks?"

"Why?"

"It could inform on where he's disappearing in the

middle of the night."

"We never had any threesomes or anything. We aren't swingers. It's always just been the two of us in the bedroom."

"Okay."

"He likes uniforms, roleplay, things like that. I doubt that'll help you."

"Probably not."

Her phone dinged, and she looked at the screen. "He's home. He wants to know where I am." She typed out a response with her thumbs and put her phone back in her bag. She made sure she zipped it before getting out of the chair. "I should get home. When are you going to start spying on him?"

"I have to get a few things set up first." I found the copy of his work schedule. "According to this, he'll be gone most of the day tomorrow."

"And night. He's working a double."

"Okay. I'll do some research and call from my personal number to let you know when I'm on my way to your house. I'll start there. I want to check his computer and set up some trackers. After that, we'll play it by ear." I nodded toward her bag. "What did you tell him?"

"I said I met a friend from group therapy for coffee."

"It's true enough. The less lies you tell, the better off you'll be."

She chewed on the inside of her lip. "Y'know, I changed my mind. I want proof of his cheating. Photographs, if possible. I want to see what she looks like. I don't want him to be able to deny it or act like I'm crazy. I'm not crazy."

"No, you're not."

"Sometimes, I feel like it."

"Me too."

"Is it terrible to hope she's drop-dead gorgeous?" She let out a bitter laugh. "I'd hate it, but I'm hoping he's bonking one of those car girls."

"Can I ask why?"

"That would be more understandable, I think. Like a hall pass or fulfilling a fantasy. It'd be worse if she were old and ugly or even if she was just your average Jane. That would mean he really cared about her or he didn't care who he was with as long as he wasn't with me."

Unsure what to say to that, I kept my mouth shut while Iris made her way out of the office. Frustrated by my assignment working for the scarlet letter brigade, I scanned and uploaded the signed contract to the server and checked to see if Amir had found any dating profiles for Theo Stapleton. He hadn't gotten any hits, but with a million different online sites and apps, it could take days, possibly weeks.

Checking the time, I wondered when my first interviewee would show up. He was already more than an hour late. L.A. traffic was a bitch, but first impressions were important. If nothing else, he should have called to say he'd be delayed, especially after he'd called the main office to find out why he hadn't heard back from us.

While I waited, I found a number of waiting background checks and security assessments Cross wanted me to complete for one of our corporate clients. So I went to work on those. After finishing in record time, I reviewed my notes on Theo Stapleton, but until I could gain access to his home and car, there wasn't much I could do. The man would be spending the next eight hours at work, which meant he wouldn't have a chance to cheat, or so I assumed.

Since there wasn't anything else to do, I made some calls to the different shelters Sophie Marshman had frequented. Most places couldn't tell me anything I didn't already know. I tried her ex-husband, but he didn't answer. I was halfway through dialing the next number on my list when the door opened.

"Sorry, I'm late." A man strode toward me with his hand extended. "I'm Skylar Lenes. You're expecting me."

"Alex Parker." I gestured to the empty chair in front of me. "Please."

He took a seat, gripping the arms as he looked around the office. "This is not what I pictured from Cross Security." He looked at his watch. "What time does the office usually close? Is today a slow day?"

"We're not closed." I'd made more than my fair share of bad impressions, but even with the benefit of the doubt, this guy rubbed me the wrong way. "And every day is a slow day. We just opened."

"Two months ago, right?" He leaned back, crossing one leg over the other. His skinny jeans stopped at his ankles, revealing a pair of flip-flops. Welcome to California. "I figured business was booming. Why does Cross Security need an office manager if there's nothing to manage?"

"Do me a favor." I held out the desk phone. "Call Lucien Cross and ask him that. Go on. I'll wait."

Skylar chuckled. "Don't get me wrong. I could use something less demanding, but with Cross's reputation and client list, I pictured something a lot different than this."

"This is a satellite branch. The main office is more impressive."

"I bet it is."

"Unfortunately, the main branch is three thousand miles away."

"I'm open to relocating."

"There aren't any positions available."

Skylar squinted at me. "I'm off to a bad start, aren't I?" He adjusted in the chair, placing both feet back on the floor and tugging on his dress shirt, which only emphasized the open top buttons and the hemp necklace around his neck. "Give me a redo."

"Sure."

He smiled. "I'm sorry I'm late. My current gig ran over, and I couldn't get away."

"What are you doing?" He hadn't listed a current job on his CV.

"I'm a personal assistant to an A-lister. I can't mention any names. NDAs. I'm sure you understand. But he's filming a TV series, so I've been running his household and taking care of whatever needs to be done. I had to get his car serviced and detailed. But the mechanics found a problem with the brakes and had to change them, which put everything else behind schedule. I rushed straight here as soon as I could get away."

"Why do you want this job?" I asked.

"Cross Security is legendary. My previous employer used Cross's teams to provide personal protection. They know everything about security and what's going on. I watched them all the time. I've even heard some of Cross's people have consulted on films and stuff."

"Uh-huh. But the opening isn't for a security position. This is an office job. Answering phones, making coffee, scheduling appointments."

"But wouldn't I have access to the security information too? Wouldn't I get to assign the protection details and keep track of security codes and things like that?"

"No."

"No?"

"No. Why would you want that kind of access?"

"I don't know. In case of an emergency."

"What kind of emergency? Are you planning a heist?"

He laughed uncomfortably, but he didn't deny it. I pulled a printed copy of his resume from the top drawer, double-checked the spelling of his name, and opened the security check we ran. Skylar didn't have a criminal record. He graduated from UCLA and majored in communications. Wanting access to our security info meant he was up to no good. The guy was right. He was off to a bad start.

"What makes you think you're qualified for this job?" I asked.

"I've been the personal assistant to at least three Cross Security clients. I've seen how the teams work. I've had to coordinate with them. I'm used to seeing what they do. I could make things run smoother from inside Cross Security."

"Have you ever worked in an office?"

"Five years." He pointed to the bullet point on the sheet of paper. "That was my first job out of college. I have the experience."

"How fast do you type?"

"Seriously?"

"Humor me."

"I don't know. Fifty-five words per minute." He glanced at the equipment. "I even know how to use that." He pointed to the multifunction copy machine.

"Wonderful, but do you know how to make that work?" I pointed to the coffeemaker.

"Yeah."

"Great."

He cocked his head to the side. "Shouldn't you be asking me something more important?"

"Like what?" I preferred conducting interviews that involved a two-way mirror or a table with a bar in the middle. But Skylar didn't need to know that. Also, I didn't like him. Maybe it was the flip-flops or hemp necklace. But I could learn to live with those things. It was his comment about security codes that worried me.

"How well I work under pressure or what my greatest strengths and weaknesses are. Y'know, things like that."

"You've spent the last six years working as a personal assistant for various celebrities which means you're used to working under pressure and in hostile conditions."

He snickered, grinning. "True."

"As far as weaknesses, I'd say it's your shoes. If you're coming to the office, you have to prepare for insane things. You need to be able to run. Those pose a liability. Liabilities around here could mean death."

He laughed, erroneously believing it was a joke. "I own real shoes with laces and everything."

"Great."

"That's two greats." He grinned. "Does that mean I get the job?"

"If you get it, what's the first thing you'd do?" My money was on breaking into a client's house or using their private information as blackmail.

He quirked his lips to the side, contemplating the question and sensing it was a trick. "Whatever you asked me to do."

"Let's say you're the first person in the office. Everything's already been scheduled for the day. We don't have any pressing issues. What do you do?"

He looked around, hoping to find the answer written on the wall or taped to the desk. When he couldn't find anything, a smug look came over him. "Make coffee."

"Good answer."

"Not great?"

"We'll be in touch."

NINE

After Skylar left, I mulled over the interview. It could have gone worse, though I wasn't entirely sure how. We were the same age, but he acted like a kid. Again, I might have been dwelling on the flip-flops, which made no sense. I loved shoes. I owned dozens of them, including impractical, strappy heels. They were one of the few designer items I didn't mind Martin buying for me.

The problem wasn't the shoes. His comment about security codes should have been a joke, since he already had access as a PA. But I couldn't help but think he wanted to commit an inside job and pin it on one of the private security teams.

In case my imagination wasn't running wild, I called Cross to give him the heads-up, but he didn't answer my call. He might have gone home for the day. But I suspected he was screening his calls, so I left him a long-winded voicemail detailing every aspect of the interview and suggesting he conduct the rest of them on his own.

After that, I cleaned out the fridge and locked up. Martin wasn't home. I texted, asking if I should wait dinner, but he told me it'd be another late night and not to wait up.

Rush hour ended a few minutes ago. If I left now, I could get to San Diego before the shelters shut their doors. Most of the staff would still be around. It wouldn't be a bad time to ask about Sophie and dig into Robert's death. If I didn't, the alleged suicides would distract me from my paying client. This was my one shot. After tonight, I'd be too busy tailing Theo.

I packed an overnight bag and left Martin a note. As long as I made it back to the office in time for the next interview, I'd be fine. Theo wouldn't be home until late tomorrow night. That would give me plenty of time to search his house and set up surveillance.

But as I drove toward the setting sun, Mark's words replayed in my head. He warned me not to do this. Cross warned me not to do this. Didn't I say I was going to listen to my friends from now on? Maybe that could be next year's resolution.

To quiet the voices in my head, I hit the speed dial on my phone and pressed the speaker button.

"Hey, what are you doing calling me? Are you home?" Detective Derek Heathcliff asked.

"No. I'm heading south."

"To Mexico?"

"San Diego."

"Why?"

"Are you at work?"

"What's wrong?"

After spilling my guts on the two suicides, the intel I'd gathered on Sgt. Will Russo, and the background I'd run on Det. Trevitt, I asked, "What do you think?"

"Trevitt did his job. He investigated, failed to find evidence of foul play, and ruled the deaths suicides. I would have done the same thing. No one was surprised by their deaths. Without a witness coming forward or forensic evidence on the murder weapons pointing to another person's involvement, there's nothing to investigate. You know this. Why are you asking me for my opinion?"

"Because the two scenes can be read a few ways, and you said murder weapons. Do you think we're right? Do you think they were murdered?"

"Parker," Heathcliff said in that tone which meant I was venturing onto thin ice, "I just said Trevitt was right to rule them suicides, but I know you. You have this annoying habit of being right about most things. What does your gut say?"

"I'm not sure."

"Ah, that explains the phone call. You wanted a professional opinion."

"I called because you're my favorite detective. And I miss you."

"I miss you too. Are you still going to meetings?"

"I have been, but I've decided to take a break for a while. What about you?"

"I've gotten busy with work."

We both knew the only reason Derek had been going to those meetings was to keep me company. "Me too."

"I find that hard to believe. You wouldn't be poking around in this if you were busy. Hang on." He came back on the line ten minutes later. "Trevitt's plate isn't overflowing. He has a few open cases, but he would have stuck with Sophie's case if he thought there was something to it. There isn't. He spoke to her ex-husband, her children, and every social worker and volunteer she interacted with. He even canvassed the homeless encampments where she stayed when she didn't find a bed in one of the shelters. Sophie was depressed. She'd repeatedly said she didn't want to go on. Her suicide was no surprise."

"How do you know that?"

"I'm a detective with a phone."

"You called Trevitt? What did you say?"

"I fudged on the details, telling him a distant relative had expressed concern over the situation."

"Do you believe him?"

"He e-mailed me a copy of the report. I'm looking at it right now, but nothing stands out. Do you want me to forward it to you?"

"I've already read it, but it wouldn't hurt to have my own copy."

"Okay. Done."

"You didn't happen to ask him anything about Robert

Devers, did you?"

"I can have O'Connell call him in a few days, if you really want me to."

"That probably won't be necessary, but I'll get back to you if I change my mind."

"I was being facetious."

"But it's a good idea."

"Good night, Parker."

"Night, Derek."

I hit end call and kept my eyes peeled for the next mile marker, wondering if I should turn around. But I was halfway to San Diego. And spending the night in front of the TV or setting up surveillance outside the Stapletons' house didn't hold much appeal.

Derek asked what my gut said. Will convinced me these suicides could be murders. I didn't disagree. Even Derek didn't disagree, but there was no smoking gun. Finding one would jam up Trevitt, but it could save lives. That's why Will had been so adamant about it. He didn't want anyone else to die, especially those on the fringe with the least amount of protection.

Why would a dirty cop or cold-blooded killer care about such things? He wouldn't, unless he wanted to make amends. And cold-blooded killers rarely changed that drastically. That didn't mean Will was innocent, but he might be hoping for a chance at redemption.

I'd be a hypocrite if I condemned him for one bad act. But I had no way of knowing if it was one bad act since he wouldn't talk to me. Again, Mark's voice entered my head, but this time it wasn't his warning, it was Lucien's. I shouldn't piss off the police or trust them. So I'd do this on my own, quickly and quietly.

* * *

The eighteen people I spoke to about Sophie all said the same thing. She was troubled. She'd been prescribed medication, but she would have benefitted from more talk therapy. Except she rarely showed up. Counselors volunteered, but Sophie didn't want the help. She never made real friends or bonded with anyone. She kept to herself.

She hated how derailed her life had gotten. She felt like too much of a failure to confide in anyone, and she'd been too prideful to ask for help. Whether that was her personality or part of her illness was anyone's guess.

I left the fourth shelter wishing she'd gotten help or admitted she needed help. But she'd burned so many bridges, she'd been afraid they were beyond mending.

Deciding that asking the social workers and volunteers for more details regarding Sophie's last few days wouldn't lead to anything more than heartache, I shifted topics and focused on the recent violent attacks against others in the unhoused community. A few of the counselors had noticed an uptick in assaults and one had heard about the dumpster incident, but they didn't have any leads. I didn't know if they were too overwhelmed or if the attacker had been careful, so I took my questions elsewhere.

A large homeless encampment was set up a few blocks from the shelter. I kept my jacket zipped, hoping I wouldn't need to grab my gun in a hurry. A trash can fire burned near the center. Several people huddled around it. A few had camping equipment they used to heat canned foods.

"Hello," I called, not wanting to startle anyone.

A few people looked up at me.

"Hi." A lady in a pink fur jacket waved.

"You lost?" a guy in an army surplus coat asked.

"No. I have a few questions I hope you won't mind answering."

"We'll see," he said.

"I wondered if any of you heard about the recent attacks. A couple of people were forced inside dumpsters. A guy almost got crushed."

The guy with the army coat nodded, focusing his attention on the can of beans he held near the fire. "Are you a reporter?"

"No."

"Then why are you asking?"

"A friend told me about it. He was concerned."

Army Coat patted the empty crate beside him. "Sit

down."

"Thank you." I took a seat, glimpsing movement near the edges. Some people shut themselves into their tents to avoid me. Others appeared cautiously curious, not wanting to turn their backs to me. "Do you know anything about that?"

"A lot of bad things happen out here. Fights. Drugs. But we gotta stick together. Not everyone gets it. When something bad happens to one of us, it could happen to any of us." He stuck a spoon into the can and gave it a stir. "I saw one of the attacks happen. Usually, shit like that doesn't go down this close to the shelter. The police patrol regularly around here, mostly to hassle us. It's a pain in the ass, but it keeps the real crazies away. That's why this camp is usually pretty damn safe."

"Where did it happen?"

He pointed behind him. "Ten blocks that way. It was the dumpster behind the donut place. They donate their leftovers to the food pantries, but if you show up before they leave for the night, you can get a handout. I was on my way back when I saw three teenagers kicking the shit out of someone. I yelled at them, and they ran off."

"Did you tell the cops that?"

He shook his head. "You're funny."

"You ever see anything else like that happen?"

"No, but after that, I started asking around. We got it hard enough without stupid little shits thinking they can rough us up for fun. That's when I heard they'd been doing it for a while."

"Can you describe them?"

He scrutinized me for a few minutes while he scooped pork and beans into his mouth. "You're not a cop. You drove a rental here. And you said you weren't a reporter. What are you?"

The woman in pink had been edging closer. She took a seat on the crate beside me, leaning over to get a better look at me.

I glanced at her, offering a friendly, non-threatening smile. "I'm an investigator."

"What does that mean?" Army Coat asked.

The woman touched my hair, and I flinched at the unexpected contact, stopping myself from reaching inside my jacket. She jumped backward. “Don’t do that,” she scolded.

“Sorry. You surprised me.”

“Surprise.” She clapped her hands together.

“Myrtle, leave our friend alone,” the man said.

“But her hair’s pretty and soft, like a squirrel.”

“Thanks.” I wasn’t quite sure that was a compliment, but it might have been.

The guy gave me a barely perceptible headshake. “It’s dark, Myrtle. Shouldn’t you get to sleep?”

She pointed to the fire. “Lights out.”

“Soon,” he said.

She smiled and waved at me again. “Bye.”

I watched as she headed to a pile of blankets beside a sideways refrigerator box with a dusty blue tarp draped over it.

“You’re skittish,” he said, finishing the last of his dinner. “You were trained. Soldier?”

“No, sir. Former federal agent.”

“That explains the questions. And to answer them, no I can’t give you a description. They ran off before I got a good look at ‘em. But there were three. Maybe white or Latino, possibly Asian. Young.”

“Gang colors?”

“I can’t be sure. Why do you care what’s going on out here? You’re not local.”

“I’m a private eye. A friend told me what’s been going on and wants to stop it from happening. In the meantime, I heard of two recent deaths in your community. Sophie Marshman and Robert Devers.”

“You got pictures? I’m not great remembering names. Faces are another story.”

“Sure.” I took out my phone and found the photos of Sophie and Robert.

His expression fell. “Yeah, I know them. She hated it out here. Hated everything. Herself, mostly. The kid, he needed to get his shit together. I told him to get his shit together. But it doesn’t look like he listened.”

"You knew both of them?"

"I know a lot of people. I keep an eye out for them."

I noticed the ripped stitching where the patches had been. This wasn't a surplus coat. It was his. "How many tours did you serve?"

"Four, but who's counting?"

"Do you always stay here?" I asked. "Is this where Sophie and Robert stayed?"

"Sophie did a few times when she got desperate. She preferred sleeping indoors at the women's shelters. She didn't talk much and made it clear she didn't want anyone talking to her either. You can't help someone who doesn't want it."

"Did she need help?"

"We all need help."

"Fair enough. What about Robert?"

"He came to this camp once, looking for drugs or anything he could steal and pawn. I found him trying to empty out Dan's tent. I scared the daylights out of him and made sure he knew he wasn't welcome here. But I kept tabs on him. I kinda felt bad for him."

"Why?"

"He was stealing everything and anything he could find because he needed his next fix. He'd do anything to get it. I'm sure he did all sorts of things for it. I saw him several times after I scared him away, always begging for money. He'd hang around the dealers. Half the time, they'd give him a few pills so he'd leave them alone. But he was like a cat. He never forgot who fed him. And he kept going back for more. Eventually, they got tired of it and had to get more aggressive."

"Did they threaten him?"

"More than a few times. He was desperate, but he wasn't stupid. As soon as he saw a gun or knife, he'd take off."

"Do you know anyone in particular who'd want to harm him? Names would be good."

"I'm not great with those, remember? But plenty of people had it out for the kid. He was a pain in the ass, but he didn't harbor any malice towards others, except not everyone out here is level-headed or rational enough to realize that. If he pissed off the wrong person or tried to steal from someone, I could see him getting stabbed."

"He wasn't stabbed."

"How did he die? Was he shot?"

"Suicide."

"Overdose?"

"No."

The guy in the coat raised an eyebrow. "Are you sure you got your facts straight? I don't believe a kid like that would intentionally off himself."

"Maybe it was an accident. Some kind of heightened autoerotic thing."

He gave me the same look he gave Myrtle. "You're telling me he choked himself out."

"He hung himself."

"I don't see it."

"Do you think any dealers might have strung him up to make an example out of him?"

"If they did, you wouldn't have confused it with a suicide."

"That's what I figured too." I thought about what he said. "Do you know anything about a church?" I had to look up the name and gave him the address.

"I hear they do a lot of charity work, but I steer clear of anyplace that has conditions to get a handout."

"What kind of conditions?"

"Any."

He finished his dinner and stared at the fire.

"I'm Alex, by the way."

He nodded. "Nice to meet you."

"And you are?"

"You should get going. It's late. People around here aren't always comfortable when strangers show up."

Reaching into my pocket, I pulled out my card and whatever cash I had on me. "Thanks for the help. I'll let you get some sleep."

"No sleep for me. I keep watch at night to make sure everyone at the camp is safe. What happens outside the camp, I can't control. But here, I can do some good."

TEN

I didn't sleep well that night. The hotel bed was lumpy, and the air conditioner made a high-pitched hum. I'd set my alarm and requested a wake-up call, knowing I had a habit of sleeping through the buzzer on occasion, but that wasn't a concern. I was still awake when the alarm went off.

After a shower, I picked up an extra large cappuccino and headed to the church where Robert's body had been found. Surprisingly, the church remained open for business. I walked in during the tail-end of the daily mass. A couple dozen people were scattered throughout the pews.

Staying near the back, I looked around. The door that led to the balcony was locked, but it wouldn't take much effort to jimmy it open. The frame was marred and cracked from what appeared to be a crowbar. That's probably how Robert had broken in.

I peered up at the balcony. The rafters were a good fifteen feet above the balcony floor. Robert would have needed a decent-sized ladder.

Silently, I wandered back the way I came, checking the other areas of the church. Down a hallway, I spotted a paint-splattered ladder beneath a light fixture. The bulb had blown out, and the fixture panel had been removed. But the bulb hadn't been replaced yet.

I'd seen the crime scene photos, but I didn't remember paint stains on the ladder Robert had used. Was this the same ladder? Had the police taken the other into evidence? After pulling the phone out of my pocket, I took a few snapshots, but I didn't think this was the same ladder.

"May I help you?" a voice asked from behind.

I spun, coming face to face with the parish priest. "Is mass over already?"

He smiled. "I saw you sneak in five minutes before we finished and walk out two minutes later. I have trouble believing that's the reason for your visit. What can I do for you, my child? You look lost."

Priest speak always made me uneasy. O'Connell usually dealt with men of the cloth, figuring I'd burst into flames the moment I stepped foot on holy ground. "What time do you unlock the doors?"

"Around five a.m."

"The man who hung himself from the rafters two months ago, did you know him?"

"Not well. We have a community outreach program. We gave him clothes, food, and information on rehab programs. We only spoke briefly once or twice. He was always in a hurry to leave. The collar made him nervous, I think."

"Who found his body?"

"Sister Mary. When I heard her scream, I came running. We called the police. It was a real tragedy."

"Is that the ladder he used?"

"No."

"He brought his own ladder?"

"The church was having work done on the stained glass window. The crew left a ladder outside. He must have carried it in and up the stairs."

"Wasn't it heavy?"

"I'm sure it was."

"No one heard him banging around with a heavy ladder and breaking down doors?" I tapped the ladder, which caused it to make a rattling metallic sound. "With those high ceilings, I'd think someone would have heard the noise."

"I'm sorry."

"What about Sister Mary? May I speak to her?"

"She's in Rome, but she'll be back in a few weeks." He held out his hand. "I'm Father Miguel. And you are?"

"Alex."

"Did you know the man who killed himself? Are you family?"

I hadn't wanted to reveal anything in case the priest or someone inside the church was involved, but lying didn't sit well with me either. Lying was a sin. I wasn't sure if it was an even bigger sin to lie to a priest, but it'd be best to err on the side of caution. "I'm a private investigator."

"So you're looking into his death. That must mean you don't believe he committed suicide."

"I don't know what to think. Robert had a bad knee. I can't figure out why he'd choose to hang himself from the rafters if all he wanted to do was end his own life. Did he have a beef with you or anyone in the church? You said he wasn't fond of you."

"He wasn't fond of the collar or my position in the church, but I didn't take it personally. A lot of people are uncomfortable around priests."

"Did he tell you that?"

"No, but that was the vibe I got the couple of times we spoke."

"What did you speak about?"

"His sobriety."

"Robert was an addict."

"He was suffering from a disease. We did our best to help him. We knew he had problems. He blamed the world, but that's only because he blamed himself and hated his physical weaknesses. I overheard him talking to a volunteer one afternoon. He told him he dropped out of college and ran away from his family. He didn't think he deserved their love or forgiveness. He didn't seem concerned with making amends. He just wanted to escape the pain, the hunger, the cravings. And the only way he knew how to do that was by feeding the beast. He begged for money. We never gave it to him. We gave him food and clothing. We offered to help him find shelter and get help.

But he wasn't ready yet."

"Did your offer of help come with any requirements or conditions?"

Father Miguel gave me a strange look. "No."

That wasn't what I'd heard. "What about the big guy?" I pointed to the ceiling. "Was Robert angry with the man upstairs?"

"I'm sure he was, but he never spoke to me about it. He never wanted to speak to me at all, but I did what I could to make myself available to him."

"You make it sound like he hung around here a lot." I cringed. "No pun intended."

Father Miguel stifled a scowl. "He did, but he usually interacted with the volunteers, not me or other members of the clergy."

"Do you remember who he spoke to?"

"I don't. It could have been any of our parishioners. Robert used the church as a sanctuary. I've worked hard to make this a safe place for everyone. He took advantage. We have a donation box, which Robert often helped himself to, along with whatever else he found. All I can say is the young man was troubled."

"But you don't think he was at rock bottom?"

"I've seen plenty of people in turmoil over the years. This young man wasn't ready to change. He'd gone down a wayward path but wanted to see where it would take him. He wasn't ready to get off that path yet or find a new one."

"Do you think he killed himself?"

The priest shrugged. "Evil exists and can take many forms."

"What kinds of forms were here the morning of his death?"

"You're asking if anyone else was here. The answer is no, aside from the Sister and me."

"Are you sure? Do you have surveillance or security devices in place?"

"On the doors, but that's it."

"And outside?"

"The police checked. Most of the cameras were disabled or blocked due to the work being done."

That would have given someone the perfect opportunity to drag Robert inside and kill him, but his lack of defensive wounds gave me pause. "When he visited the church, did he usually hang around anyone specific?"

"No. He'd interact as much as was needed to get a handout, and that was it. When he entered the church for mass or to join us for fellowship dinners, he'd keep to himself."

I blew out a breath, dizzy from spinning myself in circles. "May I see where he died?"

Father Miguel stared at me for a long time. "Why do you concern yourself with things you cannot change?"

"I'm stubborn like that."

He smiled, a gentle laugh escaping. "Nothing wrong with a bit of righteous fire." He led me back to the door. "The police checked everything already. They didn't find any evidence of foul play."

"They have a lot on their plates."

The priest removed a large silver keyring from his pocket. It only contained three keys, each gold and ornate. He slipped one into the almost comical lock. The door creaked and moaned as he pulled it open, revealing a dimly lit staircase. It was narrow and winding, just like the photos Will had shown me.

"Who else has a key to this door?" I asked.

"This is the only key. It mostly hangs on the pegboard in the office. Sister Mary, the choir director, and the deacon all have access."

I pulled out the flashlight on my keyring and shone it against the walls. No scuff marks. "When's the last time you painted?"

"Two years ago."

"Really?" I ran a finger over the splintered parts of the doorframe. "The walls are exceptionally clean."

"Only the choir uses the balcony. They used to perform from up here every week, but this last year, they've been setting up at the side of the altar."

"Why?"

"The choir director has vertigo."

"I could see how that could pose a problem." I went up

the stairs, keeping an eye out for nicks or scratches, but it didn't appear the ladder had made contact with the walls. "Is it possible the ladder was already upstairs? You said work was being done on the stained glass window. Maybe the repairmen needed to work on the window from the inside."

"No."

"You're sure?"

"I am."

When I made it to the top, I was met by a waxed wood floor and sixteen cushioned chairs in two neat rows. A large round window overlooked the balcony, streaming in the morning sunlight with an almost ethereal quality. "A choir of angels."

"What?" the priest asked.

I shook my head and approached the railing. The air smelled like dust, incense, and wood polish. A few dark scuff marks marred the otherwise shiny finish. I took a few snapshots, figuring that's where the bottom of Robert's shoe made contact after he stepped off the ladder and onto the railing before dropping himself over the edge. But I didn't find any marks on the hardwood floor from the ladder's feet.

Looking down made me dizzy. I never liked heights. Shifting my focus upward, I studied the rafters. From here, I couldn't see if the rope had caused any damage, so I pulled out my camera and zoomed in. But I didn't see anything. The police would have performed a more thorough examination of the area.

From what I'd seen in the photos, the rope had been folded in half and tossed over. The ends had been pulled through to form a simple loop around the rafter. The two hanging ends had been twisted together into a noose.

"Has the church had any problems in the past?" I asked.

"Graffiti was a problem when we first started the outreach program, but the police took care of it. Those were isolated incidents."

"What about nearby gang activity? This isn't the safest neighborhood."

"On two separate occasions, young men have entered

the church injured. One had been shot. The other was stabbed. I drove them to the hospital. I've been very vocal to the gangs that this is neutral ground. We do not condone violence, but we will help anyone in need. No questions asked. The gangs know to respect that." The hard look in Father Miguel's eyes made me wonder what he'd done before he put on the collar.

"I'm sure the police had questions once the hospital notified them about shooting and stabbing victims."

"I did my part. The rest is out of my hands."

"Do you think Robert showed up that morning because he needed help?"

"I don't know. He usually begged for cash. That's all he ever wanted. Money and anything worth selling. I would have thought he hoped to empty the donation box. But we always empty that after the last service. He might have gotten frustrated and upset. Perhaps he had an epiphany, realized what he was doing, and..."

"Overcorrected?"

"There was nothing correct about it."

I stared at the priest, wondering what secrets he had. "You said Robert attended mass. Did he show up every day?"

"He showed up a lot. Most of the time, I found him asleep in the back pews. I don't think it was because my sermon was boring. The boy had nowhere else to go. He wanted somewhere safe to rest or ride out his high."

"What about confession?"

The priest held my gaze, unwavering in his resolve. "You know I can't divulge that."

"I didn't ask what he said. I asked if he went."

The priest didn't answer.

"Did he ever seek your counsel concerning the topic of suicide?"

"No."

"You happen to hear any good murder confessions lately?"

Father Miguel rubbed the back of his neck and adjusted his collar. "I cannot provide the answers you seek."

"How about we pop downstairs and go into that little

booth? I'll share my secrets. You can share yours. We'll say the rosary a couple of times and call it a day. No one has to know."

"If you're seeking absolution, I'd be happy to help, but I will not violate the sanctity of the confessional."

I strode across the balcony, peering beneath the chairs and in every crevice before heading for the stairs. "Maybe next time."

"Are you sure? It helps to unburden yourself."

"I'll be unburdened once I figure out what happened to Robert." I went down the first two steps and paused. "Is there any other way down?"

"No, but the church has three exits on the main level. The police checked each of them. They don't believe anyone else had been inside the church."

"A bottle of pills rolled beneath the ladder Robert used to kill himself. Why would he have been so desperate if he already had his next fix in hand?"

"I can't answer that. I have no idea."

"Any idea where he got the drugs?"

"It could have been from anywhere. You already pointed out this isn't the best neighborhood. Dealers work a lot of these corners."

"Any one in particular that hangs around the church?"

"No."

"One final question," I said as he led me to the exit, "how did the congregation react to a suicide inside the church?"

"The archbishop arrived to discuss the matter and provide guidance. We've mourned the loss of life, but it hasn't interfered with church functions, aside from the minor police interference and your visit today."

"I'm glad I was only a minor interference. Good day, Father."

"Our doors are always open," he called after me, "at least from the hours of five a.m. to eleven p.m."

ELEVEN

After leaving the church, I circled around a few times but failed to spot any local dealers. Inspiration didn't strike, but since I was on a time crunch, I didn't have time to wait for brilliance to hit me. Instead, I stopped at the nearest coffee shop since my extra large cappuccino was now empty. Strangely enough, they weren't suffering from any coffee shortages. I picked up a few double chocolate donuts to take with me on the ride back. If the caffeine couldn't keep me awake, the sugar would.

The drive took a lot longer. People were getting a jump on their weekend plans and I'd chosen to venture back at the worst time of day. At least I had the foresight to pick up coffee and donuts.

By the time I made it to the office, my bladder was on the verge of exploding. Better it than my heart, I reasoned. After answering the call of nature, I logged onto the computer and ran a background check on Father Miguel.

He had a sealed juvie record, but that hadn't stopped him from entering the seminary at thirty-three. He was now forty-five. After more searching, I found a few photos of him from high school. He wore a sideways ballcap and gang colors. But I hadn't seen any of the telltale tattoos on him. Maybe he hadn't made it very deep into the gang before he got pinched, or he'd been a wannabe who messed up and turned his life around in time.

According to his employment history, he stocked shelves while working his way through night school to earn his high school diploma. Afterward, he moved on to fulfilling orders for an online retailer by working inside a distribution center. He did that for twelve years before becoming a priest. A bit more digging disclosed the list of charities where he volunteered. They were mostly aimed at distributing food and necessities to the homeless. He'd worked at food pantries, clinics, and shelters, just none of the ones Sophie frequented.

Next, I looked into the church, but it hadn't been targeted by any group. The online reviews only had positive things to say. This was getting me nowhere.

I pulled open the bottom drawer and eased back in my chair, using the open drawer to prop up my feet. Damn, I was tired. Was any of this worth it? Yanking a pad of paper off the desk, I wrote down everything I'd learned.

More than likely, Trevitt was right about Sophie Marshman's death. The only positive thing to come out of investigating was learning about the three teenagers who'd been seen beating up a homeless person. I'd pass that along to Will the next time we spoke. Of course, he wouldn't be happy I hadn't gotten a name for his witness, but at least I could point him in the right direction.

However, the big question mark that remained was whether Robert Devers' death was a suicide. I hadn't spoken to Robert's parents, but I had a good idea of how he'd spent the last few months of his life. COD was a toss-up. Without hard evidence or an eyewitness, I couldn't fault Detective Trevitt for reaching that conclusion. Surely, Robert had enemies. Dealers he'd annoyed. Friends he'd betrayed. Acquaintances he'd stolen from. Any one of them could have snapped.

But the lack of defensive wounds and the scene suggested Robert trusted his killer, assuming he'd been killed, but I wasn't sure digging into this would result in finding any answers. Robert had been in a bad situation that would have continued to get worse. The people in his life had already written him off. Without their help, I wasn't even sure where to look. I could say the same about Sophie. Even though the method and victimology of the two suicides were different, I couldn't help but think the circumstances were the same, and I'd found someone they had in common. The guy in the army coat.

I made a note to tell Will about this the first chance I got. After spending forty-five minutes conducting database searches which didn't result in me finding a name for Army Coat, I yawned. If I kept this up, I'd fall asleep at my desk, and I didn't have time for a nap today.

Forcing myself to sit up straight, I checked my inbox for updates. Amir hadn't found any dating profiles for Theo Stapleton, so he combed through his social media posts and analyzed the conversations. Based on the data the computer spit out, Theo didn't appear to be intimate with any of the people he interacted with. But what did a computer know about human emotions?

I didn't trust programs, but the analysis also provided data on who Theo spoke to most often and who was most likely to respond or interact with his posts. That would give me some idea of who might be romantically interested in him.

I looked into the top candidates, knowing if Theo were smart, he and his paramour wouldn't openly interact. In fact, they might not even be friends on any of the platforms. The lack of scandalous photos and coded messages didn't prove anything.

Since Iris granted me access to their phone records, I compared his online friend list to the people Theo called and texted. The same names popped up. In fact, Theo didn't make any calls outside of his listed contacts, except for business-related calls.

Based on that, Theo should have been predictable. But when I checked his recent charges and spending patterns, I was surprised by what I found. The guy didn't frequent the same takeout places. When it came to pizza alone, he'd gone to four different joints in the last month. And that didn't include the million other places he went for Chinese, tacos, and burgers. For someone with a tightly knit group of friends, who had a limited number of hobbies and interests, he went out of his way to be spontaneous and unpredictable when it came to his takeout options.

Variety was the spice of life, but Theo was a native Angelino. Why did he act like a tourist relying on Yelp? At the least, he should have had one or two favorite places. But he hadn't gone to any of the restaurants more than once. Could he be meeting his mistress there?

I'd just pulled out his work schedule to figure out the best time to tail him when the office door opened. I looked up to find a woman in a blazer, jeans, and boxy grey t-shirt standing in the doorway. Her short, curly hair clung to her scalp.

"Sabina Rater." She held out her hand as she approached my desk. "I'm here for the office manager position."

"Alexis Parker." I shook her hand and indicated the chair in front of the desk. "Have a seat. Can I get you anything? Coffee, tea, water?"

"I'd rather get straight to it."

"Sure." I rocked back in my chair. Theo's phone logs caught my eye. "If you had a rocky marriage and planned to have an affair, where would you go?"

Deep lines emerged on her forehead. "A hotel."

"Where would you find a person with which to have the affair?"

"Oh." She thought for a moment. "A hotel bar. Those are usually good for one-night stands."

"Any particular hotel bar?"

"One not too close to where I lived or any place my friends and colleagues went. I wouldn't want to risk running into someone who might report back to my spouse."

"Good answer. Logical. Reasonable. How would you pay for the hotel room or the drinks?"

"Assuming I couldn't convince my date to shell out, I'd pay cash, which I'd get from my regular visits to the ATM."

"To avoid attracting suspicion."

"Yes." She smiled. "Is that the right answer?"

"Possibly." I clicked a few keys and opened the file with her CV. "Why do you want this job?"

"I could use something steady."

"What do you do now?"

"I'm a relief driver for an armored car company." She nodded toward the screen. "It should be listed there."

It was, but I hadn't scrolled down that far. She'd served four years in the Army before joining the reserves. Aside from her required duties, she didn't have any other responsibilities that would keep her away from the office. "What do you carry?"

"A nine millimeter Luger."

"You ever have to use it stateside?"

"No, ma'am."

The ma'am thing might be hard for her to kick. "Why do you want an office job? I'd think armored cars would be more fun."

"I worked in the office when I was in the service." Again, she leaned closer to the screen. "Isn't that listed?"

"How do you feel about breaking the law?"

The look on her face answered that question.

Luckily, my phone rang, saving us both from the awkwardness. I smiled. "Thanks for coming in. I'll be in touch."

She stood up and nodded. "Thank you, ma'am."

That was definitely worse than flip-flops. I waited for her to leave before I answered the phone. "Cross Security and Investigations. If this is about a crime, you should call the police. We can't help you."

"You can't answer the phone like that," Cross said.

"Why not? It's company policy. We don't investigate homicides or step on toes."

"Dammit, Alex."

I smiled. That made the two interviews I'd conducted almost worth it. "What's up, boss?"

"I listened to your voicemail and thought you might need some guidelines for conducting these interviews. Apparently, you also need guidelines on how to conduct yourself professionally. I'll have Justin send over the basics."

“Great.”

“Given your history, I assumed you’d been on the other side of the table enough times to have the questions memorized. Clearly, I was mistaken. In your inbox, you should find a list of questions to ask. The applicant’s answers should inform your decision on selecting the best candidate for the job. Of course, I’ll have final say.”

“Let me cut to the chase. You don’t need an office manager. You have Justin.”

“Justin’s here. You are there.”

“But he coordinates everything. This office doesn’t have a stable of investigators or cases, and your security teams have been doing just fine on their own for who knows how long. This office isn’t large enough to need a manager. What are you doing, Lucien?”

“Preparing for an expansion. You should know that by now.”

I sighed. “Fine.”

“The fact you signed a new client indicates a market exists for our services.”

“I met Iris Stapleton at a bar. If I hadn’t, she never would have signed with us.”

Even though I couldn’t see Cross, I suspected he had a smug grin on his face. “Did you keep the receipt? I’ll reimburse you for the drinks since they were a business expense.”

“I don’t need you to buy me a drink.”

“Fine. Have you gotten started on her case yet?”

“Only the research. Her story checks out. She suspects her husband’s cheating, but I haven’t found anything online to indicate that’s true. His phone records didn’t show anything either. No flirtatious texts or nude photos have been sent or received. Iris said she checked his computer but didn’t find anything either.”

“You should ask her for access. I’ll have Amir send you tracking software to install on his computer and phone.”

“He already did that. I’m going to install it this afternoon.”

“How do you plan to conduct surveillance?”

“The usual. I’ll put a tracker on his car and keep tabs on

him that way. I'd prefer to monitor his movements in person, but that's not feasible twenty-four seven. I'm one person. And conducting surveillance isn't something an office manager can help me with."

"That's why I'll be looking at hiring additional investigators after you have an office manager in place. Is there anything else?"

"Nope."

"Really?" The tone of his voice told me he expected me to say something.

"Not that I can think of."

"Why did you spend the night in San Diego?"

"Did you ping my phone?" Again, we'd have to have the boundary conversation. "You had no right."

"I didn't ping your phone. Cross Security paid for your rental car. It has GPS tracking."

"So you pinged my car. That does not make it better."

"I didn't ping your car, Alex. The rental agency called me to make sure it hadn't been stolen. I told them I didn't believe so. Do I need to call them back and tell them I was wrong?"

"No."

"Do you want to tell me what you were doing?"

"Nope."

Cross cleared his throat, letting out a frustrated growl. "The last case I asked you to work turned into a shitshow. That was on me. If this thing with that cop turns into something, that's on you. I warned you to stay away from him. Like you pointed out, you're the only one in the office. You shouldn't take unnecessary risks."

"That's kind of my schtick."

"Tell Nero or Omar where you're going and what you're doing. I don't like this, but if you need backup, I want them in a position to provide it."

"Damn, Lucien, that might be the nicest thing you've ever said to me."

TWELVE

I checked the time. Theo Stapleton had left for work, at least that's what his wife had said. And since he had another ten hours of his double-shift, I had plenty of time to lay the groundwork for my surveillance. After a quick trip to the electronics store, I headed to the hospital.

The vast parking lot and garage wouldn't make finding his vehicle easy. I followed the signs for employee parking and circled around a few times before finding the white sedan. After pulling into the next nearest spot, I activated the tracking device, made sure it was synced with my phone so I'd receive updates, and got out of the car.

Since the hospital had dozens of security cameras posted all over the place, I zipped up my sweatshirt and pulled the hood over my head. Leaving my sunglasses on, I headed for the garage entrance, stopping behind Theo's car to tie my shoelace. Carefully, I stuck the tracker to the underside of the rear fender.

As I headed into the hospital, I checked the app on my phone. The tracker showed on my screen as a red dot. Perfect.

"How may I help you?" the woman at the information desk asked.

"My uncle's recovering from surgery. When I came to visit him last night, he kept talking about one of the nurses, um," I crinkled my nose and squinted, "Theo. Theo Stapleton. He's an OR nurse. I know he's probably in the middle of a surgery right now, but I wondered if you could tell me when he'll be finished. I wanted to thank him personally for taking such good care of Uncle Bill."

"Give me a sec." She clicked a few keys. "Nurse Stapleton's been assigned back-to-back surgeries today. He's off tomorrow. He should have a few hours Monday afternoon from eleven to two, if you want to stop by then."

"Thanks."

I returned to my car and checked the schedule Iris had given me. Theo didn't lie to her. That was a good thing. He told her exactly when he was working and when he wasn't. Most men who had affairs liked to work late or had to go to the office at random times. Jeez, Martin checked off more of the boxes than Iris's husband.

Shaking that pointless thought away, I decided now was the perfect time to pop in on Iris. Taking the surface streets proved to be much faster than the freeway. The Stapletons lived in a small house in a decent neighborhood. I pulled into the empty space in front of their house, which must have been Theo's spot, and peered out the windshield. A home security sign had been planted to the left of the front door.

Did I want Theo to see me? In case he got suspicious, I ditched the hoodie, exchanged my wraparound shades for a pair of Jackie O's, and pulled my hair into a high ponytail. With the spyware Amir had sent stored safely on a USB drive, I tucked the device into my pocket and approached the front door.

The Stapletons didn't have a doorbell cam. From what I gathered, they didn't have any outdoor security cameras, but they had motion sensor lights. The front door creaked open, revealing only a sliver of the person behind it. Iris stood on the other side of the wrought-iron bars, one hand out of sight.

"Hi," I smiled, "it's Alex from your grief support group. I thought I should stop by and check on you. How are you doing?"

She quirked an eyebrow, confused by my words.

"Is now a bad time?" I asked. "If your husband's home or you have company, I can stop by another day."

"No." She pulled the door wide open and unlocked the gate in front of it. "Why are you here? I thought you were going to call first."

"I told you I wanted to check on you. After the last time we spoke, I was concerned. I thought you could use the company."

She wasn't getting it. "Theo's not here."

"What about your home security system?" I pointed to the sign in the yard. "Any cameras?"

"No." She pushed the door open. "Come in. Theo's not expected back until late tonight. He's supposed to pick up dinner on his way home from one of those twenty-four hour places, so I'm off the hook from having to cook."

I entered the house, leaving my sunglasses on. "What about virtual assistants? Group therapy is about anonymity and respecting one's privacy. I don't want Siri or Alexa spying on us. Did you know they can record conversations?"

Iris shook her head. "We're low-tech around here."

I couldn't be certain Theo hadn't set up surveillance to keep tabs on his wife, but if he had, she didn't know about it. And since he was the one acting suspiciously, I didn't see any reason why he would have gone to those extremes, unless the attack had triggered his protective instincts. Then again, I might be projecting. The men in my life never had any qualms when it came to spying on me.

"I'm sorry to intrude. I didn't plan on showing up unannounced." Part of me had done it just to make sure Iris wasn't keeping secrets from me. "Can I get a look at his computer? I haven't found any dating profiles or suspicious online activity, but the internet's a big place."

"I get it." She led me through the house and into one of the back rooms. "This is our office." She pointed to a corner desk made out of glass and steel. It didn't have any drawers, which didn't give Theo a lot of places to hide things. "That's his computer there." She tapped a key which brought the computer out of sleep mode. "How many dating sites have you searched?"

"All of them, I think."

She laughed, though it sounded bitter. "And you haven't found him on any of them? Am I supposed to be relieved?"

"That's up to you." I checked his internet history, which only showed the last forty-eight hours. He conducted a few searches on how to build a motor and had looked at a dozen different types of wrench. Besides that, he'd listened to a few episodes of a true crime podcast. I opened the tab for the podcast and scanned the comments. He hadn't left any, but it had a broad audience from all over the world who were obsessed with a series of unsolved murders in the Cascade Mountains. Theo hadn't made any posts, and I didn't find any cryptic messages indicating a time or place to meet. Then again, I wasn't dealing with trained spies. I was dealing with a forty-year-old nurse from Los Angeles.

She watched the screen from over my shoulder. "Why were you saying all those things about group when I opened the front door?"

"You didn't want him to know you came to me, so I figured we already had a valid cover story. We met in group therapy. If you want, I can be your sponsor."

"For real?"

I glanced back at her. I had said it as part of establishing a cover story, not as a legitimate offer. Most days, I was lucky if I could manage my own craziness. "I can listen if you ever need someone to talk to."

"I think I'm good."

"Okay." I checked for hidden files on his computer, but when I couldn't find anything, I stuck the USB into the side. The techs at Cross Security would have a better time finding these things than I would. Once the upload began, I turned to face her. "Do you mind showing me the rest of the house?"

"What are you looking for?"

"I have no idea. But since you think he's hiding something, between the two of us, we should be able to find it."

Iris led me into the bedroom and opened Theo's closet.

"This isn't exactly what I hired you to do. I want to know where he goes when he leaves here. I want to know who he's with and what they're doing."

"I get it, which is why I'm curious to see if he keeps an overnight bag packed or has some mad money stashed somewhere."

"You mean in case he decides to leave and not come back?" The look on her face told me she hadn't considered the possibility and didn't want to think about it.

"It's best to be prepared for anything."

She nodded, biting her lip to keep her emotions in check. "Do you need my help?"

"That's up to you." I studied her. "I'm surprised you haven't already torn this place apart. That's the first thing I would have done."

"It's weird." She opened several of his drawers and sifted through his underwear and socks. "I always trusted him. We always trusted each other. I never had any reason to worry or think otherwise. But lately, he's a different person. I guess I should have looked."

She closed the top drawers and moved on to the next row while I checked for packed suitcases and hidden cash boxes. Iris finished with the dresser and joined me at the closet. I hadn't found anything, but she would know better if something was amiss.

"It looks like it always does," she said.

"What about the other rooms of the house? Does Theo have a mancave?"

"Only the garage. The rest of the house we use equally. I'm sure I would have noticed if he moved or changed something in the TV room or kitchen."

"You don't go in the garage?" I asked.

She shook her head. "We have street parking. Neither of us use it for our cars. The garage is mainly storage and where he fiddles with things. The last time I went in there was Christmas, when I pulled out the decorations. I swear, it looks different every time I go in there. I doubt I'll be of any help."

After grabbing the USB from his computer and making sure the spyware was running and hadn't tripped up any of his antivirus software, I put the computer back in sleep mode and met Iris at the garage door. She stood in the doorway, her arms wrapped around her middle, as if she were hugging herself. The workbench was nothing more than four sawhorses topped with plywood. A circular saw sat on top of it, along with several wooden pieces. A jigsaw sat on a metal table to the side. Various sizes of wooden gears had been cut out and placed in a stack. An instruction manual on how to build a wooden gear clock was open on the metal table.

"It looks like he's trying to make some time," I quipped.

Iris picked up the book, leafing through the pages. "I didn't know he was working on this." She put it back where she found it. "I bought him that book a few years ago after we toured a clockmaking exhibit at the museum. He'd been fascinated by the clocks, but he never showed much of an interest in building one himself."

While she examined the intricately carved gears and the different clock pieces he cut out, I searched the rest of the garage. Theo had all sorts of tools and equipment hanging, as if on display. Beside the pegboard was a metal cabinet. I checked the drawers, finding nails, screws, nuts, and bolts in assorted sizes. Inside the middle drawer was a metal tackle box. It was locked.

Using my lockpicks, I unlocked the box. The top layer revealed more screws and bolts. "Does Theo like to fish?" I asked.

"No."

That would explain the lack of lures and hooks. I lifted up the top tray, pausing at the sight of the six-shooter. After putting on a pair of gloves, I picked up the gun, finding a box of ammunition beside it. Smith and Wesson. Four-inch barrel. Black handle. "Do you own a gun?"

"No."

"What about Theo?" It hadn't popped up during the background check I'd run, but occasionally, things got overlooked.

"He hates guns."

"Even after what happened to you?"

"Especially after."

"The two of you never discussed buying a weapon for protection after you were attacked?"

She let out a shaky exhale. "Theo mentioned it, but the thought terrified me."

"Do you think he'd go behind your back and get one anyway?"

She spun, seeing the weapon in my hand.

"Jesus." She stumbled backward. "Where did you find that?"

"In his tackle box."

"He doesn't fish."

I checked the weapon. It was unloaded. But the serial number had been filed off. Whoever had done it had been in a rush. I could nearly make out a few numbers. An acid wash or the right equipment could recover the number in no time. But that told me one thing. The gun wasn't registered. I took out my phone and photographed it. "I'm guessing he doesn't have a license or permit for this."

"Are you sure it's his?"

I stared at her. "Maybe he's holding it for a friend. One who likes to fish."

The look on her face told me she didn't realize I was being sarcastic. "Yeah, maybe."

"Do you have any idea why Theo would have a gun?"

She shook her head.

I checked the box of ammunition, but it was full. More than likely, Theo had never fired the weapon. "Are you sure he didn't buy it for protection?"

"I don't know. I told him I didn't want a gun in the house."

"So you had that conversation."

"Yes, but we agreed." She stared at the weapon, her pupils dilated, her breathing shallow. Her knees knocked together.

I stowed it securely back in the box, made sure it was locked, and shut the drawer. "Iris, it's okay."

She trembled, sweat pearling on her forehead. She gasped, backing herself against the wall. Sliding to the floor, she hugged her knees to her chest and rocked back and forth, her eyes never leaving the metal cabinet.

I kept my distance. I knew a panic attack when I saw one. "Iris, take a deep breath. In and out. Slow and even." I demonstrated. "You're safe. Tell me what you see."

She blinked, forcing her eyes away from the cabinet. She described the tools and the wood.

"What do you smell?" I asked.

"Sawdust, metal, and that gross whatever it is." She crinkled her nose. "I always say it smells like dog shit."

I laughed, and she did too. I waited for her to calm down before I said, "Are you okay?"

She nodded, slowly pulling herself off the floor. "Just bad memories."

"I get it." I checked the time. "We should get out of here."

"What about the gun?"

"Do you want me to take it with me? If he looks, he'll know it's gone, that someone was here. But I'll do whatever you want."

She thought for a long moment. "Leave it."

"Are you sure? Do you think he plans to harm you?"

She shook her head, ready to leave the garage and the horrors it contained behind. "If he did, he wouldn't need that. He'd probably poison me or inject an air bubble into my heart or something." She wiped her eyes, finding her hands a little shaky. "It turns out I'm living with a complete stranger, and I'm just now figuring that out."

THIRTEEN

I'd sent the photo of the gun to Cross's techs to analyze, but my case wasn't a top priority. So I fired up the fancy photo manipulation program Martin had and played around with the shadows and contrast, hoping to digitally restore the filed off serial number.

I adjusted the settings up and down before tugging on a point on the curve and moving it around the box. I wasn't sure exactly what I was doing, but the image kept changing. Eventually, I was able to read most of the numbers.

Grabbing a legal pad, I wrote down all possible permutations, twenty in total, and entered them into the computer. But without access to the state's criminal database, I didn't know if the gun had been used in local crimes. If only I had a cop friend who could help me out with this.

Before I could phone-a-friend, my cell phone beeped. Theo Stapleton was on the move. I watched the red blip leave the hospital. He stopped by a vegan restaurant before going home. I wrote down the name of the restaurant and checked my records, but Theo had never been there before. Maybe he really was a spy. That would explain why he never went to the same place more than once. But I didn't think he was a spy. For one thing, the spies I knew had better hiding places for their weapons. And they had much better weaponry.

Since I couldn't figure out why Theo always went to different restaurants and didn't stick with much of a routine, besides going to work, I mapped out his routes. It was a good thing I had fifty different colored pens. The places he went were always on different streets. "What are you up to, Theo?"

As far as I knew, he had no reason to believe he was being followed or under surveillance. I'd never known anyone to go to these extremes unless they had a reason. Since I couldn't come up with a logical explanation for his behavior, I took my laptop into the bedroom, but in my absence, Martin had transformed our bedroom into a file room. Binders covered seventy-five percent of our bed. The floor wasn't much better.

I scanned a few tabs. *Fiscal year. Quarterly earnings. Division projects.* Deciding it'd be best to wait for him to clean up the mess, I grabbed his pillow off the bed and went into the spare room.

After propping myself up, I searched for any popular restaurant challenges. The current trend was to eat at a different restaurant every day for a month. People were always posting about doing things like this, and while I hadn't noticed anyone daring Theo to participate, I suspected that might be what had led to his odd behavior.

Twenty minutes into my dive, I found several of his friends had taken it upon themselves to post restaurant reviews for the places they tried. The ones they raved about looked like the same ones Theo had visited. That couldn't be a coincidence. Unfortunately, Theo didn't appear to be going in a specific order or following just one of his friends' recommendations. That would make tailing him harder. If he kept going to new places, I wouldn't be able to scout ahead or figure out if he was meeting someone special there. The only way to find out where he was going was to follow him from work or home.

The thought of that much legwork made me tired. In

fact, I was already exhausted, but that had more to do with not sleeping the night before. I considered calling Will to tell him what I'd learned, but he'd been adamant that we avoid communicating via internet or phone.

Too bad. I dialed the police station and waited for someone to answer. "May I speak to Sergeant Russo?"

"One moment."

While I waited, I closed my eyes. *Don't fall asleep. Don't fall asleep.*

A minute later, Will picked up. "This is Sergeant Russo. What can I do for you?"

"I thought you didn't like the title. I figured you'd answer the phone with a simple 'Hello' or maybe 'This is Will.' You really surprised me with that. I'm glad I didn't make a bet. I would have lost a bundle."

"What do you want?" He didn't say my name.

"I have a tip for you concerning the string of assaults on the homeless."

"Hang on. Let me grab a pen. Okay. What do you know?"

"Three teenagers were seen beating up a guy near the donut shop." I gave him the address.

"When was this?"

"I'm not sure. But another member of the homeless community scared them off. He's the one who told me about it, but he hasn't seen them since. He didn't get a good look at them." I described the teenagers the same way they'd been described to me. "It doesn't sound like these are organized attacks, but they could be designed to look that way."

"Did you get a name?"

"He didn't offer."

Will scoffed. "Where did you find this guy?"

"Near that camp by one of the shelters." I told him which shelter but left out why I was there. I didn't know if our call was being recorded or if anyone else could hear us, but since I wanted a favor, I didn't want to get Will in trouble. "There's more to it. He knew our two friends."

"Friends?" Will asked.

"Yeah, the woman and the college kid."

"Oh."

"Yeah."

"Both of them?"

"Yes."

"That's interesting."

"I thought so too. And since I've been so helpful, I was hoping for a reward of sorts."

"What kind of reward?"

"I need to find out about a gun."

"Do you have the serial number?" he asked.

"Sort of."

"What does that mean?"

"It was filed off. I recovered most of the number. Filling in the blanks will require some guesswork."

Someone called to him. "Let me see if this pans out first. I'll be in touch." He hung up.

"Bastard."

That left me with no other choice. I called Mark. Unfortunately, I didn't have any friends in ATF who could run the serial numbers for me, so he'd have to take care of it. When his voicemail answered, I asked him to call me back and promised to make it worth his while.

Scrolling through my contacts, I hoped I'd find a saved number that I'd forgotten about. But I had no such luck. Unsure what to do at this point, I called Nero. "Hey, this is Alex Parker. I was wondering where to go for an unregistered weapon."

"We have a cache and a few lockers. Are you looking for anything in particular?"

"I don't need a weapon. I need to figure out where someone would get one. My client's husband is in possession of an illegal firearm. I'm guessing he bought it on the black market. He doesn't have a license or permit. His wife didn't know anything about it, and he keeps it hidden."

"What kind of gun?"

"S&W revolver." I described it.

"Those are easy enough to come by. He could have gotten it anywhere. Have you tried area pawn shops?"

"Not yet."

"Do you think he's planning on using the weapon?" Nero asked. "If he's dangerous, I'd be happy to assist."

"I got this. Aren't you already short-handed on account of providing twenty-four hour security for our last client and his girlfriend?"

"I can change up the rotation and find someone we can spare. Lucien wants to make sure everyone's safe. That includes you."

"That's okay. I got this." Again, I returned to the profile I'd built. Theo Stapleton had never been violent. No professional complaints or investigations had been launched, which indicated he'd never killed a patient on the table. More than likely, he didn't plan to use the gun to kill his wife so he could ride off into the sunset with his mistress. The gun was there to provide protection, which meant he still loved Iris or he feared for his own safety.

Did Theo have any enemies? Could the attack on the ambulance have been a way to send Theo a message? I hadn't considered that, but maybe the shooter had ulterior motives besides stealing drugs. Again, I searched the Stapletons' background. Theo didn't owe anyone money. He'd never received any overt threats over the internet or strange calls or text messages. No, that didn't feel right. Truthfully, nothing about this situation did.

"You're losing it, Parker." I closed the laptop and put it on top of the dresser. It was after midnight. I was dog-tired. My brain had turned to mush, and whatever brilliant thoughts I had were no longer brilliant.

Tying back my hair, I paced in front of the bed. The view of the beach caught my eye, and I watched the reflected moonlight get swallowed up by the ocean waves. Better it than me.

What was I doing? I checked the tracker again, but Theo's car remained parked in front of his house. According to Iris, he usually didn't disappear after a long shift. She figured he was too tired to bang some hottie after spending all day in surgery. Since he had off the next day, I'd stake out their place and follow him if he left.

I pulled the drapes and climbed onto the bed. With my legal pad in hand, I wrote down everything I knew about

Theo Stapleton. Cross Security had pulled Theo's employment history and financial records. He rarely called in sick and never left early. Besides the mortgage, they didn't owe anyone anything. They'd paid off their student loans and their cars. Theo didn't have any online dating profiles, and I had yet to find a single dick pic on the internet, his phone, or his computer.

Grabbing the laptop off the dresser, I checked to see what Cross Security had uncovered from the spyware I'd uploaded to Theo's hard drive. But the computer geeks hadn't found anything damning either. At the moment, Theo was watching a video on how to rebuild an engine.

For someone seemingly that boring and humdrum, I had a hard time picturing him having an affair. Maybe he couldn't deal with being at home and fighting or not fighting with his wife, so he'd leave. But since I hadn't found a favorite hangout, I wondered where he went every time he left. Did he drive around aimlessly?

I pulled up his credit card history, wondering how often he had his car serviced or if he performed his own oil changes and tire rotations. There were dozens of car-related charges, but I couldn't figure out if any of it was relevant.

I hated this. Why couldn't he go to a bar or hotel like a normal cheater? No, Theo was too smart. Maybe he'd leave his house and go to her place. That would mean she had to live locally. I re-examined his contacts, hoping to find someone who fit the bill. For him to show up at all hours, she'd have to be single, possibly unemployed or self-employed, so she could make her own hours. Or she had a steady nine to five. Maybe she worked at the hospital with him.

I scrolled through the possibilities, checking profiles and building a list. But there were too many variables. This was another waste of time. Everything I'd done this week had been a waste of time. From surfing to interviewing potential office managers to looking into the two suicides.

Deciding it'd be best to cut my losses before I spun myself into the ground, I closed the laptop, stripped down, put on one of Martin's shirts, and crawled under the covers. Tomorrow I'd do something productive. I just had no earthly idea what that would be.

"Alexis, are you home?"

I opened my eyes and looked at the clock. It was just after two. Obviously, tomorrow had come. My new goal was to sleep. Maybe I'd work on that productive thing the following day. "In here."

Martin turned on the hall light and stood in the doorway. He wrapped his tie around one hand and unbuttoned his shirt. "You didn't come home last night."

"I left you a message."

"I was afraid you flew the coop after what happened the other morning." He put the rolled up tie on the dresser and sat on the bed beside me. He brushed my hair back and kissed me. "What are you doing in here?"

"Sleeping."

His brow furrowed. "This isn't our bed. But that is my pillow."

"I rescued it from the binders that tried to eat it."

"Shit. I was supposed to move that stuff before you got back."

"Don't worry about it. This place has plenty of bedrooms. I can make do for now."

"What about your pillow?"

"It was eaten. But that's okay. I like yours better. It smells like you, which helps me sleep. However, that talking thing you keep doing isn't helping much."

He crawled onto the bed beside me and wrapped his arms around me. "Where were you last night?"

"Walking the streets. I didn't get paid, but we're working some things out in trade. At least, I hope so. When I asked, he left me hanging, completely unsatisfied."

"Should I be concerned about the hooker references?"

"Nope, because I went to morning mass to make up for it."

"Are you going to tell me what you were actually doing?"

"Looking into a couple of deaths which occurred under suspicious circumstances. I interviewed a stellar candidate for the office manager position, except she's squeamish about breaking the law, and then I went to see Iris."

"How is she?"

"She was better before I showed up." I ran my hands along his arms. "What did you do last night? It looks like you threw quite the rager. Did you invite the lady with the dog?"

"Oh yeah. We had a blast." Martin tightened his grip as he spooned me. "In fact, I had tons of company in bed. Expense reports, projected earnings, progress reports, project assessments, employee reviews."

"Wow, an orgy. You must be exhausted."

"You have no idea."

I closed my eyes, settling against the pillow and feeling Martin's warm breath against the nape of my neck. He kissed my shoulder and pulled the blanket up around us.

FOURTEEN

I started my day by driving by the Stapletons' place. Theo's car remained parked in front of the house. Since I didn't have anything planned, I found a space at the end of the block and waited to see what would happen.

Around noon, Theo went outside to get the mail. He leafed through the envelopes as he made his way up the walk and back into the house. He wore an opened button-up shirt over a faded blue t-shirt. He looked relaxed.

Idly, I wondered if Iris would confront him about the gun we found, but she didn't want to rock the boat. She wanted her life to go back to normal. I checked to see if anyone from Cross Security had left anything in my dropbox, but it was empty.

After scanning the radio and finding the music selections annoying, I started my engine and headed for the office. If Martin could spend his day behind a desk, I could too. I was halfway there when my phone rang. I glanced at the number, but I didn't recognize it. Hopefully, Will had gotten smart and picked up a throwaway phone in order to make our lives easier.

I hit the speaker button before returning my eyes to the road. "Hello?"

"How did you know? Who asked you to look into this?"

I frowned, glancing down at the phone. "Who is this?"

"Jenna. Jenna Roth. Sophie Marshman's sister."

"What's wrong?"

"Like you don't know?" she huffed. "I was just going through my mail when I found it." She paused for effect. "How did you know?"

"Know what?"

"My sister was murdered."

I nearly slammed on my brakes in surprise. "What?"

"For god's sake. Stop pretending. You came to my place of business to ask me about it. What game are you playing this time? Did you have something to do with her death?"

"I assure you I'm not playing any game. Where are you?"

"I'm at home."

"And you received a letter in the mail?" I was having trouble following along. I hoped that had more to do with Jenna's inability to accurately tell a story than my cognitive functions.

"Yes. Sophie sent me a letter. An apology. She was terrified. She wanted to come home. She needed help. She said someone was following her. She was scared. So scared."

"When was the letter postmarked?" Sophie died two weeks ago. It shouldn't have taken that long for her letter to get to Jenna.

"It's dated the second. I'm not great about checking my mail. Don't give me shit about that. I get to it when I get to it." She exhaled again. "But I should have noticed this one sooner. I just thought it was a coupon or flyer or something."

I pulled to the side of the road, searched for Jenna's address, and entered it into the GPS. I would have asked, but she had gotten lost in her own commentary about opening mail. I'd never been great about keeping up with it either, but three weeks seemed extreme, even to me. "What does the letter say exactly?" I asked when she paused for breath.

"Sophie apologized for everything that happened

between us and missing our mom's funeral. She'd never admit she was wrong unless she was desperate."

"What else does it say?" That might have been her sister's way of making amends before offing herself.

"She goes on to say that Nathan kicked her out. She couldn't find a place to live or a job. Blah blah blah." Jenna scanned the note as she read the highlights. "She said she's been staying in shelters, but she noticed someone following her when she'd leave during the day. She got freaked out, so she found some other places to stay. She thought it would be okay. One night, she was attacked. The guy took her stuff. She was afraid he wanted more than that. She found someone to help her, a counselor, I'm guessing. She doesn't say who, but she said that her attacker got scared off."

"Did she call the cops?"

"It doesn't say. But she begged me to come get her and let her stay with me. She was afraid he'd come back. She said he had a knife."

"What kind of knife?"

"It doesn't say."

"Sophie had a phone. Why didn't she call you?"

"I changed providers and got a new number six months ago. She didn't have it."

I slowed as I crept down the residential street, reading the addresses on the mailboxes. 32A. I wedged the rental into a space that wasn't quite big enough, leaving the nose of the car sticking out. "Does she describe the man who followed her or the one who attacked her or the person who helped her?"

"No."

I locked the doors and jogged up the walkway. Jenna had left the storm door open. I tugged on the metal security door, but it was locked. Jenna heard the rattling and edged out of her kitchen and peered at me. Hanging up, she tucked her phone into her back pocket and opened the door.

"May I see the letter?" I asked.

"What are you doing here?"

"I was in the neighborhood."

She looked at me suspiciously before gesturing toward the kitchen. "It's on the table."

I put on a pair of gloves as I made my way into the kitchen. Two miniature schnauzers and a tiny, fluffy tan dog ran toward me, yipping excitedly. They jumped up on my shins, barely reaching my knees.

"Mitsy, Cupcake, down." The two schnauzers dropped down, continuing to bark at me. "Baron, behave."

"You were supposed to bark when I showed up at the door," I said to them.

"They're too chicken to bark at people outside the house. But now that you're on their territory, they don't have a choice."

Jenna tidied up, placing her lunch dishes in the sink while I read the letter. Sophie hadn't said anything more specific than what Jenna had already told me. I checked the postmark. San Diego. Pulling out my phone, I took a photograph of the envelope and the letter.

"How did you know?" Jenna put her hands on her hips and stared at me. "The police said Sophie killed herself. Why would you think anything else?"

"A friend expressed concern. Homeless people are being attacked. He thought the suicides might be related."

"Suicides. How many other people died?"

"One that I know of. I don't think they're connected. At least, I didn't. Now, I'm not sure." I told her everything I knew about Sophie's death and the things the social workers and volunteers had told me. I studied the letter, wondering if the veteran I'd spoken to had been the one who scared off the person who attacked Sophie. But he hadn't mentioned anything about it to me. Could Robert Devers have been the guy who attacked her and stole her things? I filed that thought away for later consideration.

The autopsy didn't show any marks on Sophie. No bruising. Nothing. But since this letter was three weeks old and I had no idea how long it took Sophie to write it after that incident, I had to assume no other attacks occurred between then and her death.

"When we spoke the other day, you were convinced your sister had every reason to kill herself. Why the sudden change of heart?" I asked.

"Isn't it obvious?" Jenna stabbed at the letter with her pointer finger. "She was scared. Someone attacked her. Clearly, I was wrong." She fished my card out of her pocket. "You work security and investigations. That's what the card says. Cross Security and Investigations. You deal with this sort of thing all the time, right? So what do I do?"

"Show it to the police."

"In San Diego?"

"Start with the cops here. Let's see what they have to say first. C'mon," I jerked my head toward the door, "I'll go with you."

Jenna wasn't convinced she could trust me, but if I were a charlatan, I wouldn't be offering to go to the police station with her. While she grabbed her stuff, I put the letter and envelope into a zippered sandwich bag and crouched on the floor to pet the tan dog that kept prodding me with his nose. Once he had my attention, he ran into the other room and returned with a ball for me to throw. At least he trusted me.

After a few rounds of fetch, Jenna was ready to go. "I'll follow you," she said, "since you blocked me in." She narrowed her eyes. "Are the police going to think I'm crazy?"

"Possibly, but that doesn't matter. Finding out what happened to your sister does."

"If Sophie hadn't been such a bitch and so damn stubborn, she'd be alive right now."

"People make mistakes."

She rolled her eyes and shook her head. "That's an understatement."

"Is there any chance Sophie could have hallucinated the attack or lied about it?" I asked as we made our way out of her house.

"I wouldn't put it past her. She might have said all this just to get me to help her. But for her to swallow her pride and ask for forgiveness, she'd have to be really scared or desperate. Something was going on. She wouldn't have wasted her time otherwise."

"And you're sure she wrote the letter?"

"I'd recognize her perfect penmanship anywhere. Teachers always compared us, saying I should be more like her. Boy, were they wrong."

FIFTEEN

I looked around the police station. I wasn't used to so much sunlight, but by now, I should have been. The officer working the front desk recognized me from our brief run-in on my last case, so after Jenna explained the situation and was taken to speak to a detective, the officer pulled me to the side.

"New client?" she asked.

"Not exactly."

"What exactly?" Her eyes narrowed. "Last time, you didn't even have a valid P.I. license."

"I do now." I held it out for her to inspect.

"That's great, but this isn't one of our cases. The death occurred out of our jurisdiction. I'm guessing that's why she got you involved, but why bring her here?"

"She's a local. I thought that might mean something. You serve the people of Los Angeles. That makes her one of yours."

The officer peered at her computer screen. "But it's a San Diego case. A closed case. The detective of record ruled it a suicide. ME signed off on it. It's done."

"The letter Jenna received suggests otherwise."

"It's not a smoking gun or confession. I don't see how

it'd be enough to reopen a case, especially one that was never ours to begin with. You should take it up with San Diego. You'd have better luck."

"That's a hell of a drive."

She held up her palms in surrender. "I'm just calling it like I see it. The most robbery-homicide will do is make a couple of phone calls, possibly send them a copy of the letter, and say they did what they could. Detective Trevitt will decide what to do with it after that."

"All right. I'll take that under advisement."

I sat near the door, wondering how long they'd humor Jenna before making a few empty promises and sending her on her way. While I waited, I pulled up the photo I'd taken of the letter and zoomed in, rereading each word carefully. Sophie Marshman claimed someone followed her every time she left the shelter. Given that she stayed mainly in women only shelters, that explained why he waited outside for her. But she never mentioned how long this went on or what he looked like.

Dialing the shelter, I stepped outside while I waited for someone to answer.

"Hi, this is Alex Parker," I said. "We met the other evening."

"Right. You had questions about Sophie Marshman," Diana, the shelter's director, said. "Is something wrong?"

"Did Sophie ever mention anyone following her?"

"Not that I remember."

"What about an attack? It would have happened a month or two ago."

"Hang on while I pull my records." Diana hummed while she flipped pages. "Sophie didn't report anything, but I remember hearing something about it. We do what we can to keep everyone safe, but it's an uphill battle."

"You don't remember any details?"

"Not off the top of my head. The only thing I remember is a few of her personal possessions were taken. She used to set out a picture frame beside her bedroll. One night, I didn't see it and asked what happened to it. That's when she told me."

"Do you remember when this was?"

"Probably two months ago. I didn't think much of it. Things get stolen or misplaced often. I'm sorry I didn't mention it the other night. I didn't think it was relevant."

"What about bruises or other injuries? Do you remember if she was attacked?"

"I don't think I ever saw her injured. She didn't report anything or ask us to call the police or an ambulance, so I don't know what to tell you."

"All right, thanks."

Right about now I wished I'd gotten Army Coat's name. For all I knew, he attacked her or knew who did. Our brief exchange hadn't set my radar buzzing, but people could be deceiving and I wasn't necessarily an expert judge of character.

"What are you doing here, Parker?"

I turned at the question to find Detective Dean Petrocelli, RHD, heading toward me. He carried a takeout bag in his left hand, making sure to keep his dominant hand free in case he needed to pull his weapon. I wondered if that was because he always followed protocol or if he'd seen shit and was always on alert.

"I'm waiting for a friend."

"Friend?" He tilted his head so he could eye me over the rim of his sunglasses. "I hope you don't think we're friends."

"Not yet, but I'm keeping my fingers crossed."

His brows knit together. "Don't block the door."

"Is that a punishable offense? Are you going to write me a ticket?"

"Don't tempt me."

"I wouldn't dream of it." I stepped to the side, allowing him to enter, and followed him into the police station.

He glanced at me, unwilling to turn his back to me. "Why are you here? Don't tell me you found another body."

"I didn't find it. It found me."

He stopped in his tracks, placed his lunch on the counter, and put his hands on his hips. "You've got my attention. Enlighten me."

"A woman died under suspicious circumstances. Three weeks prior to her death, she sent her sister a letter. In that letter, she told her sister she was being stalked and had been attacked. Whoever attacked her also stole her things."

"Sounds like a mugging."

"Possibly, but she was scared, desperate. She begged for help. Before her sister could help her, she died."

Petrocelli exhaled. "I know I'm going to regret this, but how did she die?"

"She bled to death from knife wounds to her inner thighs."

"Any sign of sexual assault or attempted sexual assault?"

"No. She was fully clothed."

"Was the knife recovered?"

"It was in her hand." I held up my palm and drew a line with my finger. "She had a deep cut right across here. It could have been defensive."

"Or the blade slipped." He rested one elbow on the counter, shifting his weight to one leg while he considered the scenario, as if this were a logic puzzle. "What about forensics?"

"No other fingerprints on the knife. Considering she was found outdoors, in an alley, I'm not sure how thoroughly they checked everything, but no fibers or foreign DNA were found on her body."

He picked up his bag. "It's probably a suicide. Though, most of those don't cut through clothing. Since you said she was fully dressed, I'm guessing she was cut through her clothing."

"Yep."

He shrugged. "Happens."

"What about the letter?"

"Coincidence."

"Not possible."

"Just because you believe that, it doesn't make it true. Frankly, if I bought into that, I'd arrest you for murder because you've been too close too many times."

"I'm not a killer, Detective."

"I'm not entirely sure what you are, but like I told you last time, it'd be best if you stay out of police investigations. I warned you if you interfere again, I will arrest you." He turned, entering the code to go through the door.

"While I have you, I was hoping you could do me a favor."

He wedged the toe of his shoe beneath the door to keep it from closing. "You've gotta be fucking kidding me."

"I need information on a gun. Can you run the serial numbers?"

He didn't even dignify my question with a response before going through the door and making sure it closed behind him. So much for our budding friendship.

"Do you have the number handy?" the officer at the desk asked. She peered to the side, making sure Petrocelli was out of sight before she said it.

"It's actually a list of possibilities. The number was filed off. I just want to make sure the gun wasn't used in the commission of a crime, and if it was, I'd like to know more about the crime and the suspect."

She lowered her voice. "Yeah, I can do that."

I dug through my pockets for the list I'd made the night before. After copying it down on another sheet of paper, I handed it to her. "You're sure you don't mind?"

"Give me your card. I'll call if I find something."

"Thanks." I handed her my card, and she paperclipped it to the top of the sheet. At least my encounter with the cranky detective hadn't been a total waste of time.

I'd just taken a seat and fished out my phone, checking to make sure Theo Stapleton hadn't gotten antsy in the last hour, when an officer escorted Jenna to the door. She thanked him, though I could tell it was insincere.

"A detective will be in touch," he said.

"What happened?" I asked, joining them. Jenna shook her head and pushed open the door. I offered the officer a polite smile and followed Jenna. I grabbed her arm. "Hey. Talk to me."

She spun. "I don't even know you."

"What did the police say?"

"They'll make some calls, but they don't think the letter is proof of anything, not after a thorough investigation has already been conducted."

"What do you believe?"

"I don't know." She stabbed a finger into my collarbone. "This is your fault. If you hadn't shown up at my place of business, I wouldn't have given this a second thought. Maybe I would have felt guilty. Maybe. But that would have been about it. I wouldn't be wondering if my sister was murdered because I didn't open my damn mail fast enough."

"That's not on you."

"I'm one hundred percent certain Sophie wouldn't agree. That stupid bitch. Even now, she's still screwing up my life." She stared up at the sky and yelled, "I hope you're happy."

A few people turned to look at us, but Jenna didn't notice.

"Do you want to come to my office and talk about it?" I asked.

She turned her gaze from the heavens and stared into my eyes. "Why are you involved? If someone told you the police missed something, why aren't you fixing it instead of sending me to deal with this? This isn't my problem. Sophie's dead. It sucks for her, but she's been dead to me for years. This shouldn't matter. It shouldn't hurt. I shouldn't have to waste my day off addressing these things."

"I'm sorry. Someone dropped this into my lap. I didn't want to be involved either."

"Who? Who brought this to you?"

"A sergeant. He's investigating crimes against the homeless."

She shoved a copy of the letter into my hands, since the LAPD held on to the original. "Take this to him and let him figure it out. I'm done." She backed down the two concrete steps, almost falling in the process. Holding up her hands, she backed away from me. "I'm so over this. Stay the hell away from me. I don't want to see you again. Do you understand?"

"Yeah. I got it. Again, I'm sorry for everything."

She exhaled, nodded a few times, and went back to her car.

Deciding there was no such thing as a good deed, I got

into my car and headed for Malibu. Being productive was overrated. I'd gotten halfway there when my phone rang. It was the office.

"Parker," I answered, wondering why building security was calling me. If a body had fallen out of the ceiling tiles, Petrocelli would arrest me on principle alone.

"Hi, Alex. I'm sorry to bother you, but I caught a guy trying to break into your office," Buck said.

"Did you call the police?"

"Funny thing about that. He has a badge. What do you want me to do?"

"Where is he now?"

"He's sitting beside me, eating a donut."

"I'll be right there. Don't let him out of your sight."

"Yes, ma'am."

We'd had a conversation about that, but the close proximity to the donuts must have made Buck forget I hated that word. I made the next turn and headed for the business district. Weekend traffic sucked, but the closer I got to the office, the less congested it became. After parking in the garage, I jogged to the building. As I entered, I pulled off my shades to find Will Russo seated behind the security desk. He propped one foot up on the trash can while he wiped powdered sugar off his fingertips.

"Is this the guy you caught trying to break in?" I asked Buck, ignoring Will.

"Yeah. Do you want me to call the LAPD to pick him up?"

I stared at Will, who tossed the napkin into the trash. That's when I realized his hands were bound with a ziptie. "Why were you trying to break into my office?"

"I was not," he said.

Buck gave me a look. "Mm-hhmm," he mumbled with more sass than I expected.

"Why?" I repeated.

"I wanted a cup of coffee," Will said.

"Not this again." I pulled out a pocket knife and cut him free. "We need to talk, and those damn well better be chocolate crème. I've had a hell of a day."

SIXTEEN

Will read the letter again. "I told you." He dropped it to the desk. "From the way this reads, I'm wondering if that homeless guy who gave you the tip is responsible."

"Possibly. Or it could have been Robert Devers. Army Coat said Devers was looking to steal whatever he could find. Sophie had a nice life before things went south. She might have taken a few things with her, like an expensive picture frame."

"Wouldn't she have pawned the items herself? People get cold and hungry. Under those conditions, sentimentality is usually the first to go out the window."

I'd been wondering the same thing. "You could ask her ex-husband what she took with her when he kicked her out. If you figure out what happened to those items, you might have a better grasp of determining what happened to Sophie and if she really was attacked."

"You don't believe the letter?"

"I don't know what to believe." An unsettling thought percolated in the back of my mind. "Did you find anything after I gave you the tip?"

"I sent a few officers to perform a canvass. No one remembered anything about the alleged incident involving the three teenagers. I couldn't find the victim or any CCTV footage to back up your source's story. I figured the cameras at the donut shop would have caught something, but they didn't cover that alleyway, just the front door." Will's face said more than his words.

"You think it's a bad tip."

"I'm not sure I'd call it bad. I'm guessing the tipster sent us on a wild goose chase to throw us off his scent. We're probably not even looking at three teenagers. He probably committed that assault, mugged Sophie, and staged these two murders to look like suicides. He admitted to knowing both victims. So far, he's the only connection we've found. And now we can't find him."

The nagging itch in the back of my brain increased at his words. "Did you check the camp? Myrtle, the woman in pink, might know where he went."

"No one at the camp would tell me where he was or answer any other questions. I scouted the neighborhood, but I couldn't locate him."

"What about a name?" I asked.

"No such luck, but patrol is keeping an eye out. At some point, he'll return, and we'll bring him in."

"I'm surprised you didn't round up everyone else in the meantime."

Will's brow furrowed. "Why would I?"

"Oh, come on. We both know you could have come up with a reason, no matter how bogus, to try to convince someone to give him up. Why didn't you?"

"I don't work like that."

"You pulled the trigger on a stun gun without announcing. Why is this any different?"

"You're never going to let that go, are you?"

I rocked back in my chair. "There's just one problem with that scenario. If the tipster's responsible for Sophie's death and had made a previous attempt, like her letter implies, she would have had defensive wounds. She would have tried to run or scream for help. But she didn't." I pointed to the letter. "This proves she knew someone was following her. If the same guy tried again, she would have fought back. As far as we can tell, based on the crime scene photos, none of that happened. She stayed near the dumpster, letting the life drain from her body."

"Maybe she was afraid. He could have had a gun and threatened to kill her if she tried anything."

"But she was already dying."

Will rubbed at his upper lip. "You said whoever attacked her stole her picture frame."

"That's what the woman at the shelter said."

"A picture frame might have been the only thing she had left of her old life. It could have been a family photo or a snapshot of her kids. Whoever took it could have used that as bait to lure her into the alley. Maybe he apologized, said he was off his meds, and wanted to give it back. That could be how he regained her trust and why she didn't realize the danger until it was too late. He could have surprised her."

"She wasn't stabbed in the chest. She was cut and left to bleed out. Her death wasn't instantaneous. It took time. At least six minutes, maybe more."

Will thought for a moment. "There was no blood trail. She never tried to move from that spot. He must have cut her and threatened to kill her if she screamed. He must have waited until she passed out from the blood loss before leaving her to die."

"She should have fought."

"She was scared, Alex. Everyone said it. Fear can be paralyzing."

I wondered if that was what happened to him, but I didn't ask. "I still think, if she was murdered, whoever did it was someone she trusted."

"Trusted enough to let him cut her open and sit there instead of running or calling for help?" Will asked. "That's a hell of a lot of trust."

"Unless he told her to stay put because help was on the way, or one guy attacked her and another tried to render assistance, but failed to save her."

"Like a team. One plays the villain and the other plays the hero."

"It's one possibility. But she still should have screamed for help or fought back against the initial attacker."

"So the only way that works is if the person who cut her

convinced her what he was doing would help her. Would she have believed that?" Will rubbed a donut crumb free from the side of his mouth.

"She would have if it was someone who helped her before or the person was someone she was used to seeing in that type of capacity. Y'know, like a paramedic or a cop." I stared at Will, the warning claxons growing louder in my brain.

"But to cut her, that sounds more like voodoo. Something to get the evil spirits out. Blood-letting or some kind of medieval thing."

"Did you find anything on the church or Father Miguel?" I asked.

"What are you thinking? He tried to conduct an exorcism that went off the rails?"

"As far as I know, exorcisms don't involve blood."

Will stared at me. "Sophie had a history of mental illness. Could someone have convinced her she was possessed? She might have wanted him to cut the demonic spirit out of her."

"Does Father Miguel's church offer exorcisms?"

Will shook his head. "I didn't find anything on the church. The padre used to run with a gang with close ties to a cartel in Tijuana, but he's stayed out of trouble since he turned eighteen. Supposedly, he turned his life around."

"What about his former associates?"

"Almost all of them are dead."

"Any reason to think he killed them?" I asked.

"Not that I found. Were you able to place Sophie at that church? Because I couldn't."

"I didn't ask the priest about her."

"Well, I did. He didn't recognize her."

"You went back over my work?"

"I have a badge. I thought I'd get better answers. Plus, you didn't ask about her. I did, so it's a good thing I followed up with my own questions."

I rolled my eyes.

"I like what you said about Sophie trusting her killer because he'd helped her before. That leads me back to thinking our tipster could be the killer. Let's say he's telling the truth, and three teenagers are assaulting the unhoused. One of them might have attacked Sophie, grabbed whatever he could out of her bag, and ran for it. The tipster comes to the rescue, earning some trust. He uses that to create a false sense of security. After all, he watches over the entire camp. Everyone trusts him," Will said.

"According to what he said, Sophie kept to herself. I don't think she'd go somewhere alone with him or anyone else for that matter."

"What if he came bearing gifts? Since he chased off Robert and the three teenagers, he could have told her he found the person who'd been following her and got her picture frame back. While she's distracted, he attacks."

"She would have cried out."

Will let out a frustrated sigh. "Maybe she did. Maybe he cornered her or held her down. She could have been screaming and crying, but no one heard it. Everything closed at least an hour earlier. No one was out, except the homeless community, and they wouldn't turn on their protector."

"Evidence suggests she didn't fight or struggle," I reminded Will.

"He could have waited for her to pass out and then cleaned up whatever mess they made and eliminated any evidence we would have found."

"You have nothing to back that up. It's nothing more than supposition." Usually, I was the one coming up with farfetched theories. Now I knew how my friends felt. "If Sophie was killed, more than likely the killer is the person who'd been following her."

"I'll look into it," Will said. "But don't you think Trevitt would have heard something about that when he investigated? No one mentioned it." A dark cloud settled over his features. "Unless he left that out of his reports."

"Why would he do that? You didn't think he was a dirty cop, just overworked."

"I don't know."

I studied Will. He was determined to prove these cases were murder. I'd been inclined to believe him, but that level of desperation made me wonder if he'd led me to believe that despite what the evidence said. I reread Sophie's letter. She was scared, but even her sister thought it was possible she'd hallucinated the man following her. "Will, why are these cases so important to you? Why do you think someone wants the homeless dead?"

"Look at the facts. The same thing happened to Robert Devers. He didn't fight back either, which means he thought he could trust his attacker too. More than likely, our Good Samaritan tipster is really a wolf in sheep's clothing. He could have a crew. For all we know, those teens could be working for him. Hell, the tipster could have stopped the original attack, gained Sophie's trust, and later killed her. He said he roughed up Robert, but he tried to keep an eye on the kid too. Why would he do that?"

"It sounded like a tough love situation." I powered on the computer. "He's an Army veteran who served four tours. I'm guessing he must be from San Diego or has family there. He looked about forty."

"He could be younger. The streets tend to age people."

"Just like war."

"What about identifying marks?"

"I didn't see any tattoos or anything. But he was covered up. You must have brought him in before. He complained about the police harassing the homeless."

While I searched the databases, Will made a few calls. He snapped his fingers at me and covered the mouthpiece. "Try Captain Roland Jordan," he said.

I entered the name and waited for a photo to pop up. "That's him."

Will returned to his phone conversation. "Does he have a criminal record?" He paused. "Uh-huh. LKA?" He waited. "That fits. Issue a BOLO. I'd like to speak to him in connection with the recent string of assaults." He grunted. "Yeah, I know. I wouldn't expect anything less." He hung up.

"Aren't you afraid they'll ping your phone and find out where you are?"

He glared at me. "Jordan has been brought in a few times for assault. Each time, we kicked him. The DA never wanted to prosecute, especially when he claimed self-defense and defense of others. He's a decorated war hero. We had no reason to doubt his word. But he might have snapped."

"I don't think he's our killer. Making a woman bleed out and hanging a young guy from the rafters in a church isn't exactly what I'd expect from a soldier, particularly one who claims to avoid that church." I thought back to the conversation.

"People lie all the time for all sorts of reasons. But even if Jordan isn't our killer, he may know who's responsible. At the very least, he must know more about the teenagers he said were behind the assault. From everything you told me, I'm convinced he's dialed in to what's going on with the homeless community and where the threats are originating. He keeps tabs on everyone. Protects them. He's been trained to gather intel and perform threat assessments. And now, he's gone missing. I'm thinking, after your conversation, he realized we were on to him or he went to take care of the people hurting members of his community." He stared into my eyes. "What's wrong?"

"I don't know. Something doesn't fit. He seemed genuinely surprised to learn Robert hung himself. I don't think he knew Robert was dead."

"When I first brought this to you, you told me the same person couldn't be responsible for both crimes. Maybe you're right. Or he thought Sophie Marshman and Robert Devers posed a threat, so he had no choice but to kill them or convince them to kill themselves. He told you Robert threatened the camp. And Sophie hated everyone and everything. Maybe that's all it takes."

I focused on the whiteboard where I'd scribbled my notes concerning the two suspicious suicides. "Why were you trying to break into my office?"

"I wasn't."

"Buck said otherwise."

He sighed, exasperated. "Fine, I was. But you make it sound so sinister. I figured I'd let myself in, give you a call, and make some coffee while I waited for you to show up. I had a feeling you wouldn't be working the weekend. It turns out I was right."

"Are you sure you didn't want to steal my files or check the progress I was making?"

"Wow. You seriously have trust issues."

"Again, trust has to be earned. And you're doing a lousy job."

"I'll work on it." Will reached back to grab the coffeepot, stopping before pouring. "If I get a refill, are you going to accuse me of stealing your coffee too?"

"Help yourself."

"That's what I was trying to do earlier. I already explained to you I don't want to risk talking on the phone."

I unlocked one of the filing cabinets and pulled out a prepaid phone. "Here. It's clean. The next time you want to chat, call me." I input his number into my phone. "I don't know why you didn't think to do this yourself."

"I've been busy." He made sure he had my number and that the battery had an adequate charge before tucking it into his pocket. "But that would have saved me some time."

I pulled another donut out of the box and took a bite. "Yeah, me too."

"On the plus side, your side trip to San Diego resulted in a solid lead. Frankly, I'm surprised. I guess I shouldn't be, but you did what I couldn't, what the officers under my command couldn't, in less than forty-eight hours. I'm not used to working with consultants or private eyes. Is it always like this?"

"Flattery will get you nowhere."

"Right. Only donuts work." He tapped his temple. "Got it." He grabbed another one and considered pulling out a second, but finding only three left, he closed the lid on the pastry box. "I guess it's time I pay up. What was that favor you wanted? Something about a serial number."

"Never mind. I got someone else to look into it."

"The LAPD?"

"This is Los Angeles. It makes sense when you think about it."

"I would have done it. I just have to be careful how I go about things." He dipped the donut into his coffee before taking a bite. "I've got eyes and ears on me."

"But you refuse to tell me why. Maybe I can help. You

said how amazed you were by my skills."

"I don't think I used the word amazed." Will wouldn't talk unless he wanted to, which he didn't.

"If you're being watched, how is it you can show up at my office without worry?"

"You're not local, and surely, I would spot a tail during the course of the drive here. Plus, I have the day off, so I can always say I decided to take a mini-vacation, if I were confronted."

"Why is the brass keeping tabs on you?"

Will didn't answer. Instead, he pulled a notepad from his jacket pocket and reached for the marker on my desk. He approached the whiteboard, poised to write. "May I?"

"Go ahead."

"Scenario one, the tipster told you the truth. He saw these teenagers attack another member of the homeless community. He spooked them, so they now avoid that neighborhood. That might explain why reports of attacks have slowed to a trickle, but they haven't stopped. The attackers are being more careful. They're plotting and planning. Maybe they went so far as to—"

My phone beeped. "Hold that thought." I tapped the screen a few times, finding the red blip moving away from the Stapletons' house. A second later, my phone rang. It was Iris.

"Hello?"

"He just left. He said he promised to help a friend with something and wouldn't be back until late. That's all he'd tell me," Iris said.

"Okay. I'm on it." I hung up and looked at Will. "I have to go."

"Was it something I said?"

I pointed to the door. "I don't have time for this."

"What's wrong? Where are you rushing off to?"

"I'm conducting surveillance, possible cheating husband."

He laughed, as if it were a joke.

"I'm serious. I have to go, and I don't trust you to stay here by yourself. I need you to leave. Now."

He eyed me, realization dawning on his face. "Shit. You

can't be serious. I didn't kill Sophie Marshman or Robert Devers. Why would you ever think that?"

"I didn't say that."

"No," he pointed a finger in my face, "but you think it."

"I'm not ready to rule anything out yet, including the possibility Trevitt was right, but I don't have time to debate this right now."

"Tell me why you think I could be the killer." He crossed his arms over his chest. "I'm not leaving until you do."

"Our first encounter was in an alley. You said you were looking for the assailants, but you could have been looking for your next victim. Since then, you've been keeping tabs on these cases even though no one else in your department has any interest. You're being monitored for some reason you won't disclose. Despite the risk, you brought me two closed cases to review, and you don't want anyone at the department to know about it. Add to that the officer-involved shooting and your reassignment to desk duty, the circumstances surrounding the suicides, and how, if they were murders, neither victim put up a fight. I can't help but wonder if you wanted someone on the outside to review these cases because you're afraid you left evidence behind that another investigator might find or that IA might find if they link the suicides back to the assaults and back to you."

"Because I'm investigating them?"

I shrugged. "I don't know. But you tried to break into my office, and I don't believe it's because you wanted a damn cup of coffee."

"I'll have to prove it to you." He put on his jacket. "Let's go."

"No, I said you have to go."

"I'm going with you. You said you're conducting surveillance. You might need help, and you keep insisting I prove myself and earn your trust. What better way to do that than by helping you with something? After all, I owe you a reward, and you went to the LAPD for help on it instead of me. So this should make us square. Then maybe you'll realize you can trust me."

I didn't have time to argue. The red blip was getting farther and farther from the house. "Fine, but if you stab me in the back, hell will rain down on your head."

"Understood."

SEVENTEEN

"I shouldn't have had all that coffee," Will said.

I glanced at him from the corner of my eye. "You shouldn't have come with me."

He opened the center console and looked inside before peering into the back seat. "Do you have a bottle or something?"

"If you unzip in my car, I will shoot you. Do you understand?"

He grunted. "What's up with all these rules? I didn't think the private sector had rules."

"There are tons of rules. My boss has a million of them. There must be a laminated copy hanging on the wall in the office. You can read it the next time you're there."

"Why do I get the feeling you ignore most of them?" He spotted a half-empty water bottle beneath the passenger's seat and reached for it.

"Don't even think about it," I warned. "Go take a bathroom break. A real one." I nodded toward the bookstore. "Bathrooms are usually next to the café. And while you're there, find out what he's reading. But don't blow this."

Will held up the bottle. "Do you want this recycled, or is

it a collector's item?"

"You can toss it."

He gave me a too bright smile and let himself out of the car.

I watched as he made his way across the parking lot to the strip mall where the large bookstore loomed on the corner, taking up more than half of the property. He placed the bottle into the blue receptacle before entering the shop. Adjusting in my seat, I watched Will walk around the raised platform surrounded by the decorative dividers, which separated the café from the rest of the shop, and make his way to the bathrooms.

Theo hadn't looked up from his book, which was opened flat on the table in front of him while he sipped a frothy, green concoction. I hadn't seen what he selected from the shelves before he took a seat, but my gut said he must have been waiting for someone. Three-quarters of the tables were occupied, mostly by women. A few had small children with them, but Theo hadn't acknowledged any of them. The only person he'd spoken to was the barista.

She looked to be in her early twenties. She'd filled his drink order. No smile. No flirtatious hair twirling. Nothing that indicated she had any interest in the older man. However, given the way she'd been eyeing the woman at the table closest to the counter, I was pretty sure Theo wasn't her type for many reasons.

When Will emerged from the bathroom, he cut through the opening in the dividers and approached the counter. After he ordered using enough hand gestures to land a 747, the barista placed two packaged drinks on the counter beside him before turning her back to him. Will took the drinks and sat at a nearby table, watching as she worked to fill the rest of his order.

He glanced back at Theo. I didn't like this. I shouldn't have sent him inside. He wasn't a detective. He was a sergeant, and a lousy one at that. What did he know about surveillance and covert missions? Surely, he must have had some sort of training, but when he opened his mouth and asked Theo a question, all I could do was watch in horror.

Since Theo's back was to me, I couldn't see his reaction.

What did Will say? Had he blown my cover or told Theo he was being followed or that his wife suspected him of cheating? Since Theo didn't turn around in order to peer at me through the window, I could only hope Will hadn't done anything irreparably stupid. Still, whatever he said was stupid.

The conversation only lasted a few seconds, maybe a minute, but it felt like an eternity. My blood boiled and my heart raced. This wasn't a dangerous situation, but I feared my cover had been blown. As a result, I was convinced something was about to pop off, but it didn't. Instead, Will grabbed the rest of his order from the counter the moment the barista filled it and headed out of the café. Theo turned, watching him walk out, but he turned back around before Will exited the shop. Still, I couldn't risk being spotted.

As soon as Will got back into the car, I started the engine and pulled out of the lot. "What the hell was that?"

"He's reading some kind of illustrated encyclopedia on anatomy," Will said.

"Is that what you asked him?"

"No. I asked if there were any dirty pictures in it."

"What is wrong with you?" I circled the block, hesitant to park again, but I didn't have much of a choice. This time, I found a spot between two SUVs. That made spotting my sedan harder, but it also partially obscured my view of Theo through the window. This is why I shouldn't have taken an amateur who thought he was a seasoned professional on a stakeout. After making a mental note to never do that again, I sunk back against my seat and glared at Will. "I'm waiting."

"There's nothing wrong with me. You wanted to know what he was reading. I told you. What's the problem?"

"You're not supposed to approach the mark."

"That sounds like another rule. Hang on. I should write these down." He put the two drinks in my cupholders, rested the bag on the center console, and pulled out his notepad. "Okay, I'm ready. Rule number one." He looked expectantly at me.

"Stop being a wiseass."

"Is wiseass one word or two?"

A frightening thought came over me. "God, it's like looking in a mirror."

Will snickered. "See, I'm not so bad." He opened the bag he'd placed on the console. "I got us sandwiches and chips. That's pretty much all they had besides cake and cookies, and I figured we might have reached our sugar quota for the day."

"Good call."

He tugged on the wrapper until the bag of chips opened. After taking out a handful, he asked, "What's the deal with this guy?"

"I don't know. He's been sneaking out after he thinks his wife's asleep. Sometimes, he stays out all night. He's been moody and irritable. It's a lot of little things that have her convinced he's sleeping around."

"He probably is. What are you supposed to do about it?"

"Find out for sure and bring back proof."

"That's a shitty assignment."

"Tell me about it."

A strawberry blonde parked her convertible in front of the bookshop. After putting on a fresh layer of lip gloss and fixing her hair, she flipped up her visor and got out of the car. She had a parking tag hanging from her mirror from the hospital where Theo worked. I pulled out my phone and snapped a photo of her license plate and the tag.

"Do you have to take cases you don't want to work?" Will asked.

"It depends."

"On?"

"How busy I am, who the client is, and if I want to get paid that week." I watched the blonde scan the clearance table at the front of the store before heading to the café. She put her bag down on the chair at Theo's table. "Bingo." I zoomed in, wishing I had grabbed the camera with the telescopic lens to take on this outing, and increased the magnification. After snapping a few photos of the woman, I lowered my phone.

"Who's the client?" Will asked.

"That's confidential."

"Do you work for celebrities?"

"I have before. But this isn't one of those cases."

"Glamorous." Will kept an eye on the woman as she waited at the counter for the barista to prepare her drink order. "Oatmilk latte, sugar-free vanilla, with a double shot of espresso. Do you think she's vegan, keto, or lactose intolerant and watching her figure?"

"The woman likes what she likes." I watched as she returned to Theo's table. She took a seat, smiling and laughing as she put her cup down and leaned in. But she didn't give him a hello kiss. Instead, she reached into her bag and pulled out a spiral notebook and pen with a fluffy purple feather sticking out of the back. She scooted her chair around the side until she was seated beside him. "Keep an eye on them while I figure out who she is."

"I bet I can get an ID faster." Will pulled out his phone and asked whoever answered to run the plate on her car. "Julie Carter. Got it. Thanks."

"Nice one, Sarge."

"Don't call me that."

I gave him a look before pulling up Theo's social media page and searching his friends list for Ms. Carter. "She's a graduate student in nursing. She's been working at the hospital these last six months." I pulled up her personal details, not finding anything to indicate she was an evil temptress hell-bent on seducing married men.

"How long has Theo been suspected of cheating?" Will asked.

"A while."

"That's vague."

"Yep." I read more of her personal details, feeling Will's eyes on me. "She's engaged to a pharmacist. His picture is plastered all over her pages. They've sent out save the date cards, and she has a million different photos from their engagement party."

"Let me see." Will took my phone and scrolled through her data. "Why would she cheat on this guy with that guy?"

"Love's blind," I suggested, but I didn't buy it. Taking my phone back, I searched Theo's profile pages for their interactions. They were limited to poking fun at stupid videos and memes. If they'd shared any calls or texts, they had been limited. I peered at the couple. They seemed friendly but not particularly romantic. "This doesn't feel right."

"He's an older man. They work together. Maybe he mentored her. She developed feelings, and he took advantage. That's how most of these things happen."

"Speaking from experience?"

"I've dated a few rookies, but I'm not married. Neither were they."

"They probably went out with you because you look like a rookie yourself."

"Thanks." Will smoothed his hair back, which was quite a feat given how short it was. "The baby face can be off-putting to some people."

"How old are you?" I asked.

"Thirty-four."

"When did you make sergeant?"

"Five years ago."

"When did you join the force?"

"Six years before that. Maybe seven. I applied to the academy when I graduated college, figuring it wouldn't hurt to have something else brewing while I looked for a job. I got called up before I found anything else, so I went."

"Interesting." I put my phone down and adjusted my seat, allowing it to lean back a little. "You might as well settle in. We're going to be here until closing."

"You're kidding."

"Nope."

"Why?"

"I don't think this is a date. I think it's a study session. Theo's an RN, who works in the OR. She's working on a graduate degree and interns at the hospital. Twenty says he offered to show her the ropes and is helping her study."

"I'm not stupid enough to bet against you, not with all these damn rules." He stared out the windshield. "You really think anyone is that altruistic?"

"You tell me." I turned to him. "Why are you investigating the attacks on the homeless? What are you hoping to get out of it?"

"That's not altruism. That's my job."

"No, it isn't."

"I took an oath. Serve and protect."

"There's more to it than that. You might as well tell me. I will figure it out."

"Not everything is a mystery. It's the right thing to do. Simple as that."

I watched Theo and Julie sip their drinks and pour over the illustrated anatomy book. At one point, Theo lifted Julie's arm and ran his finger along the inside of her forearm. Their physical contact wasn't romantic. He must have been demonstrating where something was located on the human body.

Briefly, I wondered if Theo liked to play doctor. According to Iris, he liked to roleplay, so that wasn't too farfetched. His credit cards and bank statements didn't indicate he visited any costume or sex shops, but since I couldn't think of anything else to do, I pulled up a list of places that specialized in costumes. Since this was Los Angeles, a lot of places sold and rented costumes. After making a list of shops located between the Stapletons' house and the hospital, I blew out a breath. Will had grown quiet while he ate his sandwich.

"How many years are you away from retirement? Eight?" I asked.

"I have seven and change until I hit my twenty, but I'm not planning on sticking around that long. I want to finish things up and walk out on a high note."

"Are you planning on going private?"

"If the right offer presents itself." He turned to me and grinned, hoping I'd take the not so subtle hint. "Law enforcement's the only job I've ever had. I'm not sure how well-adjusted I'd be to working in a grocery store or warehouse."

"You could learn a trade."

"Nothing's caught my fancy. Do you have any suggestions?"

"Be honest with me for two seconds."

"Sure." The look in his eyes told me he wanted to count, but he refrained.

"The reason you've been pestering me and buttering me

up is because you're hoping I'll put in a good word for you at Cross Security."

"Your office needs two more investigators since you have the space for them. The website said applicants are being considered. Prior experience is preferred. I've got that. I also have connections around here, connections you clearly don't have. I'd be an asset."

"Or a liability."

"I'm not going to shoot you."

"Of course, you're not. You're not carrying. But if you work for Cross, you'll need a weapon."

"I'm sure we could work something out."

"I'm a teddy bear compared to Lucien. First off, he doesn't like cops. He has a huge chip on his shoulder when it comes to working with your kind. And corrupt cops are a whole other breed. I won't put in a good word for you until I know what happened on the job. And you refuse to talk about it."

He pressed his lips together, returning his gaze to the bookshop windows.

"You killed a fellow officer, possibly two. That could make anyone gun shy and anxious to be out in the field. I get it. But in my experience, the private sector doesn't translate into a cushy desk job. I thought it would. But I've been in more scrapes since joining Cross Security than when I carried a badge." I wasn't certain of that, but it was close. "You have to move past whatever baggage you've got and be willing to talk about it, or it will eat away at you until your dying day. Walking away from the police department might be for the best, but if you're looking for a fresh start, joining the private sector isn't the answer. A fresh start means an entirely new career. I hear plumbers make good money."

Will shook his head, rolling his eyes in disdain. "You looked into me. That's why you don't trust me. That's why you think I killed those two homeless people." He opened the car door. "I should take off. It's clear you don't need me here."

"Wait."

He stood outside the car, the door still open. "Why?

You've already made up your mind about me, just like everyone else."

"Tell me I'm wrong. Tell me you didn't do it."

"I can't."

"Then tell me what happened. Why did you fire on your own officers?"

He shook his head. "I'll see you around, Alex. Enjoy the sandwich." He closed the door and headed for the nearest bus stop.

EIGHTEEN

After Will left, I couldn't shake the look I'd seen in his eyes. He was hurt and angry. But that wasn't my fault. At least I finally knew why he'd been hanging around the office every chance he got. Still, I hated how guilty I felt, but it wasn't like I pushed him away or rejected him. I was willing to give him a chance if he came clean. But he didn't want to. Maybe he didn't trust me. I couldn't blame him. We barely knew each other.

But what if it was more than that? What if Sergeant Will Russo wasn't one of the good guys? For all I knew, he could have had something to do with the attacks on the homeless and the suicides. Truthfully, nothing Will was doing made much sense to me. And the internal investigation into the fatal shooting that took his gun and ability to function in the field made even less sense. Sure, all Cross Security investigators were broken toys, but until I knew how broken Will was, I couldn't trust him and neither would Lucien.

Forty minutes before the bookstore closed, Julie and Theo made their way to the counter, purchased a few more books, and left the store. He walked her to her car and stood beside it while she tucked her purchases behind her seat. She gave him a hug and got behind the wheel.

Once she started her engine and backed out of the space, he headed for his car which was parked near the side of the building. By the time he pulled out, she was long gone. I held back, waiting until he was stuck at the nearest traffic light before pulling out of my space.

It was just after ten. Theo had a full day of tutoring or whatever I'd been watching for the last few hours. By now, he should have been tired and ready to go home. I knew I was.

I kept a few cars between us and an eye on my phone in case I lost sight of him. But I didn't. Two miles later, he turned down another street. Slowing, I took my time following him, afraid I'd been made. For all I knew, Will had let the cat out of the bag. However, Theo didn't appear to notice the tail.

Three blocks later, he made another turn and pulled into a parking lot. A food truck had set up permanent residence there. The lot had several tables and benches. Theo left his car on the outskirts of the roped off area and got out. I kept driving until I found some street parking on the other side. After pulling a u-turn and sliding into the space, I turned off the engine and killed the lights.

Theo bobbed a little while he read the menu. After placing his order and paying in cash, he took the oversized bag and returned to his car. *He's bringing dinner home,* I surmised.

This time, I pulled out ahead of him. Leapfrogging was a wonderful tailing tactic, but it wasn't easy to accomplish solo. Thankfully, he followed me through the next two lights. But since I was driving like a tourist with the rental stickers on my car to match, he got frustrated and blew past me the first chance he got. At least someone was willing to cooperate.

He made the next turn onto a more trafficked street, but I got caught by the red light. The GPS tracker I'd placed on his car continued straight on the path. By the time I turned, I'd lost him. So I followed the bouncing ball.

Instead of continuing toward home, Theo made an unexpected turn two blocks from my location. Speeding up,

I darted around the cars in my way. Flipping on my signal, I made the next turn onto an almost empty street.

The street lights were few and far between. Dark shadows and overgrown shrubs lined one side of the street. The sign said no parking. Dumpsters and abandoned boxes and pallets took up a long stretch on the other side, lining the road in front of a large parking garage. No wonder people didn't think garages were safe. When they were in dark, deserted areas like this, anything could happen.

I checked the blip on my phone. According to the map, Theo had stopped. I was practically on top of him. Since I didn't see his car in front of me, he must have pulled into the garage. What was he doing here?

Following him inside would compromise my cover, but I couldn't stay out here. While keeping one eye on the tracker, I continued down the street and turned left. The garage ran along that stretch with a second opening on that side. Deciding I'd do a complete circle before entering, I turned left again.

Restaurants and shops lined this street on both sides. The neon signs only added to the illumination provided by the many street lamps. The main entrance to the parking garage was situated across from a twenty-four hour pharmacy, a bowling alley, and a movie theater. Two of those were perfect venues to take someone special, and if things went well on the date, a quick trip to the pharmacy would ensure everyone was safe and protected.

A handful of people waited outside the box office, but I didn't spot Theo. Since he picked up dinner, he probably wasn't heading to the one location that prohibited outside food. More than likely, he was meeting someone at the bowling alley.

I pulled into the garage and circled around the first level, but I didn't spot his car. Then again, the parking spaces were limited, so I went up another level. The second level was only half occupied. The white sedan was parked near the stairs, but it was too dark to see if Theo was still inside.

Leaning over the steering wheel, I peered up at the concrete structure. No cameras. I pulled into a space near the end of that row and got out of the car. Again, I checked, but the garage didn't have any noticeable surveillance devices in the vicinity. Given how sketchy two of the surrounding streets looked at night, whoever owned the parking structure should have done a better job of protecting its paying customers.

I got out of the car and opened the trunk where I kept my go-bag, which contained a change of clothes and a few other necessities. I glanced around before removing my nine millimeter from my shoulder holster and placing it in the front pouch of the hooded sweatshirt I tugged on over my shirt. I wouldn't win any fashion awards, but a girl could never be too careful. The former federal agent in me would never walk unarmed into an unknown situation or willingly make myself an easy target for whatever predator might be lurking in the shadows.

However, the more important tool was my phone. Iris wanted proof of her husband's infidelity, and aside from the unregistered weapon I'd found in his tackle box, Theo didn't check any of the other boxes for violent or dangerous. I closed the trunk, grabbed my phone out of the car, and closed the tracking app before tucking it into my front pouch. Kangaroos would have made great private eyes.

Keeping both hands in my pocket, I walked along the path behind the parked cars, figuring I'd have a better chance of sneaking up on Theo and snapping a few money shots from the rear of the car instead of the front, where he'd be much more likely to notice me. As I closed in on the white sedan, I stooped a little. The high-profile SUV parked two spaces away provided a perfect hiding spot.

I peered around the side of the SUV, but the interior lights weren't on inside Theo's car. Maybe he liked the ambiance of the parking garage's dim lighting. Personally, I preferred being able to see what I was eating.

Since it was too dark to see what was going on inside the sedan from here, I adjusted the hood to conceal my features and continued toward the parked car. The windows weren't fogged up, so things hadn't gotten steamy yet. From this angle, it looked like someone was in the passenger's seat, but the driver's seat was empty.

This didn't feel right. I moved closer to the car and checked the plate. It was definitely Theo's. I went around the side of the car, cutting through on my way to the stairs. No one was in the back seat. The person I thought was in the front seat was actually a dark-colored neck pillow looped around the headrest. Since no one was inside, I gave the interior a closer look. The bag of takeout was gone.

Theo must have parked and gotten out. At most, he had an eight minute head start. I'd already scouted the nearby attractions for date venues. The movie theater wouldn't have let him inside with his takeout, so I gave the bowling alley a shot.

I pulled open the door. Immediately, the smell of feet, nacho cheese, disinfectant, and talc filled the air. The harsh overhead lights illuminated the lanes. The rest of the place wasn't nearly as bright. I didn't spot Theo near any of the lanes. He wasn't at the shoe rental counter, getting tokens for the arcade, or standing in line at the snack bar.

"May I help you?" a guy in a stained white t-shirt asked. He rubbed his beer belly and played with the box of miniature pencils.

"I'm looking for someone. I'm not sure he's here yet."

"What's he look like?"

I described Theo and what he was wearing.

"Nah, sorry. I haven't seen him. How's about I set you up at an alley while you wait? I'd be happy to let him know his party's here when he shows."

"If it's all the same, I think I'll wait for him outside. We might have gotten our signals crossed."

"Sure. Whatever you wanna do."

I glanced at the arcade, but I didn't see anyone who fit Theo's build. He wasn't here.

After leaving the bowling alley and sucking in some fresh air, I tried my luck at the movie theater. But the sign on the door said no outside food or drink. And the ushers made it clear they intended to take that rule seriously. However, I still asked if they had seen Theo, which they hadn't.

As I trudged toward the pharmacy, I checked my phone again. Theo's car hadn't moved. He was around here, somewhere. I just wasn't sure where. After perusing the pharmacy aisles, I asked one of the bored cashiers if there was anything fun to do. Besides movies and bowling, there were a few bars and restaurants. But Theo brought food with him. Maybe his side piece worked nearby, and he was meeting her while she went on break.

I dialed the office. Even though the time difference made it the middle of the night, Cross Security always had a skeleton crew of experts on duty. So I asked them to ping Theo's phone. Since Iris had given me the relevant account information, it made their jobs a lot easier.

"This isn't an exact science, but I can give you the last known coordinates," the tech said.

"Sure."

He sent them to my phone, and I checked the address. According to this, Theo was in or near the parking garage. Maybe Iris was wrong. Maybe he wasn't having an affair. Her original theory might have been correct. Maybe Theo had gotten mixed up in drugs. That would explain the sketchy garage, but to bring dinner with him didn't make much sense, unless the food truck was slinging more than Asian tacos.

Unsure what else to do, I returned to the garage, leery of Theo spotting me. By now, he might have returned to his vehicle. So I put the hood back on my head, walked around the entire lower level, getting spooked when a horn beeped twice as someone locked their car. No matter how well-lit or populated, parking garages always creeped me out. I wasn't sure if it was bad memories or too many scary movies, but the hairs on the back of my neck stood on end.

After completing my check of the ground level, I went up the stairs. Theo's car remained parked in the same spot. I circled around the other way, but I didn't see him anywhere. I even checked all the parked cars I passed for steamed up windows or couples in the midst of amorous activity. No one was seated inside their cars. The place was empty.

Feeling braver, I returned to the white sedan and peered

in the windows. A gym bag had been tossed on the floor of the back seat. On the passenger seat, beneath the neck pillow, was a thin blanket. It looked like one of the cheap throws that get discounted around the holidays. The worn fabric was practically see-through in the middle, and the hem on the edges had frayed. Peeking out from beneath that was a flat rectangular object.

Looking behind me, I made sure no one was coming before I cupped my hands against the window to get a better look. That was Theo's phone. No wonder it pinged to this location. Given its position on the floor, partially hidden by the blanket, I didn't think he'd left it on purpose.

I tried the door handle, but he'd locked his car. I examined each of the windows, but they were shut tight. Since the Stapletons hadn't invested in any roadside assistance services or automated features, I couldn't call to have the doors unlocked. Instead, I searched my phone for an illegal app I'd downloaded.

"Where are you?" I scrolled through the pages of apps before locating the grey box icon. It took three minutes before the app ran through enough combinations to unlock the car door. It also unlocked the SUV behind me and made the parked car across from us flash its lights and beep the horn.

Exiting the app before I could set off a car alarm, I opened the passenger door and grabbed Theo's phone. The first thing I did was install a hidden friend-finder, like the kind parents installed on their children's devices without their knowledge. Now, I'd be able to track Theo no matter where he went, assuming he didn't leave his phone behind again. Then I checked for messaging apps or secret ways of communicating that the phone company wouldn't know about.

Iris said he didn't play games on his phone, which was true, but he had a private messaging app. Since she hadn't mentioned it, I didn't think she knew anything about it.

Meet me at 11:30. I need you. I hope you're up for some excitement.

Theo had responded, *I'm game. I'll grab some food and meet you at our usual spot.*

I read the messages again, finding dozens more from the same unknown user sent over the course of the last few months. All the messages were just as vague. After snapping a few screenshots, I checked the time. It was a quarter to twelve. By now, Theo was in the midst of whatever exciting thing he had planned for the night.

"Damn." Poor Iris. I spent the next twenty minutes examining everything on Theo's phone and analyzing the messages for clues as to who the unknown user was. Given the way the messaging app worked, I couldn't figure out who sent the messages.

I copied down whatever identifying information I could find and sent it to Cross Security. Maybe they'd have better luck, but with the way these apps worked, I didn't think we'd get an identity that way. It'd be too easy.

After getting everything I could from Theo's phone, I put it back where I found it, locked his car, and returned to mine. By now, the SUV's doors had relocked from inactivity, so I didn't have to worry about them. While I waited for Theo to return from his exciting night, I compared the times and dates of the messages to his alleged disappearances, but Iris hadn't recorded those details. However, I was certain his disappearances from home coincided perfectly with these messages. Now I just had to catch him in the act, and it'd be case closed. Somehow, this didn't feel like a victory, more like a gut-wrenching defeat.

NINETEEN

After four hours of waiting for Theo, I had gotten distracted or possibly dosed off, which explained why I missed Theo's reappearance. The tracking app beeped, alerting me that the white sedan was heading down the ramp for the exit. Shit.

Rule number one of stakeouts, don't fall asleep unless you have someone else with you to keep watch. Shaking myself awake, I started my engine.

Theo used the main entrance to exit, unlike the way he'd arrived. Did he do that intentionally for fear someone was monitoring his movements? That's something I would have done, but the OR nurse had no reason to think like that.

I went out the side entrance and made a turn. Theo was already two blocks ahead. I kept my distance. He stuck to the main drag until he neared his neighborhood.

I hung back, killing my headlights and running dark to make sure he didn't notice me. Without missing a beat, he slid into the parking space in front of his house. I watched through the windshield as he grabbed a plastic bag out of the back seat. He locked his car, tossed the bag in the garbage can at the side of his house, and went into the garage.

As silently as possible, I got out of the car and darted down the sidewalk toward his house. The bag must have been the takeout. Maybe I'd find lipstick smears or some kind of romantic doodles on the packaging. At the very least, I hoped for a receipt. I needed a solid lead on identifying the unknown texter. I wasn't sure what kind of incriminating evidence there might be, but I hoped for something.

The motion-sensor lights remained on from Theo's arrival, so I pressed myself against the hedges that lined the driveway, separating the neighbor's property from the Stapletons' and scurried toward the trash. Before opening the lid, I glanced at the garage. The interior light was on. Theo hadn't gone into the house yet. But I didn't want to wait too long or the lights would turn off, and I'd be trapped in this position.

I flipped open the lid, holding it with one hand so it wouldn't flop over and bang against the side of the can. Theo had tied the handles of the plastic bag together in a tight knot. Dammit. I didn't have time for this.

Carefully, I eased the trash cover down against the side of the can. Once that was set, I reached for the bag. Voices sounded from inside the Stapletons' house, but I couldn't hear what was being said. The brick walls muffled most of the noise. None of the other house lights were on. Maybe Theo had turned on the TV or radio. I wasn't sure if Iris would confront him, but I didn't think she'd do it in the dark.

Hurrying, I grabbed the plastic bag. In my haste, the bottom snagged on something and ripped. A heavy object fell out, clanging against the can on its way to the bottom.

I leaned over the can, hoping to see what had fallen out of the bag. A bottle, perhaps? But it was too dark inside. The exterior floodlights weren't angled to allow me to see deep enough into the can.

Flipping over the bag, I figured I'd carry it out upside down, but I stopped when I noticed a piece of cloth hanging out of the tear. I pulled the material free from the opening and held it up. Had I known this was going to happen, I would have worn gloves. The cloth was a dirty wifebeater with permanent pit stains and a yellowing around the collar. The middle had a dark red stain. What was that? Blood? Given the amount and its central location on the shirt, this looked like a fresh kill.

The side door squeaked, the knob turning. I had no time to think. Fight or flight. The last thing I wanted was a confrontation.

I dropped my grip on the bag, flipped the lid closed, which made a much louder bang than I thought it would, and raced toward the street, keeping my body low and pressed against the hedges. Even with the floodlights, the outer edges of the Stapletons' property were barely illuminated. Theo pushed his way back outside, but he might not have seen me.

As soon as the row of hedges ended, I turned the corner and dove to the ground on the neighbor's front yard. Army-crawling, I kept to the other side of the hedge barrier, hoping to find a place between the thick, dense branches where I could see into the Stapletons' yard. Halfway up the property, I found such a spot.

Covered in dirt, I held my breath, too afraid to move. Concealed by the edgework and my dark clothing and shoes, I didn't think anyone could see me. But if the neighbors reported a prowler, that would be tomorrow's problem. Tonight's problem was Theo.

He grabbed a bat from the garage and stood near the opened side door. Slowly, he peered toward the front porch and glanced at his car. He'd heard something. He just didn't know what it was.

Dragging the bat on the ground behind him, he returned to his car and opened the trunk. After taking out a duffel bag, which he slung across his chest and tucked behind his hip, he closed the trunk.

He took a painstakingly long moment to look up and down the street, analyzing every inch of the neighborhood, from the parked cars to the pile of recently cut tree branches two houses down on the opposite side. When he couldn't figure out what was amiss, he hefted the bat higher in his hand, so it wouldn't drag, and strolled up the driveway.

From the way he continued to look around, he hadn't given up on determining what had caused the sound he heard. When he reached the trash can, he paused. Again, he looked behind him.

Taking a step back, he lifted the lid. He cocked his head to the side, confused, knowing he hadn't left the trash like that. His eyes narrowed as he strained to hear. Standing stock still, he stared directly at me through the thick foliage.

Was I caught? I didn't move or breathe. Finally, he lifted the stained shirt out of the can and took a few steps toward the house. He stopped, turned back around, and focused on the hedges again. I could practically feel his eyes boring into me. At any moment, he'd rush the hedges, jump over, and attack.

But he didn't. Instead, he put everything back inside the trash can and dragged it into the garage. Even from my position in the neighbor's yard, I heard the deadbolt slide into place. After he locked the garage door and checked all the windows, he moved from room to room, making certain no one could get inside his house.

I didn't move. For all I knew, he intended to kill any trespassers. I hadn't even had time to process everything I'd seen inside the trash can before he came outside, but the clothes looked far too dirty to be his. However, I had no evidence of anything. And whatever evidence existed was locked inside his house.

I considered calling the police, but at most, they could perform a wellness check. They'd have no reason to search his trash. Was Iris safe in there with him? Was her husband having an affair, or was he a stone-cold killer?

After ten minutes, the exterior lights automatically shut off. I crawled across the neighbor's yard. Headlights at my back nearly froze me in my tracks. A squad car was heading down the street. The officer had turned on the spotlight, aiming it at the houses.

I glanced back at the Stapletons'. Theo had some nerve calling the police, given whatever secrets he had. But if I didn't get out of here, I'd have a lot of explaining to do.

Hoping they hadn't noticed me yet, since they were

scanning the yards for prowlers, I sprinted as fast as my legs could carry me back to my car. My heart hammered in my chest. Running wasn't the answer. If anything, I should flag them down and tell them everything. Except I was covered in dirt and leaves. I didn't look like a concerned citizen. I looked like a prowler. A burglar in the making. And given my first encounter with Detective Petrocelli, who had previously accused me of being an armed robber, the odds were already stacked against me.

Since I'd left the rental unlocked, I pulled open the door and slid into the back seat. I hunkered down on the floor behind the passenger's seat, curling myself into a ball with my hood covering my face and hair. After the police car rolled past, I waited another five minutes before sticking my head up and looking out the window. They were gone.

Exhaling, I climbed into the front seat and moved my car so I could keep an eye on the Stapletons. By now, all the lights in the house were off. But I couldn't leave, not if Iris was sleeping beside a killer.

Was that even blood? For all I knew, it was ketchup or barbecue sauce. But for Theo to behave like that, it must have been blood. I knew it in my gut. Whose shirt was that, and what happened to its owner?

At six, the lights in the Stapletons' house turned on. At seven, the garbage truck came. Theo rolled his can to the curb and waited for the trash collectors to pick it up before dragging it back inside. Whatever evidence might have existed was long gone. I'd never be able to prove anything. I didn't even know what happened last night, but it wasn't good.

Theo went back inside, grabbed his things, kissed his wife goodbye at the front door, and went to work. I followed him, not bothering to go to extremes to make sure he didn't notice me. In fact, I may have wanted him to notice. It'd make him nervous, which might provoke him. But he didn't pay any attention to the traffic around him.

He turned into the hospital parking lot and found a spot near where I'd last spotted his car. Maybe it was the same spot. They weren't numbered or assigned, but people were creatures of habit. Leaving his space empty might have been an unspoken rule.

I circled around a few times, keeping an eye on him. But he grabbed his things, climbed out of the car, and walked briskly toward the entrance. Once he was inside, I parked and searched his car for anything amiss. No signs of damage. No dried blood. No stench of decaying flesh.

Unsure how to proceed, I called Iris. “Is everything okay?” I asked.

“You tell me. Theo came home late again last night. Where was he?”

“I’m not sure. He gave me the slip after he left the bookstore.” I gave her the play-by-play and the address of the parking garage. “Does he have any friends who work around there?”

“I don’t know.”

“Have you ever gone to that movie theater or bowling alley?”

“Once or twice. The movies mostly. And we’d get tapas. Is that restaurant still around the corner? We haven’t been there in over a year.”

“I didn’t notice.”

“Maybe that’s where he went.”

“What time do they close?” I asked.

“Eleven, but it could have changed.”

“I’ll look into the staff and see if Theo met someone getting off work.” But I was more concerned with the stained shirt he’d made sure to conceal.

“Whatever floozy he’s seeing must live or work around there. Unless...no...he wouldn’t.”

“He wouldn’t what?” I asked.

“You don’t think he’s screwing sex workers, do you?”

“I don’t know.” I hadn’t figured out how to broach the subject yet.

“Did he see you?”

“I don’t think so.” But the way he’d stared at the hedges sent shivers through me.

“Theo said he heard a noise outside when he got home. It freaked him out. He woke me up, even though I wasn’t really asleep, and had me reach out to my friends at dispatch, who were more than happy to send a patrol car through the neighborhood."

"Yeah, that noise was me. When Theo got home, he tossed some things into the trash. Things he didn't want anyone to see."

"Like what?" I heard the fear in her voice.

I hesitated, unsure if I should tell her what I'd found in the trash. "A bag with something heavy inside and a shirt with a red stain. Did Theo have blood on him when he got home?"

"No."

"You're sure? What about on his clothes? Or beneath his nails?"

"Alex, what did you see him throw out?"

"I think it was a bloody shirt."

"Maybe it was something from work."

"It didn't look like it." I described the dirty wifebeater.

"I don't know. I'll look around and let you know if I find anything like that, but I think you got it wrong. You found it inside a takeout bag. It was probably sauce. That man is the messiest eater."

"Yeah, maybe." But I wasn't convinced. "Did he shower or wash his clothes last night?"

"For the first time, he didn't. I hoped that was a good sign. Like maybe, they just talked. Maybe he finally broke it off with her."

Maybe he killed her. But I didn't say it out loud. "Did he take the gun with him when he left the house yesterday?"

"No."

"You're sure?"

"Positive. My husband may be a lying, cheating bastard, but he wouldn't kill anyone. He must have gotten the gun for protection, or it belongs to someone else. He'd never shoot anyone. Not in a million years." She exhaled. "Unless he really has become that much of a stranger to me."

TWENTY

A million thoughts went through my mind, all related to Theo, all wondering what happened to the owner of that shirt and how it came to be in Theo's possession. The only thing I knew for certain was that wasn't Theo's shirt. If he'd been injured that badly, there'd be physical indicators. And he didn't show any signs of injury or weakness.

I wasn't sure I believed Iris when she said the gun had been at home. Even if it was, Theo might have had another weapon. Squinting, I tried to recall if the shirt had any tears or holes, but I didn't remember seeing any. However, rushed in the dark meant I wasn't focused on the important things.

Kicking myself for running away, I wished I'd confronted Theo when he left the garage. But after finding the gun the other afternoon, I figured he might kill me. But that gave me pause. Why did he go outside with a bat when he had a gun at his disposal? Maybe the gun wasn't in the house. Maybe that had been the heavy object that fell out of the trash bag. Or maybe Iris was right and it was just a nasty ketchup stain.

"Dammit, Parker, why didn't you do something when

you had the chance?" This would eat at me forever. Making mistakes was a human trait, but in my line of work, it could also prove fatal. If Theo was a killer, my failure to act may have allowed him to get away with murder, and I wasn't okay with that. I just wasn't sure how to fix it. After getting some sleep and regrouping, I'd come up with a plan to find out exactly what Theo was up to last night.

By the time I made it home, it was a few minutes before eight. More than likely, Martin had already left for work, but on the off chance he hadn't, I went around the side of the house. The beach was crowded with surfers, but I didn't see him in the water or running on the sand. I entered the code and unlocked the gate that led to our fenced in backyard. A gentle breeze made the water in the pool ripple. Again, no Martin.

I disarmed the security system and entered through the back door. Going into the kitchen, I found the dishwasher empty and no coffee in the pot or a pitcher in the fridge with leftovers for iced coffee. Martin must have been pissed I'd been gone all night. I was pissed about that too.

I went into the living room to grab my laptop. Martin was sprawled out on the couch. His eyes closed, his tablet against his stomach, and his laptop open on the coffee table. The screen was blank. None of the keyboard lights were illuminated.

For a moment, I stared at his chest, willing it to rise and fall. Once I was reassured he wasn't dead, I let out a sigh of relief. Martin had an entire philosophy aimed against sleeping on the couch. I'd gotten him to break his rules a few times, but this wasn't like him.

Silently, I crept out of the room. I needed to shower, but finding out what was going on with the love of my life was more important. So I texted Marcal, asking when Martin was supposed to be at work.

Marcal responded immediately. *I'm on my way now.*

When's his first meeting?

Eleven.

Does he have anything pressing before that?

No.

You're sure? Martin would kill me for doing this, but

given the state I found him in, I didn't think I had much of a choice.

Yes. Eleven. The rest of his morning schedule is clear. Is everything okay? Did something change?

I found him asleep on the couch.

The three dots moved back and forth while Marcal worked on his response. Given how long it took to receive an answer, I assumed he was just as flummoxed by this as I was. Or he'd gotten into an accident. Finally, he wrote, *I'll pick him up at ten. That will give him plenty of time to prepare during the ride to the office.*

I set the alarm on my phone for 9:30, took a two-minute shower to wash off the dirt and debris, dried my hair on high, nearly burning my scalp in the process, and returned to the living room. Gently, I removed the tablet from Martin's chest, closed his laptop, and plugged the devices in to charge. Then I eased onto the sofa beside him.

He wrapped his arm around my waist and turned on his side, burying his face in my hair. He didn't wake up, so I closed my eyes. I was too tired to think. All I knew was he couldn't go on like this. *We* couldn't go on like this.

An hour passed before he stirred. "Sweetheart?" his voice was thick with sleep.

"Hmm?" I forced my eyes open. I'd barely even had time to fall asleep.

"What time did you get home?" He pressed his lips against my shoulder. "You smell like soap. Did you shower? It's so late."

"It's morning, handsome."

"Morning?" Panic overtook him. He released his grip on me and sat up, turning to look out the window. "Shit. I'm late. Why didn't you wake me?" He ran a hand over his face. "I have to get ready." He picked up his phone and sent a text, requesting an immediate pick-up. Before he even finished typing the message, he shut himself inside the bedroom.

I rolled onto my back, finding the cushions warm. My eyes closed. It wasn't his fault he'd fallen asleep. This couch had powers, just like the one at his estate. Right now, it was using those magical powers to lull me back to dreamland.

"Alex," Martin's sharp tone jolted me awake, "have you seen my tablet?"

I lifted it off the end table. "I plugged it in, just like your laptop. The batteries appeared dead from overuse." I handed it to him. "In case you're wondering, you looked dead too."

"Thanks." He took the tablet and headed toward the kitchen. Two steps later, he stopped and spun around. "Dead? Did you really think that?"

I exhaled and shrugged noncommittally. "It was that kind of night."

"Shit." A flash of guilt came over his features before he remembered the time and continued into the kitchen. "Can we talk about this later?"

"I think we better."

He hadn't expected that either. Usually, I avoided talking about everything. But this was different. He tore his eyes off the screen for a split second. "Are you okay?"

"Uh-huh."

"All right." He powered off the tablet and tucked the car charger into his briefcase. Before he could finish filling the espresso machine, the proximity alarm sounded. Marcal had pulled into the driveway. "I'll get coffee at the office." He didn't even bother closing the coffee can before grabbing his briefcase and jacket. He gave me a quick peck on his way to the door. "Are you coming home tonight?"

"I'll be here."

"We'll talk then." He entered the code and opened the front door. "Stay safe."

"Always." I didn't even get a chance to say I love you before he closed the door.

After that rough start to the day, I wanted nothing more than to crawl under the covers and hide. But I had too much to do.

Unfortunately, I had another interview to conduct in a couple of hours. So I pulled out the detailed notes I'd made on how to use the espresso machine, finished filling it, and pressed the button. It hissed and sputtered before expelling a vast amount of steam, which forced me to back away. When the scalding storm cloud cleared, I found the tiny mug beneath the spout filled.

I took a sip, finding it thick with grounds. "You bastard." I thought about refusing to drink the sludge in protest, but I'd been up most of the night. Caffeine wasn't a luxury. It was a necessity. So I sipped it as I made my way to the bedroom.

Martin had left the closet and drawers open. If I didn't know better, I'd think someone had broken in and tossed the place. Had he left things in such disarray because he was in a hurry or because he was mad? Maybe both. I closed the closet and drawers as I gathered my clothes. I didn't know if we were fighting, but I didn't like it. We normally didn't have exchanges like this.

Despite the more pressing issues, I found myself dwelling on Martin as I drove to work. He'd always been a workaholic. He'd spent weeks living out of his office before. This wasn't that much different. But it felt different. Whether that was due to the move was anyone's guess, but I'd never seen him this stressed over work, except for when we first met. And that was because someone was trying to kill him and take over his company.

Filing that thought away, I parked in the garage, made a note to pick up a new rental car to use for surveillance before tailing Theo again, and trudged to the office building. Howard stopped me before I could make it past security. His shifty-eyed glance told me something was wrong.

"You got a visitor," he said.

"Who?" I resisted the urge to peer down the hallway.

"An LAPD detective. The same one who came around here after your office received that special delivery."

"Petrocelli?"

Howard nodded.

"What does he want?" I asked.

"If I had to guess, I'd say your head on a pike." He sat down behind his desk as a few more people entered the building. After they disappeared into the elevator, he said, "You might want to call a lawyer. He's acting like he's itching to handcuff someone."

"That's because he has a bondage fetish. I'll be fine." I

gave him a reassuring smile, but it was for show.

As I headed down the hall, I sent a text to Jason Ganz, the criminal defense attorney Cross kept on retainer, and told him if he didn't hear from me within the hour that he should meet me at the police station and bring bail money. After tucking my phone away, I removed the key to the office and kept my hands where Petrocelli could see them. The last thing I needed was to get shot by another overzealous cop.

"Is there something I can help you with, Detective?" I approached slowly.

His eyes went to the spot on the floor where blood had spilled. But there were no stains on the white tile. The building's janitorial staff were on top of everything. "You have some explaining to do."

"I'm going to need a little more than that."

"This is about yesterday."

Shit. I eyed the handcuffs visible beneath his jacket. "Are you arresting me?"

He studied my expression carefully. "That depends on what you have to say."

"It sounds like I need a lawyer."

Petrocelli ran his finger along the steel bracelet. "If that's how you want to play this."

I hadn't done anything illegal, so even if he brought me in for questioning, he'd have to let me go. But I had too much on my plate to waste half the day or more inside an interrogation room. "Ask your damn questions."

He sidestepped, gesturing toward my office. "After you."

I unlocked the door, flipped on the light, and took a seat behind the reception desk. I didn't touch the computer. Detective Petrocelli peered around the room, making sure we were alone before grabbing a chair and placing it opposite me.

"Tell me about the gun. Where did you see it?" he asked.

"Gun?"

"The serial number you asked the officer to run."

"I take it she got a hit on one of the numbers, but like I explained to her yesterday, the serial number was filed off. I wasn't able to determine two of the digits."

"One of the possibilities got a hit."

"Who's the gun registered to?"

"I'm not here to answer your questions. Are you still confused how this works?"

"It doesn't," I mumbled.

"Where's the gun now? Do you have it?"

"No."

He nodded toward my side. "May I see your weapon?"

"Do you want to see my permit too?"

"I've already seen your permit." He stared at my jacket. "Go slow. Only use two fingers to lift it out of the holster."

"Mine's a semi-auto nine mill. The gun in question is a six-shooter."

"Let me see it anyway."

"Fine." I held up my hand and moved my jacket to the side before releasing the snap and lifting the handle with my thumb and pointer finger. Carefully, I placed it on the desk in front of Petrocelli with the serial number facing him.

Once he was satisfied, he rocked back in his chair. "Where's the six-shooter?"

"The last time I saw it, it was hidden inside a tackle box."

"Whose?"

"I'll tell you, but I want to know one thing first."

"We'll see."

"Was that gun used to commit any other crimes?"

"It'd be in evidence lockup, if it had. I'm sure you're aware how evidence works."

"Guns like that, with filed off numbers, are usually stolen. Sometimes, they have sheets to go with them. You can't tell me things don't go missing from time to time."

"Let's talk about the tackle box."

"I know, you're the one asking the questions. I just want to know if you have any reason to think that gun," I told him every detail about the weapon that I could recall, "was used in any violent crimes."

His eyes narrowed. "What do you know?"

"Quid pro quo?"

"Hell no. You answer, or I'll ruin your day. It's that

simple."

"Cops can't make threats like that."

He chuckled, refusing to budge.

"Let me tell you a story, Dean. Can I call you Dean?"

"No."

"Okay, Dean." I grinned at him, which made his expression sour. "A man's wife becomes the victim of a violent attack. He gets scared. He wants protection, but he doesn't know what to do. She doesn't want a gun in their house. So he gets one from somewhere and hides it in a locked box and doesn't tell her. When she's cleaning out the garage, she finds it. Do you understand why I don't want to give you the name?"

"You have no way of knowing if it's that innocent, and even if it is, it's still illegal. Possessing an unregistered firearm is a crime."

"Is that the only crime?" I waited, but Petrocelli wouldn't break. "Let me tell you another story. A man sneaks out of his house repeatedly, usually late at night. He's moody, prone to outbursts, but he's never been violent with his wife. No domestic calls. No abuse. In fact, let's go so far as to say he does charity work in his spare time, but afterward, he sneaks off alone and disappears only to surface four hours later. He drives home, throws a suspicious package into his trash can, worries someone may snoop through his trash, so he takes the can inside and personally passes it off to waste management the next morning. What would you say to that?"

"I need a name."

"Do you think he killed someone?"

"Did you see a body? What about his wife? Have you spoken to her?"

"She's fine. She thought the blood may have been ketchup."

"Blood?"

I exhaled. *Dammit.* "The bag contained an unknown object with a certain heft and a stained wifebeater."

"Where was the stain?"

I indicated the spot on my chest. "I don't think there were any holes, but I can't be sure."

"Name. Now." Fire burned in his eyes, but Detective Petrocelli knew I was just as stubborn as he was. I wouldn't talk until he gave me something. "The gun in question was taken during a home invasion. We believe the thief used the gun to kill the home owner and his wife. The perpetrator remains at large."

"Do you have a suspect in mind?"

"I will once you give me a damn name."

TWENTY-ONE

Petrocelli tucked his phone away. Agitated, he frowned at me. "How come you're always in the middle of my investigations?"

"Small world, but you're jumping the gun. For all you know, the weapon in question isn't even the same one from the home invasion. The serial number may not match. You shouldn't assume I'm in the middle of your investigation. However, you're getting into the middle of mine."

"Except I'm investigating an actual crime. You're doing what? Looking for dirt that a shitbag attorney can use in divorce court?"

"That's not the point."

"It sure seems like it."

I glared at him. "Iris doesn't want a divorce. She wants her life back."

Petrocelli's expression softened. "Regardless, the home invasion turned double homicide is my case. It's been cold for the last eight months, but now I have a new lead." He scratched the back of his head. "Damn."

"What?"

"I wish I didn't."

I snorted. "Whatever."

"Not whatever. Iris's life has already been torn apart. Homicide tried to put it back together for her once. Now it looks like I'm going to undo all that."

"Like you care."

"I do. Did she tell you what happened?"

"How her partner was killed and she was shot? Yeah, I heard that story."

"She was one of us. We watch out for each other. We have their backs, they have ours. It's how we survive on the streets. We remove the danger. The EMTs take care of the injured and dying. If a patrol car had escorted her rig to the hospital that day, this wouldn't have happened."

"Did you work the incident?" I asked.

"Not the call she and her partner responded to, but I assisted on nailing the guys who killed Gary and shot her. Everyone in the department did. We wanted to make it clear that killing first responders, especially EMTs, would not be tolerated. They don't pose a threat. They are there to help. It's just not right." He glanced down at the notes he'd taken. "And now she has to deal with this."

"Theo Stapleton doesn't have a record or a history of violence. I find it hard to believe he'd break into someone's house to steal a gun."

"But you think he killed someone last night and brought evidence home with him, evidence he painstakingly concealed until it could be disposed of."

"I don't know. I'm just telling you what I saw."

"You should have called it in last night." He scrutinized me. "I have half a mind to bring you in for obstruction."

"Again?"

"Haven't you ever heard of see something, say something?"

"I did say something. I told you about it."

"Twelve hours too late." He let out a growl. "Stop making my job more difficult. The next time you do, I won't be so forgiving."

"This is forgiving?"

He glared at me as he made his way to the door. "I don't want to see or hear from you again. When I need something, I'll contact you. Until then, whatever it is you do here," he waved his arm in a frustrated gesture, "better not involve the police or criminal activity. Do I make myself clear?"

"Crystal."

"You said that last time."

"You're perfectly clear, Detective. I'm the one who's usually fuzzy."

"I suggest you do something about that." He tugged on the door handle and stepped through, nearly colliding with the newest interviewee. Petrocelli cocked his head to the side. "Do I know you?"

"I don't think so," Paul Nepper muttered.

"No, I do. I never forget a face. You worked vice." Petrocelli gave him the once-over. "You still strung out? If I pat you down, what am I going to find in your pockets?"

"Fuck you," Nepper said. "You don't have probable cause. No exigent circumstances. You come at me, the city's going to face one hell of a lawsuit."

"Gentlemen," I said from my desk, unsure if I should intervene, but Nepper sounded like he could hold his own.

Petrocelli glanced back at me. "I warned you."

"Stop harassing us." I locked eyes with him, the challenge obvious. "Get out."

Petrocelli huffed, shoved past Nepper, and continued down the hallway, muttering to himself.

Paul Nepper sucked in a long breath and slowly exhaled, staring after the homicide detective. "Great first impression. Should I reschedule?"

"No." I gestured to the chair. "Don't sweat it. I already know he's an asshole."

"How often does he show up here?"

"This isn't exactly the first time, but it is the first time this week. I take it you have a beef."

"I don't. I never worked with him, but he must remember seeing me around. Like so many other assholes with badges, he's got an axe to grind." Nepper slumped into the chair and slid a printed copy of his resume toward me. "I quit the force for a reason. I worked undercover. Things got dicey. One thing led to another, and I got addicted. I haven't tried to conceal that. I worked hard to get clean. I wasn't forced out of the police department. I chose to leave. I didn't like the stress of the streets, but after I switched to a desk job, the other officers still gave me shit. They never trusted me with evidence or anything. The comments, the looks, it became too much. So I walked."

"That's why you want to work here?" I asked.

"I worked private security for a while afterward. But it was a lot like the streets. Lots of shit going down, booze, drugs, guns, whores. It was too much too soon."

"It challenged your sobriety?"

Nepper's shoulders hitched upward a few inches. "More like my resolve. I became a cop to do good. Working private security to help some boyband heartthrob with a coke problem was never in the cards."

"How long have you been clean?"

"Eighteen months."

"Good for you."

He smiled. "Thanks."

"Any friends left in the LAPD who'll trade favors?" I asked. "Or were they all like Detective Petrocelli?"

"I got a few contacts left, I guess. Why do you ask?"

I checked the friend-finder I'd uploaded to Theo's phone. He was still at the hospital. Given everything I'd said, Petrocelli would have enough to get a warrant to search the Stapletons' residence. But would he drag Theo out of the OR to question him? Or would he wait until the man came home from work?

I had to call Iris and tell her what happened. She didn't deserve to be blindsided. My gut said Theo didn't commit the home invasion, but Petrocelli had made a valid point. I was pretty sure Theo had something to do with a violent attack or murder that took place last night. At some point, he must have snapped. Whether that was last night or eight months ago or sometime before that was anyone's guess.

"Can you find out if anyone was killed last night?" I asked.

Nepper looked uncomfortable. "It's L.A. Odds are someone's killed every day."

That didn't make me feel particularly warm and fuzzy.

"What about violent crimes that happened near this address?" I gave it to him. "Can you find out for me?"

"Does this have anything to do with why that detective was here?"

"It does."

Nepper reached for my desk phone. "Do you mind?"

"Help yourself."

He dialed a number, identified himself, and asked if anything had popped off last night. "Okay. Thanks." He put the phone down. "Nothing was reported. Dispatch didn't receive any calls. Patrol didn't notice anything suspicious." He looked around the office. "Is this what the job entails?"

"Yes and no."

"What other tasks do you expect from the office manager?"

"You know how to make coffee?"

"Yep."

I smiled. "Do you know how to make coffee that doesn't taste like the burnt mud from a police station?"

"I'm willing to learn. What else you got?"

I ran through the list of duties, which didn't involve much besides scheduling appointments, dealing with walk-ins, answering the phones, and making sure the security teams were properly assigned, in case Nero decided to hand that over. "Other than that, you have to keep everything running smoothly. Anticipate what we'll need, and get it done."

"You mean get my hands on police files and see what sort of investigation law enforcement's already conducted?"

"Sometimes. Is that going to be a problem?" I asked.

"I don't know. I'm going to have to think about it. But I am curious. Is that the only reason I was considered for this position?"

"No." But I had no idea if that was true. Cross selected the candidates.

He stood and extended his hand. "It was nice to meet you. Thanks for taking the time."

"You don't want the job?"

"Are you offering it to me?"

"That's up to Mr. Cross, but for what it's worth, I'd hire you."

"Whenever you get this mess straightened out with that detective, give me a call. But I left the force to avoid this kind of aggressiveness in my life. I already dealt with plenty of guys like him. I don't want to do it on a regular basis anymore. I won't take another job like that. If this is going to be more of that, give it to someone else. I'm sorry if I wasted your time."

"This isn't a regular thing."

"How many of your cases cross paths with police investigations?"

"You shouldn't ask me that. My cases aren't the norm for Cross Security. That's why I'm a private contractor. I tend to specialize more in these types of cases."

"But you're the only person here right now. In essence, I'd be assisting you with whatever you needed, which would be cases like this."

"I won't be here forever. This is a temporary assignment."

He pointed to the closed offices. "What about the other investigators?"

"We haven't hired any yet." I cocked my head to the side. "Would you be interested in one of those positions instead?"

"Possibly, depending on the types of cases and the clientele."

"Here." I wrote down Lucien's phone number on the back of one of my cards. "Give Mr. Cross a call. He'll be better equipped to answer any questions you have. But I hope you'll consider a position here. From what I've seen today, you are more than capable of handling yourself in all sorts of situations."

"I'll think about it." Nepper tucked the card into his shirt pocket. "It was nice to meet you," he glanced down at my nameplate, "Ms. Parker."

After he left, I stared at the tracker on my phone. I didn't have time to procrastinate, so I called Iris and told her what was about to happen. "I'm sorry. Detective Petrocelli ambushed me. I..."

"You would have reported it, anyway," she said. "It's what I would have done in your position." She sighed. "I'm not mad. I get it. A part of me wonders how many secrets Theo's hiding. We found a gun in the garage. A gun. In my house. That is not something the man I married would ever consider."

"Shit happens."

"Yeah."

"What do you want me to do?" I asked.

"Nothing. I'll tell Theo I found the gun and freaked out. No reason he needs to know I hired you to look into his odd disappearances."

For a woman who'd been on the edge, she had it together in this situation. But training and muscle memory may have kicked in. "I'll return your retainer," I said.

"No. I want to know where Theo goes and what he's doing. Now more than ever."

"Don't you think the police will want to handle that?"

"Only if his actions have anything to do with the illegal firearm. But like you said, they don't even know if Theo's gun is the same as the one stolen and used in that home invasion. And even if it is, he probably picked it up from someone else. Once he tells the police where he got it, they'll leave him be. I know how these things work. I figured you did too."

"Yeah, but—"

"But nothing. I hired you to find out if my husband's cheating. That hasn't changed. Unless you want to back down because of what Detective Petrocelli said, in which case, I understand, but I'll need to hire another investigator and could use some recommendations."

This was a bad idea, but I was never one to back down. "No. I got this. But it'd be best to give the police some space to work."

"I agree. While they're keeping an eye out, Theo will be on his best behavior. I'll give you a call and let you know what happens."

"All right. Be careful."

"I may not know my husband, but I don't believe he'd ever harm me." She laughed cynically. "That's probably what all those murdered women said before it happened to them."

"I wouldn't be too sure they believed it."

"That's the difference. I do. I just wish I was that confident he hadn't harmed someone else."

"Has Theo been having any problems or disputes?"

"No."

"Bar fights or anything like that?"

"No."

"He's never come home bruised or injured?"

"I've seen a few scratches on his back once or twice. I figured those were from her."

"But nothing else?"

"No."

I thought about what Iris said, but the facts only made this scenario I'd created in my head seem even more insane. "Do you know of anyone Theo would want to hurt?"

"Besides the fuckers who killed Gary and shot me, no."

"But the police arrested them."

"Yes."

"All of them?"

"Yes," Iris said. "What are you thinking? Theo's seeking revenge, like a vigilante?"

"I don't know. But there was a whole lot of something on that stained wifebeater. If it was blood, I'm not sure the owner survived."

"Why would Theo take the shirt home? Wouldn't he have left it on the victim?"

"Not if he was afraid forensic evidence would point back to him."

Iris mulled that over. "He's an OR nurse. He'd consider body fluids and skin cells. That's just how he's wired." She swallowed. "Do you think I've been blind to this all along?"

"If Theo hurt someone, he must have snapped. Most violent criminals have a rap sheet a mile long. Theo's clean. He's never been arrested for anything. If he's been doing this for years, you would have noticed the warning signs a long time ago."

"You're probably right. I don't think he's ever even been in a fight," Iris said. "We shared all our crazy stories from childhood onward. I've spent every other holiday with his folks. I've seen baby pictures and little league photos. His mom and dad would have told me if he'd gotten into a scuffle."

"Then that's probably not what's going on here. I just don't know what is."

"Are you saying that to make me feel better?"

"Maybe."

"At least I know you won't lie to spare my feelings."

TWENTY-TWO

Despite Petrocelli's warning, I found myself parked outside the Stapletons' house in a brand new rental car. This one was a shiny blue, two door. It'd be great for nighttime surveillance, but in the day, I worried the color would make it more noticeable than the silver sedan Cross Security had leased for my use. However, Theo didn't act like he'd seen me following him home from work.

Since the tracking device on his car was still transmitting and the app on his phone showed me exactly where he was, I knew his paranoid behavior from the previous night hadn't leaked into any other aspects of his life besides hiding his trash. There must have been something in that bag he didn't want anyone to find.

The tiny voice in the back of my head told me Petrocelli had been right. I should have called it in the previous night or flagged down the cruiser. But I'd been too afraid what would happen to me if I did. I couldn't do this job and think like that, especially when the worst that would have happened would have been spending the night and part of the day in lockup.

But I was worried how that would impact Martin, his project, and his company. I'd never admit this to Lucien, but I didn't want to cause too many problems for him either. He sent me here as a favor. And I wanted to do a good job. I just didn't want him to know that. The wiring in my brain was screwed up, which explained my inconsistent attitude and behavior, but that was something a professional with a bookcase full of psych journals would have to figure out. And I had no intention of allowing that to happen.

The police cruiser and the unmarked remained double-parked outside the Stapletons' house. They'd been waiting for Theo when he got home. But Theo didn't act like a guilty man when he saw the police vehicles. Instead, he pulled into the driveway and jogged toward his open front door. That wasn't typically how a guilty man behaved.

One of the patrol officers stopped him at the door. They spoke, and then Theo entered the house. That was forty-five minutes ago.

In the interim, I'd seen the patrol officer step onto the front porch to answer a radio call. And I'd seen his partner check the exterior. He'd searched the shrubs, the crawlspace, and the barbecue pit in the back. He didn't find anything.

An hour later, Petrocelli appeared in the doorway. I slumped down in my seat, but he had no reason to think I'd be stupid enough to go to the Stapletons' after our earlier exchange. He carried an evidence bag which contained the six-shooter. He also confiscated the ammunition and what appeared to be a receipt.

After shaking hands with Iris and Theo, Petrocelli returned to his car, put the items inside the box in his trunk, and spoke to the uniformed officer who'd searched outside the house. Theo put his arm around his wife's shoulders and pulled her close. From where I was sitting, he looked genuinely concerned. The way he held her and kissed her temple told me he was worried about her, not himself. Since this was L.A., I couldn't dismiss the possibility he deserved an Emmy, but my gut said he loved her.

She waved to the police as they headed for their vehicles. Then she turned fully into her husband's embrace and hugged him. Theo held her tightly, rocking her gently back and forth. After they finally broke apart, a few minutes later, Theo closed the front door.

I remained parked outside their house for another hour, watching the lights in the living room and kitchen. Finally, Iris called.

"Theo bought the gun from a pawn shop," she whispered. "He had the receipt and everything."

"When did he get it?"

"Almost eight months ago. Theo freaked out. He said he had to do something. He apologized. He swore the gun's been locked in that tackle box ever since, and I believe him. He just wanted to do whatever he could to keep us safe."

"Okay."

"Dean thinks the killer was in a rush to lose the gun, took it to one of the more disreputable pawn shops, and Theo happened to be the first idiot who walked in looking to buy. Given the cheap price and cash sale, the pawn broker must have figured Theo was desperate. He probably saw him coming a mile away."

"I didn't know you and Detective Petrocelli were friends."

"We're friendly. We've known each other a while. He's a good guy."

That hadn't been my experience, but I didn't argue. "What's his next move?"

"Dean will make sure Theo's story checks out, press the pawn broker, and see where that leads."

"And Theo?" I asked. "Petrocelli was adamant that possessing an illegal firearm is a crime, which according to the attorney I spoke to isn't true if the firearm is kept within the home."

"Lack of registration isn't enough to warrant charges, but since the firearm was used to commit a crime, it's up to the DA to determine what they want to do. Dean thinks, if everything checks out, that given the circumstances, no charges will be filed."

"I'll give you the name of a good attorney. I'll make sure he knows you're a Cross Security client and to expect your call. He'll do whatever he can."

"Thanks."

"How are you holding up?"

"Okay," she said. "Theo just stepped into the shower. He's been so attentive since he got home. We let the police search our house. They didn't find anything else. Theo's been by my side the entire time. He was afraid seeing cops around would be too traumatic. I think he still loves me, Alex. I really hope that's true." She sniffed, her voice cracking. "I've missed him so much. I didn't even realize how much until tonight. I told him I found the gun and called a friend about it. That's how the police got tipped. I didn't say I hired you. I didn't say anything about that."

"Did Petrocelli ask where Theo was last night?"

"Yeah." She inhaled an unsteady breath. "He said he was helping a nursing student study for her boards. Afterward, he got takeout and went to see a movie. He even had the ticket stub. He went to a double feature. It let out around three."

"Was anyone with him?" I asked, since no one at the theater had seen Theo.

"No, he went by himself."

"And the stain on the shirt in the trash?"

"I didn't ask about that, but he probably spilled something. He said he got chili dogs. Maybe that's what you saw on the shirt."

"Why wouldn't he bring it in the house to get washed?"

"He didn't want me to know he was at the movies. That's what he told Dean when he was asked for his recent whereabouts. I'm guessing he must have gone with her, and that's why he didn't want me to know."

"Did he have the receipt for the movies?"

"No, just the torn stub." Iris hesitated. "You think he's lying about that too, right? Like you think he went with her and that's why he didn't want me to know and why he threw out the shirt. Because if he told me he went to see a movie by himself, I'd call bullshit. And he'd have to confess to the affair."

"Maybe."

"I'm starting to hate it when you say maybe."

"How about perhaps?"

"That's not much better."

"I'll see what I can do." I peered at the house, noticing a silhouette against the window shade in the bathroom. Theo had gotten out of the shower and was drying off. "Do you think he's in for the rest of the night?"

"I'm sure he is. We have a lot to talk about. I'm glad he isn't mad. I feel like I'm finally getting my husband back."

"Do you want me to hang around here?" I asked. If he was dangerous, he wouldn't be happy his wife tipped off the police.

"No. We're fine. If something changes, I'll let you know."

"Are you sure you feel safe?"

"As safe as I've always felt at home."

"Okay." But I promised myself I'd keep an eye on Theo's position remotely in case anything changed.

The police had everything they needed on the gun. After I provided this helpful tip, Petrocelli owed me. However, I didn't expect him to see it that way. Still, I'd hold on to that chit for a rainy day. A storm was brewing.

Instead of returning to the office, I went home. Since Martin got a late start today, I wasn't sure when he'd show, so I ordered dinner from the Italian place he liked and asked them to deliver. Unsure how our conversation would go, I prepared for the worst by adding a few slices of cheesecake to the order.

Once my duties as devoted and loving girlfriend were fulfilled, I set up shop at the kitchen counter. I'd already looked into the ambulance ambush once, but I gave it a second glance. According to eyewitnesses, three men were involved. The police made three arrests. The case hadn't gone to trial yet, but Theo had no reason to think someone had gotten away with murder.

Again, I brought up his background history, going as far back as high school. He'd never been a rulebreaker. He didn't stick out in the crowd. He was the guy with his nose in a book, who enjoyed going on fictional quests to fight dragons in his spare time. But people change. At least, that's what I'd been told time and time again. However, I wasn't sure I believed it.

It was always the quiet ones. Maybe his violent streak wasn't new. After all, he had no problem finding a sketchy pawn shop to buy a gun. Why would any upstanding citizen purchase a weapon with a filed off serial number that didn't require a background check? Only one reason came to mind. He intended to use it, and he didn't want to get caught.

I called the main branch of Cross Security and waited for someone in IT to answer. We went over everything on Theo's computer with a fine-tooth comb, searching for the smoking gun.

"He obsessively cleans his browser history every few days," Stuart said.

"Porn habit?"

"No."

"None?"

"Not according to his ISP."

"That's weird."

"Most times, it's the type of porn that's weird, not the lack of."

"He isn't Amish. And his wife hasn't exactly been in the mood. I'd think his browser history would be full."

"It's not. I guess that's why she thinks he's cheating."

"Probably, but if he's not hiding filthy secrets, what is he hiding?"

"No secretive communications. I haven't found any messaging apps or anything like that."

"What about his web searches? What is he looking for?"

"Mostly, how-to videos. He watches a shit ton of them. And podcasts on unsolved murders."

"What kind of how-to videos? Anything about disposing of a body?"

"A few."

"Shit." I hadn't run across any of that. "What else?"

"Cleaning up crime scenes, removing blood, destroying different types of evidence, things like that." Stuart clicked a few keys. "He doesn't watch a lot of those, and he doesn't do it that often. Most of his video views are about building and repairing cars and appliances."

"Those might be to cover up his more disturbing

viewing habits."

"You don't think...nah...that's out there."

"What?" I asked.

"Nothing."

"You're wondering if he's a killer."

"Actually, I was thinking he might be looking at ways to plan the perfect murder. He learns about these unsolved murders, figures out why they were never solved, and researches how to keep from getting caught in those types of situations."

"That sounds like serial killer training 101." But I'd never heard of a serial killer doing research.

"He probably just has a morbid fascination, like a good deal of the American population. Something about murders and true crime really gets a lot of people going." He laughed. "It gets ninety-five percent of the people at Cross Security going. I bet it gets you going too. That's why you do what you do."

"That's not what gets me going."

"No?" Stuart asked. "So why are we having this conversation? Most of the investigators who look into cheating spouses don't end up using words like killer. Isn't this the second time that's happened to you?"

"Let's not count. It'll make Cross anxious. And you know how he gets when he's anxious."

Stuart laughed.

"Theo likes to window shop. Have you seen him browsing for weapons of any kind?" I asked.

"Nothing."

"Okay." I thought about the messages I'd read on Theo's phone. "Have you made any progress on determining who he was communicating with last night?"

"It's always the same user. He's been messaging this person on a regular basis, at least a few times a week, for the last seven plus months."

"Seven plus?"

"Not quite eight, but close."

Which meant this started around the same time he bought the gun. "Has Theo looked up any information on removing serial numbers from firearms or destroying ballistic evidence?"

"There's nothing related to guns or gun violence in his search history."

"What is his preferred method of killing?" I asked.

"You mean based on his video searches?"

"Unless you know something I don't."

"The more recent searches have to do with stabbings. Before that, it was strangulation."

The proximity alarm sounded, alerting me that the delivery driver had pulled up. "Send me a list of those links. I want to see those podcasts and how-to videos. Let me know if you make any progress identifying who Theo's been talking to on that app."

"Will do," Stuart said. "But Alex, I'd say this is probably a hobby. Something he does to pass the time."

"Did he always look into these things?"

"From the data we received, I'd say so. It's become more frequent. What used to be a few times a month turned into an everyday thing, but like you said, he and his wife are on the rocks. It makes sense he'd need to find something to fill that time."

"Yeah, or someone."

"I can't help you with that. There's nothing on his computer. No dating profiles. No browsing hookup sites. Nothing like that."

"What about the dark web?"

"I don't think he knows how to access that."

"Any searches for pawn shops?"

"No."

"Check back eight months and make sure."

"I have. It's not here."

"Okay." The doorbell sounded. "Thanks."

After tipping the delivery guy and resetting the security system, I put dinner in the fridge and set the table. When Martin wanted to show his romantic side, he'd go all out. I wasn't nearly that mushy, but I found the candleholders and a few tapers and put them on the table.

I was searching for a lighter when the alarm sounded again. A quick glance at the screen told me Martin was home. Despite how tired he looked, he had a bounce to his step. With any luck, we were no longer fighting, if that's even what was going on this morning.

"Are you mad?" I asked when he entered. "Because I'm prepared to wave the white flag." I grabbed one of the napkins off the table and held it up.

Martin cracked a smile. "Come here."

"I take it you accept my surrender."

Devious thoughts flitted behind his eyes. "I do rather enjoy that." He brushed my hair back and tilted my chin up to face him. "I'm sorry about this morning. I didn't mean to snap at you. I didn't even realize I had. I'll try not to do it again."

"It sounds like you're surrendering."

"If that's what you want." He leaned down and kissed me, sending that bolt of lightning through me and making butterflies take flight in my stomach. After all this time, the fact that he still had that kind of power astounded me. He grabbed my hips and lifted me onto the counter. "This morning, you said you wanted to talk." He pressed his forehead against mine. "I'm all ears."

Distracted by the scent of his cologne and the tickle of his fingers against my sides, I found it hard to think straight. "You're in a good mood."

"I am."

"Why?"

"That can wait." He stepped back, so he could look me in the eyes. "This morning, you said you thought I was dead. I hope that was a joke."

"It was. Sort of."

"Explain."

"You never sleep on the couch, unless I beg and plead. You never sleep through the alarm, and you rarely skip workouts."

"I was tired."

"I know. I'm afraid you're working too hard. I moved out here to be with you, and—"

"We haven't had time to do anything outside of the house, besides the occasional dinner and grief counseling meeting."

"You mean the hour you spend sending and receiving

work e-mails while sitting in an uncomfortable chair?" I shook my head. "It's okay. I don't mind. I get it. This is about saving jobs and keeping the L.A. branch operational and starting new projects and new research. You have a lot on your plate right now. But you haven't slept more than five hours in a single stretch since you've been here."

"That's going to change. Groundwork is laid down. I have a few things to finalize, but we're moving forward. I just have to get the Board to sign off. I'm flying home in two days."

"We're going home?"

"Hold your horses, sweetheart. It's just for the day, maybe two. I'm presenting everything to them and getting the backing I need for our investors. After that, I'll be back here to oversee the project getting off the ground. Once everything is up and running, we can go home and stay home." He stepped between my legs. "Do you want to fly back with me this week? It's a short trip, but we can take the company jet."

"No more commercial flights to save money?" I asked.

"This is entirely company business. And quite frankly, I'm tired of not flying private." I laughed, but he swallowed it with a kiss. "What do you say?"

"I can't. Lucien has interviews scheduled every day this week. And now I'm in the midst of god knows what." I looked at him, finding the disappointment on his face. "Do you know when we can go home for good?"

"My best guess right now is six weeks."

"I can deal with the California sun until then."

"Are you sure you don't want a quick reprieve? You can tell Cross you're sick."

But I couldn't risk taking the time away when I hadn't figured out what Theo's deal was. "Rain check?"

"How about a compromise? Saturday. No work. Just you and me, out on the town."

I walked my fingers up his chest, finding the first two buttons of his shirt already opened. So I started on the third one. "We don't have to go out."

"Humor me. Wherever you want to go, whatever you want to do, we'll do it. But we're going somewhere. Let's mark something off our list." Martin had been building a list of tourist things to do while in California. So far, we'd only done one of them.

"Anything?"

He grinned. "Anything."

"Santa Monica Pier, on one condition."

"Name it."

"No Ferris wheel."

"You drive a hard bargain."

"I could make it harder."

He smirked. "I know you can." He stole another kiss. "Deal."

TWENTY-THREE

When the phone rang, I waited for Martin to answer it. But the cheesecake had his full attention. He glanced at me, like he'd been doing throughout dinner, but the sexy smile and mischievous gleam were gone. He gestured with his fork, pointing it away from the plate. "Do you want to take that?"

"What?"

He laughed, his head shaking. "I'm not the only one suffering from sleep deprivation." He pointed at the counter. "It's for you, sweetheart."

I got up to see who it was. *Heathcliff.* I wasn't expecting that. For a moment, I considered sending the call to voicemail, but Martin scooped the last morsel of dessert into his mouth and started clearing the table.

"Hey, what are you doing up so late?" I asked.

"How'd you know?" Heathcliff asked, his tone akin to the way he spoke to suspects inside the interrogation room.

"Know what?"

"That Sophie Marshman's suicide wasn't a suicide."

"It wasn't?"

"Not according to Detective Trevitt. Since the last time we spoke, he's changed his tune. Sophie's sister received a letter, which drew the circumstances surrounding her death into question. Trevitt has decided he should reopen the case and give it another look. He wanted to know what Sophie's distant relative had to say and why I'd called to ask him about the case before the LAPD called with questions. What am I supposed to tell him?"

"Tell him a P.I. lied to you about being a relative because she was investigating Sophie's death and needed help getting access to the records."

"I don't like this."

"Regardless, you shouldn't get in trouble. I can take the hit."

Derek grunted. "Do you have any idea what's going on with the suicide? The more intel I can provide, the less pissed he'll be."

"Jenna, Sophie's sister, received a letter which detailed a prior attack. According to what Sophie wrote, she was scared. She wanted Jenna to pick her up and take her home. She didn't feel safe on the streets."

"Any theories?"

"A few, but none that hold water. It's all guesswork. I don't have anything in terms of hard evidence, just a few accounts and the letter Sophie wrote."

"What about that other alleged suicide you told me about? Did you find any connection between the two victims?"

"A homeless vet encountered both of them. Will and I tossed around a few ideas. The vet is a potential suspect, but the last I heard, he's gone to ground. He left the camp he usually guards after I spoke to him. The police are keeping an eye out, but I don't know if they ever found him."

"Do you have a name?"

"Roland Jordan." I could hear Heathcliff typing in the background. "Why do you ask?"

"Is Jordan the only connection you found?"

"So far, but I didn't do that much digging. Jenna made it abundantly clear I shouldn't stick my nose in her business. The LAPD reminded me of the same thing, and Will and I had words last night. No one wants me to continue looking into this."

"You're still exceptional at making friends, I see."

"That's why I have to do my best to hang on to you."

"You always got me. You know that." Heathcliff paused. "Are you backing off this case?"

"For now."

"That's a first."

"Let's just say something else has my attention at the moment."

"Okay. That's all I needed to hear."

"Derek, wait. What do you know? Is there a reason I should stick with this?"

"Shouldn't your San Diego sergeant keep you apprised of these developments?"

"I already told you we had words."

"Regarding the case?"

I glanced toward Martin who had stopped loading the dishwasher to reply to a text message. If it hadn't been my phone that interrupted us, it would have been his. However, I resisted the urge to shout, *Ha!* Instead, I ducked into the game room for some privacy. "Will's not cleared to carry. There was a recent incident. He won't talk about it. He was annoyed I kept pushing him to disclose."

"Sounds like someone else I know."

"Me?"

"No. Me." Derek exhaled. "Y'know, from before we met. He needs to follow orders, do what he's told, and find his way through it. That's all he can do."

"I don't think he has any intention of doing any of it. He's not planning on sticking around the department after he figures out who's behind the attacks on the homeless. As soon as that's settled, he says he's turning in his badge."

"Okay, that does sound more like you. Still, I thought he'd want you to know another alleged suicide victim surfaced a few hours ago. TOD is estimated around one a.m. The guy cut his own throat."

"And the SDPD thinks that's a suicide?"

"The vic wrote a note, addressed it to his daughter. They found it in his pocket. He said he was sorry he was such a disappointment. He could never get clean and never had enough desire to try. His family deserved better. She deserved better. He didn't want to drag this out any longer, so he killed himself."

"Why?"

"He was already dying. Stage four. It would have been excruciating."

"But to slice open his own throat, that's not how addicts usually choose to go."

"The guy didn't have much of anything, except a rusted, old straight razor."

I cringed. "Did Trevitt tell you this?"

"That's why he's reopening Sophie Marshman's case and a few other ones. He wants to make sure nothing else is going on here. He's afraid he could be looking at a serial killer."

"Give the detective my contact info. I told Will I'd keep him out of it, but everything else is fair game."

"Trevitt will want to know how you got involved in this."

"I'll figure something out."

"Alex, be careful. Make sure you have someone watching your back."

"It's a good thing Cross has dozens of security specialists operating in the area."

"I'm serious."

"So am I. Thanks for looking out, Derek."

"Yet, I'm wishing I hadn't bothered to tell you any of this."

"Too late now."

I tucked my phone into my pocket and stared at the wall. The empty space begged me to tack my notes to it. But I didn't have enough notes. Not yet. But now would be a good time to get started on that.

Heathcliff hadn't disclosed the most recent suicide victim's name. I doubted Detective Trevitt had provided it. But there must be a news story covering it. If it bleeds, it reads, as the saying went. So I scanned for breaking news updates. Two of the San Diego news outlets mentioned a fast-food worker discovering a body behind the dumpster. Police were investigating, but the man was believed to be homeless. No identification had been made, and the police had yet to determine if foul play was involved.

The only thing I learned was the man died near a dumpster. Dialing Will's burner, I wondered if he was at the scene. Was he even working tonight? I could barely keep up with my schedule, much less his. All I knew was the sergeant usually worked nights.

"Answer your damn phone." I waited another two rings, but after eight, I doubted he'd pick up by ten. Hanging up, I sent a text. *Call me*. Then I waited. "Fuck."

"Alex," Martin poked his head into the game room, "is everything okay? Did something happen at home?"

"No. Derek's fine. Everyone's fine."

He almost let out a sigh of relief, until he saw the look on my face. "What's going on?"

"Another suicide in San Diego." Something Heathcliff said made me pause. "TOD was around one a.m." I rubbed a hand over my mouth, hating the thought that went through my mind. "Oh god."

Martin came toward me, stopping short of touching me. "Talk to me. Whatever it is. Talk it out."

"Will."

"What about him?"

"He left before the mark exited the store. That was around ten. By the time I pulled out, he'd already gotten a ride back to his car. It was definitely before eleven." I opened the browser and checked to see if there had been any major accidents or tie-ups, but I didn't find anything. "It takes two, maybe two and a half hours, to get to San Diego without traffic." My stomach knotted, causing me to regret eating dinner.

"I don't—"

"He could have gotten back in time." I brushed my hair back, forcing myself not to jump to any conclusions. "Shit." Sucking in a breath, I called the office. Will had a burner phone, but he also had his phone. Despite everything, he was a cop. He'd have his regular phone with him. "This is Parker. I need to know where Will Russo was at one a.m. last night. And I need a rush on it." I gave them Will's phone number before hanging up. All I could do now was wait.

I blinked a few times. My mind everywhere at once. The room spun with the rush of thoughts. Grabbing the notepad off the bar, I scribbled down everything that came to mind. Where was Will when Sophie Marshman died? He said he was at work when the call came in. That should be easy enough to verify. Detective Trevitt would remember, but I couldn't ask him until he called me. And I didn't know when that would be.

Martin's phone buzzed. He glanced at it before silencing the call. "Is there anything I can do?"

"I need a map of San Diego. A big one."

Martin didn't even ask. He went into the other room and returned with a stack of tourist brochures, maps, and travel guides. "How big?"

"The biggest you have."

He unfolded the travel guide to San Diego and flipped it over. On the other side was a city map with the popular attractions starred. "I can have Marcal find something larger and bring it over."

"No, this is good. Thanks." I spread it out on the pool table and grabbed my pen, marking down the relevant locations, including the police station where Will worked. All three suicides were spread out, but the latest took place just off the highway exit Will would have taken to get home. A chill went through me, and I shuddered.

Martin went into his office and returned with markers, pens, a few legal pads, sticky notes in assorted colors, tape, and a stapler. He put them down on the pool table beside me and ran his hands over my shoulders. "Are you all right?"

"I will be, if I'm wrong."

His hands fell away. A moment later, he put one of his sweatshirts on the edge of the table. "You were shivering. I don't want you to get cold." His phone chimed, alerting him to a waiting voicemail. "I'll be in the living room if you need anything. Let me know if you have to leave." He kissed my cheek. "And we are not falling asleep on the couch again. Two hours, and then we call it a night. No arguments."

Three suicides. How many more had there been? I

resisted the urge to call Derek back and play twenty questions. He told me whatever he knew.

After I taped the map to the wall, I picked up the legal pad and wrote down every tidbit of information I knew about Will Russo. Was he responsible for these deaths? I'd practically accused him of it last night. Did that cause him to lash out and find another victim? I glanced at my phone, desperate for it to ring. Why hadn't Will answered when I called?

The TOD could have been off. Those were hardly ever accurate when bodies were discovered. So I looked up details on the restaurant. The dining room closed at ten. The drive-thru closed at midnight. A worker found the body when he showed up to work the breakfast shift at five a.m.

I rested my head in my hands for a moment. "You are not a homicide detective." But it sure felt like it. Taking a step back, I wondered if the dead man had any connection to Roland Jordan, Marshman, Devers, or that homeless encampment. Again, that would be Detective Trevitt's job, not mine.

My phone rang, and I lunged for it. "Parker," I answered.

"Russo's phone was in Los Angeles last night. He used his phone around seven, local time. It pinged in this vicinity." He gave me the cross streets near the bookstore. "The next time he received a call was five a.m."

"Where was he at five?"

"Still in Los Angeles. I checked the address and his credit cards. He booked a room at a motel."

"Who called him?" I asked.

"Gabriel Trevitt."

"How long did they speak?"

"Seven minutes."

"Did Russo leave after that?"

"I don't think so. He made and received several calls after that, but his phone didn't ping different cell towers until ten a.m., which coincides with checkout time."

"Where is he now?" I asked.

"San Diego."

"Thanks."

It looked like I owed Will an apology, but the gnawing at the back of my brain hadn't stopped. It'd only gotten louder. Why didn't Will answer when I called?

TWENTY-FOUR

I hadn't slept the night before, unless the brief nap in the car or on the couch counted, which it didn't. But I couldn't sleep now. Was a serial killer picking off the homeless population? At least the warning bell had been rung. The police were investigating. They'd figure it out, or so I kept telling myself.

However, that hollow reassurance did nothing to squelch the other wayward thought that popped into my head every time I told myself Will Russo was no longer my problem because then I'd start thinking about Theo Stapleton. That one was my problem.

Martin hadn't moved in the last forty-five minutes. His slow, steady breathing told me he'd fallen asleep. But when I tried to shift away from him to grab my phone earlier, he opened his eyes and asked what I was doing. I didn't want a repeat of that, so I'd been waiting to make sure he wouldn't wake up again. But I couldn't wait any longer.

Carefully, I untangled myself from his arms and reached toward the nightstand. He sniffed and rolled over. That was easy enough.

According to the various trackers, Theo remained at home. He hadn't gone anywhere. Iris hadn't called or sent any crazed texts. At least someone was having a calm night after an insane day.

Yawning, I tucked my phone beneath my pillow for easier access and rolled onto my back. When I could no longer stare at the ceiling, I closed my eyes. My thoughts unraveling into nothing more than vanishing wisps as sleep approached.

Where did Theo go after he left the parking garage? Had he left his phone intentionally? Since I missed his return, I didn't know how he'd made it back. But regardless of what he told his wife and the police, the stain wasn't from a chili dog or ketchup. Every cell in my body knew that shirt wasn't his. And that the stain had been blood. A lot of it.

I thought about the bloodstain. The way it ran from the neck of the wifebeater halfway down the middle. I would have seen a bullet hole. What about a stab wound? No, the material would have puckered outward or inward at the tear. There hadn't been any tears. It's like blood had come from a neck or chest wound above the fabric. But it didn't run in streaks. It had pooled and spread, soaking in. Was it still wet when I found it?

I'd seen red inside the takeout bag. It had been wet when Theo put it inside. But the fabric itself could have dried. He hadn't used a gun. So what did he use? Did he bludgeon someone? He could have gotten into a fight, broken someone's nose, and knocked out some teeth. But that looked like too much blood. Then again, I'd seen some nasty street fights, but this looked much worse.

The shirt's owner could have already been injured and the wound reopened. That would explain the lack of tears. Or the owner had gotten his throat slit.

Shit. I opened my eyes and swallowed a lungful of air. Was it possible to make it to San Diego and back in that span of time? It could be done, but the person would have to be quick. In and out. No waiting. No hunting.

Theo had no ties to San Diego that I knew of. For him to ditch me in that parking garage, hitch another ride south, kill someone outside a fast-food restaurant, and return was absurd. How small of a world would it have to be for Iris's husband to be the assailant killing the homeless in a city two hours away?

"No fucking way," I mumbled. Things like that weren't possible. Were they?

Martin rolled over again, wrapping his arm around my waist. "Stop," he mumbled.

"What?"

"Stop. I can hear your wheels spinning. You need to sleep. That's the only way you're going to make sense of whatever's going on." He kissed my temple and settled onto my pillow, stretching his free arm out beneath us. His fingertips brushed against my phone. "We can't go on like this."

"I mentioned that earlier."

"I know." He released my phone and curled both arms around me. "But you made it sound like I had the problem. It looks like we're equally afflicted."

"It must be contagious. I caught it from you."

* * *

I put the free weights down and picked up my ringing phone. *Russo.* Exhaling, I wiped my face with a towel and pressed answer. "I didn't think you'd call."

"I was working. You should try it some time."

"Bite me."

Will huffed. "What do you want, Alex? I just got off shift. I'm too tired to deal with this."

"How was your shift?"

"I take it you heard. The attacks have escalated to murder. Again. There's no denying it. This is the third one I've heard about, but Trevitt thinks there might be more. He's reexamining the closed cases. Sophie's letter helped, so thanks for that."

"I want this stopped as much as you do, but there's not much I can do from here. I'm hoping Trevitt will call me for a chat. Until then, I'm not sure how I can help."

"Except by pointing the finger at me, right?"

"That's not fair. I'm working from what I know. You have an interest in these cases, which you still haven't explained."

"I don't have to. I get enough of that at work. I don't need it during my off hours too."

"Are you waiting for an apology?"

"I still haven't heard one."

I licked my lips. "I'm sorry. Are we good?"

"Yeah, sure." He sighed.

"Do you want to tell me about this newest alleged suicide? Have you located Roland Jordan yet?"

"Not yet. Patrol's still looking for him. We issued a BOLO."

"The department sounds sure it's him."

"It could be. Trevitt suspects the latest vic may have spent some time in the same homeless encampment where you met Jordan, but it's conjecture. No one's come forward to substantiate it."

"Did you question the people at the camp?"

"I've been behind my desk all day."

Despite Will's assigned desk duty, I found that odd. "Where were you when the call came in?"

"Again?" he asked, exasperated. "I don't care what you or anyone has to say. And for the record, I didn't do it."

"I didn't say you did."

"It sounds like that's where this conversation is headed. After all, you said you thought I killed Sophie and Robert. I doubt you've changed your tune."

"Maybe I have."

He snorted. "Let me guess, you checked to see if I had an alibi. So you know, I was in L.A. when the latest body dropped."

"Were you?"

"Was I what?"

"In L.A."

"Yeah. I got a motel. I didn't want to drive back in the middle of the night."

"But you work nights. That's your usual time to be awake."

"Not after I've been awake all damn day," he growled. "I said I wasn't going to explain myself to you. So I'm done. I'm hanging up."

"Wait, Will. What's the vic's name? The police

department hasn't released any information yet. All I know is his throat was sliced open with a razor and the suicide note was found in his pocket. Have the police found any solid connections between him and the previous vics, Roland Jordan, or the camp? Or is Trevitt just making shit up in his head?"

"Joel Curry, sixty-seven, he and Jordan went to the same VA hospital. They could have crossed paths there. Other than that, Curry was a loner, stayed near the shore, and panhandled. As far as I can tell, he never stepped foot in that camp or any of the shelters, kitchens, or pantries that Sophie and Robert frequented. But Trevitt thinks otherwise. We don't know much yet. The homeless don't like cooperating."

"What about the church?"

"Sophie never went to the church."

"But Robert did, and the church has an outreach program for addicts. Joel was an addict, and he was dying. Father Miguel might have tried to persuade Joel to get help, or Joel may have gone there in search of answers."

"I'll make sure someone looks into it."

"Is there anything I can do?"

"I doubt it." Will exhaled, his tone shifting. He must have realized he was also running low on friends. "I'll let you know if anything changes. How did things go with the cheater after I left? Shouldn't you be wrapped up in that?"

"Don't ask."

"That good?"

"He ditched me." It was too early in the day to hold my tongue. "Are you sure you didn't tip him off?"

"For fuck's sake. Goodbye, Alex."

The hang-up didn't surprise me. I would have done the same thing.

I finished my workout, grabbed breakfast, and got ready for another fun-filled day at the office. Martin had left two hours earlier, after swimming twenty laps in the pool. For him, that was taking it easy.

Instead of going straight to work, I drove to the Stapletons' house. Iris hadn't texted me since last night. The trackers assured me Theo remained at home, but I wanted to make sure everything was okay. When I arrived outside their house, I texted Iris and fed her a cover story in case she needed to provide Theo with an excuse to see me.

I'm fine, she texted. *No need to stop by.*

I have to see for myself. Can you come to the door? I replied.

A few minutes later, she opened the front door to put a letter in the mailbox. Theo stopped her in the doorway, offering to do it for her, gave her a quick peck, and jogged to the box. He didn't give the letter a second glance as he shoved it through the slot. He didn't appear concerned that his wife was conspiring against him. Most paranoid people would have examined the envelope and address, but he didn't care. Then again, it might have been a bill payment or something innocuous. But since I was assured Iris was alive and well and Theo hadn't gotten wise and disabled the trackers, I went on my way.

No one was waiting for me when I arrived at work. Security wasn't even at the front door. I wondered if they'd been called off since no incidents had occurred in the last few weeks, but Howard would have told me. The guards may have been on a bathroom break, coffee run, or dealing with some issue on another floor. Hoping something insane wasn't about to happen, I went past the elevators and down the hallway.

Unlocking the door, I let myself inside. My inbox was full of messages from Cross, Justin, and Stuart. Stuart, the tech I'd spoken to, had sent me all the videos and links I'd requested. While I scanned the comments on the how-to videos, I let them play in the background.

As far as I could tell, Theo hadn't interacted with anyone who posted comments or messaged the content creators. Before I went through every page of Theo's shopping history, I hit play on the latest true crime podcast episode he'd listened to. This one focused on another unsolved murder that happened in the Cascade Mountains. The body of a missing hiker had been found two months after he vanished. It appeared he'd lost his footing and fallen, hit his head on a rock, and died, but the narrator argued the angle was wrong. Blood was found beneath the rock. Someone had picked it up and bludgeoned the hiker with it, placed it back down, and erased whatever evidence existed that he'd been there. That's what led Theo to search for how-to videos on eliminating footprints and minimizing the chances of leaving trace evidence behind.

This appeared innocent enough, except Theo had gone on to window shop for snowbrushes. Almost every car owner I knew had at least one of these, but this was Los Angeles. Snow was a rare occurrence. He'd have no use for that here, unless he expected another freak storm to sweep the region. It didn't hurt to be prepared, but since brushes like that were used to dust the ground and eliminate footprints in the how-to video, I didn't think his reasoning was that innocent.

After online browsing for other suspicious items like car mat protectors, duct tape, rope, tire irons, plastic car mats, seat covers, cleaning wipes, handheld vacs, and other car centric items that could also serve a purpose when it came to body disposal, Theo stopped online searching. However, a few days later, he charged five hundred dollars on his credit card at one of the big box stores. Originally, I figured he bought groceries and other household necessities since stores like that stocked everything, but now I had doubts.

Theo had made a similarly large purchase a couple of months ago. I hadn't seen any of the things from his online browsing inside the garage. Again, I wondered if I could be jumping to conclusions. The police searched the house. They would have noticed anything suspicious, unless he kept everything inside his car.

The cops had no reason to search it. They hadn't even asked. They found the gun. Iris and Theo cooperated. That was it.

I thought back to the duffel bag I'd seen Theo carrying on several occasions. I assumed that's where he kept his stuff for work, but he could have more than one bag. I checked the time. Theo had just left for the hospital.

I watched the tracker take nearly the same route to work. Considering how Theo mixed it up every day on his way home, I wondered why he stuck to the same path to get there. This man was a mystery I intended to solve.

The door creaked open. "Hi," a tall, lanky guy said. "I'm Monty Earles. I'm supposed to have an interview with Alex Parker." He peered at the closed office doors, but there were no signs. "Is he available?"

"She is." I gestured to the chair I had yet to move back to the waiting area. "Have a seat."

"Oh, I'm sorry. I shouldn't have assumed."

"No big deal." I took the resume he offered me, and we got down to business. "You used to work at a law firm."

"Assistant office manager."

"So you've done this job before and know a thing or two about protecting a client's privacy."

"That I do."

I scanned the rest of the page. "Any particular reason you left that job?"

"The newest name partner and I had a personality clash. But before that, things were great. You can see I have several letters of recommendation in there."

I scanned the sheets. "You seem more than capable." I checked the time. "I have somewhere to be, but I'll pass this on to Mr. Cross. He'll be in touch."

"Okay." Earles stood and held out his fist, waiting for me to bump it. I stared at it for a moment before obliging. "Between us, how do my chances look?"

"Pretty good."

He smiled. "Have a wonderful day."

"You too." Once he was gone, I called Cross. "Did Paul Nepper call you?"

"This morning. He had some questions. I don't remember telling you to find investigators. Right now, you're looking for office managers."

"He didn't want that gig?"

"He thought I'd want him to use his contacts to assist on investigations."

"What did you tell him?" I asked.

"That the office manager position requires him to do whatever tasks are asked of him."

I rolled my eyes. "He turned it down."

"Yes."

"Are you going to offer him one of the other spots?"

"We aren't filling those yet. Why are you in such a rush? Do you need help on your case? Kellen Dey has offered to fly out."

"Tell Kellen thanks, but I can handle it."

"Fine." But Cross didn't believe me. "Why are you calling?"

"I had a question."

Cross cleared his throat. "Go on."

"Do we have to interview all the candidates, or can we stop as soon as we find one?"

"You found someone?"

"Yeah, Monty's great. Let's give him the job."

Cross clicked a few keys, reading the man's resume out loud as he scrolled down the screen. "He's qualified. And you like him?"

"Yep."

"Is this your way of getting out of conducting more interviews?"

"He's a good fit," I said, checking the time. "What do you say?"

"I'll call him and set up a video interview. If I like him, legal will draw up the contract. I'll let you know what happens."

"But what about the other interviewees?"

"Once we've locked in an office manager, Justin will cancel the rest of the appointments. Not before."

"Great. Do us both a favor, and woo this guy, Lucien. He's a catch. But right now, I gotta go."

TWENTY-FIVE

I kept my head on a swivel, but most people appeared more concerned with their own activities than mine. Despite that, breaking into a car in broad daylight in a crowded parking lot wasn't the best idea. However, I couldn't wait for Theo to return home. He might take the bag inside with him before I got a chance to search it, and I'd already spooked him once. I didn't need to do it again.

Moving between his vehicle and the minivan parked beside it, I peered through each of the windows. The crumpled blanket and neck pillow remained, but there was no duffel. If he kept his work clothes or a change of scrubs in that bag, he would have taken it inside. But I was betting he kept that bag handy for something else. Or he had multiple bags.

I didn't stop on that first pass. Instead, I cut through the rows of cars until I reached the sidewalk and looped around the parking lot. No one was watching me, except the security cameras. More than likely, the bored security guards inside weren't paying that much attention to the feeds. Even if they were, they'd assume I parked in the wrong section or forgot something in my car, which would explain why I was heading back the way I came.

On my second pass, I crouched down low enough to keep my body concealed from view as I crept to the back of Theo's car. A green pickup truck sandwiched Theo in on the passenger side. The long truck bed made it easier to stay hidden from the cameras, but it did nothing to shield me from the mother and child headed back to their car.

The kid pointed at me. "Look, Mommy. What's that lady doing?"

"Shh," the mom scolded. "It's not nice to point." But her eyes settled on me.

I stretched my arm out beneath the truck. "Gotcha," I announced loud enough for her to hear. Holding my keys up triumphantly, I stood, hating that I'd have to perform another complete pass to get back into position. I brushed the dirt off my jeans and kept walking.

"She dropped her keys," the mom said.

"No, she didn't," the kid insisted.

Smart kid, I thought. He'd make a great cop or a decent lookout. Returning to my car, I unlocked the door and got inside. While I waited for the woman and kid to leave, I pretended to search for something in my glove box.

Once they were gone, I looked around and checked my mirrors. Finally, a lull. Sliding out of my seat, I got out of the car, slung a jacket over my arm, and headed across the parking lot. Let's try this again.

Given the dozens of vehicles packed so tightly together, I didn't want to risk using the app on my phone to break into Theo's car. My lockpicks would work just as well and not arouse suspicion. I held them beneath my jacket. Once I was out of the camera's line of sight, I knelt beside Theo's trunk.

Keeping the picks partially hidden beneath my jacket, I stuck them into the keyhole, determined to get the trunk open. It didn't take much to get it to unlock. Not wasting any time, I lifted the lid.

Theo's trunk was a mess of emergency items. Flares, first aid kits, blankets, towels, bottled water, and protein bars stared up at me from a large crate. Beside the crate were two duffel bags. One in blue, like the kind first responders carried, and the other was black.

Curious, I unzipped the first bag. It contained everything from syringes to bandages to scalpels. Based on the equipment inside, I couldn't help but think Theo was stealing hospital supplies. Most people stole drugs. It looked like he'd taken everything else.

After zipping the bag, I opened the next one. Inside, I found clothes. But they weren't Theo's. They were all different sizes, ranging from women's yoga pants to children's sweatshirts. I rifled through the bag. The items weren't new. Were these his trophies? Where did Theo get these, and what was he doing with them? Maybe they were donations. Or maybe they belonged to his girlfriend or girlfriends, who appeared to have children. How many secrets was this guy keeping?

Unsure what to make of the oddities inside the two duffel bags, I zipped them closed before giving the crate of emergency items a more thorough look. Near the bottom, I found the snowbrush. Dirt, dust, and clumps of mud clung to the bristles.

A chill went through me as I recalled the podcast Theo had watched before purchasing the snowbrush. Who was this guy? Was he recreating these unsolved crimes?

Digging deeper in the crate, I found thick rope which had started to fray at the cut end and an old plastic drop cloth. Images flashed behind my eyes of Robert Devers swinging from the rafters. This looked like the same type of rope. It was the same color, but again, I knew that was insane. Yet, Jablonsky's voice played through my head. *There's no such thing as coincidence.*

A car door slammed, breaking me from my trance. I had to move. Shoving everything back where I found it, I closed the trunk. Keep walking. Remain calm. Do not draw attention to yourself. No one will notice.

A man went down the row I'd just vacated. I only caught a glimpse of him between the vehicles. But he looked like he was in a hurry. The hairs at the back of my neck stood at attention.

I didn't dare turn until I was inches from the hospital entrance. When I looked back, I couldn't see anyone past the truck. The hollow sound of a trunk lid slamming echoed off the concrete. A moment later, it was followed by the sounds of a car door closing and an engine starting.

The voice in my head urged me to keep walking, so I did. This was a crowded hospital. People came and went all the time. Patients, doctors, nurses, visitors, and staff. I had no reason to think Theo would be leaving work early or that I'd nearly been caught, but that was the only thought running through my mind.

Pulling out my phone, I checked the tracker. Theo's car hadn't moved. It wasn't him.

I let out the breath I hadn't realized I was holding and entered the hospital. The lobby had a coffee stand. That would serve as the perfect cover while I figured out my next move. But opening that trunk had only left me with more questions than answers.

While I waited in line, the elevator doors opened. Several people exited. I glanced up, but none of them looked familiar. *You're paranoid, Parker,* the voice in my head said. I wasn't going to argue with it.

With my coffee in hand, I turned to leave. My heart caught in my throat, and I spun back around, reaching for napkins and sugar packets. Busying myself with adding creamer to my coffee, I kept my eye on the distorted reflection provided by the metal pole which held the roof on top of the coffee stand.

Theo had just entered through the automatic doors. He had on a pair of light blue scrubs and a surgeon's cap. Sweat made the shirt cling to his chest, leaving a dark sweat stain in an exaggerated horseshoe shape halfway down his front. He had matching pit stains and wiped at the beads of perspiration that dripped from his forehead and temples.

What was he doing outside? Had someone from security alerted him about the strange woman loitering near his car? Had I been caught? Did he have a security system I missed?

When I ran out of things to add to my coffee, I secured the lid, cleaned up the mess I made, tossed everything in the trash, and turned around. Theo was waiting at the end of the line. His focus was on the board with the daily specials. The flavors of the day were hazelnut and Irish cream.

Without breaking stride, I left the lobby and returned to my car. Theo didn't follow. But I couldn't risk hanging around here. That had been too close.

I left the hospital and drove until I found a place to park. Once I did, I checked the tracker I'd put on Theo's phone. He was still at the hospital. Maybe he'd gone for a walk after surgery. That would make sense. Doctors and nurses did things like that all the time. Okay, maybe not, but they did on TV, so it was possible.

Once I got over the jitters of nearly being caught again, I climbed out of the car and tossed the now too disgusting to drink coffee into the trash. The last thing I needed was caffeine. What I needed was a refresher course on conducting surveillance. Clearly, I sucked at it. I could almost hear Will mocking me. Truthfully, I deserved it.

Since I didn't want to risk getting caught again, I returned to the office. Part of me wanted to call Iris, but she sounded so hopeful last night and looked so happy this morning that I didn't want to burst her bubble, not when I had no proof. Instead, I did what I should have done from the beginning and listened to all the true crime podcasts Theo obsessed over.

I'd filled a legal pad with notes on the victims and methods of killing. The latest victim had been bludgeoned with a rock. Prior to that, the alleged Cascade Killer, as the podcast commentator dubbed him, had sliced open several major veins of another of his victims, tied him up, and left him for the wildlife.

Aside from the occasional coyote and big cat, Los Angeles didn't have too many predators from the animal kingdom wandering around city limits. Still, I found myself comparing Theo's shopping habits to when he listened to that episode, wondering how he'd want to reenact that one. After all, he already had the rope.

Turning to a new sheet, I made a list of everything I found in Theo's trunk. He could have pulled off that murder. He had the scalpel, rope, and snowbrush to wipe away his tracks. Did Theo hike? This area was lousy with trails.

I checked the recent missing persons list. Several people had vanished while hiking, but that didn't mean any of them were dead or that Theo killed them. But my imagination was running rampant.

I went into the middle office and stared at the tourist map of San Diego that I'd marked with the suspicious deaths. I couldn't wait another second. Digging my phone out of my pocket, I called Iris. She answered on the third ring, a little out of breath.

"Is this a bad time?" I asked, finding myself checking the tracker to make sure Theo hadn't left the hospital.

"No, I was just working out. I woke up today and felt like doing something. I haven't felt like this in a while."

"That's great."

"Do you want to try that again with more gusto?" she asked.

"Sorry. It is great. Really. I'm just wondering if Theo has any friends or relatives in San Diego."

"Not that I know of. Why?"

"Just curious."

"Bullshit. Do you think that's where he disappears when he leaves? He's not usually gone long enough for that to be the case."

"Has he ever stayed out all night?"

"Sure, but he usually waits until he thinks I'm asleep to leave. It's pretty late when he sneaks out, and he comes home before I get up."

"He'd only need five hours to get there and back."

"It's possible. But that'd be a hell of a drive for a quickie, wouldn't it? I mean, if he's cheating, he'd have to jump out of the car, jump on her, get in, get out, and get back home. That's barely enough time for a wham bam. Theo would have to pregame. I'm sure she would too."

"Iris," I said, hoping to stop her from going too far down that road when it wasn't relevant to my question.

"For him to be that attracted to someone to go through all that, I don't think I want to know who she is. How could I compete with that? Unless that's the only woman he could find who'd put up with his antics, knowing he has a wife at home."

"Iris," I said again, "I don't think Theo's having an affair with a woman in San Diego."

"You don't?"

"No."

"Why are you asking about San Diego?"

"I was working on something else and had this weird thought there could be overlap."

"The only time Theo and I ever went to San Diego was on our way back from TJ. We were young and carefree then. We spent the weekend in TJ and a couple of days holed up near the beach. It was a mini-vacation."

"Tijuana?"

"Yeah." She laughed, though it sounded a little forced. "Are you going to ask me if I think he's been sneaking over the border?"

"No." I tapped my pen against the points I'd written on one of the sheets of paper. "Has Theo gone back to San Diego since?"

"Not that I know of. He never had any reason. When we vacation, we usually head north, if we don't want to travel too far. And if we're looking for a beach getaway, we go to some island in the Caribbean or Hawaii. That's where we went on our honeymoon."

"What about hiking?"

"We used to do quite a bit of that."

"Ever go to the Cascades?" I asked.

"No. Camping and roughing it aren't my thing. We only hike around here. Griffith Park, mostly. Have you been?"

"Not yet." It was on Martin's list, along with a million other places. "Does Theo ever go by himself?"

"On occasion, but I don't think he's gone for a hike since the incident. Neither of us have."

"Okay, thanks."

"Alex," she stopped me before I could hang up, "my husband's finally acting like he sees me again. I don't want to lose him. He needs to break it off with her if he hasn't already. I need to know whatever he's doing is over. That we can move forward together."

"Did you confront him?"

"Not about the affair. After the police left, I asked why he didn't ask me to go with him to the movies. He said it was an action movie, and he didn't know if that would trigger me. I'm not sure if that's thoughtful or patronizing."

"Both."

"Probably." She sighed. "Then I asked what he's doing every time he disappears, but he brushed it off. I told him I felt like I was married to a stranger, a stranger who bought a gun. He apologized for that, came up with good reasons for his actions, but I know better. It's not just that. There's someone else. There has to be. I didn't want to push too hard. But he said he'd try to be better about everything. I need that proof."

"I'll get it." Even if Iris couldn't use it, Detective Petrocelli could.

TWENTY-SIX

I left the office in time to catch Theo on his way home from work. I didn't pull into the hospital parking lot. Instead, I kept circling while keeping an eye on the tracker. As soon as it went into motion, I made another turn. Theo had just pulled out and was eight cars ahead of me. Perfect.

Settling into my seat, I kept my distance. Traffic at this time of day was horrendous. But Theo stuck to surface streets, which made things easier. Halfway home, he detoured off the most efficient path to his house. I wasn't surprised. Instead of following him, I kept going straight for another two blocks before turning. I'd just made it to the stop sign when he drove past me.

By the time I turned, the tracker had come to a stop. I spotted his car in a reserved space. The sign said order pick-up only. Theo had changed out of the sweaty scrubs I'd last seen him wearing and into a plaid shirt over a dark t-shirt and jeans. He looked rough, like he'd had a long day.

After waiting his turn in line, he fished out some cash and took the three pizza boxes the guy put on top of the counter. Theo didn't wait for change before heading back to his car. Once he got inside, he peered behind him and pulled into traffic.

I dropped back, afraid of getting spotted again, but I wanted to stay close enough to see if he took anything out of his trunk when he got home. By the time I caught back up to him, he was halfway to the front door. He had a different duffel bag draped across his chest and a pair of sneakers with the laces tied together, hanging over his shoulder. If I hadn't known what his day entailed, I would have thought he'd just come back from the gym or a pick-up game of basketball.

Iris opened the front door, grabbing the boxes out of his hands. Theo kissed her cheek, dropped his shoes and bag near the door, and pushed it closed. For a cheater or a killer, he didn't act guilty or suspicious.

Deciding the coast was clear, I drove past the Stapletons' house and parked on the other end of the street. Since the sun hadn't set yet, I had a hard time determining if Theo turned on any lights in the house. Was he showering? Were they eating? Had he locked himself in the garage or home office?

I continued to watch the house for signs of activity. Forty minutes later, the sun had set, and I was able to see the lights through the blinds. It looked like they'd finished eating.

A few minutes later, the front door opened. Iris palmed her keys and headed for her car. She put on her headlights, made a u-turn in the middle of the street, which required backing up twice, and drove toward me.

When she made it to the stop sign at the end of the street, she called me. "I need you to follow Theo. He said he's going out."

"I'm already here."

"Where?"

I flicked on the dome light before quickly turning it off. "Did you see me?"

"Yeah. Thanks. I was afraid you wouldn't be available. You know, on account of tonight's meeting."

"I'm skipping it," I said, out of habit.

"Good."

My thoughts exactly. "What's going on? You sound

freaked."

"Theo said Frank invited him out for drinks. He's going to meet him at a bar. When I asked which one, he told me they hadn't decided yet. He's waiting for Frank to text him the details. This isn't like either of them. Theo hardly ever goes out on a work night."

"Did he say why he was going?"

"They lost a patient during surgery. I told Theo he should come with me instead, but he won't even consider it."

"It sounds plausible. People have different coping mechanisms."

"I know, but that's not the problem. Frank's a recovering alcoholic. He's been sober for twenty odd years. I find it hard to believe he'd throw that away, particularly with witnesses around. He could lose his job if someone reported him."

"Do you think Theo's lying?" I asked for clarification, though I was certain of that fact.

She snorted. "That's a big fat hell yes. I would have expected him to come up with a better lie. I don't even know why he told me he was going out tonight, unless he's not planning on getting back before I do. Maybe I should stay home. Maybe then he won't go."

"Do you think that will stop him?"

"I don't know. Maybe."

"What about next time?" I asked. I hated to do it, but I had to know what Theo planned. Every fiber of my being thought he was dangerous.

"You're right. I just...yesterday was great." She exhaled loudly, hoping to hide the emotion in her voice. "I thought we were on the right track. No more secrets. No more lies. How can he do this to me? How can he lie to my face? Does he think I'm that stupid?"

"Take it easy and try not to jump to conclusions. Go to your meeting. I'll keep an eye on your husband."

"You mean my cheating bastard of a husband."

Iris had completely changed her tune since this afternoon. But that was due to Theo getting her hopes up for a reconciliation, only to crush them again with this announcement. Hope was the worst four letter word. Now his wife wasn't just hurt; she was mad.

Ten minutes after Iris drove away, Theo left the house and climbed into his car. He left his lights off, letting it idle while he checked his phone. This went on for another five minutes before he put the phone down and reached for his seatbelt.

I called the office, hoping someone would be able to tell me if Theo had spoken to someone and what was said. Iris's anger made me determined not to lose him again. But the techs at Cross Security weren't able to help.

"We're seeing real time updates. He hasn't sent or received any texts or calls. He might be using that messaging app," Stuart said. "It wouldn't show in his phone records."

"Dammit. Have you made any progress figuring out who he's been talking to on it?"

"Negative. Amir thought he could track the user's location, but the closest he's gotten is somewhere in Los Angeles."

"That doesn't help much."

"That's why I didn't mention it," Stuart said.

"Keep trying. And thanks."

"Sure, no problem."

Theo's brake lights came on as he stopped at the sign at the other end of the street. Once he started going again, I pulled out of my parking space and made an immediate right. The street two over ran parallel. That would have to do because I didn't want to risk giving Theo so much breathing room he could ditch me again.

The voice in my head warned to be cautious. I'd almost been made once today. I didn't need to get caught a second time.

For a civilian, Theo had the best tactical awareness I'd ever seen. That could have been a consequence of the attack on his wife, or he was paranoid by nature. Maybe he'd been mugged or stalked. But I found those explanations unlikely.

I moved parallel to him, peering down each cross street to make sure I kept pace with his sedan. The moving red dot on my map helped me adjust my speed and timing. But as we traveled away from the neighborhoods to more commercial areas, traffic and pedestrians kept getting in my way.

Someone blared his horn as I zipped around him, nearly getting dinged as he attempted to pull out of a parking space. *Sorry,* I waved, but I didn't slow. I didn't have time. Leaning forward, I looked down the next cross street, glimpsing Theo's sedan barreling through the intersection.

I kept pace like this for another half mile before he made a turn in the opposite direction. I slammed on my brakes and turned at that intersection, relieved it wasn't a one-way. My back tires squealed, and I hoped he didn't hear me coming.

Theo picked up speed. The erratic way he drove made me think he knew he was being followed. Maybe he heard my tires. By now, we were in a heavily trafficked area. He shouldn't have been able to spot me, given the precautions I'd taken and the cars I kept between us. But he seemed determined to flush me out.

I wanted to drop further back, but with the way he was driving, doing so would guarantee I'd lose him. And after the other night, I had to keep him in my sights without giving myself away. He was three cars ahead when a slow moving convertible cut in front of me. As soon as that happened, he gunned the engine, weaving in and out of the lanes and putting as much distance between us as possible. In the dark, identifying his vehicle was harder, but I kept my eyes on his taillights as I maneuvered around the convertible.

Theo made a sharp turn without signaling, nearly losing me in the process. I'd come too far to let him vanish like he did the other night. He wasn't going to get the best of me again, so I sped up and made the turn, realizing too late he had pulled onto a secluded street.

The sedan zipped around a curve, the rear tires skidding before disappearing from sight. With no other drivers on the road, he'd make me if I followed him. The smart thing to do would be back off and let him get away. I could always get to his location once he stopped, but my gut said he'd be long gone by the time I found his car.

That thought irked me. This asshole had been playing games since before I even started following him. He always took different routes home. He went to different restaurants. Maybe I wasn't the only person following him. But no one else was out tonight.

Weighing my options, I decided to push him. We'd had a few close calls. For all I knew, he already made me, which would explain his erratic driving. But it was a bad idea, and I knew it. I just didn't care.

Instead of backing off, I sped up until I was right on top of him. At first, he drove faster, more erratically, but he couldn't shake me. So he did the smart thing and slowed down. He rolled down his window and waved me past him, like I was just another pissed off motorist.

"You bastard." I had to give him credit. He was smart. Too smart.

I flashed my headlights and zipped around him, wondering where we were after all those turns. A glance at the GPS told me we were approaching the arts district. But this neighborhood didn't appear as busy or bustling as the images on the tourist websites.

I kept my eyes on my mirror, wondering what Theo planned to do now. The next intersection led to a main road. Unsure which way to turn, I waited to go left, figuring it'd buy time and give Theo a chance to catch up. Once the light changed, I turned.

Theo went right. I kept my eyes on the mirror, moving at a crawl. Just like the other night, Theo turned into a nearby parking garage. Since there was another car in front of him, he had to wait to enter.

Slamming on my brakes, I yanked the steering wheel hard and turned around. Luckily, the other motorists had seen my insane driving and kept their distance from me. By now, Theo had pulled into the garage.

I followed suit, pressing a button and waiting for the machine to spit out the ticket. From my position, I could see Theo's taillights as he maneuvered up the ramp. As soon as the boom gate lifted, I killed my lights and followed him. He went up to the fourth level before pulling into a space.

I kept my eyes on him while I parked on the opposite side of the garage. With my lights already off, he might not have seen me. At least, that's what I was hoping.

He opened his door and got out. After checking his phone, he typed out a message with his thumbs. He did a little one-legged dance as he shoved the phone into his pocket and headed for the stairs.

As soon as he started going down, I ran after him. The rubber soles of my shoes barely made a sound against the concrete floor. Slowing, I hesitated at the stairwell door. He didn't take anything with him, but that didn't mean he wasn't armed. His pockets might have been full of something if he had that much trouble stowing his phone.

But the police searched the house after I did. If he had another firearm, someone would have found it. Still, I had to be careful. Theo was on edge. When backed into a corner, animals usually attacked. More than likely, he'd do the same.

Once Theo reached the bottom level, I went down the stairs at a fast clip. *Don't fall,* my internal voice warned. Visions of me falling face first down the concrete steps played through my head as I raced to the bottom. It hadn't taken me more than ten seconds to get down the stairs. Theo should still be close.

I paused at the door, which was held open with a wooden doorstop that had seen better days. Dirt and debris had collected at the bottom of the stairs and around the doorframe. Carefully, I stepped around it, not wanting to make any noise and alert Theo to my presence.

But when I stepped out of the stairwell, I didn't immediately see him. The garage lights provided enough illumination to see all the way to the exit, but Theo wasn't walking toward it. I scanned the vicinity. No Theo. He couldn't have made it out of the garage that quickly, even at a dead run, so I turned to look behind me.

A large support pillar blocked most of my view. As soon as I made my way around it, Theo stepped out of the shadows. He cleared his throat, making sure I noticed him. He held a metal pipe down near his side. I wasn't sure where he'd gotten it, but he hadn't brought it with him.

"Who are you? Why are you following me?" He didn't lift the pipe, but he adjusted his grip. The metal of his wedding ring clicked against the pipe, causing a high-pitched echo to reverberate a few times in the garage.

I looked behind him. I didn't spot another human being, but I saw a few security cameras. "I don't know what you're talking about."

He took a step toward me. "You were behind me. I saw you."

"Whatever you say, man." I held up my palms. "That doesn't mean you can threaten me."

"No?" He took another step closer. I backed up, my hand moving slowly toward my shoulder holster, beneath my jacket. Too sudden of a move, and he'd lash out with the pipe.

He forced me into the stairwell. Again, he was smart. The security cameras were outside the stairwell door. If he attacked me here, it wouldn't get recorded. But it'd be pretty damn obvious what happened.

"I saw you at the hospital, lurking around my car. I know you've been following me for days. You came to my house. You told the cops about the gun." He took another step closer, kicking the doorstop out of the way. "What do you think you're going to find?"

My fingers wrapped around the solid handle of my nine millimeter. "You need to back off."

"Who are you?" he asked again. "Why are you following me?"

"I'm not, but if you don't get away from me, I'll call the cops."

"And tell them what?" His eyes narrowed, and he took a step back, his hands coming up to hip height. "Fine, but if I ever see you again, you'll regret it. Stay out of my business. And stay the fuck away from my wife. If you go near her, I'll kill you." Without warning, he lunged forward, grabbed the door handle, and pulled it closed. He slid the pipe between the push bar and the door, leaving one end sticking out at a diagonal so I couldn't get the door open. He held the bar tightly, making sure I couldn't get out while he looked from side to side for a way to secure it in place.

"Son of a bitch." I rammed the door with my shoulder, making the glass and metal rattle. "Let me out."

Theo glared at me. "I won't tell you again."

Headlights bounced off the concrete floor behind him. A moment later, a dark SUV stopped beside him. "Help." I banged against the door, but the person in the vehicle didn't get out. With the SUV's tinted windows, I couldn't see who was inside. Theo sneered at me before letting go of the pipe and racing toward the car.

I kicked the door, causing the pipe to fall free from the push bar. It clanged against the floor, making a rattling noise as I pulled the door open. By the time I cleared the stairwell, Theo had gotten into the waiting SUV which was now gaining speed as it headed for the exit.

Sprinting after it, I assumed it'd have to stop at the boom gate, but the arm rose like magic, and the SUV sped off. I tried to get the license plate before it disappeared around the corner, but it didn't have a plate.

I looked around, wondering where the SUV had come from or how long it'd been waiting. For Theo to have a getaway driver, whatever he was doing behind Iris's back was a lot worse than any affair. This was some serious shit.

Reaching into my pocket, I pulled out my phone and checked the tracker I placed on his phone. I'd be able to pick up his trail, but I needed to change cars first. I didn't want him to see me coming. The only way I'd find out what he was up to was by sneaking up on him. So far, I hadn't had much luck.

I jogged back to the stairwell and went up the steps to my car, angry at myself for getting caught. Before leaving, I decided to check his car. Smashed on the ground beside the driver's door was the device I'd planted beneath his rear bumper. Theo had found it. He must have looked after he spotted me at the hospital. But why would he have thought to do that?

Since I'd already been burnt, I pulled out my lockpicks and opened his trunk. Everything that had been inside was gone. He hadn't unloaded it when he got home, so he must have done it while he was at the hospital. Where did he put that stuff, and why was he in such a rush to get rid of it?

The last thing he said echoed in my brain. *Stay the fuck away from my wife*. Fearing for Iris's safety, I called Nero and asked if he could send a couple of guys to guard her from a distance. Since I didn't know what Theo was up to, I had no way of knowing what he was capable of doing, but if the items in his trunk, the clothes in the garbage, or the podcasts he listened to were any indication, Theo Stapleton was a very dangerous man.

TWENTY-SEVEN

I kept an eye on Theo's movements while I waited in the garage. He'd been circling the city for a while, stopping periodically for a few minutes before moving farther from the garage. His route made no sense. He'd double-back and circle several times before moving on. Even now, he feared he was being followed.

From what I could tell from his crazy trajectory, Theo was headed west toward the beach. He wouldn't be back anytime soon. A part of me wondered if he'd be back at all. He knew he was caught. Okay, he wasn't exactly caught since I had no idea what he was doing, but he knew I was on to him. He suspected Iris was on to him. And so were the police. He had to tread carefully. Assuming he killed someone the other night or had been killing people for a while, which was where my thoughts were leaning, he'd cut and run. That'd be the smart move, and Theo was no dummy.

I checked the time. It was getting late. Iris would be getting out of the meeting in a few minutes. Was Theo planning on showing up there?

"Hey, Parker." Omar, another of Cross's security specialists, walked up the ramp. "I brought a new tracker for Theo's car. Which one is it?" Omar had come prepared with surveillance equipment and trackers. After setting up a few pinholes cameras throughout the garage and installing a low jack under the hood where Theo would be unlikely to find it, he exhaled. "You always get made?"

"Not usually, but this guy has me off my game. He was supposed to be a bored, philandering husband. Instead, he's looking more like a killer. And a paranoid one at that." I showed Omar the red blip circling one of the sketchier downtown neighborhoods.

"Blame it on the jet lag."

"I've been in California too long for that."

"The Santa Ana's then. They call them the devil winds for a reason. They cause all kinds of problems. They're worse than any full moon with the way people and animals react."

I laughed. "Isn't it the wrong time of year?"

"I'm trying to help you by coming up with some excuses."

"In that case, can you do me a favor?"

"What's that?"

"I need to trade cars." I held out my keys.

"The SUV's bulletproof. Artillery is in the trunk. We got a locker in there. Let me give you the combination. Zero, four, seven, nine, two, one."

"Got it."

"You need backup?"

"I hope not."

"Just say the word."

"Right now, I need you guys to keep an eye on his house and his wife. If you head to their address now, you might have time to set up surveillance."

"You think he's going to hurt her?"

"I have no idea. She doesn't think so, but I don't think she has any idea who she married."

"All right." He bumped his fist against the side of my crossed arms. "You got the number. Call if you need anything."

"Will do." Getting behind the wheel of the SUV, I adjusted the seat and mirrors and followed Omar out of the garage, getting a feel for driving such a heavy vehicle. The armor weighed it down, as did whatever the security team kept stashed in the back.

The tracker on Theo's phone showed he'd finally stopped circling that neighborhood. He'd moved on, heading in a straight line. After a few minutes, the blip stopped moving at such a fast speed. Theo must have gotten out of the car. I checked the address and headed to his location. This time, he wasn't going to see me coming.

Theo needed to believe he scared me off. That's the only way I'd figure out what he was up to. After I collected evidence or found proof he was involved in something illegal, I could call Detective Petrocelli, but he'd probably arrest me for interfering in a police investigation or for conducting illegal surveillance. I could call Will, but this was out of his jurisdiction. And I didn't think he'd want to help anyway. It'd be best to play this by ear.

Before I reached Theo's location, he took off again. "Dammit." But he wasn't headed home. He kept moving farther west. A sinking feeling came over me. Was he headed to Malibu? That didn't seem likely. He asked who I was, which meant he didn't know, unless he used a phone-a-friend. But I didn't think Iris would give me up. However, she had plenty of first responder friends, many of whom were cops. Theo must have known a good deal of them for Petrocelli to act the way he did during the search. Any one of them could have gotten my name and given it to Theo, or he'd found me in hospital records since I'd spent a good chunk of Wednesday morning in the ER. They'd have my address, phone number, and Martin's information.

Realizing I was paranoid, I pushed the thought aside and continued to where Theo had stopped. The area was sketchy. A single street light flickered, casting eerie shadows against the buildings. The neon open sign buzzed and sizzled as it blinked. It hung from the pharmacy door, but with the graffiti, boarded-up window from a recent break-in, and what might have been bullet holes in the brick, it looked like something out of a slasher film.

Reluctantly, I got out of the car, unzipped my jacket, and kept my hand on my gun. When I pushed the door open, the buzzing of the overhead fluorescent lights was the only sound in the place. No music. No talking. Nothing. A woman sat behind the register, reading a magazine.

I went down the first aisle, glancing up at the curved mirror which was positioned for added security. The razors were locked behind a case, as were most of the expensive items and contraceptives. Near the back, a man with a vest and name tag mopped the floor. The reddish-tint to the water made me curious.

"Excuse me," I said.

He looked up, wary of my presence. "Yes?"

"Is everything okay?" I nodded toward the floor.

"Just a little accident. Do you need something?"

"I was looking for the feminine care aisle." That usually kept men from asking too many questions.

"Aisle four."

"Thanks."

On the ground, I spotted blood droplets. A few had smeared, leaving behind shoeprints. I followed the trail, which led to a door marked authorized personnel. Glancing behind me to make sure no one was paying attention, I stood on my tiptoes and peered through the tiny square window. A brick kept the back door from closing. Through the tiny crack, I could see the alleyway behind the pharmacy.

By now, Theo was miles away, but he'd been here. I went to the front counter, picked up a pack of gum and a candy bar, and handed them to the woman. "Exciting night?" I asked.

"Does it look like it?"

"It looks like someone bled on the floor."

"Nah, that's ketchup." The look on her face told me not to press the issue.

I stared into her eyes. "Are you sure? I'm on my way out. I could call someone."

She put my change on the counter. "Have a nice day," she said sharply.

I went outside and around the side of the building until I reached the back door. I pulled it open and stepped around the brick doorstop. A few blood droplets had fallen on the tile here, but given the way they landed, whoever had been bleeding had been on his way out. Was this Theo's doing?

I checked the off-limits area. Bloody bandages had been tossed into the overflowing trash can inside the restroom. *No body, no crime*, but I didn't buy it.

Sneaking out the back door, I turned on my flashlight and held it beneath my gun as I made my way down the alley. After a few steps, I didn't find any more blood. I checked the dumpster, but it was empty. No body. No bandages. And with no witnesses, I had nothing.

I called in an anonymous tip to the police, reported suspicious activity, and returned to the SUV. Thankfully, it hadn't been jacked or stripped in my absence. Theo's phone showed him still on the move. The blip paused briefly, but he might have been stopped at a traffic light.

I expanded the map. If he kept on his current trajectory, he'd be in Malibu in twenty minutes.

Martin. I had to get home. I couldn't risk Theo coming after the man I loved. Rational thought told me that wasn't the case, but I had to be sure. Theo could have gotten my info if he wanted it, and with the way he came at me in that garage, he wanted it bad.

I arrived home before Theo reached his destination. He wasn't more than five miles from here, but he was circling again. However, it looked like he was heading north. I decided to wait until Theo settled before leaving the house. The last thing I needed was for him to notice another tail. But given his erratic driving, he already suspected a tail, even if it wasn't me. Who did he think was out to get him?

How had things gotten so out of control? How could I have let myself fall into his trap and get caught, not once, not twice, but three damn times? Mark would give me such an ass-chewing for this.

"Stupid. Stupid. Stupid." I wasn't a rookie. I'd served my time as a federal agent. And I'd been at this private sector thing long enough. But when it came to surveilling Theo Stapleton, I'd made every mistake in the book, starting with not taking the case seriously enough and underestimating the target.

Maybe Theo was smart enough to get away with murder. I feared what he'd do to Iris. He knew she was the reason I was sniffing around. It wouldn't have taken much for him to figure that out, but if he was as dangerous as I suspected, her life could be at risk.

Nero would protect her. But what if Theo did something to her in the middle of the night? He could suffocate her with a pillow, and the security detail outside would never know. We needed to get cameras inside their house. I sent a text to Omar, hoping he found a way inside.

We got this, he replied.

I tried calling Iris, but she didn't answer. I'd seen her turn her phone off during meetings before. Maybe she forgot to turn it back on. By now, the meeting should have wrapped, unless she was talking to someone or had gone to get a drink. That could go on for hours. So I called Nero for an update.

"I'm looking right at her," he said. "She's at a bar with a bottle of wine to keep her company."

"All right. Keep an eye out for her husband."

"Yes, ma'am."

I rubbed a hand down my face, wondering if I told Iris what was going on if she'd warn Theo. Given how she reacted when I told her about the bloody shirt, I had a feeling she'd side with him. In her mind, he was cheating. That was the beginning and end of it. She didn't believe he was capable of hurting anyone. But his stunt in the stairwell and the bloody shirt in the trash proved otherwise.

Martin came into the room, watching me pace back and forth, occasionally taking out my frustration on the free-standing bag with a jab or kick. "You should wrap your hands and wear gloves. You're going to shred your knuckles or break your hand."

"I don't care." I took a step back and kicked the bag, letting out a frustrated grunt. "I'm a moron."

"Careful. You're talking about the woman I love." He reached for the training gloves, but I shook out my arms and stepped away from the bag. It was smaller than the one at home, but it came with the house, like the exercise bench and free weights. It wasn't much of a home gym. It didn't even have a treadmill. But Martin had made use of it when he wasn't surfing, swimming, or running. "What's going on?" He eyed me. "You're still in your work clothes. Are you going back out?"

"Yes, soon." I didn't want to admit the reason for returning. It'd make him worry. "I'm trying to figure out what to do. I've really fucked this case up. It was supposed to be simple. Follow the cheating spouse. Take photos. Turn it over to the wife. Case closed. Instead, I'm chasing Jason Bourne."

"He doesn't remember who he is?"

"No, he knows exactly who he is. I, on the other hand, have no fucking clue who he is. I don't think his wife does either. He made me tonight. Actually, he made me the other night and again this afternoon at the hospital. I'm oh for three."

"Hospital? Are you okay? Is this about the other morning? Are you having issues or symptoms?" He reached for me, cupping my cheek in his hand while he assessed my appearance.

"I'm fine. The hospital is where he works." I didn't know how Theo knew I was outside. His car didn't have a security system. I checked. How did he know I was messing with it? I didn't think the mom and kid narced on me. Maybe hospital security had, but they should have had better things to do.

Martin let go of my face and lifted my right hand, examining my knuckles. Since I'd only thrown a few punches, my flesh remained intact. Martin pressed his lips to my hand and stared into my eyes. "You think he's a spy?"

"He's...something."

"Trained?"

"Aware." A stray thought crossed my mind. The night Theo heard me inspecting his trash, he came out of the garage with a bat. Today, he came at me with a pipe, which he found somewhere in the parking garage or stairwell. Why didn't he have a knife or gun? Pipes were distance weapons, like bats. He didn't want to get too close. Most assailants had no problem getting up close and personal. Was he afraid? Could he have attacked someone else with a club-like weapon? Could that be how the blood got on the shirt? It seemed unlikely, but anything was possible. Again, thoughts of the homeless being attacked, beaten, and held at gunpoint came to mind. "Stop it," I hissed.

Martin looked concerned. "Stop what?"

"Not you. Me." I pulled my hand out of his grip. "I need to figure out what Theo's doing." I checked his location, finding he had drifted farther north. "Now that I know it's safe, I should head out."

"I was hoping you changed your mind."

"About what?" I left the room, heading for the bedroom to grab a spare magazine and change into something more appropriate for nighttime maneuvers.

"Flying home with me."

I stopped abruptly in the doorway. My suitcase was on the floor. Martin's bag was opened on the bed. It looked like he'd stuffed half of the closet into his garment bag. "I thought you were coming back."

"I am."

"When?"

"Two days."

"Why are you taking all your clothes? You have clothes at home. In fact, there's no reason why you need to pack anything." I entered the room and tapped the suitcase with my foot. "What are you doing with my bag?"

"I figured I'd change out my wardrobe and grab some of your things while I was at it."

"A suit is a suit."

He scowled at me, not bothering to respond to my astute observation. "You always pack light, and no matter how many times I've offered to take you shopping, you refuse. You could use a few more things. We have several weeks left in this house. Don't you want anything?"

I unzipped my suitcase, finding it empty. "I don't need much. This looks about right."

"You need work clothes and light layers. Every time we go out on the beach at night, you steal my sweatshirt."

"I didn't think you minded." I gave him a sly smile. "And

when we come back inside, that oversized sweatshirt is all I'm wearing while I lounge around, bored and lonely."

"I do enjoy taking it off of you." His eyes twinkled. "Stop distracting me from my point."

"What is your point?"

"We live here now. Even if it's temporary. You should have the things that make you comfortable and the necessities."

"I got it covered."

He didn't believe me. "I'll grab a few of your things from home, unless you'll let me take you shopping."

"We went shopping and you bought me that t-shirt that says Los Angeles. If you play your cards right, I could be persuaded to get something that says Santa Monica. Other than that, I have everything I need right here."

"Hardly." He put a few more things in his suitcase before zipping it shut. He turned, finding me searching the drawers. "What are you looking for?"

"Dark colors."

"See, this is why you need more clothes."

"Fine." I pulled a black form-fitting outfit from the dresser. After changing, I secured my shoulder holster, filled the pockets with the essentials, and shook out my shoulders.

Martin stopped what he was doing to watch me. "Are you planning a strike or conducting surveillance?"

"I'll be fine."

"You didn't answer the question."

"That's because I don't know." I gave him a kiss. "In the event you have to leave before I get home, have a safe flight. Call me when you land."

"I'm not sure I can do that. Here's my counter. Get home before I leave."

"No promises, but I'll do my best."

"Alexis, I'm serious. It's my jet. It leaves when I tell it, so I'm not going anywhere until I know you're safe."

"You can't do that. You have meetings."

He shrugged. "Too bad."

"Martin."

"Alex."

I exhaled. "You can be so damn stubborn sometimes."
"What can I say? I learned from the best."

TWENTY-EIGHT

I parked the SUV and waited. Theo had circled this neighborhood twice already. It was far enough inland that the sight and smell of the ocean was nothing more than a distant memory. Given the overpowering scent of hot trash, urine, and something rotten, I wondered what Theo hoped to find here.

The tinted windows made me invisible. Only a handful of vehicles had passed since I'd parked. The young men I spotted across the street wore gang colors. The sideways caps, baggy pants, and excessive bling made me think this was where Hollywood came up with the stereotype.

After they disappeared into one of the apartment buildings, I shifted my focus to the other end of the street where a sex worker and a drug dealer were haggling over the price of something. The sex worker wasn't willing to back down. Eventually, the dealer put something in her hand and gave her a kiss.

"I'll get you next time," she promised, tucking the item into her brassiere and walking away.

As soon as she disappeared down one of the dark alleys, the SUV that had picked up Theo approached the corner where the dealer remained. It came to a stop, the passenger window sliding down. I checked the tracker to make sure Theo was inside. He was.

I couldn't hear their exchange, so I lowered the back windows another inch, but that didn't help. Their voices were muffled. The dealer rested his elbows on the window frame and leaned in to talk to them.

I zoomed in with my camera, but besides spotting the dealer gesturing vehemently, I couldn't see through the tinted windows of the SUV. Obviously, Theo and his pal had the same advantages I did, which proved to be a disadvantage for me. After thirty seconds, the dealer stepped away, but Theo called him back to the vehicle and handed the dealer a small paper bag.

Cash? I had no idea what was in the bag, but I clicked the shutter on the camera a few times, capturing as much of the exchange as possible. The dealer handed something to Theo so seamlessly I couldn't tell what it was, but it had been contained within his palm. I guessed it was something Theo couldn't get from the hospital. Cocaine? Meth? I wasn't sure.

Before the SUV pulled away, I closed the windows. They drove past me, oblivious to my presence. This time, they didn't circle. They kept going straight. It looked like they'd concluded whatever business they had here. Theo had gotten what he wanted, whatever that was. Now where was he going?

The dealer rolled up the paper bag and shoved it into his pocket. The tracker on Theo's phone showed he was moving straight down the street. It looked like he had a destination in mind. No more circling or backtracking. Perhaps, he was on his way home. I watched the blip continue north, briefly slowing or stopping at intersections. If Theo was headed back to the garage, he was going the wrong way.

Deciding not to follow blindly after Theo, I got out of the armored vehicle and moved down the street. The dealer had returned to his spot near the fire escape of an apartment building. He'd taken a seat on the bottom rung of the ladder and sucked on the end of a vape pen.

"Hey." I approached with my hands where he could see

them.

He nodded, his eyes narrowing. He knew I was carrying. “Something I can do for you?”

“I was hoping you could hook me up.” I moved into the alleyway, finding the smell had only gotten worse.

“You got the wrong idea.” He blew out a puff of vapor. “Best if you keep moving.” He peered at my parked car. “Have a nice night, officer.”

“I’m not a cop.”

“Funny thing, they always say that.”

“I’m not.”

“Yeah, whatever.”

“I was hoping you could tell me what you know about the guy who gave you that bag in your pocket.”

“What bag?” He looked down. “I don’t see a bag.”

“I’m not a cop,” I repeated. “Look, let’s make this simple. I’ll pay you for information.”

“I’m listening.”

Holding up one hand, I reached into my jacket pocket with the other and pulled out the cash I kept there. “Where’s he going?”

“Do I look like a mind reader?”

I didn’t believe him for a second. “It looked like you were giving him directions.”

“Nope.”

“Okay.” I held out a hundred dollar bill. “What’s in the bag?”

“Seriously?” He snatched the cash out of my hand and shoved it into his pocket.

“Show me.”

“You’re crazy, lady. But I kinda got a thing for crazy.” He pulled the bag out of his pocket and opened it, holding up an inhaler. “Dude brings me my medicine sometimes.”

I stared at him. “You have asthma?”

“Yeah, so?”

“You’re vaping.”

He snorted. “You sound just like him. Dude needs to chill out. So do you.” He glanced back at my parked vehicle. “I’d offer to help you with that, but y’know, I don’t want to get arrested.”

I didn't argue. "What else is in the bag?"

He reached in a pulled out some Narcan. "He doesn't want things to get dicey out here."

"Does he buy drugs from you? Is this a barter system?" I held out another hundred dollar bill.

"You really think I'd admit to selling. Jeez, you are crazy. Man can do whatever he wants as far as I'm concerned. What he wants to put in his body is none of my business. And as far as bartering goes, I wouldn't mind bartering with you." He made a kissy face.

"What did you give him in exchange for the bag?"

"I gave him what he wanted," the guy said, but he wouldn't go into detail.

"How often does Theo come around here?"

"Theo? Is that his name? I didn't know."

"Cut the bull."

"About once a week. Whenever he needs something."

"Does he have a problem?" Since the dealer was too careful to admit to committing a crime, I had to find another way to ask the question.

"For sure. No matter what he does, he can't quite shake it. Works out for me, though."

"Thanks." I took a step back. "Do you know if he owes anyone or if someone's got a score to settle?"

"I mind my own business. You should do the same. It's not worth getting in the middle of other people's shit."

"That's my job."

"Shitty job."

"You could make it easier by telling me where he's going or who's after him."

"All I can say is he's chasing his demons while they chase him."

That vague answer didn't help, but it looked like Iris's initial fear may have been correct. Her husband had a drug problem. That explained why he bought the gun. He'd need the protection. But for an addict, he was good at hiding it from most of the world. He didn't miss work. As far as I knew, he'd never gotten pulled over for driving while intoxicated. But that would explain why he'd disappear for hours at a time. He'd know better than to go home high.

"What about the other person in the car?"

"Person?" the dealer asked.

"Who was driving?"

He shrugged. "How should I know?"

"Have you seen him before?"

"Him?"

"Her?" I tried again.

"I don't pay attention. It's best not to. Now if you'll excuse me." He climbed the steps to the fire escape and kept going.

I checked my phone, finding the tracker had finally stopped. By now, it was approaching midnight. Traffic had lessened. I followed the GPS until I found the SUV parked on the street. The dark windows made it impossible to tell if the driver remained with the vehicle, but the tracking app on Theo's phone told me he'd gotten out. The red dot hadn't moved in the last five minutes.

I parked on the next cross street, grabbed my surveillance equipment, made sure my gun was easily accessible, and got out of the armored vehicle. I headed for Theo's location on foot, growing more uneasy the closer I got.

The tracker led me to the side of a condemned building. The notice on the door said it was unsafe. Given the scorch marks and burn patterns, it must have been the scene of a fire.

Assuming Theo and his buddy had just scored, they'd want to go somewhere secluded. But the door was chained and locked. I backed away, reading what little was left of the sign. All I could make out was *Clinic*. I went around the side, looking for another way in. Pieces of broken glass littered the ground around the building.

Voices sounded from within. Two men. One of them was laughing or crying. I couldn't be sure, but the hysterical gasps came at random, frantic intervals. A high-pitched wail followed that made my blood run cold. It sounded like a dying animal.

Avoiding the jagged glass shards hanging from the frame, I climbed through the broken window and tiptoed along the corridor. Everything was covered in ash and soot.

I avoided the broken pieces on the floor, not wanting to give away my presence as I made my way deeper inside.

The building was set up like most walk-in clinics. A doorway from the waiting room led to a hallway with several exam rooms. Following the sound of voices, I stopped when the hallway branched sharply to the right.

I pressed against the wall and peered around the corner. Theo and another man, perhaps the SUV's driver, were seated side by side on the floor of a large, empty room. It might have been a lab or some kind of testing facility, but with all the damage, I couldn't be certain what it was. Whatever equipment it once contained had been removed.

"I got you," Theo said. "Let me help." He bit the cap off a syringe before injecting it into the other man's upper arm.

"Shit," the guy slurred.

"Give it a minute." Theo leaned his head back against the brick and closed his eyes. It looked like he was praying. The other man took an uneasy breath, but he didn't speak. "Let me know when you feel it kick in."

Theo remained with his eyes closed, his face skyward. The other man's hysterics came less frequently. From where I remained hidden in the shadows, I could hear him panting. Theo appeared to have passed out. He hadn't moved since he injected his friend.

This was bad. I hated seeing it, but there wasn't much I could do at this point. Theo needed help. But given the extremes he went to keep his addiction a secret, I didn't think he was open to the idea of rehab.

After making sure the flash wouldn't go off, I snapped a few photos. Iris had her proof. Maybe she'd take some solace in seeing Theo with another man instead of a woman. But this wasn't how she imagined I'd find him.

I tucked the camera away, wondering who the unidentified man was. He looked ragged. His clothes were dirty, like he'd fished them out of the dumpster. He kept his face obscured with a worn Dodgers' cap. The bill had been pulled down low, making it impossible to see anything above his upper lip. All I could see was a layer of unkempt scruff. How did a man like that afford the fancy SUV?

On appearances alone, I didn't think he could. Did they steal the car? Is that why they'd been so careful all night? How many places had they gone to score before arriving here? I thought about the blood droplets at the pharmacy. Was the man injured? When did that happen? How did it happen?

I squatted down, searching for a closer vantage point that wouldn't give away my position. But the debris and rubble didn't offer any cover. I glanced up, realizing a section of the roof was missing. No wonder the building was condemned. A strong enough quake would make the rest of it crumble in on itself.

How often did Theo come here? If he wanted to get high, why didn't they park in some garage and stay in the SUV? It'd be safer than this.

The man beside Theo finally stopped making those random noises. Theo opened his eyes. "How are you feeling?" Theo asked, shifting a little and sitting up. He turned toward his nearly unconscious friend. Something in the hallway caught his eye, and he looked up.

Immediately, I pressed my back against the wall. But I didn't think he'd seen me. It was too dark inside. But I didn't move. I didn't even breathe. I waited for him to settle. Shuffling noises sounded from within that room, followed by the screech of a table sliding across the floor. I hadn't seen one, but I could only see partially into the room. Was someone else in there? Was Theo coming out to investigate?

I clutched my flashlight in one hand and my gun in the other. I didn't know if he was armed, but he'd surprised me one too many times for me to be unprepared for our next encounter. But the shuffling stopped. Another metallic groan sounded within the room.

"This won't be so bad," Theo said. "Try to relax."

The other man screamed in agony.

Tightening the grip on my gun, I peered around the corner. Theo held something shiny in his hand.

"No. Don't. Get away. Please. Don't touch me. Leave me be," the other man begged for his life. Another scream escaped his lips.

I couldn't let this happen. I clicked on my flashlight and spun around the corner, aiming into the room. The scalpel glinted back at me, blood dripping from the tip of the blade. "Drop the knife, Theo."

The other man was no longer on the ground, but atop an exam table, which Theo had moved closer to the hole in the roof in order to see what he was doing. The man let out a shrill gasp, using the distraction to roll off the table. He landed hard on the floor, swallowing his scream and scrambling to put some space between himself and Theo. But he couldn't quite get his feet underneath him. A dark stain covered the side of his shirt, leaving a thick wet smear along the ash-covered floor as he dragged himself toward the doorway.

"You heard me," I repeated. "Put it down. Now."

"You don't understand." Theo's grip tightened on the surgical tool.

The man let out a pitiful sound, clutching his side while he rolled onto his back.

"Drop it or I'll drop you." I stepped around the corner. I couldn't risk calling for help until Theo dropped the scalpel.

Theo squinted, but he couldn't see me clearly with the light in his eyes. "I told you to stay away from me. You're gonna regret this. Get away from me while you still can."

"You're the only one with regrets." I took a step toward him, hoping to put myself between him and his next kill. He wasn't high or stoned, at least not to a noticeable level. But he'd acted like it only minutes before. That must have been how he lured out his victims. What kind of sick bastard did Iris marry?

Theo stepped toward me. "You don't get it. I have to do this."

"No, you don't." I spoke calmly, forcefully. The way I'd been taught at Quantico. Take charge. Deescalate the situation. "A gun in a knife fight wins every time. You're at a disadvantage. I don't want to hurt you, but I will if you don't put the blade down."

Theo didn't let go of the weapon. Instead, he looked around, searching for another option or a better weapon.

"This is none of your business. Walk away before things get worse. You being here is making it worse. Go. Now."

"Worse?" I didn't think he had a gun, but I couldn't be sure. I glanced down at the man who'd crawled to the doorway, but he hadn't moved in the last few seconds. Placing myself between him and Theo, I pointed the barrel of my gun at Theo's chest. "I won't let you hurt him."

"Hurt him? I'm helping him."

"By cutting into him?"

The man moaned, the panting getting louder. I knelt down, wanting to call 9-1-1 but afraid to drop the flashlight and lose sight of Theo. While keeping one eye on him, I lifted the guy's shirt, but there was too much blood to see how deep the cut was.

Theo stepped toward me, changing his grip on the scalpel from holding it like a precision tool to the way one would hold a dagger. Glass cracked beneath his feet. I leveled the flashlight and gun at his chest.

"Back up," I ordered. "Lose the scalpel now. I won't ask you again."

He caught the look on my face. "Take it easy. It's okay. I've got this under control." His tone changed, like he was dealing with a distraught patient.

Glass crunched beneath his shoe, except Theo hadn't moved. It sounded again. This time, behind me. I turned in time to see a figure rushing toward me.

TWENTY-NINE

I barely had enough time to shift my weight and pivot before the figure crashed into me. Even after compensating, he nearly knocked me to the ground before colliding with the wall. But that didn't slow him down. He bounced off the ashy surface and came at me again, shouting a battle cry.

The gun in my hand didn't deter him. He rammed me with his shoulder, his head down, like a charging bull. The force knocked me against the wall. I let go of the flashlight, needing a free hand.

"Stop," Theo shouted.

The assailant grabbed something off the ground and swung at me. I jumped back. Without the beam of light to guide my aim, I didn't want to fire my weapon. Instead, I shoved it into my holster and raised my hands, prepared to fight. Nothing could ever be simple.

The shuffling sounded again from within the room. Theo was moving. I couldn't let him finish what he'd started. The man with the stab wound let out another wail, but I couldn't get to him. The figure who'd attacked me from behind came at me again.

He raised his arms overhead and swung downward. I

dodged, sliding to the side and kicking my right leg into the air. The ball of my foot impacted against his solar plexus, resulting in a satisfying oomph. Nearby, something buzzed.

"Stop," Theo tried again.

"Fat chance," I mumbled, sliding across the floor toward the dropped flashlight.

Just as my fingers latched around it, the assailant, who I thought I'd put down, got back up. He ran at me, knocking into me sideways. I moved with his momentum. We rolled on the ground. The pieces of broken glass bit into my skin as we wrestled on the floor. Throwing an elbow at his face, I heard the hit connect with a resounding crunch to his jaw.

Instantly, he went limp. I rolled him onto his stomach and ziptied his hands. One down. One to go.

The buzzing I'd been hearing for the last few seconds stopped. I pulled out my gun, creeping through the shadowy hallway toward the room. My flashlight remained on the ground, painting a cone of light on the soot covered floor. The injured man had been yanked back inside the room.

"Come out, Theo," I said. "You don't want to make matters worse than they are."

Theo edged to the doorway and grabbed my flashlight off the ground before I could and shone it in my eyes, temporarily blinding me. I aimed at the light.

"Take it easy," he said. "I don't want to hurt you." He pointed the light at the man I'd subdued before turning it back on me. "Who the hell are you?"

"Like you don't know."

Theo edged backward. "Are you a cop?"

Maybe Martin was right, and I needed to update my wardrobe. "I've gotten that a lot tonight." I aimed at him. "Get that light out of my eyes. Now." I didn't know if he had the scalpel. I had to assume he did, which meant if he came toward me, I'd have to shoot him. Cross wouldn't like that. Iris would like it even less, and frankly, I wasn't too keen on the idea either. But it was him or me. And Martin made me promise I'd always come home.

"Who sent you?" Theo asked.

Taking a risk, I lunged forward and grabbed the flashlight out of his hand and pointed it at him. “On your knees. Hands on your head. Don’t make me ask a second time.” The sound of crunching glass came from deeper within the room. I cast my flashlight toward the noise, finding another doorway on the other end. “Who’s with you?”

“No one.”

I circled around, keeping my gun pointed at him. I peered through the open door. A stray soda can rattled as it rolled on the floor. The boards had been removed from another gaping hole in the building just beyond the doorway. Whoever else had been here was now long gone.

I knelt down, checking the stab victim’s vitals. “Hang on, buddy. I got you.”

“So you are a cop,” Theo said, watching as I pulled out my phone.

“I’m not.” The screen showed a missed call. *Will.* But I didn’t have time to worry about that now. Instead, I dialed 9-1-1. “But if that’s what it takes to get you to comply, then fine. But those are your words, not mine.”

Theo lowered to one knee. “Don’t do this. You’re making a mistake. Let me help him.” He jerked his chin at the man he’d stabbed.

“And let you carve him up? I don’t think so.”

“He’ll die if I don’t.” Theo stared at me, determination in his eyes. “He’s been shot. I’m trying to save him.”

I tossed my handcuffs to Theo. “Put those on and lie flat on the floor. Don’t try anything or your friend here won’t be the only one with a hole in him.”

Theo did as I asked. I patted him down, but I didn’t find any weapons. The scalpel had landed on the floor beside a blue duffel bag, the same one I’d seen in Theo’s trunk earlier in the day. Finally, an operator answered. While I spoke to him, I pulled out the first aid supplies. A pool of blood had collected around the victim.

“Let me help,” Theo said. “We’re too far out. It’ll be eight minutes before anyone gets here, if they hurry, which they won’t. He might not have that long.”

“Don’t play innocent. You did this. I saw the blood on

the scalpel. He's not your first victim, is he? What about your friend?" I jerked my chin toward the man I'd knocked unconscious. "Do you take turns? Is this how you get your kicks? Is this what you do every time you sneak out of the house? How many people have you killed?"

"Killed? Whoa, lady, you've got this all wrong. I help them. And that guy," he jerked his chin toward the unconscious man, "is not my friend."

"That's not what the evidence suggests." I grabbed the gauze. "What about your other accomplice? The one who escaped. Is that the SUV's driver?"

"You've been watching me." He stared at me from his spot on the floor while I packed the wound, hoping to slow the bleeding to buy this guy enough time for the paramedics to arrive. "But you haven't been paying attention. I'm a nurse. I took an oath to help people. It's not always easy, but I do what I can, however I can. I won't apologize for that."

"Really? It doesn't look that way to me."

He nodded toward the wounded man. "We came out here to save lives."

"Right, that's why your friend with the broken jaw attacked me."

"He's not my friend. He's in a gang. He's the reason we're out here tonight." Theo watched as I applied pressure to the wound. "There's duct tape in the bag."

"I'm not going to duct tape him together. Are you insane?"

"It'll help."

I glanced back at the unconscious man, making sure he was down for the count.

"Why would I carry first aid supplies if my goal was to kill him?" Theo asked.

"I don't know. Why'd you stop to score before coming here?"

"He needed something for the pain." Theo sighed, his eyes on the victim. "Check his pulse."

I pressed my fingers to the victim's neck. "Fast."

"That means he'll bleed out faster. His heart's pumping extra hard on account of the blood loss. I can help."

"Help's on the way. You and your buddy have done more than enough." I jerked my head toward the unconscious man. "You say he's not your friend. Who is he?"

"Damien."

"That doesn't tell me much."

"I still don't know who you are."

"I'm a private investigator, hired to keep an eye on you."

"By whom?"

"It doesn't matter."

"Certain people want me dead. It matters very much who hired you."

Theo's good guy act was pretty damn convincing. No wonder Iris thought she was losing her mind. "I'm not a gun for hire," I said. "If you're that afraid, you should have gone to the police."

"I have my reasons."

Of course, he did. He couldn't go to the police when he spent his nights reenacting his favorite slasher flicks. "Why don't you tell me how you ended up here? Maybe I can help."

He hesitated. His jaw clenched.

"You can tell me now, or tell the cops when they arrive. They are on the way. If you are as innocent as you claim, you're gonna need someone to back your story, and it doesn't look like your getaway driver is coming to save you this time."

"I saved someone I shouldn't have. A gunshot victim. He showed up at the hospital parking lot. He refused to come inside. He didn't want the police involved. It's illegal to treat a patient like that, but he would have died. A few days later, he shows up with some of his pals. They'd also been hurt, just not as badly. They threatened to kill me if I didn't keep my mouth shut. So I did."

"When was this?"

"Eight months ago."

"Is that why you bought the gun?"

"I needed a way to defend myself. These aren't nice people or nice neighborhoods."

I wasn't sure I believed it, but I let Theo continue.

"One day, a few of them showed up at the hospital and tried to follow me home. I'd been careful, but not careful enough," he said.

"Does your wife know you're moonlighting as a back-alley surgeon?"

He shook his head. "She doesn't need to. I just have to make sure they never figure out where I live. That's the only way to keep her safe."

"That doesn't explain why you didn't go to the police."

"What I did was illegal. I'd lose my job, at the least. Worse, I could face criminal charges."

It sounded reasonable, but Iris had connections. Theo should have come forward. "That was eight months ago. What did I walk into tonight?"

"Today, Damien showed up at work. He said I had to help him or else. He gave me a time and place to meet. When I got there, I found this guy bleeding out. GSW means it'll automatically get reported to the police. He begged me not to take him to the hospital. So I brought him here. That's it."

"Is this how the gang always reaches out to you? No phone calls or messaging apps?"

"Sometimes, they leave notes on my car. I hate it. But I don't think they know who I am. And I'll do whatever it takes to keep it that way."

"Do they text you in the middle of the night?" I asked.

"No."

"Someone does."

Theo licked his lips. "It's complicated."

"Simplify it."

"I can't."

"Did Damien or his crew have anything to do with your wife's accident?"

"God, no. I'd never help those sons of bitches."

"But you're helping these guys who are just as bad, if not worse."

"I'm keeping them from killing. Don't you get that?"

"You're not. At best, you're keeping them from dying."

Theo took an uneasy breath. "It's not just them." He sucked in a breath. "We come out to help other people too.

Those who are afraid or unable to get help through any other means. Illegals who are afraid they'll get reported. People without insurance. The homeless. A lot of times, we save victims of gang violence. Sometimes, that means helping these guys too. And sometimes, the victims and the perpetrators are one and the same. We can't pick and choose. Saving a life is saving a life. I don't want anyone to die. Period."

I filed that away for later. "How did Damien know what time things would pop off?"

"They had some kind of negotiation. He figured it'd result in a double-cross."

"Where did Damien tell you to meet him?"

"The pharmacy." Theo gave me the address. It was the same place I'd found the blood droplets. "That's where we picked up this guy. He's one of theirs."

I blinked, shaking my head which was starting to spin. "He's another banger? Like Damien?" I jerked my chin toward the unconscious man. "Are they part of the same gang?"

"I think so. Why else would Damien want me to save him?"

I narrowed my eyes, not sure what to believe. While I kept pressure on the man's abdomen, I searched his pockets. Once I found his wallet, I checked his ID and called Omar.

"Can you run a name for me?" I asked.

"It's not really what I do."

"But you know how?"

"Yeah."

"Great." I gave him the guy's name and date of birth.

"He's got a record. Vandalism and grand larceny."

"Nothing violent?"

"I'm not seeing anything."

"Run another name for me. Damien—" I waited for Theo to give me his last name, but he didn't know it.

"You mean the first guy's older brother?" Omar asked.

"That explains it." It must have been an initiation gone wrong. "What's his gang affiliation?" I asked.

"He's with the Slayers." Omar chuckled. "Do you want

to ask for backup, or should I show up and pretend it's a coincidence?"

"I'd say show up, and put a rush on it. Police are en route, but I don't want to walk outside to find a gang war brewing."

"Gotcha. Me and a couple of guys are five minutes out. Keep your head down until then."

I disconnected, giving Theo another look. The man with the gaping hole in his side suddenly gasped. His eyes opened for a moment, and then he convulsed.

"Let me help." Desperation leaked from Theo's voice.

"If he's one of them, why do you want to help him?"

"Look at him. He's just a kid."

There was a fifty-fifty chance Theo was lying to me. But the things he said made sense. And the dying man didn't have time for me to verify the facts. "Fine. I'll cut you loose, but if you try anything, these guys will be the least of your problems."

"Okay."

Reluctantly, I unhooked the handcuffs. "Keep him alive. Make a move for anything sharp, and it's the last thing you'll ever do."

"I got it." Theo knelt beside the guy who'd been in and out of consciousness for the last couple of minutes. He pressed hard against the hole in his abdomen, causing him to let out a shriek. Theo whispered apologetic and encouraging words to him. "He needs fluids. I have saline and an IV in my bag." I pulled them out and handed them to Theo. He ran a line, wide open, holding the bag on his shoulder while squeezing it. "Now, we wait." Theo peered in Damien's direction. "How is he?"

"He'll be eating out of a straw for a month. Glass jaw." I made my way toward the unconscious man and searched him more thoroughly. Besides removing the gun he'd dropped during our fight, I found a push dagger on the ground beside him with fresh blood on it. I felt behind me, finding the back of my shirt wet beneath my shoulder, the fabric ripped and shredded. I didn't realize tonight was going to be one of those nights or I would have worn a vest.

THIRTY

"Police. We're coming inside," an officer announced a moment before I heard the crunch of glass beneath heavy boots. They'd surrounded us by using the broken window at the side of the building that I'd used to enter and the rear door.

Two beams of light bounced off the floor before I spotted the officers. They hadn't drawn their weapons, but they each had a hand on their holsters. I held up my hands, instructing Theo to do the same, but he wouldn't let go of the victim.

"I called it in. That guy attacked me," I pointed to Damien, "and this guy isn't doing so hot."

"A little help over here," Theo said.

The other officer peered at the hole in the roof. "This place looks like it's on the verge of collapse. We should evacuate."

"Great idea, except we have a problem." I indicated Theo, who remained on the ground beside the victim. "GSW to the abdomen, followed by a knife wound."

"I was helping," Theo insisted.

"Watch them both," I suggested.

"Who are you?" the officer asked.

"A concerned citizen."

"What about this guy?" The officer nodded at Damien, who'd regained consciousness and glared at me. His jaw was swollen to the size of a grapefruit where I'd hit him. "How did he get tied up?"

"He tried to kill me." I indicated the gun and dagger I'd found on him. "I had to subdue him."

"And you came prepared? What's your name? What are you doing inside a condemned building?"

I reached into my front pocket and handed him my ID and credentials. The cop shone his flashlight at them. "You made the 9-1-1 call?"

"That's what I said."

He pointed the flashlight at the ground, noticing the blood droplets pooling near my feet. He moved the beam of light upward, finding the slash on my back. "He got you pretty good."

"Bitch," Damien hissed from between his clenched teeth.

"Manners," the officer warned. He turned to me. "I'm waiting for an explanation."

"I saw those two men enter the premises." I pointed to Theo and the guy with the stomach wound. "One appeared injured. I thought they might need help and followed them inside." Damien mumbled several angry phrases, all unintelligible. I resisted the urge to kick him. "This guy jumped me from behind. I don't know if he's alone or if he brought friends, so I thought it best to wait for help to arrive."

The cop gave me a cockeyed look. "That's it? You got lucky?"

"I used to be a federal agent."

"That makes a lot more sense." He listened to his radio. "A second patrol car is on scene. Let's continue this outside, ma'am."

"What about the ambulance?" I asked.

He hit his radio, giving the all-clear and requesting two additional RA units. Another officer joined him to secure the scene and set up some floodlights while paramedics got the victim stabilized. Theo and I were escorted out of the building separately.

From the corner of my eye, I spotted my rental pull to a stop a block away. Omar got out of the car with another member of the security team. While he jogged over to see what was going on, the other member of the team pulled a spare set of keys and got behind the wheel of the armored SUV. Cross had taught them not to get implicated or stopped by the police. Our boss wouldn't want one of his expensive bulletproof trucks impounded or the cache of weapons discovered or seized. It's a good thing he splurged on having more than one key made.

"Stay back, sir," the cop said. "This is a police matter."

"She's bleeding," Omar pointed out.

"She'll be taken care of. Were you here? Did you see what happened?"

"No, sir," Omar said.

"Then I suggest you move along."

"I'm good," I said, catching Omar's eye.

He nodded, stepping back.

Another team of paramedics entered the condemned building, they returned with Damien. After they loaded him into an ambulance, an officer climbed in beside him. The ambulance took off, leaving me and Theo with a growing number of police personnel.

"Ma'am," the officer led me toward a third ambulance, "tell me what happened, starting with who you are and why you followed those men inside that building."

I sat on the edge of the gurney while the EMTs cut the back of my shirt and peeled it away. "That looks nasty," one of them said. "What happened?"

"The guy with the broken jaw rushed me. He slashed me with a push blade."

"I'm still waiting for you to tell me how you ended up inside the building," the cop said.

"That's a long story. I was hired to follow Theo Stapleton. I'm not sure how he's involved in any of this, but he's the reason we're all here."

* * *

I drank burnt coffee from a brown paper cup. The label said it was made from recycled materials. I wondered if that meant the cops were reusing old paper cups to save money and cut down on waste. Frankly, that might have improved how the coffee tasted. I refilled my cup and took another sip, thinking it might have gotten better. Nope, still terrible.

A member of the gangs unit had taken Theo into one of the interview rooms. In the meantime, the police didn't want me going anywhere. The perks of being a material witness.

After checking the vending machines and grabbing a stale donut from the box in the break room, I called Jason Ganz. The attorney wasn't happy to receive a call at two a.m. Nor was he excited by the prospect of traipsing down to the police station at this time of night. He gave me the same fundamental advice I'd heard from Mr. Almeada, Cross's attorney, to do my best to keep my mouth shut. The less I said, the better off I'd be. Unless the situation changed and the police decided to place me under arrest, he figured I should be fine on my own.

I couldn't blame him. I wouldn't want to check on a client in the middle of the night for a non-emergency. Plus, from the background noise, the attorney wasn't sleeping alone. Staying in a warm bed with a friendly face was far more enticing than schlepping across town in the middle of the night to drink really bad coffee under buzzing fluorescent lights.

I settled into one of the chairs lining the wall. For a city this large, I expected more action from the graveyard shift, but things were quiet. A few detectives worked at their computers.

Two a.m. Martin should be asleep by now. The last thing I wanted to do was wake him, but a part of me knew that was just an excuse. Calling from the police station would lead to loads of questions, most of which I couldn't answer.

Hey, handsome. Just wanted to let you know I'm safe. But I'm not sure I'll make it home before you have to leave. Some things came up at work. I love you. Go to sleep. I deleted that message and typed another one. But it didn't sound right either.

"Ms. Parker," Detective Turner poked his head out of the interview room, "I need you to verify a few things. This is Detective Montoya." A woman stepped out of the interview room, grabbing the folder from his hand as she exited. "She'll go over your statement with you in there." He pointed to the interview room across the hall.

She pushed open the door, gesturing for me to go ahead of her. Once we were settled at the table, she put the folder down. Her eyes resting on the cup as I brought it to my lips. "I can't believe you're drinking that."

"I've had worse."

"I didn't think that was possible." She rested her arm over the back of her chair, turning sideways to face me. "I've warned the guys to wash the pot and change the grounds, but they never listen. I'm just waiting for a judge to rule a confession inadmissible on account of torture."

"It'd only be torture if you force-fed him the coffee. If he drinks it willingly, you should be in the clear."

She smiled. "You were law enforcement."

"FBI."

"I've heard about you." This was her way of building a rapport. "We pulled your file."

"You got that pretty damn fast."

"Homicide's been fascinated with you."

"Only Dean."

Her eyes went wide for a millisecond, the expression giving away her surprise. "I didn't realize you were on a first name basis."

"Neither did he." I put the cup down. "Let's cut to the chase. It's late, and I'd like to get home before the sun comes up. What do you need from me?"

"Who hired you to keep tabs on Mr. Stapleton?"

"His wife, Iris."

"Why?"

"She was afraid he was cheating."

"Is he?"

"I'm not sure. I haven't found any indication of it, but I've only been at this a few days. It's possible."

"You called 9-1-1 twice tonight."

"That's not a crime. I didn't make a false report."

"No, you didn't." She pulled out the transcripts of my two calls. "The first time, you reported suspicious activity at a pharmacy. 9-1-1 received reports of gunfire in the area prior to your call. A man was shot. He took refuge inside the pharmacy until Mr. Stapleton arrived. Stapleton and an unidentified man we now believe to be Damien Everst loaded the gunshot victim into the back of an SUV and drove away. A few minutes later, you arrived and called 9-1-1."

"Bad timing," I said. "And Damien wasn't driving the SUV."

"How can you be sure?"

"Did you find it parked outside the condemned clinic after you picked us up?"

She made a note in the margin. "Any idea who was driving?"

"Nope." I wondered if the garage surveillance would show anything. "Did you ask Theo?"

"Mr. Stapleton never mentioned another party's involvement."

Even now, Theo was still keeping secrets. I adjusted in my chair, wondering who he was protecting and why. My gut said that was the person he'd been texting via the app. My phone rang again. "Sorry about that."

"No," Detective Montoya waved a hand at the device, "please, go ahead."

I checked the display. *Will.* Twice in two hours. Something was up. But answering a call in the middle of an interrogation room wouldn't serve either of our interests. Instead, I silenced the call and waited to see if he'd leave a voicemail or text message. After he hung up, my screen went back to the home page. No messages.

"Was that important?" she asked.

"I guess not."

"Who was it?"

"It might have been a wrong number."

She glanced down at my phone before going back to the notepad in front of her. "Was someone else at the clinic?"

"I'm not sure. I thought I saw someone slip out the rear

door, but the lighting inside was less than ideal."

"Uh-huh." She wasn't buying it. "But you already pointed out the SUV took off, leaving Theo and the GSW victim at the clinic. Someone else must have been there."

"I never got a good look at the driver."

"But you're sure Mr. Stapleton wasn't driving?"

"Yes."

"How do you know that?"

I explained the situation from the parking garage.

"What happened afterward?"

"I followed the SUV. Eventually, it led me to the condemned clinic."

She reread the rest of my statement. "Prior to tonight, did you ever encounter Damien Everst?"

"No."

She checked her notes. "According to a statement you provided to Detective Petrocelli, you followed Theo Stapleton to another parking garage two nights ago, the same night you found a bloody shirt in Stapleton's garbage can."

"It wasn't a statement."

"So you didn't say that?"

"No, I did, but I didn't realize we were on the record."

"And yet, you call him Dean." She cracked a smile. "Do you have any idea whose bloody shirt it was?"

"No."

She scribbled something in the margin. "Have you observed Stapleton exhibit any other odd or violent behavior?"

"Not really." I told her about every encounter I'd had with the man and the close call in the hospital parking lot, leaving out the parts about me breaking into his car and planting a tracking device on it.

"How did you know where he was going to be?"

"His wife gave me access to their phones."

"Find my phone," Montoya said. "Clever." She made one final note and closed the folder. "Damien Everst is looking at hard time. But I was told you didn't want to press charges. Why not? He could have killed you."

"I have my reasons." I glanced toward the door. "You

should have a solid case, assuming Theo Stapleton cooperates."

"He will. He knows what's at stake."

The police would use the attack on Iris's ambulance to force his hand and guilt him into it. But I wasn't sure that'd be enough to get Theo to give up his accomplice. "How much trouble is he in?"

"That depends on a number of things. You being one of them. You discovered the gun in his house. You followed him tonight. You should have some idea what's going on."

"I don't."

"C'mon," she wheedled.

"It could go either way. The only weapon I found on Theo was the scalpel. He had it to cut the bullet out of the gunshot victim."

"What about the other night?"

"It's my understanding the six-shooter Detective Petrocelli confiscated is the only firearm Theo possessed. Ballistics can tell you more than I can. But he bought it because he thought he needed protection."

"From whom?"

"I'd guess Damien and his buddies."

"You're telling me this is an ongoing situation?"

I shrugged. "I haven't found any evidence. All I know is his wife says he's been sneaking out of the house late at night."

"Damn." She tapped her nails on the table. "We're looking into recent GSWs. The Slayers, the gang Damien Everst and his brother Dwayne are connected to, are a bunch of street thugs. They're small potatoes. They can threaten a man and his family, but they don't have the reach or membership to do much more than that. You really should consider testifying. We can keep you safe, and putting Damien behind bars will keep others safe too."

"I'll think about it." But the answer was no.

"Good." She stood. "For now, you're free to go."

THIRTY-ONE

I tried calling Will back, but I didn't get an answer. Something was up. Had the SDPD found another body?

Martin came into the bathroom, wrapped his arms around my waist, and kissed my naked shoulder. He exhaled before letting go and stepping back to assess the large bandage taped beneath my other shoulder blade, to the right of the bruise caused by the surfboard. "What happened?"

"Nothing. I'm fine."

"This doesn't look like nothing." He gently peeled the gauze off, finding a neat line of stitches underneath. He pressed the tape back in place and adjusted my bra strap. The other cuts and nicks from the broken glass were covered with pieces of rolled up gauze beneath strips of tape. He kissed a path halfway down my spine while I braced myself against the bathroom vanity, my heart breaking at his tenderness.

"I'm okay," I said, my voice hoarse.

He straightened, finding my eyes in the mirror. "It's late. Come to bed."

"Soon."

He pressed his lips to my temple and squeezed his eyes

closed before stepping back into the bedroom.

I ran a hand through my hair and stared at the LAFD t-shirt the EMT had given me to wear. At least I'd gotten something nice out of the ordeal. Iris couldn't exactly say the same, but she already had dozens of LAFD t-shirts.

My phone buzzed. But it wasn't Will. It was Iris. We'd been exchanging messages for the last thirty minutes. The police had shown up at her door with questions, and since they'd let the cat out of the bag, I couldn't let her questions go unanswered. After responding to her latest text about the gang and her safety, I slipped into one of Martin's t-shirts and climbed into bed.

"Come with me," Martin said. His eyes remained closed, but he reached for my hand and hooked his fingers between mine.

"I can't, but know that I want to." I pulled my fingers free from his grip and wrapped my arm around him, letting my hand rest against his chest. Beneath my palm was the steady beat of his heart. By the time my phone buzzed again, Martin had fallen asleep.

Carefully getting out of bed, so as not to disturb him, I grabbed my phone and went into the game room. Iris had more questions about home security systems. She hadn't noticed the Cross Security team outside her house when the cops showed up, but she'd been preoccupied.

I'd already contacted Nero. They had gotten some basic equipment installed earlier in the night. But Iris was terrified of a repeat of what happened ten months ago. She'd already lost one partner. She couldn't lose another, especially her life partner—her spouse.

After making arrangements to have a security team keep an eye on their house, I relayed those details to Iris, along with the promise that I'd stop by tomorrow afternoon to discuss upgrading her home security system. What she had was an outdated keypad alarm which would alert the security company if someone entered without inputting the code. She needed something with a faster response time, particularly if Damien or his pals paid her a visit.

I researched a few options for something that directly notified the police. After putting together a list of recommendations and seeing which companies had contracts with Cross Security, I turned the sound off the pinball machine, needing to do something to decompress.

I was on my third game when Martin padded into the room. "You should have woken me up."

"I didn't see any reason to do that. It's nearly morning. You have to leave soon."

He waited for me to finish the game before pulling me away from the table. "I have two hours. Until then, I'm yours."

"You should be asleep."

"So should you." He ran his thumb across my cheek. "I'll sleep on the jet. When are you going to sleep?"

"Later."

"In that case, I'll make pancakes."

He'd just finished mixing the batter when the proximity alarm alerted us to a car pulling into the driveway. I grabbed my gun and checked the surveillance feed. But in the dark, I didn't recognize the vehicle. A moment later, a man in a police uniform stepped out.

I disarmed the security system and pulled the door open, gun at my thigh. "What are you doing here, Will?"

"Were you asleep?" he eyed me, his eyes stopping on my bare thighs.

I tugged on the hem of Martin's t-shirt, aware of my half-nakedness. "How did you know where I lived?"

"I'm a police sergeant. I have access to records."

"That's a violation."

"What are they going to do? Fire me?" Will laughed cynically. "Do you want to file a complaint? You can drive down to San Diego and ask to fill out a form on police misconduct. But they'll probably laugh at you."

"Up yours," I mumbled.

Will stared at me. "I heard you were a victim of a violent crime. I was worried. When I called to find out what was going on, someone said the victim had taken a shot to the gut and was in critical condition." He eyed me again. "That wasn't you?"

"No."

"Knife wound to the shoulder?"

"Yes," I hissed. "Now shut up." I waved my hands, hoping he'd lower his voice.

Will eyed my gun. "Is this how you always greet guests?"

"It is at this time of the night."

"It's technically morning."

"You should have called first."

"I did. You didn't answer." He raised his hands in defeat. "Are you okay?"

"I'm fine."

"I'm glad."

"Why didn't you answer when I called you back?"

"You did?" He checked his pockets. "Shit. I forgot the burner at my desk. Two phones are too many."

I folded my arms across my chest, feeling exposed. "You drove all the way here to check on me?"

"Pretty much. I guess, since I'm here, I'll make myself useful, but I wanted to make sure you were okay. I didn't know what happened, but the details I heard sounded grim."

"The last time we spoke, you hung up on me. We're not friends. Why do you care what happens?"

"What do you mean we're not friends? I thought we were friends. Best friends." He crossed his fingers and held them up. "We're like this."

I laughed, despite myself, and he smiled, glancing behind my shoulder. "Don't you want to invite me inside?" He stepped back, looking up at the house. "This must have set you back quite a few pennies. The private sector is looking better and better all the time."

"The house isn't mine. It's a rental. And it's not even in my name." I stared at him. "How did you track down my address?"

"The forms you filled out to work as a P.I. and carry that weapon required an in-state address."

Martin joined me at the door, the whisk in his hand. "Alex, is everything okay?"

"I don't know." I stared at Will. "You checked on me. I'm fine. Why are you hanging around here? San Diego's that way." I pointed in a random direction.

"That way," Martin corrected, moving my hand to the

right.

"Is this the cupcake man? This must be the cupcake man." Will grinned, extending his hand toward Martin. "You're a lucky guy."

"I know." Martin's tone remained cordial, but it could turn on a dime if he deemed Will to be a threat. "And you are?"

"Will Russo."

"Aren't you out of your jurisdiction?" Martin asked, ignoring Will's offered hand.

"What gave it away? Was it the uniform? Or did Alex mention me?"

"Both."

Will glanced at me. "I'm flattered."

"You shouldn't be," I said.

Martin moved closer, prepared to put himself between me and Will. "Is this official police business?"

"No, sir." Will held that annoying grin but retracted his hand. "I heard what happened tonight. I was worried about Alex, especially when she didn't answer my calls."

I interrupted, afraid what Will would say next. "How about you pick up some coffee and donuts, and I'll meet you at my office?"

"No need," Martin said, his voice contained an edge. "Sergeant Russo should join us for breakfast. We have plenty of pancakes."

I stared into Martin's eyes, but he wasn't backing down. He wouldn't fly home until he knew I was safe and what Will's intentions toward me really were.

"Pancakes sound great. And there's no need for formalities. You can call me Will." He followed us inside. "I'm sorry. I didn't catch your name."

"James Martin."

"Huh." Will looked around the house as he followed Martin into the kitchen. "Lovely place you have."

"Thanks." Martin gestured to the kitchen table. "Have a seat. Would you like some coffee?"

Will pulled out a chair and sat down. "Please."

Martin glanced at me. "I'll get to know your friend while you get dressed."

I pulled on a pair of jeans and returned to the kitchen, afraid to leave Will alone with Martin for more than a few seconds. Will turned and smiled when I took a seat beside him, like we were best friends sharing a secret. I didn't like it. We'd been at each other's throats the last few times we spoke. The sudden change worried me.

"Shouldn't you be in the middle of a shift?" I asked.

"Technically, I am." He checked his phone. "I volunteered to make the drive here. I'm still on the clock. With the way things look, I'll be earning some OT."

"Why?"

"We received a report Roland Jordan boarded a bus headed for L.A."

"When?"

"Earlier this evening." Will glanced at his watch. "At this point, I guess I should say last night or yesterday."

"I haven't slept yet. Earlier this evening makes more sense."

Will nodded. "That's how I see it, too."

Martin put a mug down in front of me. I picked it up, surprised to find hot chocolate instead of coffee. I gave him a cockeyed look. *Sleep*, he mouthed. But with Will's appearance, that didn't seem likely. Martin put another mug down in front of our unexpected guest. "Who's Roland Jordan?"

"A suspect in three suspicious deaths." Will reached for the steamed milk and poured a splash into his cup. "He vanished after Alex spoke to him. An hour ago, we confirmed he left town. By town, I mean San Diego."

"Why do you think he's in L.A.?" Martin asked.

"That's where the bus was going."

Martin stared at him. At least it wasn't just me. Will could drive anyone crazy. "That's not what I meant. Why would Roland want to come here, to Los Angeles?"

Will turned and stared at me over the rim of the mug. "Did you give him your card?"

I couldn't imagine why a homeless veteran would come looking for me. I didn't threaten him. I asked a few simple questions. That was it. "Yes, but he has no reason to come looking for me."

"Are you sure he sees it that way? You come around, and the next thing he knows, cops are searching for him and questioning his neighbors. As far as he's concerned, you caused him a lot of grief. He just wanted to be left alone."

"You brought me the damn cases."

Martin scooped the pancakes off the griddle and added them to the large stack. He put them down on the table, grabbed the syrup and butter, and sat across from me. "How dangerous is this guy?"

"It'd be best if we keep him away from knives," Will said. "Anything sharp, really. And rope. We definitely don't want this guy playing with a piece of rope. Twine would probably be bad too. And ladders. He should stay away from ladders."

That's why Will had called twice before showing up. He must have called to warn the LAPD, found out about the attack inside the clinic, and decided to make the drive to find out what happened. It was sweet, but a little stalker-like. I chuckled. He'd fit in great at Cross Security.

"What's so funny?" Will asked.

"Nothing." I piled pancakes onto my plate and doused them with syrup.

"You don't seem worried."

"She's not." Martin hadn't taken his eyes off of me. "I hate that look, sweetheart."

"I don't have a look."

Will shifted his gaze from Martin to me and back again. "Roland could be searching for you, Alex. The LAPD's been alerted. They've issued a BOLO."

"Great," I said, eyeing Martin. "See, nothing to worry about. It's fine."

"You still have that look. And you know damn well what look it is," Martin said. "I leave in an hour. Like you said, there's no reason to pack. We go home. I take care of business. And by the time we return, the police will have found this guy. It's simple. Everyone stays safe. And everyone's happy. What's the problem?"

"What about Iris?" I asked.

Martin leaned back. "I bet she'd enjoy an all-expenses

paid vacation. Getting away from her husband and her problems would do her some good."

"Theo was arrested tonight. She's already scared."

"Perfect. She'll appreciate you looking out by relocating her for a few days."

"No."

"Why not? Give me one good reason."

"I have a job to do."

Martin reached for his phone. "We'll see."

"Don't you dare." I slammed down my fork. "Roland Jordan didn't come to Los Angeles to hurt me. We don't even know if he's responsible for those deaths. There is zero evidence." I glared at Martin. "If you contact Lucien, I—"

"I'm not." He put his phone down. "I was going to have a new flight plan filed with an updated manifest."

"I'm not going. Neither is Iris."

"Why are you always so damn stubborn? You came home less than four hours ago with ten stitches. I'm afraid what will happen next."

Will cleared his throat. "Umm...about that evidence thing...it's not exactly zero."

"What do you mean?" I asked, ignoring the searing look Martin continued to give me.

"Forensics pulled a partial print from the handle of the straight razor Joel Curry allegedly used to kill himself. It matched Jordan."

THIRTY-TWO

Will and I left the house before Martin. A part of me wondered if my beloved would still get on the plane. I hoped he would, but I hated parting ways on bad terms. Before I'd left the house, he'd cornered me in the bedroom and kissed me like he'd never see me again. "I love you," he said. "Always."

I almost changed my mind about going home with him based on that alone. The last thing I wanted to do was make him anxious or unhappy, but I had responsibilities here. He couldn't fault me for them. I just hoped he wouldn't fault himself for them either if any worst case scenarios played out in his absence, though I didn't think getting attacked or killed by Roland Jordan was particularly likely. My money was on getting dragged out to sea by a catastrophic tsunami or dying in a building collapse due to a disaster movie level earthquake. Roland Jordan didn't even make the list of top ten things I feared most in Los Angeles, but I had a vivid imagination and had seen far too many movies for my own good.

"Was cupcake guy a former client?" Will asked.

"Don't call him that. In fact, don't talk about him at all."

"Those pancakes were really good."

"What did I just say?"

"I can't talk about pancakes either? Jeez. Fine, I'll pick another topic." Will adjusted the badge on his uniform. I wasn't used to seeing him like that. Oddly, it suited him.

"How about we talk about the real reason you made a two hour drive in the middle of the night?"

"I already told you what happened. Jordan boarded a bus to Los Angeles. I made the trip to verify his ID and read in the LAPD."

"Who did you speak to?"

"The bus driver."

"What about the other passengers?"

"They were long gone, just like Jordan."

"How can you be sure he didn't hitch another ride?"

"He might have. I don't know." Will exhaled, his good mood waning. "The LAPD is on alert in case any bodies drop under suspicious circumstances."

"Does Jordan have any ties to L.A.?"

"Only you."

"And Jenna."

"Who?" Will asked.

"Sophie Marshman's sister, but that's assuming he's responsible for her death. We still don't have any evidence."

"A partial fingerprint isn't nothing. It's something." Will opened the folder he'd brought in from the car and handed it to me. "That's a copy of the Joel Curry case file. But you didn't get it from me."

I flipped through the sheets. The police had gathered as much intel on Curry as they could. They had his DOB, military record, information on the VA clinic, and as much as they were able to collect concerning his medical records. Curry had decades on Jordan. They didn't serve at the same time, so there was no overlap there.

"Did the two ever have appointments at the VA hospital on the same day?" I asked.

"Once. Eleven months ago."

"But we don't know if they crossed paths. This is circumstantial at best."

"The fingerprint isn't. That connects Jordan to the

crime scene."

I examined the forensic report. "Jordan's fingerprint is on top of Curry's. The blade was found on the ground to the left of the body."

"So?"

I rocked in my chair. "Curry was right-handed, just like Jordan. If Jordan attacked, he could have slashed left to right and tossed the blade, which would put it to the left of Curry's body."

"I told you he's our killer."

"Most Americans would cut left to right, the same way they read, and his fingerprint was found on top of Curry's. He touched the razor afterward. He might have found Curry, moved the blade to render assistance, realized he was too late, and ran before he could get blamed."

"Why are you defending this guy?" Will asked. "You're the one who brought him to me as a suspect. We've already discussed this. Jordan knew Sophie and Robert. He's the only connection we have to all three victims."

"The only connection we know about. We could be overlooking someone else." I stared at the crime scene photos, grabbed the letter opener off the desk, and held it in my right hand before switching it to my left. Placing it near my throat, I pulled across before switching hands and trying again.

"Hey, let's not play with sharp objects," Will said. "I'm starting to think you're trying to frame me for murder."

Rolling my eyes, I put the letter opener down. "According to this, Curry had tendonitis in his right wrist. It would have been hard for him to slit his own throat using that hand. He would have had to use his left, even though he wrote with his right."

"This isn't a suicide. I thought we were in agreement on that. Why do you change your story every damn time I talk to you?"

"Chill. I'm not saying it's a suicide. But someone put the blade in Curry's left hand before Jordan touched it."

"Or Jordan wore gloves or forced Curry to off himself, just like he forced Sophie and Robert to off themselves."

"Maybe, but we don't know that they offed themselves."

"Right," Will said sarcastically.

"Did Curry wear a brace on his wrist?" The photos didn't show one. I didn't see any indentions on his skin or find one listed in the items found with the body.

"No."

While I pondered who would have known to plant the razor to the left and make sure the prints on the blade matched Curry's left hand, Will's phone rang. I glanced up when he gave the caller our current location. After he hung up, he reached across the desk for the folder.

"What's going on?" I asked.

"Trevitt will be here in five minutes. He wants to speak to you."

"It's about damn time. Why didn't he call me?"

"He's been busy. Interviewing you wasn't one of his top priorities. But things have changed. This case has leaked into the LAPD's jurisdiction. Detective Trevitt needs local help to apprehend our suspect, so we're working with the LAPD until Jordan is taken into custody. As far as anyone knows, you spoke to Jordan last. You may be able to provide valuable intel."

"You know everything I do."

"In case you weren't paying attention, the cops I work with don't trust me. Trevitt knows I had concerns about the recent string of violent attacks against the homeless, so he's been kind enough to loop me in, but he wants to talk to you himself. I'd appreciate it if you didn't throw me under the bus."

"The one Jordan took to get here?"

"Yeah."

"I'll do my best. Does Trevitt know we have a connection?"

"Only that you gave me the tip about Roland Jordan. You were looking into Sophie Marshman's death and I thought there might be overlap."

"What about Robert Devers?"

Will shook his head. "I had no reason to bring that up."

"Jordan connected to both of them. Maybe I can push that angle and mention the person who attacked and robbed Sophie could have been Robert since Jordan found him stealing from the others at the camp." This conversation with the homicide detective would not go well. Our story had too many holes. He'd see right through it. "For the record, I hate lying to the police."

"Really?" Will chuckled. "I wasn't expecting that. You're a P.I. Most of the things you do are illegal. I'd think lying would be second nature to you."

"Those aren't lies. They're misdirections and omissions."

"Still lies."

"Think for one second," I said. "Don't you think it'd be beneficial for everyone involved if we show our hand? We need Trevitt on board."

"I don't know. He wouldn't have even bothered reopening these cases if you hadn't gotten the LAPD to make the call or that cop from across the country to look into it. Trevitt doesn't give a shit what I think, at least he didn't until Curry's body was found. I'm not an asset. I'm a hindrance. Stick with the omissions."

"Fine, but for the record, I don't like it."

I made a pot of coffee. I'd need the caffeine to make it through the rest of this never-ending day. While I waited for Detective Trevitt to arrive, I made sure my notes were safe to share. Maybe they weren't, but with a killer on a spree, I wanted the right guy caught. But on this bright, sunny morning, I wasn't convinced Roland Jordan was our suspect. He'd have no way of knowing Joel Curry couldn't hold the razor in his right hand, unless Curry told him or he'd been observing him.

"Did Curry have any ties to Robert or Sophie?" I asked.

"I don't think so." Will glanced toward the door when it creaked open. "Gabe, did you get the LAPD squared away?"

"They'll keep their eyes peeled." Detective Trevitt wore an off the rack suit. The dark circles beneath his eyes told me he hadn't been getting much sleep either. "Alexis Parker?"

"Guilty." I capped the marker and crossed toward him, offering my hand. "Detective Trevitt, I presume."

"Yes, ma'am." He shook my hand. "I have a few questions. I thought it'd be best to do this in person, and since I'm in town for the day, I figured I'd save you a trip."

"I appreciate it." I gestured to the middle office. "We can speak privately, if you like."

Trevitt narrowed his eyes at the whiteboard I'd filled with notes and the map of San Diego I had hung on the wall. "That won't be necessary." He jerked his chin toward my musings. "How about you tell me why you're investigating one of my closed cases?"

"The circumstances regarding Sophie Marshman's death left a lot of unanswered questions. I assume the LAPD contacted you about the letter Jenna Roth received."

"Uh-huh."

"Sophie claimed she was being stalked. Someone attacked and robbed her. A few weeks later, she ends up dead. The idea of suicide doesn't sit right with me."

"You know Sophie Marshman had a history of mental illness. She downed a bottle of pills inside the house where her children lived."

"Regardless, I don't think she intended to harm herself." I glanced at Will, but he kept his mouth shut. "Would you like some coffee, Detective?"

"Sure." Trevitt moved closer to the whiteboard and examined the intel. "Who hired you to work the Marshman case?"

"Cross Security maintains strict client confidentiality," I said. "All I can say is that I informed Jenna Roth, Sophie Marshman's sister, to reach out to the police regarding the final letter she received from her sister. Have you spoken to her?"

"Uh-huh." Trevitt took the offered coffee cup and put it down on the desk without sipping it. "She said she didn't hire you."

"Pro bono is good for the soul."

"She said you came to her."

"I did."

Trevitt spun on his heel to face me. "Why? And while you're at it, explain to me why a detective from across the country called to ask about the case." Trevitt stared at me. "I checked. Sophie Marshman doesn't have any distant relatives."

"What about close friends of the family?"

"How about you tell me the truth? Did you know Sophie?"

"No, sir. I stumbled onto the story somehow and got obsessed. It happens. I get bored easily."

Trevitt didn't look convinced. "Detective Petrocelli warned me to keep my eye on you. He says people around you end up suffering violent deaths. He's not sure how you're involved, but he knows you are."

"He's not wrong. But like we're told in grief counseling, it's not our fault. I have terrible luck. Wrong place, wrong time. All the time."

Trevitt stared at me like I was crazy, which was exactly how I sounded. "Let me lay this out for you, Ms. Parker. You start looking into a suicide that occurred hours from here, which involved a woman you never met, for absolutely no reason. No one hired you. And while you're snooping around, you speak to dozens of social workers, volunteers, and members of the homeless community, one of whom disappeared immediately afterward and is now the prime suspect for three murders. The dots just don't connect. Would you like to start over, or should I ask my new friends at the LAPD if they can spare an interrogation room so we can have this conversation in a more formal setting?"

"I asked her to look into it," Will piped up. "We bumped into each other when Alex was looking for a missing woman. One thing led to another, and here we are."

Trevitt let out an incredulous snort, his eyes going skyward, before he sighed. "You dragged a private eye into your insanity. What's going on with you, Sarge? You used to be solid. Now this. I told you I'd give those cases another look as soon as I had some time. Why would you hire some private dick who specializes in digging up dirt on celebrities?"

Will put his hands on his hips. "This is one of the top private detective firms in the country. And she's one hell of an investigator."

"The fancy office doesn't make her a great investigator," Trevitt said.

"Maybe not, but more than half a decade with the Office of International Operations, a special branch of the FBI, does." I stared at Trevitt. "But you've made it clear you don't need my help. So ask your questions and get out of my office."

"You were a Fed?" Trevitt asked. "And you just happened to cross paths with Sarge? That's something."

"Is that a question?" I asked.

Trevitt smiled. "You're feisty. Petrocelli mentioned that too. I apologize if I offended you, but this was my case. I followed the evidence. The deaths were odd, but no witnesses, motives, or suspects turned up. I had to rule on them. Even the families agreed. If they'd pressed the issue, I would have stuck with it. But they didn't. They believed it was suicide. And until you came sniffing around and calling in tips, I was happy believing that too." He gestured to my empty chair. "Take a seat. I want to know everything."

THIRTY-THREE

"You look exhausted," Iris said when I showed up at her front door.

"Thanks."

"I'm sorry." She held the door for me. "Are you okay? The police told me what happened last night. I can't believe Theo. What was he thinking? Why was he out there? How could he—" She stopped herself and took a deep breath. "My head hasn't stopped spinning."

"That's understandable." I dropped into the nearest chair, wondering if Iris would mind if I took a nap in her living room. It'd been nonstop. First, Theo, then Will and his SDPD pals, followed by conducting another Cross Security interview, which Justin hadn't canceled, and now this. Martin was right. I should have gone home with him while I had the chance. "Where is Theo?"

"The police are holding him for now. They have lots of questions." She looked uneasy. "I don't know what we're going to do. Or what I'm going to do. He's going to lose his job over this. He might be facing jail time. I just...I don't know."

"Did you contact that attorney I told you about?"

"Jason?" she asked. "Yes. I spoke to him. He said he'd

look at Theo's case and see what he can do."

"That's good."

She tugged on a piece of string that had come loose from the sofa cushion. "Yeah, maybe. But I'm not even sure I want Theo to come home, which is crazy. He's supporting me. I still love him, I think. I don't know anymore. I don't even know who he is or why he was doing what he was doing." She stared into my eyes. "Do you know why he did any of this?"

I pulled out my phone and found the photo I'd taken of the text messages on Theo's phone. The image didn't include everything, but there was enough. "Theo had an encrypted messaging app on his phone." I held it out to her, and she read the messages. "Do you have any idea who he's been messaging? We haven't been able to figure it out."

She read the words several more times. "Maybe. I'm not sure."

"He's protecting whoever this is," I said. "Last night, someone picked Theo up inside a parking garage. They drove a dark SUV with the license plates removed. I didn't get a chance to pull the VIN. With twenty-twenty hindsight, I should have done that before I entered the clinic. The SUV circled the city for hours. They made one stop at a pharmacy and another to buy drugs."

"Drugs? Shit. Are you sure?"

"The dealer didn't admit it, but Theo gave him an inhaler and Narcan in exchange for something. Theo said he had to get painkillers for the man who'd been shot. The one he planned to perform amateur surgery on. I'm assuming those are the drugs he received. He shot the guy up with something before I could stop him."

"Theo isn't a surgeon. This is so bad. What was he thinking?"

"I know," I said, realizing Iris needed to talk this out. "Whoever drove the SUV was with him for all of that. But that person took off when I showed up. He didn't wait for Theo. He just took off. The police want to know who that is. Theo won't say. At first, I thought it might have been a member of the Slayers, but that doesn't fit."

"The Slayers," Iris repeated.

"Yeah."

She bit her lip. "Dammit." She read the texts on my screen one more time. "Have you tried sending this person a message?"

"I didn't want to tip my hand. I'm guessing the police will do that once they get a warrant and access to the contents of Theo's phone, assuming he didn't willingly hand it over. But the texts aren't incriminating. Unless the other party admits to being involved or Theo points a finger, the police don't have any proof he or she was involved. At least not at the present. Something could surface. Surveillance feeds or DOT footage or an eyewitness, possibly the GSW victim could make an ID, but that's iffy."

"But you can send this person a message," Iris said.

"Yes."

"All right. Let's do that."

I eyed her. "Do you know who this is?"

"I have a pretty good idea. But I might be wrong."

"All right." I'd already been warned one man was looking for me. No reason not to add a second name to that list. Martin was out of town. If the crazies wanted to come out of the woodwork, now was the perfect time to send the invitation. After downloading the app and typing the username into the send box, I asked, "What do you want to say?"

She thought for a moment. "This is Iris. What the hell were you thinking?"

"That's it?"

"Yeah. If I'm wrong, we can play it off. You have security teams guarding me, and we're going to discuss getting a better home security system after this, so I shouldn't worry. I'm protected."

Maybe it was the sleep deprivation talking, but it sounded feasible to me. "I can't make any guarantees. The only way to make sure there isn't a looming threat is to find out who and what Theo's involved in."

"Send it."

I pressed the button and waited. We stared at the open

app for forty seconds before receiving a response. *Theo offered. Ever since, he's been wanting to do something. I'm not sure why. I told him no. I told him to stay home. But he needed to do something, and I thought we'd be able to make a difference. Things got messed up and out of control. I said I'd take care of it, get them off his back, but you know how stubborn that man of yours is. I'm sorry. How can I fix this?*

Iris pressed her palms into her eyes and let out an angry grunt. "I'm gonna kill that man. Those men. Ugh." She grabbed my phone and typed out a reply before I could stop her.

"Who is it?" I asked.

"Calvin Waites. He's a resident, who works in the ER. He's got a chip on his shoulder the size of Texas." She put my phone down and got up to pace. "I'm going to kill him."

"He's a doctor?"

"Yeah. He grew up in Compton and saw a lot of gang violence. He lost his father, his brother, an uncle, and two cousins to the streets. His mother knew she had to get out of there before she lost another son." Iris cringed. "They moved to some farmland in the middle of nowhere. But he made his way to the city. Better neighborhood, more money, but he always said he wanted to make a difference. He'd ask me all kinds of questions about paramedicine and emergency medical services. I suspected he was moonlighting, but I didn't think my dumbass, moron of a husband would be stupid enough to go with him. How could Theo do that after what happened to Gary? Doesn't he realize how dangerous it is? Doesn't he realize what's at stake?" She was so angry she shook.

My phone chimed. Iris snatched it off the coffee table. After reading the message, she put the phone down, glaring at it. I picked it up to see what it said. *Theo believed what we were doing was making a difference. It's what you used to do.*

"This is not on me," she huffed.

"No, it isn't. It's not your fault."

"Damn straight." She dropped into the chair, pulled her knees to her chest, and hugged them. "Is this what he's been doing when he sneaks out?"

"It looks like it."

"Why?" Her voice cracked, but she wouldn't give in to the emotion. In this instance, holding on to the anger helped.

"Theo told me a member of a gang showed up outside the hospital eight months ago. He'd been shot. He wouldn't go inside. He didn't want the cops involved. Theo saved his life. After that, he and his buddies kept coming back. They expected more from Theo. They knew they had him. He couldn't report anything because his job was on the line."

"Do you believe him?"

"I've seen plenty of security cameras at the hospital. If the footage hasn't been deleted, it won't be hard to verify. Theo acted while under duress. He could argue he continued to do so for fear of retaliation. Mr. Ganz might be able to spin it and negotiate a deal. Besides criminal trespass and possessing an unregistered weapon, he hasn't committed any crimes, unless the police found the drugs and charge him with possession or the GSW victim claims assault."

"Could he?"

"I didn't see exactly what happened, but your husband cut into him with a scalpel." I narrowed my eyes at the phone. "Why didn't the doctor do that?"

"Should I ask?" Before I could answer, Iris sent another message. "Calvin said his hands were shaking too much. He's not a surgeon. He's not steady. Theo assists surgeons. He works in the OR. His hands are always steady." A tear rolled down her cheek. "He's supposed to be the steady one. He held everything together when I fell apart. He wasn't supposed to fall apart too." All the tears she'd never cried threatened to burst forth, but she forced them back. And then she laughed. "Why couldn't he have an affair and buy a stupid sports car like everyone else?"

"You said you couldn't afford the kit car."

"If we make it through this, he can have the damn car. I just want to go back to the way we were."

I spent the rest of the day at the Stapletons' house, supervising the home security installation. They upgraded her system and changed every lock in her house. Nero assigned a team to keep an eye on Iris, but she was nervous.

"You're all set. A two-man team will monitor the situation from out here. They'll keep you safe. If you have a problem, you have their number. You know how to contact them. You also have my number. And I'm sure this goes without saying, but don't hesitate to call 9-1-1."

"Do you have to leave?" she asked. "You could stay for dinner."

"You're going to be okay. You're safe."

"Yep." She wrapped her arms around her waist and bit her lip.

I knew that look. "I have some things to take care of at the police station. If you're not comfortable and would prefer staying with a friend or family member, tell the team outside. They'll go with you."

"I don't know."

"You could always check into a hotel. Room service, spa treatments, think about it." I gave her an encouraging nod. "You'll get through this."

"Thanks, Alex."

THIRTY-FOUR

Jason Ganz was waiting outside the police station when I arrived. As usual, the attorney didn't look happy to see me. "Why are you handing out my card like candy on Halloween?"

"I'm not. The Stapletons are Cross Security clients. I'm not sure how things work here, but back home, when a client fucks up, Mr. Almeada or someone from his firm handle it. Was I wrong to assume the same rules apply here?"

He sighed. "Generally speaking, Cross Security clients don't ask how much I charge."

"Bill me," I said.

Ganz's eyes grew wide. "Are you crazy?"

"Why? Do you charge that much?"

"Haven't you ever heard of professional boundaries?"

"Yes, but Iris isn't a typical client. She's in a tough spot. Whatever they can't cover, I will."

"This doesn't mean I can violate attorney-client privilege."

Almeada would break that rule for Cross, but I kept the thought to myself. "Are they willing to offer Theo a deal?"

"Only if he names his accomplice, which he won't."

"Is the gunshot victim talking?"

Ganz shook his head. "He's in critical condition. They removed the bullet, but he lost a lot of blood and now he's battling a serious infection."

"Shit."

"If he dies, they could push for murder, but without intent, it won't fly. Manslaughter's still on the table." Ganz looked at me. "Theo's done this before, hasn't he? I only ask because once the police locate previous victims, it's going to get a lot worse. Detective Petrocelli's sure there must be at least one more."

"The one I pointed him to."

"Why would you do that if you were going to cover this guy's legal fees? Wouldn't it have been easier to set your money on fire? At the very least, it would have saved me some work."

"Theo told me he was repeatedly threatened. He was acting under duress."

"The encrypted texts he sent and received tell another story." Ganz checked his watch. "Here's some free advice. Find proof of these threats and turn it over to the authorities. The sooner you do, the faster we can take control of the narrative and negotiate a deal. We need to get this taken care of before matters get worse."

"I'll see what I can do."

"Don't make it worse." He got up from the bench. "I have to be somewhere in forty minutes. From the chatter I heard inside, you've become quite popular with RHD. Try not to get arrested until after dinner. I don't want to have to duck out early to save your ass."

Hoping I wasn't walking into a firing squad, I entered the police station. A different officer was at the desk. "How can I help you?" he asked.

"I need to speak to Detective Turner or Montoya. It's about Theo Stapleton. I have some information on their case."

He picked up the phone and relayed what I said. "Detective Montoya's waiting. Officer Cortez will take you to see her."

The door opened and a rookie stood on the other side

with a freshly pressed uniform. He gave me a tight nod and led me to the gangs unit. Before he opened his mouth to say anything, Montoya swiveled to face me.

"You saved me a dime," she said. "I was about to call you." She thanked the rookie and led me down the hallway. After finding the interview rooms occupied, she kicked another detective out of the break room and closed us inside. "We retraced Stapleton's steps and pulled the relevant footage. You didn't mention the assault in the garage."

"Theo didn't attack me. He wanted me to back off. He did it for my own protection."

Montoya snorted. "Tell me another one."

"Have you spoken to his wife?"

"Not personally. Turner handled that. But I'm up to speed. While I'm sorry for everything she's going through, that has no bearing on what becomes of her husband."

"Eight months ago, Theo was leaving the hospital when a member of a street gang approached him for help. The banger had been shot. He wouldn't go inside the hospital, but he was dying. Theo saved him. But he was afraid to report it. A few days later, more members of the gang showed up. They needed patching. They forced Theo to help them. After that, anytime they needed medical care, they reached out to him. Yesterday afternoon, Damien showed up at the hospital, told Theo he needed a favor, and threatened to kill him and his wife if he didn't comply."

"Do you have proof?"

"Hospital security footage."

"I need to know exactly when this happened."

"Yesterday. Pull the entire day's feed. It has to be there."

"And the inciting incident?"

"It was right before Theo bought the gun from the pawn shop. That's what set him off. That's why he's been behaving so erratically. It's why his wife thought he was having an affair. He was afraid these dangerous men would follow him home and kill his family. He almost lost her once. He was desperate not to let it happen again."

"You've changed your tune."

"If you'd spoken directly to Iris, you'd understand why.

You need to look into this, Detective. Theo's done some stupid things. Dangerous things. He's made a lot of mistakes. But he didn't think he had a way out. Reporting would have cost him his job. Without it, how would he and his wife support themselves?"

"Let's say I buy into this sob story. We know Theo's been communicating with someone. Based on everything I've seen and heard, that someone is his accomplice. And it sure as shit wasn't Damien. I need to know who that is. Until I do, my hands are tied."

"Do you think the techs will be able to get an ID off the username?" I asked. "Cross Security didn't have much luck."

"It's too soon to say. But something tells me you already have the name."

"I'm not sure."

She rolled her eyes. "Tell me this. Why is Theo protecting this third party?"

"Rumor is, it's a young doctor who's seen a lot of street violence and wants to help those who are too afraid or unable to get help. I'm guessing Theo doesn't want to tarnish someone else's career or reputation."

"You understand their actions are illegal for a reason."

"I do."

Montoya looked at me. "Things would go a lot better for Theo and everyone else involved if this doctor comes forward without the police forcing his hand."

"Okay," I stood, "but I need your word that Theo will get a fair shake."

"He needs more than that. He needs a miracle." She glanced around, but we were alone except for the hum of the vending machine. "It's a good thing I have a reputation as a miracle worker."

I didn't leave the police station. Instead, I ducked into the ladies' room and sent an encrypted text to the unknown user. Since Iris had used my phone, Calvin Waites would think she was sending the messages. But that didn't matter. As succinctly as possible, I explained the situation, asked him to do the right thing, told him which police station, and gave him Detective Montoya's name. The rest was out of my hands. If this guy was serious about helping, he'd come forward.

But on days like today, I wondered how many good people were left in this world. Even now, I had more than a few doubts about Theo. Had he made the situation up because he enjoyed being a back-alley surgeon? Was he getting paid on the side? Was he a crazed killer or helping the street gangs dispose of the bodies they dropped? The only way to know for certain was to get his accomplice to speak up. In the meantime, the police would comb through every part of his life. I'd already done it but found next to nothing. I didn't think they'd have much better luck.

Returning to the front desk, I smiled at the officer. "Do you know if Detective Trevitt from San Diego is in the building?"

"Didn't you ask to speak to Detective Montoya?"

"Yes, but now I need to speak to Trevitt, if he's here."

"Trevitt's assisting robbery-homicide."

"I'm aware."

The officer picked up the phone and made the request. He covered the receiver. "What's your name?"

"Alex Parker."

He nodded and put the phone down. "Go on up. I was told you know the way." He buzzed me through the door, wondering why I hadn't made the detour myself. But I didn't want to risk walking into RHD unless Trevitt was there. If not, Ganz would miss dessert, and the last thing I needed to do was piss off the lawyer.

"I was wondering when you were going to join us." Trevitt met me at the top of the stairs. "Petrocelli wanted to send officers to pick you up."

"How thoughtful."

Trevitt gestured to a chair at the conference table. I sat down, eyeing the empty coffeepot on the other side of the room. I'd already passed the thirty-six hour mark on being awake. Caffeine wouldn't help. Only sleep would. Or some serious amphetamines.

"Where's Sergeant Russo?" I asked.

"He's gone for the day. The captain approved him to liaise between the two departments, so he hasn't gone far.

He'll be here in the morning." Trevitt looked like he wanted to say something, but thought better of it. "I'll let Petrocelli know you're here."

"Great." I scanned the intel on the corkboards which lined two walls inside the conference room. The first few were devoted to the three alleged suicides—Sophie Marshman, Robert Devers, and Joel Curry. The next two boards contained details on Roland Jordan, his last known whereabouts, friends, relatives, and anything that might be useful in apprehending him. I stared at the surveillance photos from the bus terminal. Roland Jordan carried a large backpack and that was it. Everything he valued he kept with him.

"When I spoke to him, he didn't strike me as a killer. He struck me as a protector," I said when Trevitt returned.

"That could have been what led to the attacks. Jordan wanted to protect his people. Marshman and Devers threatened their way of life," Trevitt said.

"Devers more than Marshman. But Jordan said he kept an eye on the kid, on Robert. I don't know why he'd harm him."

"Maybe he talked him into committing suicide. He could have encouraged it. Pushed the idea. Waited for Devers to be in an altered mental state, gave him the necessary tools, and sent him to hang."

"Anything's possible." I turned away from the boards. "How many suicides have you reopened?"

"Just those two, plus Joel Curry's case. I don't think any others connect to Jordan, but it's possible."

"Sergeant Russo said he was going to check. Did he?" I asked.

Again, Trevitt gave me that odd look. "He pulled files for the last six months, but he would have caught on to anything suspicious when the deaths occurred. He's been like a dog with a bone when it comes to crimes against the unhoused. Any idea why?"

"How would I know?"

"You know an awful lot for an uninvolved third party."

"Doesn't she?" Petrocelli joined us inside the conference room. "Since you're omnipotent, Ms. Parker, why don't you tell me where Roland Jordan is hiding and save us all some time?"

"How would I know where he is? I only spoke to the man once."

"Let's see, in the last week, you've been instrumental in turning an eight-month-old case hot, accusing an otherwise upstanding member of the community of being a serial killer, one who is now being questioned by the gangs unit, and you had a grieving sister turn over a letter which has now not only complicated Detective Trevitt's life, but mine too. The sooner you come clean, the happier I'll be."

"My job isn't to make you happy. If you're looking for someone who can, you might want to check Sunset Boulevard."

Petrocelli snorted. "I'm sure vice would agree. But in the meantime, let's get back to the matter at hand. You knew these deaths were murders. I'm guessing you know a lot more than that. Share what you know before things get worse. The last thing I want is another killer loose on the streets."

"Are you sure Jordan's even responsible? All you have is a partial fingerprint. That's it. That isn't proof of anything."

"You sounded the alarm," Petrocelli said. "You can't unring that bell now."

"It's all we have to go on. Jordan knew the three most recent victims," Trevitt said. "He was at the scene of Curry's death. Afterward, he fled San Diego. That's pretty damn convincing to me. Jordan's dangerous. Have you seen his military record? Most of it is redacted, but he was a tracker who also trained in psy-ops. He knows how to play mind games. Even if he didn't pull the proverbial trigger, he handed each of them a loaded gun, knowing damn well how to convince them to do it themselves. He's a threat to the homeless community."

Petrocelli pointed at me. "And to her."

"It's sweet you're worried about me," I said.

"I'm not." Petrocelli dropped into a chair. Leaning back, he rested his heels on the edge of the table and grabbed one of the folders. "But since you insist on being a thorn in my side, I thought I'd return the favor. How's protective custody sound?"

"Go screw yourself."

Petrocelli almost grinned. "You want to go with the second option then?"

"What is it?"

"We want to set up at your office. You gave Jordan your card. As far as we know, you're the only person he knows in Los Angeles. And Sgt. Russo thinks Jordan came all this way to see you. We want access to everything listed on this card." Petrocelli pulled out one of my business cards which he'd saved from our first encounter. "E-mail, phone, your office." He flipped the card over, so I could see the front. "Did you give him any other information besides what's printed here?"

"No."

"We'd like access to your home too," Petrocelli said.

"No."

Petrocelli's face pinched. "Fine." But I couldn't stop him from posting a unit outside, and he knew it. "We'll get set up overnight at your office. That should be sufficient. In the meantime, do you have any idea where Jordan might go?"

"I keep telling you, I don't know this man. We met once. We talked for less than twenty minutes. That was it. It's ridiculous that any of you think he came here for me."

"Sgt. Russo thinks Jordan's out for revenge, since you upended his routine." Trevitt rocked a little in his chair.

"Has the sun fried your brains?" I asked, too tired to find a nicer way of asking the question. "You're assuming this man is guilty with nothing to back it. Do you even know why he'd want Joel Curry dead? Joel was dying. He didn't stay at the homeless encampment. He didn't go to the same food pantries. He didn't do anything that would interfere with Jordan's life. Why would Jordan harm him?"

Trevitt opened his mouth to say something, but Petrocelli shook his head. "She should be considered as much a suspect as Jordan. For all you know, she's responsible."

"Bite me. I wasn't anywhere near San Diego when those deaths occurred."

"It doesn't mean you didn't put someone up to it. Someone like Jordan," Petrocelli said.

I rolled my eyes. "I'd get checked for syphilis. It's known to cause insanity. At least then you'd have an excuse."

Trevitt cleared his throat, leaning forward and blocking my view of Petrocelli. "The hotline received a tip. Dashcam footage from a passing car caught Jordan running through the fast-food parking lot after Curry's death. He had blood on his hands and splattered on his shirt."

"That doesn't mean—" I began.

"Play the footage," Petrocelli said. "If not, she'll argue with us the rest of the night."

THIRTY-FIVE

"Ms. Parker?" Detective Trevitt gave the rung of my chair a gentle kick.

I startled awake, reaching for my holstered weapon.

"Take it easy." Trevitt twirled a keychain around his finger. "We're all set. Undercovers will be waiting when you arrive at work tomorrow to keep an eye on things. Petrocelli said you can go home. I thought you might like a ride."

"I'm fine."

"Are you sure you're gonna be able to keep your eyes open? I saw you nod off three times in the conference room before you finally fell asleep out here."

"I'm sure Malibu is out of your way."

"I don't mind." Trevitt tucked his thumbs into the sides of his waistband. "I'm not taking no for an answer."

"All right. Thanks." I climbed out of the chair and followed him out of the station.

Once we were on our way, Trevitt glanced at me. "I wanted to talk to you in private. First, I want to say that I don't think you had anything to do with those deaths. You explained everything to me earlier. We're good. Whatever issue Petrocelli has with you, that's his problem. It's not mine."

"I appreciate that."

"Sure. No problem. So you used to be a Fed?"

"Yep."

"Used to be. As in, you aren't currently?"

"Nope."

"Uh-huh." The way he said it made me think he didn't believe me. "A Fed from the East Coast goes private and happens to end up in an alley where she runs into Sgt. Russo." His tone gave it away. "Talk about a small world, particularly when Russo's on desk duty."

"I've been meaning to ask, if he's not authorized for field work, how come he got cleared to come to Los Angeles?"

"He didn't ask permission. He was supposed to brief the LAPD on the situation, but when he heard about the attack, he thought it was related. That's how he ended up here, and since he's already here, the brass can't be bothered to recall him."

"Russo strikes me as stubborn."

"Indeed." Trevitt glanced at me from the corner of his eye. "He used to be a solid cop, as solid as they came. Now, I'm not sure. Do you think Russo could be responsible for these deaths?"

"He was in Los Angeles when Curry died. I already checked. Russo has an alibi, plus you have the fingerprint and dashcam footage. Russo wasn't anywhere near Curry."

"You're wrong. He was in San Diego, not far from the crime scene."

"That's not possible. He was with me until ten that evening. He checked out of his hotel at ten that morning. He didn't go anywhere else. I pinged his phone."

"He left his phone," Trevitt said. "We pulled DOT footage after the tip came in. I wanted to verify the witness's story. I saw Russo's car getting off the highway at that exit twenty minutes before the dashcam showed Jordan fleeing the scene. Russo couldn't have gotten far because DOT cams showed him heading back to Los Angeles thirty minutes after he arrived in San Diego."

I swallowed, feeling as though I'd been punched in the gut. "You're sure it was his car?"

"Pretty sure. I got the plate to prove it."

"Did you see him on the dashcam?"

"No."

"What about other traffic cams?"

"No luck yet. It looks like he pulled off the highway, disappeared in a blind spot, and doesn't reappear until he gets back on the highway. I have no idea where he went or if he even went anywhere."

"Why would Will kill Curry? Or any of the other potential victims?"

"You tell me. Why's he obsessed with the homeless population?"

"He hasn't always been like this?"

"Hell no." Trevitt checked the mirrors. "He did his job, handed out assignments, supervised scenes, and assisted in tons of investigations. But he never conducted his own. If something didn't smell right, he'd take it to the detectives."

"Maybe he's bored. Desk duty can do that to a person."

"I guess." Trevitt fell silent.

I stared out the window, forcing my eyes to remain open. I didn't know Trevitt well enough to fall asleep in his car. Frankly, I didn't quite trust him. But I didn't trust Will either. "Do you know why he's on desk duty?" I asked.

"Do you want the official story or the rumors?"

"Whichever version you believe."

"I don't know what I believe," Trevitt said. "Patrol stumbled onto a cartel stash house. They called for a supervisor. Sarge shows up, but the cartel must have too. Two officers were killed in the line of duty. Sarge got wounded, and the bad guys got away. That's the official story. The unofficial version is Sarge is on the take. Cartel paid him to keep us away from their business. Patrol's blunder would have cost Sarge everything, so he shows up, calls his friends, and makes sure no one's left standing to contradict his story."

"Is that what you think happened?"

Trevitt shrugged. "You tell me."

"How would I know?"

"Like Petrocelli said, you seem to know a lot about everything. More than an innocent bystander should. And remember, I've seen your office. I have trouble believing that's one of the best private security firms in the country."

"Did you see the coffeemaker and pantry? It's swanky."

"Don't worry. I'm not going to burn your cover."

"Cover?" The sleep deprivation must have been worse than I thought.

"The Feds are investigating what really happened. They planted you with this lame-ass cover story. That's why you pinged Russo's phone and how you crossed paths with him in the first place."

"That's not..." I sighed. "You're wrong."

"Right." He winked at me. "All I ask is you tell me what you know about Russo's involvement with Jordan and if he played a part in these deaths."

That was the one thing I'd been wondering since the start. "As far as I know, he's not involved. He just wants to keep everyone safe."

"But why? He never cared about the homeless before he got assigned desk duty. Why should he care now?"

Unfortunately, I didn't have an answer. Will was the only one who could provide one, and when I'd asked, he failed to give me a satisfactory answer.

* * *

The constant chiming forced me awake. I blinked, my eyelids heavy and uncooperative. My eyes closed again, but the chiming didn't stop. What was that noise?

Forcing myself upright, I looked around the room, seeing the notification on the home security panel. It was the proximity alarm.

I stumbled out of bed, bleary-eyed. A quick toggle of the exterior cameras didn't reveal a car in the driveway or anyone at the front door. Things looked quiet.

I switched to the cameras at the back of the house. A dog was sniffing around the fence. Changing the camera angle, I saw his ball had landed inside and rolled along the patio. On the bright side, Roland Jordan wasn't attempting to break in and kill me.

After putting a hoodie on over my t-shirt and pajama

shorts, I tucked my gun at the small of my back and went to the rear door and entered the code. Cautiously, I pulled open the door and peered outside. The dog let out an excited yip when he saw me. His tail whipped back and forth.

Bending down, I picked up the ball and headed for the fence. "Lose something, buddy?" I dropped it over the gate. He caught it in his mouth and gave it a squeeze, making it squeak.

The brunette jogged up the beach toward us. "Hi." She paused when she realized I wasn't tall, dark, and delicious. "Oh, it's you."

"Sorry to disappoint. I take it you were looking for James."

"Not really." But her expression said yes. "I haven't seen him in a couple of days. Is everything okay?"

"Peachy."

She knelt down to clip the dog's leash back to his collar. "I'm not sure if you remember me from the other morning."

"I do."

She stood up, brushing sand off her knees and then her palms. "How are you feeling?"

"Better."

"I'm glad. All surfers get tossed around. I know it's scary for a newbie, but you should stick with it. Is that why you guys haven't been out on the beach lately?"

"It has more to do with work."

"Oh. Okay." She smiled. "I'm Tiffany, by the way."

"Alex."

She patted the dog, who continued to squeak. "This is Milo. We were playing fetch, and the wind picked up. I hope we didn't disturb you."

"I had to get up anyway."

"You just missed your friend."

"Friend?" I tilted my head.

"Yeah, he had a camouflage backpack over his shoulder."

"What was he wearing?"

"It looked like military gear."

"When did you see him?"

"Forty-five minutes ago, maybe. He was asking if anyone had seen you or knew where you lived."

"Did you see where he went?"

"He headed down the beach." She turned around. "I think he left."

I scanned the beach, but I didn't see anyone matching that description. "Have you seen anyone else creeping around, asking about me?"

"Only James, but he doesn't creep." She smiled. "Tell him we miss him."

"We?"

She patted the dog again. "We."

"The last time you saw James, did he have a lint roller?"

"What?"

I shook my head. "Never mind. Have a nice day." I returned to the house, locked the door, and made sure the security system remained engaged.

When did the proximity alarm first go off? The system detected a presence almost an hour ago and attempted to alert me. I had slept right through it. I'd never done anything like that before. A mistake like that could have killed me. At least Martin wasn't around to see it.

I pulled up the recordings. A man trekked up the beach. He wore a grungy camouflage cap, which matched his coat and backpack. He moved past the property before making his way up the beach to the road. He circled around the front, possibly to check the address or look for surveillance units, before knocking on the front door. He didn't ring the bell, but the doorbell camera still got a look at him. Will was right. Roland Jordan came to L.A. to find me. Now it was my turn to find him.

THIRTY-SIX

"Are you all right?" Will asked when I arrived at the office.

"Not really." I studied him, unsure what to think about any of this. Cross would murder me if he found out the police were using his satellite office to conduct a sting operation. "Why did you drop this in my lap?"

"I needed a second set of eyes and thought you could help."

I lowered my voice, afraid of being overheard. Two undercover LAPD officers were keeping an eye on things from the third empty office. On the bright side, I'd moved everything out of there before the police set up, but since they'd been here when I arrived, I didn't want to think about how much snooping they might have done at Petrocelli's request. Hopefully, he was as much a stickler for following the rules as he was for enforcing them. "Jordan came to my house this morning."

"What?"

"Shh." I cringed, hoping the cops hadn't overheard. They'd have questions, but I needed to figure out what was going on before they confused things. I waited, but neither of them poked their heads into my office. Pressing my finger to my lips, I grabbed a notepad and pen and wrote down my question. *How do you think he got my address?*

"I don't know," Will said.

"You got it." I stared at him.

"I have resources." He thought for a moment. "Maybe he does too."

"How?"

Will pulled up Roland Jordan's police file on my computer. "He lives on the street, but he gets a pension. He has an account with some money saved. He doesn't access it often, but it's how he paid for his bus ticket. See this," Will pointed to the other name on the account, "she's active military, stationed in Washington, works in intelligence. We've reached out, but she doesn't know anything about any of this."

"You don't believe her."

"I have no idea, but we weren't able to pull her phone records. Given her position and current location, no judge around here would order them. But I'm guessing she found you and told him where to look."

"Phone records, huh?" Cross Security had plenty of friends at the various providers who'd let us take a look. I entered her phone number and scanned the page of recent calls. "Three calls from an unknown in the last week. Two of them occurred two days ago, after Curry died. One of them was made before he'd been found." I read her name again, remembering it from the intel plastered on the board. "Who is she to him?"

"I'm not sure. They were in the same unit."

"Was she his girlfriend?"

"I don't know. But she received a medal for her act of bravery and a promotion and fancy duty assignment, so—"

"So she saved his bacon," I said. "And he wanted to say thanks."

"That doesn't mean they weren't knocking boots," Will said.

"It doesn't matter. She's there. He's here." I unlocked the cabinet and grabbed one of the throwaway phones. After activating it and making sure it was charged, I tucked it into my pocket. "I'm gonna get some breakfast. I'll be back."

"Do you want company?" Will asked.

"No, but if you run interference for me, I'll get you something to eat."

"Deal."

As soon as I was out of the office, I spotted the surveillance van. They followed me down the street to the café. That wouldn't work. After picking up two bags of breakfast burritos, I returned to work. Instead of continuing past the elevators, I pressed the button and went up to the fourth floor. Once I reached 4L – Risk Management, I pushed open the door.

"Hey, it's the detective lady," a guy said when I walked in.

"Alex," I reminded him. "Eric, right?"

"You remembered." He grinned. "I haven't seen you lately. What brings you up here?"

"My office is a little cramped at the moment." I held out one of the bags of breakfast burritos. "I was hoping you could do me a few favors. First, I ordered way too much, so you need to take these off my hands."

He took the bag, opening it and grinning. "No problem. I can do that."

"Second, I need to make a phone call, but it's private. Can I hide in one of your closets for a few minutes? It shouldn't take long."

"I can do better than that." He glanced around the corner. "Jett's not coming in until twelve. You can use his office."

"Thanks."

"Just don't touch anything. He's weird about his stuff getting moved."

"No problem." Once I was shut inside the office, I called Mark Jablonsky. Since it was an unknown number, I wasn't sure he'd answer, but Mark being Mark picked up on the second ring because he didn't recognize it. "Hey, it's me. I don't have a lot of time, but I need to run a few things by you." I told him about Roland Jordan showing up at my house and the woman listed on his bank account.

"It sounds like she gave him the intel," Mark confirmed. "Why would she risk her position to help a serial killer?

Surely, someone with that level of training would have to know how unstable Roland Jordan is."

"He's not unstable," I said. "And I don't think he's responsible. But the police aren't listening to me."

"They rarely do."

"Careful," I warned, "you're starting to sound like Lucien."

"Bite your tongue," Mark said. "I'm looking at Jordan's previous arrests. He's only ever resorted to violence to protect people."

"That's what he said. That's why the police think he'd want to kill Robert Devers."

"Devers was sick. Addiction could make him desperate, which could, in turn, make him violent, but it hadn't happened yet."

"I didn't really call to talk about this. I wanted to tell you what Detective Trevitt told me last night."

"I've already spoken to Marty. He said Will Russo showed up at your house in the middle of the night. Didn't I tell you to stay away from him?"

"We both know I never listen. Yell at me about that later. I don't have a lot of time right now. Trevitt said Will was in the vicinity of the latest suicide. I pinged Will's phone, but it showed he was in Los Angeles. According to Trevitt, Will left it behind."

"He needed the alibi."

"Possibly. Another thing, Trevitt doesn't know why Will's been obsessed with these cases. I've been wondering the same thing. Can you see if he has an alibi for either of the two previous TODs?" I gave Mark the case numbers.

"I'll see what I can dig up."

"I owe you."

"Be careful, Parker. I mean it. If anything happens to you—"

"I know. I will."

* * *

The phone rang. I glanced at it, waiting for the cops to give me the okay before I answered. "Cross Security and

Investigations," I said. "This is Alex."

"You finally learned how to answer the phone," Cross said.

"I thought it might be you." I checked the time, but the next interview wasn't for an hour. "What happened with Monty Earles?"

"He looks promising. He's got a handle on a lot of things and knows how to find information quickly. With a little training, he'd be an excellent office manager. I made him an offer a few minutes ago. He'll get back to us by the end of the week."

"Did you cancel the rest of the interviews?"

"Not yet."

"C'mon, Lucien. We found a guy. Let's not waste any more time. I'm slammed as it is."

"I heard." Cross cleared his throat. "Mr. Ganz called me late last night. He wanted to know how much more work you'd be throwing his way."

"That depends. Iris's situation wasn't what she thought it was. It wasn't what I thought it was either."

"I did some digging, figuring you might need the help." The condescending way he said it made me want to slap him. "Amir accessed the hospital's video files. Theo Stapleton wasn't lying. We forwarded the relevant timestamp to the LAPD. That should help his case."

"What about his extracurricular activities?"

"You haven't heard?" Cross asked. "His accomplice, Dr. Waites, came forward. He's provided sworn statements, dates, times, locations, everything."

"What's going to happen to him and Theo?"

"Ganz will take care of our client. I believe he knows Waites's attorney. They'll work on coming up with a defense. But given the circumstances and Theo's home life, the DA ought to consider appearances before prosecuting. We'll see how it goes. But Theo's getting arraigned and released on bail today."

"That's better than nothing. Thanks for the assist."

I put the phone down, wondering how that conversation would play out with the LAPD. But once they'd realized who was on the line, they stopped listening in. At least, that's how it appeared. Whether that was true was anyone's guess.

"Was that news about this morning?" Will asked.

"No, that had to do with Theo."

"The cheater?"

"He's not a cheater."

"Well, damn. That's good to hear, unless he's a killer."

"No. He was playing mob doctor, but without the mob or the medical degree." I picked up my phone and sent Iris a text. "Depending on if his patients survived, he should be in the clear."

"He could be facing assault charges or criminal charges for practicing without a license," Will said. "It'll depend on if his patients want to press charges. If they aren't breathing, that's a whole other can of worms."

"That's what the defense attorney said." I checked the reply I received. Theo would be home in a couple of hours. At the present, the gunshot victim remained in stable but critical condition. Assuming he pulled through, Theo would have a chance.

"How's the wife feel about all this? She must be relieved he wasn't cheating."

"Actually, she might have preferred it."

"Why was he doing it? Was it for the money? Drugs? Other favors?"

"They threatened his life and hers. I'm not sure he ever got paid." All the crimes he'd committed had been minor, but they related directly to the duress. Theo wouldn't have had to buy drugs or illegally trespass if it hadn't been for Damien's demands. It all connected back to the gang forcing him to act. I wasn't sure Waites had the same excuse, which worried me. Waites wanted to get involved. He'd helped Theo and talked him into providing additional medical assistance to others who didn't hold them at gunpoint, literally or figuratively. That's where the problem would come in, and that's what Ganz and Waites's attorney would have to figure out.

Will snapped his fingers in front of my face. "You still with me? You zoned out."

"What did you say?" I asked.

"I said that's a better reason than throwing away a career for a few dollars." Will didn't hide the contempt.

I went into the break area and opened the fridge. But I couldn't shake the question from my mind. My phone chimed, but it wasn't the burner, it was my regular phone. Iris wondered if I'd be willing to speak to Theo about the current situation once he got home. I told her I would and put the phone down.

"What are we doing, gentlemen?" I asked.

The three cops looked at me, but no one said a word.

"Are we going to sit around all day, waiting and hoping Roland Jordan didn't throw away my business card? We have no reason to think he's going to show up here."

"You can go," one of the cops said. "We don't need you here to make an arrest."

"What happens if a client walks through that door?"

"We'll tell him to come back tomorrow," the cop said. His partner snickered.

"Fine," I turned off the computer, "but fair warning, my boss has a lot of money and way too much time on his hands. He likes it when his attorney sends him a bottle of something nice as a thank you for the seven and eight figure lawsuits he files."

"Is that supposed to scare us?" one of the undercovers asked.

"No, but it sure as shit worries me." I stared up at the ceiling. "Remember, there are eyes everywhere."

THIRTY-SEVEN

"I thought you liked cops," Will said as I drove us to Iris's house. "Why are you threatening them?"

"I wasn't." I checked my mirrors again. Ever since we left the office, I could feel someone watching. It was probably the LAPD. The surveillance van remained parked outside my office, but the police could have an unmarked assigned to follow me. "I'm ambivalent toward your kind. Don't get me wrong, some of my best friends bleed blue, but I've had enough run-ins with dirtbags who put me in the hospital."

"Is that how you got the scars on your thighs?" Will stared at me. "Not that I was looking."

"Yes, you were. And no."

"How did you get shot?"

"Which time?"

The creases on his forehead deepened. "You're serious."

"I don't like getting shot. And I don't like getting shocked either. Some sadist tortured me with a cattle prod once. That was a really bad day. Really bad."

"Jesus. I'm sorry."

I drove into a parking lot, keeping my eye on the mirrors. No one followed me in. No one parked on a nearby street. But they might be circling.

Mark hadn't gotten back to me yet, which meant he was having trouble getting the information or he'd gotten busy. But since he wouldn't want me driving around with a killer, my favor would be at the top of his to-do list. So what was taking him so long?

"I saw your face in the office when we spoke about the possibility of Theo being on the take. That bothers you," I said.

"Damn right, it does."

"You gotta give me something more than that. I can't keep doing this."

"Did Trevitt say something to you?" Will read the answer on my face, cursed, and stared out the windshield. "And you believe him."

"You told me you didn't kill Curry."

"Trevitt said I did?" Will's eyes went wide. "Why would he say that?"

"You went back to San Diego. He spotted your car near the exit, the same exit that was a hop, skip, and jump away from the fast-food restaurant where Curry died. You were in the vicinity at the time of his demise."

"Do you have any idea how pissed off that makes me? I was right there. And I had no idea what was going on."

"What were you doing there?"

Will pressed his lips together, his jaw muscles bunching. He closed his eyes, trying to control his breathing. "Fuck it." He opened his eyes and exhaled. "I had to meet an informant."

"Why did you drive all the way back to Los Angeles afterward?"

"I forgot my phone in the motel." But his eyes gave him away.

"You left it on purpose."

"Drop it, Alex. This doesn't concern you."

"You wanted to have an alibi in case someone pinged your phone."

"Drop it."

"I can't. You brought this to me. You made this my problem. I haven't slept in days. Now some guy is creeping around my house, asking my neighbors if they've seen me. Undercovers are hiding in my office, and you expect me to let this go. How?"

"That's part of the job."

"That's the part I tried to leave behind." I stared at him. "My gut says Roland Jordan isn't the killer. He protects people. He chooses to stay at those camps and keep an eye out. He provides for them. Takes care of them. He wouldn't kill them. But I bet he knows who would. And as soon as he heard the cops were looking for him, he took off. That doesn't read well for you."

"Fine, tell Detective Trevitt that. He'll buy whatever crazy theory you spin, even though he knows I was at my desk when Sophie Marshman and Robert Devers died. But we don't need facts. The rest of the department will fall in line, and they'll railroad me. It's no big deal. They'll have a villain, and you can have your office back. Everyone wins."

"Why aren't you fighting to prove you're innocent?"

"Because I shot those two officers." Will looked sick. "It was them or me. I had to, but they were my friends. I don't want shit like that to happen again. I'd do anything to prevent it. I can't... I just can't."

Unsure what to do now, I put my seatbelt back on, pulled out of the parking lot, and kept my eye on traffic, hoping to spot a tail.

"Where are we going?" Will asked.

"I'm taking you with me to see Iris and Theo. At this point, I don't know what else to do. I want to believe you, but my mind's not there yet. And you refuse to help yourself. Until I know for sure, it'd be best for everyone involved if we stick together."

"You think I might need another alibi?"

"I don't know what to think. And that's the problem."

"Do you think Roland Jordan's stupid enough to stop by your office?" Will asked.

"No. He'd spot the surveillance team a mile away. I'm guessing that's why he came to my house. He wants to tell me something. I wish I could make it easier for him, but I don't know how." I checked my mirrors again.

"The LAPD assigned a few patrol units to check Skid

Row and other popular homeless areas within the city," Will said. "They figure he'd go somewhere that felt familiar."

"It'd be like looking for a needle in a stack of needles. They'll never find him."

"That's what I said. But Trevitt's keeping track of that, which should keep him busy."

"What are you supposed to be doing?" I asked.

"Coordinating and updating the SDPD on our progress."

"That's why you've been hanging around my office all day?"

"Yep."

When we made it to the Stapletons' house, I hoped I wasn't making a mistake. Sgt. Will Russo could be a killer, which is why I didn't want to leave him unsupervised, but bringing him to meet Iris might be an even worse mistake. Exhaling, I opened my car door and stepped out. I guess I'd find out.

No one had followed me, or they were so good at surveillance I hadn't been able to make them. Will watched me from the other side of the car. "Are we good?" he asked.

"I think so. When we get inside, follow my lead, and keep your mouth shut."

He followed me up the walkway and waited a polite two steps behind me while I rang the doorbell. I smiled at the doorbell cam, figuring Iris would check it before opening the door. Her house now had state-of-the-art security. With any luck, it'd keep her and Theo safe.

A moment later, the door opened. "Hi, Iris." I indicated the man standing behind me. "This is Will Russo. He's shadowing me today."

She smiled at Will before unlocking the metal gate in front of the door. "Nice to meet you. Are you a private investigator?"

"No, ma'am," Will said. "I'm a sergeant with the San Diego police department. But I'm hoping to make a career change. Alex just needs a bit more convincing."

"Will's a client of sorts." I glanced back at him, communicating with my eyes that he keep his mouth shut. "Y'know, it might be better if he waits in the car."

"That's okay. The police know everything. We don't have anything left to hide." She glanced toward the kitchen. "At least, we better not."

"Is Theo in there?" I asked.

Iris nodded. "He's starving." She lowered her voice. "It serves him right."

"Are you okay?"

"Ask me when my head stops spinning."

"Does Theo know you called me?"

"He does."

"Okay." I patted her arm and went into the kitchen. "Mr. Stapleton?"

Theo turned away from the fridge, a sandwich in one hand, a plate in the other. "Yhmm." He finished chewing and swallowed. After drinking from the orange juice container, he closed the fridge and put the plate in the sink. "You were there the other night. How's your back?"

"I've had worse."

"I warned you."

"May I sit?" I gestured to the kitchen table.

"Go ahead." Theo glanced into the living room, but Will and Iris remained in there. Will had found something of interest on the coffee table, and Iris was telling him about it. "Is that your bodyguard?"

"I don't need protecting. But you and your wife do."

Theo nodded. "I'm sorry."

"You should tell her that." I jerked my head in Iris's direction.

"I have."

"Good."

Theo studied me for a moment. "Iris said you met at grief counseling." He stared out the back door. "I didn't know she felt the way she did, that she was losing me. I didn't realize she even noticed I was gone. She's been like a shell for so long, and now..."

"I'm not a therapist. I've used every trick in the book to avoid talking to them, so don't expect me to solve your marital problems or absolve you of your sins. That's not why I'm here. I want to know what Cross Security can do to help. We've updated your home security system and put additional measures in place. Right now, a team of security personnel is keeping an eye on your wife. I can arrange an additional team to guard you."

Theo stared at the table for a long time. "Why are you helping me?"

"Iris loves you. She might not like you or trust you right now, but she loves you. She needs you to be okay, like you needed her to be okay. At least, that's the story I keep hearing."

"I was afraid they'd kill her. The things they said, the threats they made—" Theo swallowed. "I didn't know where to turn or what to do. I wasn't sure how to get myself out of it."

"Digging deeper is never a solution. Take it from someone who's screwed up more times than she'd ever admit." I reached for my phone. "I'll assign a detail for your protection until we know the threat's been removed. Detective Montoya told me they planned to arrest every member of the Slayers that you identified. Please tell me you didn't leave anyone out."

"I didn't."

"What about Dr. Waites? How does he figure into this? Is he the only person you were protecting by keeping silent? Because speaking up is the only way you and Iris survive this. Do you understand?"

Theo nodded. "Calvin came forward. He told the police everything I didn't. After that, I didn't see any point in holding my tongue."

"How did Calvin end up involved?" I asked. "I saw the hospital footage. The night Damien showed up in the parking lot, shot, you were alone."

"I was already going through a tough time. I'd only been back to work a couple of weeks. Every second I spent away from home, away from Iris, I worried. A lot of my friends and coworkers noticed. Calvin had been really great about checking in. He understood what it was like to go through something like this. He'd come over for dinner once or twice a week and talk to Iris. I don't know if it made a difference, but it made me feel better to get his opinion on how to help my wife."

"You should have gone to therapy with her," I said.

"The first time she went, she cried for a week. She wouldn't talk. She wouldn't eat. I hated seeing her in that much pain. I didn't want her to go back. I just wanted her to get better. Calvin stopping by and talking to her helped. After my run-in and repeat encounters with Damien, he could tell something was wrong. He thought it had to do with Iris. That's when I told him what happened, what they were forcing me to do. Calvin used to work with an outreach program, volunteering his time and expertise to bring care to those who couldn't afford it or those who had problems getting access to the healthcare they needed. The program was shut down for safety issues. But Calvin stuck with it. He knew some of the Slayers I'd patched up. He thought he could convince the gang to leave me alone."

"But he couldn't?"

"No. Instead, he came with me anytime Damien called. And since he was risking his neck and career for me, I would go out with him. Those are the texts you found."

"Wasn't Calvin worried about losing his medical license?"

"He wasn't charging his patients. He was providing care. He'd spoken to a lawyer about it, and a lot of what he did was in a gray area. The licensing board could have a field day, but his actions weren't criminal. But mine were. As a nonphysician, practicing medicine and performing the advanced procedures I did could be considered criminal. That's why I was afraid to come forward. Now I feel terrible because Calvin's facing the firing squad too."

"He'll figure it out. The focus now has to be on making sure Damien and his Slayer buddies don't retaliate against you."

"I'm planning to testify. So is Calvin. Detective Turner promised we'd be safe. It's the only way."

"Have they been arrested yet?" I asked.

"I'm not sure, but Detective Turner said they might be released on bail. That's why Iris is worried. As far as I know, they don't know where I live. They only know where I work. I've been careful."

"I noticed." But Theo's arrest would be part of the public

record. Damien would be able to find him if he wanted. "Cross Security will keep an eye out until we come up with a better solution."

"The police will keep watch. Detective Turner promised they'd beef up patrols and monitor the street chatter. Everyone in dispatch and a lot of cops know my wife. They'll do what they can, but with a city this large, they can get overwhelmed and short-staffed. I don't want to think where that would leave us. It'd be like Calvin's patients who got cut from care. If volunteers didn't bring them food and check in on them, I'd hate to think where a lot of those people would be. As it is, a good portion of them are living in their cars or on the streets. They need people like Calvin helping. Frankly, being able to do that, to do what Iris and Gary used to do, made me feel good inside, like all this shit was worth it."

"Iris used to help the homeless?" I asked.

"They'd perform wellness checks, make sure everyone had the medicines they needed, and they'd bring them food and water. It was routine, but every one of those people expected to see Iris and Gary. They thought of them as friends or family. What happened to that ambulance didn't just end one person's life and ruin another's. It hurt a lot of people."

THIRTY-EIGHT

My mind had latched on to a few of the things Theo Stapleton had said. The people in need trusted Iris and Gary. They trusted Calvin and Theo. Even that bastard Damien and the Slayers let Theo and Calvin treat their injuries, knowing the police could roll up or Theo could let a knife slip or overdose his patient on whatever pills he picked up that day. But they trusted the medics and medical professionals enough to let them help.

"Police are first responders," I said.

"What an astute observation," Will replied. "I've got one for you. The grass is green."

"Smartass." I glanced at him. "We've gone over this a million times, but Theo said something that stuck. On the off chance the suicides are murders and you didn't kill them and Jordan didn't kill them, whoever did was someone the victims were used to seeing. Someone like a social worker, volunteer, or EMT."

"Haven't we been over this already?"

"We have, but I don't know how deeply you dug into it. I didn't have much time, but the few names I researched came up inconclusive."

"I ran everyone's name. I checked the social workers,

the clergy, the people employed by the pantries, soup kitchens, and shelters. Only a few didn't have alibis, but after Curry dropped, everyone alibied out."

"You're sure?"

"That's what the patrol officers Trevitt assigned to look into it said."

"Why didn't he handle that himself?" I asked.

"You can ask him, but I'm guessing it's because we'd already settled on Roland Jordan as our prime suspect. And Trevitt tends to follow his best lead and delegate the rest."

"What about a volunteer who worked off the books?"

"Sure, that fits. But how exactly are you going to figure out who that is?"

"A lot of legwork." I stopped at the red light, wondering if it was worth checking in at the police station. "We'll have to question everyone at the camps again. Or we find Roland Jordan and ask him."

"You think he wants to tell you something?"

"He came to my house for a reason."

"To kill you."

"Maybe, but I don't think that's what this is. He's not that guy."

"I'll try not to take that personally, since you think I could be. But fleeing the city while being wanted for questioning is not the way to go. I get that most people on the fringe have trouble trusting the police. But if Jordan is trying to protect people, or so it seems, why didn't he come to us and tell us what was happening? We could have stopped it or made an arrest."

"Would anyone have believed him?"

"Point taken." Will turned in his seat, reading the street sign I drove past. "You missed your turn for the station."

"No, I didn't."

"Yeah, you did. It was right back there." Will tapped against the window.

"We aren't going to the station. We're going to find Jordan."

Martin and I had run miles along the beach. My gut said Jordan had found a secure place to bunk down and wait for nightfall. I had a few ideas of where he might have gone, places where he wouldn't be noticed. Places he'd feel safe. I'd find him, or he'd find me. Nightfall was coming. He'd make another approach under the cover of darkness, if I didn't find him before then.

The first thing I did when I got home was check the security feeds. Roland Jordan hadn't made another approach. But the beach had gotten busy. A lot more people were out, and with the bright sun overhead, he'd be easy to spot.

"I'm surprised the police aren't sitting on this place," Will said, peering out the front window.

"Me too." But I wasn't going to look a gift-horse in the mouth.

Deciding our best bet was retracing Jordan's steps, Will and I headed in the direction Jordan had gone. At some point, we split up to cover more ground. Jordan had to be here. Somewhere. He came all this way. Why hadn't I heard the proximity alarm and let him in earlier today? Why didn't he ring the doorbell?

By the time the sun set, I was tired, thirsty, and cold. The wind had picked up. Will pointed to a spot farther down the beach. "What about over there?" he asked. "Have you checked there?"

"It's too close to the water. He wouldn't set up down there."

"You can't be certain of that." Will continued toward it. "Let's check it out, and then we'll call it quits."

"Go ahead," I said. "I'm gonna check over there before we head back." I indicated an area with tall grass poking out of the sandy terrain. It was close to a house, which had a lockbox and for sale sign out front. The back of the property faced the water, and the landscaping made anyone behind the house invisible from the street.

A ringing phone caused me to turn. Will stopped, fishing the device out of his pocket. "This is Russo," he said. "No. We haven't seen or heard anything. Alex had business to take care of, so we've been running errands most of the day. Did anything turn up? Did the hotline receive any new tips?" Will turned, noticing me watching him, and waved me off. "Uh-huh."

I continued toward the house, glancing back to see Will had drifted farther away with the phone pressed to his ear. "Hello?" I kept my voice low, not wanting to draw attention to myself, but afraid I'd get shot if the owners hadn't moved out yet or if the realtor was in the middle of showing the house to prospective buyers.

The wind made the gate rattle as it blew past. The fence was a white wooden construction. Beyond the fence was a covered pool surrounded by a few dead potted plants.

More rustling sounded off to the side. Two tall palm trees stood on the left side of the house, providing shade and additional privacy. The trunks left a narrow path to the front of the house. In the growing darkness, I couldn't see past the trees.

Turning, I squinted, but I'd lost sight of Will. Reaching for my flashlight, I turned it on and aimed at the stepping stones which led around the side of the house. Sand and debris covered the stones. No one had been here recently.

Before I could head back down the beach, a thud sounded behind me. "Don't scream."

Whipping around, I aimed the flashlight while I yanked my gun free from the holster. Roland Jordan didn't even wait for me to find him in the light before grabbing the barrel of my gun in both his hands and flipping it out of my grasp. He ejected the magazine and cleared the chamber.

"Nice trick." I stepped backward, slightly afraid.

"I'm not here to hurt you." Jordan looked from left to right. "How did you find me?"

"I could ask you the same thing."

He handed me my unloaded weapon. "Force of habit." He glanced in the direction we'd last seen Will. "The police want to arrest me. You brought them to my front door."

"That wasn't my intention."

"This is why I never should have talked to you." Jordan pulled on a string, releasing something from the branches above. Kneeling down, he tucked the material into his backpack. "The police presence used to keep the crazies away. It kept my people safe. I didn't realize the crazies had found another way to lure the unhoused community away from safety."

"Lured away?"

"That's what I came to tell you." His eyes hadn't stopped moving. "They're closing in."

I looked around but didn't see anything. "No one's here. It's just the two of us. What's going on?"

The way he looked made me think he was ready to rabbit or grab a weapon and start firing. Maybe he wasn't as stable as I originally thought. Will had warned me about this.

"He'd show up sometimes to help. He'd ask questions about our living situation, the dealers and predators in the area, and how to make things safer. I wrote him off. He was blowing hot air, like the bureaucrats and officers. They said they'd make things better, but nothing ever improved. Until you showed up, I didn't realize or I didn't want to believe it. But he was separating the weak from the rest of the herd. He was a wolf in sheep's clothing."

"Who?"

Jordan trembled, his right hand spasming at his side. "I tracked him away from the camp. Away from everything. He caught on, so he offered Myrtle dinner and popcorn to feed the squirrels."

"Roland, you're not making any sense."

His eyes grew intense. "Listen." He fastened the pack on his back. "She kept talking about the squirrels. That's her thing. I don't understand it, but it makes her happy. Before dinner, she asked me to watch her house. I thought she was going to get a hot meal. But when she didn't come back, I went looking. I followed the trail of pink fluff and found her, miles away. Myrtle knew better. She knew not to venture that far from the camp. She knew it wasn't safe."

"I don't—"

"Listen," he insisted. "I found her on a bench, waiting for the squirrels. I sent her home. But he lured her out so I would go after her, so I would be there." He stared at me. "Did she make it back okay?"

"I don't know."

"Dammit. I hope she's okay." He wrung his hands together and wiped them on his pants. "I never made it back. I stopped to see if I could salvage some scraps from a dumpster. That's when I heard the call. That fast-food joint has one of the only payphones left. I heard him calling for help."

"Who?" I asked.

"Um...Joe. No, that's not right. Jonah?"

"Joel? Joel Curry?"

Jordan shrugged. "I'm not good with names. I've told you that. But that sounds right." He froze, taking half a step back and listening. "I don't have much time. They're almost here."

"What happened to Joel? What did you see?"

"Joel was in bad shape. He was crying, begging. I didn't want to intrude. He sounded desperate, afraid. But I didn't want to leave him like that, so I lingered in the shadows. He had called a suicide hotline, I think. That's how it sounded. A few minutes later, that asshole arrived in an unmarked car. I thought the operator must have called the police to get them to talk Joel down. Forced hospitalization is the worst, but the cop didn't act like he wanted to bring Joel in. That's when I realized something was wrong. I tried to stop it, but I didn't make it in time. By the time I got close enough, the cop was gone. I checked Joel's pulse. But his throat was slit. It reminded me of the beheadings I'd seen. A lot of carnage, not much else."

"Roland," I tried to get him back to the present, "what happened to Joel? Did he kill himself?"

"No. The cop who'd been coming around, asking the questions, pretending to care, pretending to help, he killed Joel. He wanted Myrtle, but she got distracted along the way or wouldn't cooperate. Myrtle's in her own world. Joel wasn't like that. He wanted the drink. That was it."

"Do you know the cop's name?" I asked.

Jordan took another step backward, peering between the trees. "They're here."

"I need a name."

Before Jordan could utter a word, we were bathed in white light. "Freeze. Police. Put your hands in the air, and step away from the woman."

I turned, raising my hands. Trevitt and a team of

uniforms converged on us from the other side of the house. Will raced up the beach toward us, his badge catching the light as it bounced from the chain hanging from his neck.

"Stay right there," Will yelled. "We have you surrounded."

Jordan backed against the trees. "It's him." Forcing himself between the two trunks, he turned and ran, disappearing across the street before the police reached our position.

Trevitt keyed the radio. "Suspect fleeing. We need to box him in." Trevitt gave the coordinates while the uniforms chased after Jordan. Will grabbed the flashlight from my hand, planning to follow. "He could be armed, Sarge. It's best if you stay here. Let us handle this."

THIRTY-NINE

I stared out the back door. The manhunt continued, but it had been ten hours since Roland Jordan had been spotted. He knew they were there. He knew how close the police were and how to escape. When we'd been talking, I thought he was paranoid. Now I realized that wasn't the case. He had everything timed perfectly. He wouldn't get caught, and if he did, he wouldn't go down without a fight.

"That's all he said?" Detective Trevitt asked.

"That's it. He said he didn't do it and wants to be left alone."

"You're sure?" Petrocelli asked. "He didn't say how he found you or why he came here?"

"No."

Petrocelli rolled his eyes. "This is a citywide manhunt for a suspected murderer. If he reaches out to you again, we'll be ready. Are you sure you aren't interested in protective custody?"

"Positive. If Jordan wanted to hurt me, he had his chance. I don't think he's a killer."

"Because he didn't kill you?" Trevitt asked. "That's the stupidest thing I've ever heard."

Will watched me from the corner of his eye. He'd been

on the phone with San Diego for a good chunk of the night and most of the morning. "All right. I'll see you soon." He hung up. "The captain wants me to come home. He thinks the situation is too hot for me to handle."

"All right. Go home and see what you can dig up. Find us some answers, Sarge," Trevitt said.

"That's the plan." Will put his jacket on and headed for the door.

"I'll walk you out," I said.

Will opened his car door, which an officer had dropped off earlier this morning. "Do you want to tell me why you're lying to everyone?"

"I'm not."

"Bullshit." He glanced back at the house. "You had time to talk to Jordan. He told you something. Something you aren't saying."

"He's worried about Myrtle. That's all he wanted to talk about."

"Myrtle?" Will arched an eyebrow. "The one with the pink fur coat?"

"How did you know that?"

"You must have mentioned it."

But I didn't think I had. "He thinks whoever's been harming the homeless targeted her but settled for Joel Curry instead."

"I'll check on her and see what she has to say." Will stared into my eyes. "Anything else?"

"That's it."

"Okay." He opened the car door and climbed inside. "For the record, I'm sorry."

"For what?"

"Everything."

I watched Will drive away, the sinking feeling only getting worse. Jablonsky had called hours ago, in the midst of this mess, to tell me he verified Will had been on duty when the bodies had been found, but no one could pinpoint Will's exact whereabouts at the times of death. He'd been on shift, but he'd stepped out to get coffee around two a.m., the same night Sophie Marshman died. And no one recalled what he'd been doing the morning

Robert Devers died. Combined with Roland Jordan pointing the finger at a cop, one who he believed had been present last night, and Will's knowledge of Myrtle's coat, I couldn't help but think I'd been wrong to trust him.

"Fuck."

"Do I want to know?" Petrocelli asked, creeping up behind me.

"Probably not."

He shrugged, continuing toward his car.

"Actually," I called after him, "do you have a minute?"

"No." But he stopped beside his car. "What is it?"

"Not here." I opened the passenger side door and climbed in, which only annoyed him further.

"I'm not an Uber driver," he said, joining me inside.

"I may have forgotten to mention a few details, details that our friends from San Diego don't need to know about."

"Friends? They aren't my friends."

Hoping that meant he wouldn't divulge what I was about to say, I filled him in on everything that happened with Roland Jordan. "He said a cop killed Curry."

"I'll look into the payphone angle. If that's even true, there will be a record of it with the suicide hotline. Police dispatch should have been notified if an officer or negotiator had been sent to the scene, but no one mentioned that to me. It wasn't in the file either. More than likely, this is just another bald-faced lie made by a dangerous individual."

"Or someone's covering something up."

"Who?" Petrocelli waited, but I didn't say anything. "It's Russo. He killed his own. Now he's killing more innocents."

"I don't know. But if he is, Myrtle may be in danger. He said he'd check on her."

"I'll make sure nothing happens to her."

"Thanks."

Petrocelli gave me another look, shaking his head. "Get out of my car, unless you want me to bring you in for obstruction."

"Not this again." I got out of the car and watched Petrocelli drive away. A surveillance team remained outside the house, and another one was parked closer to where we'd found Jordan. The undercovers remained at the Cross Security office. This was a mess.

I went back inside to find a few techs performing one final check. Once they were done, they let themselves out. I flopped onto the couch, glad Martin wouldn't be home until late tomorrow, but until they apprehended Jordan or found the actual killer, the police presence wouldn't be going anywhere. I'd have to find proof and fast, or Martin would be coming home to a crowded house.

"All right," Trevitt said, "we'll get out of your hair. I'm ready to knock off. Twenty-four hours on is way too much for me. You got my number, right?"

"Yep."

"Good." He exhaled. "I can't believe Jordan got away from us. How did you know where he'd be?"

"Lucky guess."

Trevitt didn't look like he was buying it. "Did Sgt. Russo tell you where to look?"

"How would he have known?"

"These last few months, Russo's spent a lot of his off hours with the homeless. He must know how they think. Maybe he knows Jordan. Do you think they could be working together?"

"I doubt it."

"Well, Jordan fled San Diego. Someone could have tipped him. How else would he have known not to go back to the camp after Curry's murder? He had to know we were looking for him. Y'know, Will was close to the scene at the time of Curry's death, just like Jordan. They could be in this together."

"You're accusing the sergeant of murder?"

"It's not much of a leap. Russo already killed two men that we know about." Trevitt rubbed a hand down his face. "Forget I said anything. That's just the exhaustion talking." But it wasn't, and we both knew it.

After everyone left, I pulled out the burner phone and called Cross. "I need help." Once he was up to speed and thoroughly pissed that his brand new office was occupied by the LAPD, he agreed to help. He also made several threats about shutting down this entire endeavor, firing me, and reminding me exactly what I was supposed to be doing in California. "Thanks, Lucien."

"This conversation isn't over."

"We're on a clock."

"I'm aware." He cleared his throat. "I'll see what we can access. But I told you not to involve yourself in police investigations. Going up against a killer with a badge is the worst thing you could do."

"I know."

"You should," he snapped. "We will talk about this later. Right now, don't get killed."

"I'm not a target."

"Not yet. But that could change. Stay vigilant. I'll be in touch. In the meantime, a security team will provide protection. As soon as the LAPD are out of my office, I'll have a clean-up crew perform a sweep for any bugs before we get back to business."

"Yes, sir."

Cross cursed a few times. "I'll fly out as soon as I can."

"That's not necessary."

"I disagree."

I put the phone down. Surveillance units had eyes on the beach house and the office. They'd keep track of me if I went anywhere, and they were monitoring the phone lines. They hadn't been granted access to my personal computer, just my work e-mail, which meant I could continue to work unhindered.

I checked all the information I had. I'd gotten the names of every officer who'd been on the beach last night. Will Russo remained a question mark. The facts could be spun in either direction, but according to Will, he had alibis for the murders. If he had met with an informant the night of Joel Curry's death, his informant could alibi him out, except obtaining information like that was next to impossible. But I couldn't fathom why a sergeant would have an informant.

Moving on to the next few names on the list, I looked into the officers who'd shown up to assist Detective Trevitt, but without access to the internal police servers, I had to ascertain alibis through other means, like tracking their activities and whereabouts through social media. I scratched out a couple of names and referred the others to my colleagues to dig into. Then I pulled up the research I'd already done on Detective Gabriel Trevitt.

Trevitt was a homicide detective with a decade and a half on the force. No reports of abuse, no domestic calls, no serious issues or complaints. Trevitt had never been married. I checked, but he only had a single social media account for networking and professional contacts. He was smart. He didn't want to jeopardize his career or himself by posting nonsense on the internet, which is how a lot of law enforcement officers got in trouble.

Since a basic search didn't get me anywhere, I ran a background check. Trevitt grew up in foster care. It had been a revolving door between stints of his mother going to jail, going to rehab, and fighting to get him back. At eighteen, he was left to his own devices. He'd gotten a scholarship and a few grants to attend college. Combined with a work study, he scraped together enough to have food to eat and a place to live for the next four years. He'd applied and been accepted to the police academy before he even graduated. Besides a ten month span at age twenty-two that I couldn't find a known address for him, there weren't any other blips on his otherwise unremarkable record.

I leaned back, the nagging buzzing in my brain getting louder. On a whim, I searched for Trevitt's mother, Natalie. Her obituary was the first thing that popped up. She'd died less than a year ago. She'd never gotten clean and gotten it to stick for more than a few weeks. Surely, Trevitt must have had to divulge this on his application. The police department required knowledge of any association with criminals.

Dialing Heathcliff, I waited, but he didn't answer. Hanging up, I sent him a text, remembering I was contacting him from an unfamiliar number. A few minutes later, he called me back.

"Do I need to get a plane ticket?" he asked.

"No."

"Are you sure? Are you okay? What's going on? Why are you using a burner?"

"The police are monitoring my phone, and I don't want them to know what I'm doing."

"What are you doing? Is this about the suicides in San Diego?"

"Yes. I found something disturbing concerning the lead detective. You spoke to Trevitt. Did he act squirrely?"

"Maybe a little anxious and annoyed. That's how anyone acts when an outsider wants to poke holes in a case."

"That was it?"

"What do you have on this guy, Parker?"

"His mom was an addict. She'd been living on the streets. She ODed. Now more homeless addicts are being picked off, and Trevitt's ruling them all suicides."

"You think his judgment's impaired?"

"Possibly, or something worse. I need to know where he was at the time of these deaths. And I don't know how to get this information."

"Why don't you ask your sergeant friend?"

"Because Trevitt blew a hole in Will's alibi. He told me Will's the killer."

"Shit. You think it's one of them, but you don't know which. What does the evidence say?"

"It doesn't say anything. The only evidence is a fingerprint on a razor blade which connects to a third party."

"But you don't think it's him?"

"No."

"Why not?" Heathcliff asked.

"Because he told me a cop did it."

"Great, which cop?"

"That's where things get tricky."

"The way I see it, your only option is to turn this over to IAD and let them sort it out."

"I turned it over to the LAPD. I'm just not sure Detective Petrocelli believes me or likes me enough to stick his neck out on this."

Heathcliff didn't say anything for a long time. Finally, he said, "All right. Let me run this by Lt. Moretti. Maybe there's something we can do on our end."

FORTY

I was waiting in the living room when Martin came home. He carried two suitcases inside, turned, and grabbed the other two from where Marcal had left them on the porch. One of these days, I'd teach that man how to pack light.

"Hey, handsome." I met him at the door, backing him against it and flipping the locks before kissing him.

"You missed me," he breathed, lifting me off the ground. "Why don't you greet me like this every time I come home?"

"Maybe I will from now on."

He grinned. "I have a surprise for you."

"How many people stowed away on your jet?" I asked.

Martin gave me a confused look. "None, although Mark almost took me up on the offer, but he couldn't take another week off. He promised he'd be here next weekend and wanted me to remind you he's only coming for vacation. No work. No more favors."

"What about Lucien or Derek?"

"I didn't see either of them. Was I supposed to?"

"No." I shook it off, disentangling my limbs from around his body so he could put me down. "Tell me about the surprise."

He gave me that look that said he knew something was wrong. "How about you tell me what's going on first? Before I left, you had to get stitches and that son of a bitch sergeant showed up at our house. What happened with that?"

"The Theo situation's been taken care of. It's a legal issue now. Iris has my number. She knows I'm here if she needs someone to talk to, but that gig's done which means no more knife fights in condemned buildings."

"I'm not sure which part of that sentence is more unsettling, knife fights or condemned building. Why didn't you mention this to me before I left?"

"Would you have left?"

Martin ran his thumb across my cheek and gave me a gentle kiss. "Not without you."

"That's why I didn't mention it. But it's fine now. Everything's fine."

"I thought we weren't keeping secrets."

"That wasn't a secret. That was one of those things that you didn't need to know about. Let's call it a surprise." I gave him a bright smile. "Speaking of, I'm waiting."

Martin's eyes narrowed. "You're damn lucky I missed you." He ran both hands through my hair. He'd always been clingier than I liked, but I didn't mind the contact.

"I missed you," I said.

He released me, grabbed his bags, and headed for the bedroom. "We've been together long enough that I know when you're avoiding telling me something. Bruiser pointed out the surveillance team stationed near our house, and Mark said you were using a burner phone. Why are you taking so many precautions?"

"That's complicated. I don't believe we're in any danger. But Lucien thought sending a security team to keep watch would be a good idea, and the police have a surveillance team out front in case anyone decides to drop by, which is also why they are monitoring the house phone, my phone, and the Cross Security lines."

"Who do they think will show up?"

"It depends on who you ask. Cops are worried about

Roland Jordan stopping by again. He's suspected of killing a homeless man, but Jordan didn't do it. Instead, he knows who did, which is why I think the person responsible is hoping to take him into custody. After which, I suspect he'd suffer some sort of freak accident in lockup."

"Custody?" Martin put one of the suitcases on top of the bed and unzipped it. As he started to put away his newly updated wardrobe, I sprawled out on the bed and sifted through the neatly folded garments, finding several of his shirts that I wouldn't mind borrowing. "That would mean the killer's a cop. Is it the guy who ate pancakes in my dining room?"

"Do you think it's him?"

Martin stopped what he was doing and stared at me. "You don't know?"

"Given the evidence and the back and forth, the odds are fifty-fifty. My money's on the second option, but you met Will. I'd like your opinion."

"I once employed a homicidal maniac."

"We all make mistakes." I picked up one of his concert t-shirts I found at the bottom of the pile. It was dark purple with blue writing and super soft.

"Hey." Martin held up a stern finger. "These are mine. You said you didn't want anything from home."

I put the shirt down, figuring I'd borrow it from his drawer when he was otherwise occupied. "Do you think Will's a killer?"

Martin finished unpacking that suitcase and switched it out for his garment bag. "I don't know." But there was something Martin wasn't saying. He smoothed the creases from his jacket and hung it in the closet. "He seems conflicted, like he's being pulled in too many directions."

"You got that from pancakes?"

"No, I got that from the conversation. He seems like a man who wants to break free and start over. Who do you think he killed?"

"The homeless, but he's been investigating these crimes the entire time, even before the deaths. He must have had some inkling something was going down."

"And he brought them to your attention." Martin

grabbed the rest of the hangers and carried them to the closet. "You're not involved. You're over a hundred miles away. He wouldn't bother making that trek or dragging you into any of this if he were responsible. There would be no point. But you already know that, which is why you've never thought he was guilty and why you've taken his claims seriously from the start."

"You summarize things so well."

Martin smirked. "It's one of my many talents. Also, I know you. You won't discount any possibilities, but it's a waste of time and we both know it." Martin put the bag on the floor and went to retrieve another one from the living room. He returned a minute later. "Since you don't think Will's a killer but the prime suspect is pointing a finger at a cop, who do you suspect?"

"The lead detective, Gabriel Trevitt." I filled Martin in on the things I'd discovered. "It's all circumstantial. I told Petrocelli. I'm not sure what he's going to do about it."

"He's the one who keeps threatening to arrest you, right?"

"Yes."

"I'm not sure you can count on him either."

"There was a time Derek Heathcliff used to threaten to arrest me too, so I called him for advice."

"That explains your earlier question." Martin went into the attached bathroom with his bag to unload his toiletries. "What did Heathcliff say?"

"He's going to get the lieutenant to call the LAPD and vouch for me, I think. I can't be sure. Heathcliff was vague on the phone. He probably didn't have much of a plan. This isn't his jurisdiction. He's already stuck his neck out for me once when he looked into the two suicides and spoke to Detective Trevitt on the phone."

"Could that be enough of an excuse for Heathcliff to ring some kind of alarm bell?" Martin asked.

"I'm not sure."

"The one thing I know for certain is Derek Heathcliff would do anything for you." Martin returned to the bedroom. "Not that I can blame him."

"We're friends," I said.

"I know. My guess is whatever he's doing will keep you safe and get the guilty party off the street or whatever."

"I wish I knew what that was."

"I'm sure he'd tell you if it was important," Martin eyed me. "How did you put it? It could be something he doesn't think you need to know about."

I made a face. "It sounded better when I said it."

Martin slid the last piece of luggage across the bed toward me. "Here."

"Is this my surprise?"

"It's not much of a surprise, just a few things I thought you'd like to have from home."

I arched an eyebrow. "This isn't my surprise?"

"No."

"Are you hiding my surprise in your pants?"

"That's got to be the worst pick-up line ever."

"But you didn't deny it."

"Sweetheart, you can absolutely have what's in my pants, but that's only because I fully intend to exceed all your expectations which shouldn't be a surprise."

"It could be if you got a tattoo or piercing. You know, they sell elephant boxers. Under the right conditions, the trunk could move. That could be surprising."

Mischievous thoughts danced behind his eyes. "Oh, I can make the trunk move."

FORTY-ONE

Martin pressed his lips to my temple, his arm tightening around my waist. "Stop looking at your phone. We agreed to take today off."

"That was before."

"Nothing's changed. You told me our lives aren't in danger. And there's nothing you can do. So we are going to have a good time." He led me to the pizza stand. "Two slices, please."

The guy slid them onto paper plates. Martin paid him, and we found a bench to sit on. Nearby, two kids chased each other up and down the pier while a mother shouted at them to be mindful of other people.

"This isn't bad, but I miss the pizza back home," I said.

Martin took a bite, chewed thoughtfully, and wiped his mouth on a napkin. "We should have tried the vegan version with endives."

I pressed the back of my hand to his forehead. "Don't move. You might be suffering from heatstroke."

He grabbed my hand and kissed the back of my knuckles. "I bet it's good."

I looked frantically from left to right. "Don't they have a first aid station around here? Hang on, I'll call for an ambulance."

Martin kept a straight face. "Would it be so bad if you had to get used to this kind of pizza? They have plenty of options for toppings. If you don't want endives, we could try the veggie combo. That'd be just as healthy."

"If I wanted healthy, I wouldn't eat pizza."

"I've seen you put salad on top of pizza before."

"I told you, that was because I was out of forks. It doesn't count. And there was ranch dressing."

"I thought it was creamy Italian." Martin laughed, enjoying watching the panic on my face. "Okay, okay." He held up his hands before picking up his plate and taking another bite. "I was going to wait until dinner to tell you the surprise, but something tells me I better do it now, before you have a panic attack in the middle of the Santa Monica Pier."

A wave of horror came over me. "We're staying here permanently."

He laughed, nearly choking on the pizza. After coughing a few times and swallowing, he shook his head. "The project's approved. The research caught the eye of the government, which I feared, but Guillot sold me on it. We qualified for research grants and additional funding. I'll be able to name a project manager who can take over. He'll run things from here, and with all this additional funding, the L.A. office is now our top performing branch."

"That's great. Congratulations."

Martin beamed. "Thank you."

I waited a beat, but he continued to eat his pizza while grinning down at the plate like a kid who just made honor roll for the first time. "What does all of that mean?" I asked.

"We can go home."

"When?"

"Somewhere between six weeks and two months."

I squealed and hugged Martin, which made a few people nearby turn to look at me. They must have thought he proposed because a couple of people clapped. "Why did you lead with the crack about the pizza?" I asked.

"I like watching you squirm." He chuckled, leaning back

and kissing me. “Did I exceed expectations?”

“Always.”

With our lunch finished, the remainder knocked onto the ground in my excitement, we toured the aquarium, rode the carousel, and explored the carnival games.

“Are you sure you don’t want to ride the Ferris Wheel?” Martin nodded toward the metal contraption. “The sky’s beautiful at this time of day with the sun nearly setting. It’s the perfect time to see everything.”

“No.”

“Are you sure?”

“I don’t like heights.” I leaned against the railing and stared out over the water. “I can see enough from here.”

He wrapped his arms around me and rested his chin against the top of my shoulder. “I’m glad we made the time to do this.”

“Me too.”

The sky performed an amazing color show for us. Watching the sun get swallowed up by the water was one of my favorite parts about being here. I’d miss the sunsets.

When I turned in Martin’s arms, I noticed all the stands and attractions now had the lights on. The white and neon made everything look fun. “Now what would you like to do?” Martin asked.

“Shooting competition.”

After investing more than we should in carnival games, we headed down the pier. The hairs on the back of my neck prickled. The breeze off the ocean always made me shiver, but this wasn’t from that. On the beach, I spotted a shadowy figure. He watched us move from one stand to another. How long had he been there?

I squinted into the dark, making out the outline of his backpack. *Roland Jordan.* How had he followed me here? Sure, he could access public transportation, but he’d ditched his phone after speaking to his D.C. contact for fear it could be traced. That meant taxis and rideshares were out. How would he have been able to keep tabs on me over the distance?

Reminding myself Jordan had been a tracker before working in psy-ops, I couldn’t dismiss the possibility he’d trailed me here. He must have figured it'd be safer to make an approach where the cops were less likely to intervene. With so many people around, no one would even notice him.

"Uh, Martin." I tried to figure out how to broach the subject. He wouldn't want me to meet with Jordan alone, but Jordan wouldn't stick around if I showed up with someone else.

"Hold that thought." Martin stopped at one of the stalls and bought me a sweatshirt. "I don't want you to catch a cold."

"You didn't have to do that," I said.

"I saw you shiver a second ago."

"It's not that."

But he wasn't paying enough attention to catch on. All the sights and sounds had distracted him. "You said I could get you something that said Santa Monica, remember?"

"Thanks, but the giant purple panda bear you won for me is more than enough."

He took the bear from my arms and examined it under the street lamps. "It doesn't say Santa Monica."

"It says you're too competitive for your own good."

"No, it says I love you."

"It does?" I looked at it, realizing a moment too late what Martin meant. "Charmer."

"How about we do something a little more high-end tomorrow? I was thinking a private tour of the art museum and a rooftop dinner."

"You'd need to make reservations."

"I did, a while ago."

Before I could reply, Martin's phone rang. He shifted the bear to one side and checked the display. "Do you mind? We agreed no phones, but—"

"It's okay. Take it." This would give me the perfect opportunity to find out who was following us. If it was Jordan, he'd be able to tell me everything and I could try to convince him to turn himself in and go on the record. "I'll meet you at the car. I want to pick up a few souvenirs for Nick and Jen. I'll only be a few minutes."

"Get something for Mark too, or we'll never hear the end

of it." Martin answered the phone, carrying the bags and bear toward the car.

Once he was a safe distance away, I hurried down the stairs and onto the beach. The security team wouldn't be far away. However, neither would the police. And that was a concern. So I had to act quickly.

"Roland?" I whispered, loud enough to be heard over the lapping waves. "I know you're here."

He edged out from beneath the pier, keeping a watchful eye on the beachgoers in the distance. He looked tense, worried.

"How did you know I'd be here? Did you follow me?" It was a stupid question, but I wondered how he'd gotten from Los Angeles to Santa Monica.

"The woman on the beach with the dog said you were coming here Saturday." He looked around. "After what happened, I didn't think it was safe to stick around. The police are everywhere."

"I'm sorry about that. You said you know who's killing the homeless in San Diego. You said it was cop. I need you to tell me which one."

Roland glanced behind him, checking the other side of the beach. "This is too exposed."

"It's out of the LAPD's jurisdiction. Santa Monica has its own police force."

"That doesn't mean they aren't here."

"Tell me who the killer is?"

"That cop," he said.

"Which one? Describe him?"

Roland kept glancing around while he described Gabriel Trevitt, everything from the detective's height to hair color. "I went to see Sophie's sister to tell her what happened and apologize for not saving her. I stay in that encampment to keep people safe. But Sophie didn't want help. At least, she didn't want my help. But Jenna said her sister sent her a letter begging for help. I never saw anyone stalking Sophie, but someone figured she'd be an easy target. She had nice things which would fetch quite a bit. And she always had cash on hand. He—"

"Detective Trevitt?" I asked.

"Yeah, Trevitt came by after she was robbed to take her statement. I thought it was odd. Cops never gave a shit before. I figured he did it to placate her and make his superiors happy. Sophie might have been someone important at some point, at least that's how she acted. I figured that was why. I didn't put it together at the time. But she trusted him. He had a badge. To her, that made a difference. He lured her away from the encampment, away from the shelters, away from safety."

"Sophie never felt safe at any of those places."

"That's what her sister said. That's why he was able to do that."

"Can you prove it?"

"I can prove he was there. I can't prove the rest." He turned to watch the water. "No one's going to believe a homeless guy."

"I believe you."

Roland laughed. "Great, but in the grand scheme of things, who the hell are you?" The sharp snap of a twig made me turn. "He's come to silence me. Don't let on you know." Roland disappeared beneath the dark pier.

"Parker," Trevitt raced toward me, "which way did he go?"

"What are you doing here?"

"My job." Trevitt aimed his flashlight near the ground, finding the remnants of Roland's footprints which hadn't been erased by the ebb and flow of the water. "What did he say to you?"

"Nothing."

Trevitt turned to stare at me. "Nothing? That's not what it sounded like to me. I was listening. You sounded convinced. You can't honestly say you believe him. The guy's off his rocker. I'd never hurt anyone without just cause."

Behind Trevitt, the moonlight caught the parabolic mic he'd abandoned beside an umbrella and blanket he'd set up on the beach. I took a step backward. "How long were you listening?"

"Long enough to wonder if you're naïve enough to fall for his lies."

"I wanted him to think I was on his side so he'd turn himself in." I glanced at the gun in Trevitt's hand. It wasn't police issue. It had a silencer. "How'd you know he'd follow me here?"

"I picked up his trail at Jenna Roth's house. After that, he caught a bus to Venice and made the trek along the beach."

"Why didn't you call for backup? You could have taken him sooner. At Jenna's house, before he got on the bus, or after he arrived in Venice."

"It was a local bus. I didn't know what his intended stop was, and I didn't want to put Jenna's life at risk. Roland Jordan's a killer."

"He has to be stopped." I edged backward, hoping Trevitt wouldn't notice. The best thing to do was put some distance between us. He already had his gun in his hand. It'd take me a few seconds to clear mine from inside my bag. "Is Petrocelli coming? What about the rest of the LAPD?"

"They'll be here soon. They got held up. Like you told Jordan, this is out of their jurisdiction." Trevitt moved closer to me.

"Don't you have to wait for permission too?"

"I'm not letting a killer go free." His eyes focused on the area beneath the pier. "I'm glad you met him down here instead of convincing him to come to you. There are less civilians. Less chance of casualties. No one has to notice anything's wrong." He looked at me. "Where's your companion?"

"He had a work emergency. He had to leave."

"Gentlemen don't leave ladies alone at night."

"He's no gentleman. And I'm no lady." I lunged forward, grabbed Trevitt by the shoulders, and kneed him in the balls. Surprised, he took the full force of the impact. I knocked the gun out of his hand, hearing it land with a thump. But in the dark I couldn't find it.

"Bitch."

As I unzipped my bag, he knocked me onto the wet sand. He clawed through the muck for his gun with his right hand while he wrapped his left hand around my throat. I grabbed his left wrist, sliding my fingers around his thumb and pulling his hand off of me and twisting it backward. I drove my knee into his kidney just as he located the silenced pistol.

He grunted, clocking me with the weapon in his hand. Things blurred. Blood ran into my eye, which was already tearing from the impact. Climbing off of me, he hovered above me. "You left me no choice."

Before he could pull the trigger, Roland Jordan rushed him from behind a pylon. Jordan bellowed a war cry as he dove onto Trevitt. Trevitt squeezed the trigger wildly. Four shots rang out, dulled by the silencer and lapping waves. They impacted above my head and to the left.

Jordan pummeled Trevitt, splashing water and sand all around as he punched him. Trevitt fired again. Jordan kept hitting, his punches getting slower and sloppier.

Scrambling to get my feet beneath me, I took a few unsteady steps, grabbing my bag and gun, as Jordan slumped to the side. Trevitt rolled him off of him and climbed to his feet.

"Put the gun down," I said.

"You first."

"Not a chance."

"Fine." Trevitt tossed the silenced weapon to the side and held up his hands. "I give up."

Cautiously, I moved closer and tossed a ziptie at his feet. "Put that on."

Trevitt knelt down, slid one wrist into the plastic band, and then the other. He raised his hands toward his mouth and pulled it tight with his teeth. "You're making a mistake."

"The only mistake I made was not looking into you the moment Will brought me the case. You were the common denominator. I should have known better."

"You've got it wrong. I'm not a killer, unlike Russo. He murdered good men in cold blood. I never killed anyone. They killed themselves with the poisons they craved. Booze, pills, it's all the same. I did my job. They were suicides. I don't care what he says," he pointed to Jordan, "there is no proof because I did my job."

"Then why attack me?"

"Attack you?" Trevitt laughed. "I didn't attack you. He did. I tried to stop him, but I couldn't."

"Except I'm the one standing, and you're not."

"Watch out," Roland moaned.

I didn't see Trevitt pull the knife. All I saw was him rushing toward me.

FORTY-TWO

Trevitt rammed me so hard I went airborne before crashing into one of the pylons. He raised the blade, his hands free. I wondered when he cut the ziptie. I ducked before he could stab me in the chest and slid around the curved wooden pillar.

I staggered backward, aiming in the dark with only one good eye. I tripped over a piece of driftwood. He took another step toward me, and I fired. But he didn't go down. Squeezing off another round, I hit him in the leg, and he dropped onto the wet sand.

Above us, I could hear thunderous sounds. Unlike Trevitt, I didn't carry a silenced weapon. My gunshots hadn't been suppressed. People on the beach, above us on the pier, and in the parking lot had heard the commotion.

I got up and moved to the downed assailant, kicking the blade out of his reach. Then I used his own handcuffs to secure his wrists behind his back and frisked him, finding his service piece in an ankle holster and another dagger concealed behind his jacket.

Trevitt whimpered each time the cold water lapped against his wound, but I didn't care. He deserved much worse.

I made my way to Jordan and knelt beside him. "How bad is it?" I asked.

"I've had worse."

"Funny, I always say the same thing."

He winced as I helped him sit up. "Do you see an exit wound?"

I checked behind him. "Yep."

"That's the good and bad news." Jordan propped himself against another pylon.

"Alex?" Martin bellowed from somewhere to my right.

I knew that tone. "Down here," I called. "Beneath the pier. Call 9-1-1. We need police and ambulances."

He ran down the steps, three beams of light bounced off the sand. "Sweetheart?" He was the first to find me. "I heard gunfire. Were you hit?"

"No, I'm okay." I spotted the Cross Security team and Bruiser, Martin's bodyguard, taking stock of the situation. The security team kept an eye on Trevitt while Bruiser put his field medicine knowledge to use to keep Jordan from bleeding out.

Martin pulled me into his arms and hugged me as tightly and gently as possible. "We agreed we would take today off. You broke your promise."

"I'm sorry."

He kissed me, his fingers brushing my hair back so he could examine the gash on my face. "Are you sure you're okay? You don't look so good."

"I'll be fine. Did you call the police?"

"ETA is two minutes," one of the security team replied.

"Ambulances?" I asked.

Before they could provide an answer, lights and sirens bombarded the beach. Officers converged on our location. Once the area was secured, they gave the okay for paramedics to move in.

"He's mine," Detective Petrocelli said, climbing out of the passenger seat of an unmarked. "Keep him handcuffed and make sure an officer stays with him at all times. He's killed at least three people."

The EMT nodded as they loaded Trevitt into the back of the rig.

"And here I thought you were just a pain in my ass," Petrocelli said, moving beside the officer who was speaking to Martin and me. "Apparently, you're a pain in everyone's ass."

"Now's not the night to push my buttons, Dean."

But the detective ignored my warning. Instead, he glanced at Martin. "Do I know you?"

"James Martin." Martin gave the cop a wary look. "And you are?"

"Detective Petrocelli, LAPD, robbery-homicide division. Did you see what happened here?"

Martin shook his head. "I only heard the gunshots and found the situation resolved."

"That officer wants to take your statement," Petrocelli said.

Martin gave me a look. "She needs medical attention."

"She'll get it. The sooner you answer the questions, the faster you can come back here and hold her hand."

"It's okay," I said, worried Martin might get himself arrested for assault. "I'll be fine."

"You better be." He narrowed his eyes at Petrocelli before meeting the officer fifteen feet away.

"You got here fast. And people say traffic in California's a bitch." I pulled the gauze pad I'd been given away from my face to see if I was still bleeding, which I was.

"I was in the area."

"Really? How come?"

Petrocelli glared at me. "Follow me." He led me toward the paramedics which were packing Jordan's wounds. "Mr. Jordan?"

Jordan looked at the cop. "Yes."

"First, I'd like to thank you for your service. Second, I want you to know that I'm going to personally ensure you're taken very good care of."

"What about the charges?" I asked.

"No charges," Petrocelli said. "Sgt. Russo phoned. He spoke to several San Diego social workers and a few other people. Together, we figured out Trevitt was responsible for killing Joel Curry. You saw it happen, didn't you, sir?"

"I did. I tried to stop him," Jordan said. "But I didn't

reach them in time. And I knew what the cop would say, how it would look."

"That's why Trevitt wanted you dead. Is that why you came to see Parker?"

Jordan nodded. "She's the only one I knew would believe me."

"We'll take good care of you. And we'll get you back home as soon as we can. For now, you're safe." Petrocelli offered Jordan his hand.

"What about Myrtle?" Jordan asked.

"Myrtle?"

"She's a homeless woman who lives in the same encampment. He thought Trevitt planned to kill her too," I said.

"Pink fur coat?" Petrocelli asked.

"Yes, sir," Jordan said,

"Sergeant Russo said she's fine but disappointed she didn't get to feed the squirrels."

Jordan laughed, grimacing as they hefted the stretcher and carried him to the ambulance. "That's Myrtle."

"Is she an addict?" I asked.

"She must be. That's the only reason Trevitt would target her." Petrocelli led me away from the crime scene and to another team of EMTs.

I sat down while they cleaned my cut and checked my eye. One of them handed me an ice pack while they grabbed supplies out of their kit.

"Despite everything, I have half a mind to arrest you," Petrocelli said.

"Try it, and Martin will hire a team of attorneys to bury you."

"You know a lot of interesting people, Ms. Parker. FBI agents, police lieutenants, police commissioners, all of which vouched for your investigative chops. Yet, none of those people have any authority over the LAPD or me. But for whatever the reason, I listened anyway and looked into what you said about Trevitt. He didn't have a history, no record of violence, nothing to indicate he'd kill, but Father Miguel told me Trevitt volunteered with the church outreach program. Trevitt spoke to Robert Devers. He was also at the church the morning of the hanging. He showed up within seconds of Sister Mary calling the police. The coffee shop across the street has footage of Trevitt arriving immediately after the hanging and rushing out the second the call went out over the radio. He didn't even order a coffee. He just sat by the door, like he was waiting for something."

"That's because he knew what was going to happen and he didn't want any other detective to take the case."

"Right, and since he was on duty, no one questioned it. The same's true of Sophie Marshman."

"Still, that sounds circumstantial," I said.

"Russo has an eyewitness who'll testify, and I'm sure Roland Jordan will be just as eager to put that bastard away. So we're done." Petrocelli spotted Martin coming toward us. "That means you're done. Stay out of police business and away from homicide cases. I don't care what jurisdiction it is. If you end up anywhere near another dead body, I'm dragging your ass to jail."

I smiled. "Face it, you're starting to like me."

* * *

Martin brought the breakfast tray into the bedroom and climbed back into bed. He kissed me, stopping to check my eye, which was bruised but no longer swollen. "Next time you agree to take the day off, I expect you to take the day off."

"You too."

"I took a phone call. I didn't place a killer under citizen's arrest."

"Same principle."

"It is not."

"Hey," I reached for his hand, running my fingers down his forearm, "we had fun before that, right?"

"Yes."

"And we made up for all the crap that happened Saturday night by doing something fun and work-free on Sunday, even though your fancy night out was with Cyclops. Plus, I got two Santa Monica souvenirs out of it.

That's a pretty big win in my book."

"I would have bought you everything in the store if we could have avoided the gunfire."

"Now you tell me."

"You knew what was about to happen, and that's why you sent me to the car." He handed me a bowl of scrambled eggs with crumbled turkey bacon. "I would have gone with you."

"I know."

"I can handle myself."

"I know that too."

"Then why?" He picked up his own bowl and took a bite.

"Roland would have run. He was scared. He'd been wrongly accused, and he didn't have a leg to stand on. Who would believe a violent, homeless guy?"

Martin didn't speak. Instead, he focused on his breakfast. "How did he end up that way?"

"I don't know. He has some money in an account. I don't know if it's enough to find a place, but when I spoke to him, he made it seem like his mission in life is to protect the others in the camp. That's what he needs to do. Trevitt tried to take that from him and use it against him."

"It's a good thing you stepped in."

"Not me. Will."

When we finished eating breakfast, Martin cleared away the tray. "Are you insisting on going to work today?"

"I have to. Lucien's coming tomorrow, and if I don't make sure the LAPD have cleared out and taken all of their surveillance equipment with them, he'll wage World War III."

"Fine, but I'm giving you a ride to work."

When I got there, I found Will sitting at the security desk, eating donuts with Howard and Buck. "Gentlemen," I said, "I hope someone saved me a chocolate crème."

"Half a dozen." Will grabbed the box off the desk and followed me down the hallway. "How's the eye?"

"Fine."

"And your back?"

"Still bruised, but it was before, so that's nothing new. At least I didn't pop any stitches." I unlocked the door, turning to look at him. "Did you make the trip just to ask me that?"

"No, I wanted to thank you."

"With donuts?" I took the box from his hand and put them down on the reception desk. "You could have had those delivered."

"I'm also bringing the LAPD the prisoner transfer orders and overseeing Trevitt's hospital release. I want to make sure he doesn't pull a fast one."

"Is your case solid?"

"Yep. Hence, the donuts." Will made coffee and poured us each a cup before taking a seat. "Are you still wondering if I'm a killer?"

"No, and I'm sorry about that. Really." I took a sip and reached for the box of donuts, making sure Will hadn't lied about the six chocolate crèmes. "Are you still planning on joining the private sector?"

"Now more than ever. The shooting was bad enough. This made everything worse."

"But you see the private sector isn't all it's cracked up to be. The job is still the job."

"Like I said, being a cop's all I've known. I'm not equipped to do anything else. But getting away from the accusatory remarks and stares will help. Starting over somewhere fresh, that's what I need."

Deciding that I needed some dessert after breakfast, I picked up one of the donuts. "Do you want to work here?"

"Are you serious?" He didn't look like he believed me.

"The job's yours if you want it. I'll smooth it over with Lucien." I wasn't sure how I'd do it, but stopping a killer with a badge should have earned Will my boss's respect.

"Yeah, I want it, but not yet. I have one case to close. Trevitt's shit got in the way and confused things. Now I have to get back on track and finish what I started. After that, I'm walking. Can you hold my spot?"

"Yep."

"Great."

DON'T MISS TROUBLE BREWING, THE NEXT ALEXIS PARKER NOVEL

AVAILABLE IN PAPERBACK AND AS AN E-BOOK

ABOUT THE AUTHOR

G.K. Parks is the author of the Alexis Parker series. The first novel, *Likely Suspects,* tells the story of Alexis' first foray into the private sector.

G.K. Parks received a Bachelor of Arts in Political Science and History. After spending some time in law school, G.K. changed paths and earned a Master of Arts in Criminology/Criminal Justice. Now all that education is being put to use creating a fictional world based upon years of study and research.

You can find additional information on G.K. Parks and the Alexis Parker series by visiting our website at www.alexisparkerseries.com

Made in the USA
Monee, IL
02 May 2023

32889581R00208